MIRACLE

Titles by Katherine Sutcliffe

MY ONLY LOVE

ONCE A HERO

MIRACLE

KATHERINE SUTCLIFFE

JOVE BOOKS, NEW YORK

To my horse trainer:
Mark Jamieson of Trademark Farms, Manor/Austin, Texas.
For caring so devotedly for my beautiful Arabian horses.
For making me proud every time you take them into the ring.
For helping me realize one of my grandest dreams.
You're one of the best in the business,
a consummate professional who treats his horses
with the respect and love for which they are so deserving.
I'm lucky to have found you.

Also, my thanks to his wonderful grooms:
Kiki Pantaze, Alison Cowden, Catherine Pipkin.
Wonderful ladies who work so hard to keep the horses
healthy, happy, and eager to show.
We couldn't do it without you.

Cover art designed by John Ruzick.

ISBN: 0-515-11546-0

A JOVE BOOK®
Jove Books are published by The Berkley Publishing Group,
200 Madison Avenue, New York, New York 10016.
JOVE and the "J" design are trademarks
belonging to Jove Publications, Inc.

PRINTED IN THE UNITED STATES OF AMERICA

Marriage and love have nothing in common. We marry to found a family, and we form families in order to constitute society. Society cannot dispense with marriage. If society is a chain, each family is a link in that chain. In order to weld those links, we always seek for metals of the same kind. When we marry, we must bring the same conventions together; we must combine fortunes, unite similar races, and aim at the common interest, which is riches and children.

from *A Grandmother's Advice*
by GUY DE MAUPASSANT

Prologue

Basingstoke Hall, Salisbury, England
1800

Ah weddings! What a *glorious* tradition. What *pomp*! What *circumstance*! *What a royal pain in the derrière.*

The dowager duchess of Salterdon gazed out over the elaborate landscape of her grandson's home, watched the harried goings-on of the servants—at least a hundred of them—as they erected the brightly colored awnings, the scores of banquet tables, the array of plush chairs, and the multitude of potted blooming plants that flanked the winding, red-carpeted aisle that led to a dais before the distant fountain of rearing marble horses. The fountain was drained and dry, but soon, it would flow with champagne—enough champagne to more than sufficiently intoxicate the five hundred guests whom she had invited to witness this most auspicious occasion.

So far so good.

With a sigh, she turned back to the vast drawing room, allowed her sharp eyes to peruse her surroundings while her ears listened to the murmur of her grandsons' voices in the next apartment. As yet, their tone sounded friendly enough—the usual sparrings between brothers. Trey, her oldest grandson and therefore heir to the dukedom when his father died so tragically those many years ago, would offer Clayton, the younger brother, a drink, a pinch of snuff, perhaps a somewhat off-colored joke or two before they got down to business. She could so easily picture them in her mind—her beloved children who she had adored since the moment they took their first breaths, only minutes apart, thirty years ago.

Who could have known on that beautiful spring day that their mother would have given birth to identical twins?

"Praise God that he has blessed us with two fine and strapping lads!" the duke (the duchess's son) had exclaimed, then proceeded to spoil the shavelings rotten.

Who could have imagined that two such adorable, cherub-faced little tykes, with flashing gray eyes and smiles that could melt iron would have grown into such scoundrels who, consciously or unconsciously, immersed themselves in the sort of mischief that gave even the gossipmongers enough wag to make them heady with disbelief.

Who would have thought that she, the duchess of Salterdon, at the age of sixty and looking forward to retiring to the country where she might die in peace (should the good Lord decide it was her time to go), would suddenly find herself, due to the boys' parents' untimely death, in charge of rearing the "arrogant monsters," as their many nannys and governesses had termed them, through the stormy years of their adolescence.

Not that it had *all* been trying.

The duchess sniffed and dabbed her perfumed monogrammed hanky to her nose, cocked her head slightly, and listened more intently to the muted conversation through the wall, then raised one eyebrow at the sudden, deep silence. *Any moment now*, she thought, and moved to another window where she could better see the activity surrounding the west wing conservatory, which was not so much an adjunct to the palatial house as a miniature Gothic cathedral conceived by a fin de siècle voluptuary a century before, with a nave and aisles formed by clusters of carved pillars, stained glass windows, and a ceiling whose glazed traceries flooded the surrounding marble pavement with light.

Guests had begun arriving hours ago: women in low-necked, high-waisted satin dresses, attended by white-stockinged gentlemen in ultrafine dress milled about the grounds sipping milk punch and, no doubt, wagering on the outcome of this entire affair. The duchess, at eighty years of age, and having spent her entire life living under the haughty, aristocratic eye of her own family and peers, knew beyond any doubt what the intrigued group would be discussing.

The bride didn't belong: not with *her* background, *her* lineage, which, if rumor could be believed, made her as nameless as she was penniless.

Ah, but the future bride was beautiful—no one could deny that. The ton could rattle their jewels and waggle their purses all they wanted, but all the shillings in their gilded coffers could not purchase her comeliness and kindness. The girl, with her surreal looks and her unique way of regarding the world without jaundice, had a way of melting the coldest of hearts and the narrowest of minds. The duchess of Salterdon, known for her unbending sense of purpose, could vouch for that. At the duchess's advanced years, one would think that she had learned all there was to know about life and people, about love, death, anger, and betrayal. After all, she had dealt with them all throughout her life. While her world perceived her as dour and stony, with a backbone as rigid as a ship's mast, she had learned over the past weeks to bend—even to weep.

Bah! She was becoming a sentimental old fool; had to be, else she would never have stooped to such a shenanigan in the first place. Must be something in the mind that became a bit crusty when one grew to her age. It somehow inhibited better logic. Turned iron will into jelly. Cold resolve into . . . a warm puddle of contrition. Perhaps it was simply an old woman's need to know her grandchildren were happy before she died, that she had not failed in her ability to mold their young minds and souls into what their world would deem as acceptable.

Not that she was terribly worried. Trey, the firstborn and therefore the heir to his father's title, was capable of attaining everything he wanted out of life—and had—*several* times, before he lost it all in bad investments or gambling or tossed it away on the incorrigible lot of ne'er-do-wells who hung upon his purse like suckling jackals. She loved Trey. How could she not? And while she was hard-pressed to approve of his hedonistic lifestyle and friends, she could not help but blame his parents—and, to a certain extent, herself—for his foolishness and foolhardiness. As heir to the dukedom at only ten years of age, he had never known a moment's uncertainty about his future, while Clayton . . .

The duchess moved to a chair and eased into it. She sat with her back erect, her bejeweled hands lying lightly upon the chair arms, her gaze fixed on the oil portrait on the wall—Clayton Hawthorne.

Clayton was and always had been her favorite. She had recognized it from early on—the differences in the lads—even when their parents had not. While the boys' mother and father had lavished the older son with everything the security of his position provided for him, Clayton had contented himself with his own kind of survival. He had been born with a gift —something that Trey's station in life, his wealth, and his security, could not buy him: honor, self-respect, and ambition. A *great deal* of ambition.

Clayton had established himself as one of the wealthiest men in England. He'd amassed enough land and estates to feed and house a good portion of five counties. He had a mind thirsty for knowledge and a heart achingly gentle enough to worship even the lowliest of creatures. While Trey reveled in society's often corrupt and jaded world, Clayton shunned it. He chose, instead, to fill his few idle hours with nature. He craved the sun on his face, became intoxicated by the smell of dirt on his hands. Undoubtedly, Clayton Wyatt Bishop Hawthorne, Lord Basingstoke, marched to the beat of a different drummer.

Therein lay his problem—and hers.

While there wasn't a woman in England or any other country who would not have swooned with the mere thought of marrying the somewhat unconventional young lord—many having contrived all kinds of ploys to win him—none had managed it. Certainly, there had been sweethearts and mistresses aplenty, but none had lasted overly long. The moment their eyes had become starry with the prospect of luring him into matrimony, he had bid them a fond farewell and sauntered off into the sunset. When the duchess had time and again called him on the carpet about it, demanding to know what, exactly, he was doing to guarantee the perpetuation of the Hawthorne name, he had responded with that typically arrogant shrug of his shoulders and lopsided smile. "I assure you, grandmother, you can feel confident that I am hardly the laggard concerning the pleasurable act of procreation. However, concerning my refusal to marry so far, I will tell you again what I've told you repeatedly: I have yet to meet a woman who was not predictable, boring, vain, vapid, and a money-hungry she-devil with the personality of oatmeal. It will be a cold day in hell before I allow some eyelash-fluttering vulture with an overly voracious appetite for bon-bons and Parisian couturiers to ride on the coattails of my success." Then he had added with a flourishing bow that was as impertinent as it was respectful, "I don't intend to pluck up just any little mouse to marry, darling, so don't bother feigning another one of your heart spells. You're healthy as a bloody mule and will undoubtedly outlive us all, much to Trey's consternation. If you're so hell-bent on seeing one of us married before you die, then you should direct your interest toward him. He, after all, is the firstborn—the duke of Salterdon. I, madam, am simply a lowly farmer."

Farmer indeed.

A door opened. She tensed and gripped the chair arms fiercely. The door slammed, rocking the windows. Turning her head, she watched through the glass as one of her grandsons stormed across the lawn, scattering servants and flocks of peacocks in his angry march toward the distant stables. Guests paused in their promenades and, with their heads together, no doubt debated in whispers if this tantrum were only a hint of the no doubt scandalous trouble that was about to erupt around them.

"Idiots," the duchess grumbled under her breath and wondered, much to her perplexity, which of her grandsons it was striding out across the lawns, white shirt molded to his body by the breeze, his hair a wild array of dark curls. Of course it was Clayton. Trey wouldn't be caught dead in polite company garbed in such a disreputable fashion.

Behind her, a door opened and quietly closed. Footsteps, then a man moved into her line of vision. Tall, elegantly dressed in his finest black tailcoat with its rolled collar of black velvet, the duke of Salterdon was breathtakingly handsome—and arrogant and infuriatingly aloof—a dignified mirror image of the recalcitrant buck stalking off into the distance. Often, throughout the years she had raised the intractable pair, the dowager duchess had pondered on the idea that, had each brother inherited a few positive traits from the other, they might have turned out to be perfect gentlemen . . . thoroughly decent human beings . . . quintessential examples of what God had intended for the aristocracy.

Salterdon walked to the window and, like the duchess, regarded his brother's exodus across the gardens.

"I fear I touched a nerve," he said, sliding his hands into the pockets of his black trousers.

"Are you surprised?" she replied.

"I thought he might take it better."

"Would you?"

At last, the duke turned to face her. His eyes, as usual, reminded her of cold steel, even as one corner of his mouth turned up in a smug grin. "He dropped the gauntlet, you know. Flung it at my feet. Demanded that we meet at dawn so he could at last have done with my 'bastardly tendencies.' I told him to name his second."

"Poppycock." The duchess drummed her fingers on the chair. "He'll marry her, of course. No reason not to."

"Certainly there is. To spite you, of course. You know Clay has prided himself on avoiding your obvious attempts to manipulate him—much better than I have, I confess—or I wouldn't be in this predicament now. I'm certain he feels quite scalded to discover you've gulled him at last."

Directing her gaze back to the portrait on the wall, the duchess pursed her lips.

Salterdon moved to her side, leaned upon her chair, and lowered his lips to her ear as he whispered, "My darling grandmother, we both know that Clay's the master of the counter blow—"

"He loves her!" the duchess barked.

"How better to gall you than to humiliate you in front of your guests—all of whom are waiting for the sky to open and hail consequences on your beautiful, noble, and devious head."

Turning her gaze back to her grandson's, the duchess raised one lofty eyebrow. "I should speak cautiously, Your Grace. With one swipe of my pen, you could find yourself penniless . . . again."

They exchanged flat smiles before Salterdon moved to the liquor cabinet and poured himself a drink. "He'll go through with it," he said thoughtfully. "He'd be a fool not to. After all, the lass is quite . . . extraordinary."

"Is that a note of wistfulness I hear in your tone?"

"Perhaps."

The duchess looked back over her shoulder at him. Their eyes met.

Setting down his drink, Salterdon said, "You have that guileful glint in your eye again, grandmother. I'm not certain I like it."

"If Clayton, that foolish boy, won't go through with it—"

"Surely you're not suggesting—"

"No one will ever be the wiser."

"Except her. The moment she suspects—"

"It'll be too late. She'll be married to the duke of Salterdon. What woman wouldn't warm, eventually, to the idea of someday becoming a duchess? Of inheriting everything I own?"

"Obviously, you don't know Lady Cavendish as well as you think."

"She's a woman, isn't she? Beneath that inculpable veneer is a fox no less eager to experience the rewards and amenities in life than the rest of us. Besides, I'll make it well worth your effort."

"Well worth?"

She nodded.

"I wasn't aware that having great-grandchildren meant so much to you," the duke said.

"I shall bounce the bairn on my knee before I die. I want to mollycoddle him. Indulge him. Cater to his every desire."

For an instant, humor lit the depths of Salterdon's gray eyes, and he threw back his handsome head in laughter. "My darling grandmother, you never mollycoddled us, nor catered to our every whim. In truth, had we ever been treated to anything other than your strict obedience to aristocratic norms, we might have turned out to be passably decent human beings."

"My reasons for coddling the children are hardly estimable, my impertinent and disrespectful young pup. I simply wish to raise them in a way that you—as their parent—will be forced to deal with their militantness, as I have had to deal with yours for the last twenty years. Now, tell me, how would you really feel married to the girl?"

Salterdon stared down into his port, a smile still on his lips.

"That's what I thought," the duchess declared. She pushed up from her chair, straightened the velvet sleeves on her tunic, then patted the plaited coil of gray hair that was wrapped around the back of her head. "The wedding will take place three days from now, with or without—"

"A bride," came the unexpected, breathless voice from the door.

The dowager duchess, as well as the duke, turned abruptly toward the intruder. Clayton Hawthorne stood in the threshold, long, black-clad legs planted firmly apart, his hands fisted at his sides. His lace-up, finely sewn shirt of India cotton lay open over his brown chest, and his shoulders were dusted with hay particles as was his mass of dark hair. He breathed heavily. Hot color suffused his high, sun-kissed cheeks as he regarded them both with eyes the color of hot ash.

"Where is she?" he demanded in a threatening tone. "What have you done with her? If this is another of your bloody attempts to manipulate me—" Focusing on the duchess, he moved across the room, his stalk menacing, causing her to back away until, coming up against a table, she was forced to stand her ground, to raise her chin and meet his intimidating glower. "You told her already," he said through his teeth. "You meddling old witch. I should strangle you. Have you any idea what you've done? She's gone. Got away. No doubt returned to that despicable old haunt where I found her, all because you couldn't mind your own bloody business. Can you not see what you've done? She'll never forgive me for this, damn you. She'll never trust me—the lot of us—again, and I don't blame her."

"You'll go after her, of course," said the duke in a calm voice.

"Oh yes," Hawthorne said, still staring into his grandmother's eyes. "I'll go . . . for whatever good it will do me."

To love someone is to be the only one to see a miracle invisible to others.

FRANÇOIS MAURIAC

Chapter One

Wyndthorst Hall, Cheltenham, England
Three Months Earlier

Clayton Hawthorne stood by the elaborate Renaissance mantel that was burdened by their grandmother's outrageous collection of porcelain cherubs and gold-plated clocks adorned by Roman winged messengers. One broad shoulder was propped against the stone fixture, and his arms were crossed over his chest. Clay's gray eyes regarded his twin brother wearily. In truth, he was exhausted. Having been summoned to Wyndthorst by his grace on the pretense of extreme urgency, Clayton had departed Basingstoke, his home in southern England, at just after midnight, arriving at the dowager duchess's estate just after daylight, only to discover that what he had anticipated as bad news concerning the aged duchess's health had turned out to be Trey's usual manipulations. The duke of Salterdon was up to something; Clayton was certain of it.

"I realize this all sounds like madness," said Trey as he critically studied his own reflection in the framed looking glass and adjusted his linen stock so it lay perfectly against his white shirt. Raising one dark eyebrow, he then focused on Clayton's image in the mirror, obviously regarding Clay's attire: his mud-spattered Hessians, patched breeches, and a shirt that had yellowed with age and too many washings. His brother hadn't so much as bothered to brush his hair. It lay mussed and feathered all over his head, and was in dire need of trimming. Clayton could so easily read the thoughts swimming behind Trey's stone-gray eyes: *You've dressed like that just to spite me.*

Absolutely, Clay grinned back with that devil-may-care glint in his eye that told his brother his exact feelings on the matter. Clayton Wyatt Bishop Hawthorne, second son of Harry William Dillion Hawthorne, the duke of Salterdon before his untimely death in a shipwreck off the coast of Africa, was unequaled in his ability to mask his true thoughts and feelings. Grown wagering men had been known to sweat before the iciness of Clay's demeanor.

Facing Clayton at last, the duke continued, "A fortnight ago, I would've agreed. However, circumstances being as they are, I firmly believe that I have little choice. I swear upon the king's crown, Clay, that the dowager continues to live just to see me agonize."

"The dowager continues to live because she's perfectly healthy and obliged to see her first great-grandchild born into his proper place in the world—that being the future duke of Salterdon, of course. In short, my dear brother, she won't die until she sees you respectably married with a half-dozen brats tumbling about the floor like little rug rats."

For another long moment, Clayton's hooded eyes regarded Trey's, his hard body at ease and suited to the cavernous and austere surroundings of their grandmother's home. "Get to the point," he finally said. "You didn't hoodwink me into making that hellish jaunt from Basingstoke just to prat on about grandmother. You want something from me. What is it?"

"Ah, Clay. As always you're painfully direct, an almost enviable trait . . . had we been born into the socially or economically inferior classes. Obviously, somewhere in our distant past, you forgot to embrace the lesson of tact. But then, perhaps that's what makes you so infamous among our circle. There's something about your dark good looks and bucolic *virility* that is apparently incredibly alluring to the weak-hearted women who find themselves the focus of your attention. I suppose your reputation as a lover doesn't hurt."

Rewarding Clayton with a derisive smile, Trey lowered his voice and added, "I wonder what it is about women who find themselves drawn to a ruffian like you. Obviously, there's some feminine sexual appetency that causes them to risk an occasional dance with the devil. You've broken hearts from one continent to the next, and yet . . . there isn't a woman who has ever fallen under your spell who came away from your fiery affairs with anger and regret. As a wife of a mutual friend recently proclaimed, "If every husband who neglected his lonely wife would treat his spouse with as much consideration and affection as the superbly handsome and scandalous Lord Hawthorne, there would be no unfaithful wives. They would all be too deliriously satisfied to climb out of bed."

"I'm certain you didn't have me ride here throughout the night just to discuss my love life," Clayton said.

"You're absolutely right. I've brought you here to inform you that I've hatched a plan to get exactly what I want—and need—from the duchess."

"Don't tell me you again plan to sneak into her room and smother her while she sleeps," Clay teased with a laugh. "I bet you a hundred pounds last time that you wouldn't go through with it, and you didn't."

"Nothing so dramatic. I simply intend to give her what she wants. A granddaughter-in-law."

Silence.

"You?" Clayton replied at last, and somewhat smugly. "Marry? I beg your pardon, but I'll believe *that* when I see it."

"You needn't look so shocked. It's done every day. Occasionally, compromise must be employed if one wishes to achieve what one deserves out of life."

"So tell me . . . have you someone in mind?"

His Grace removed a snuff box from his coat and flipped it open. "Yes, as a matter of fact," he replied with a flourish.

Silence again while Clayton pondered the surprising possibility. "Well? Don't keep me in suspense. What little featherbrain is so desperate as to consider marriage to *you*?"

"I shouldn't spar too loudly. Not with your reputation. There isn't a father in England or the Continent, for that matter, who would trust you five minutes unchaperoned with his daughter, not for all the guineas in your coffers nor your seven estates. The fact is, you're an incorrigible gambler—"

"Who wins. Who *always* wins. Who can spy a fraud a stone's throw away. Who, therefore, is not at the mercy of our guinea-pinching grandmother who continues to defy death in order to force you, the eldest Hawthorne, to marry and produce an heir. In short, I don't require the dowager duchess's money and therefore can happily invite her to burn in hell, should I choose to do so."

"But you wouldn't, of course. You like the old crone." The duke touched a pinch of snuff to each nostril before slipping the blue crested porcelain box back into his pocket.

"I can honestly say that, yes, I do," Clayton replied. "I find her amusing, if not predictable. Besides, I was always her favorite."

"That's putting it mildly. I could never understand it, actually. You were always the troublemaker, for her, and for me. You were quite the scalawag, you know. Still are, I daresay. I wouldn't trust you as far as I could throw you."

The brothers exchanged dry smiles, then turned at once and walked in unison to the immense double French doors overlooking the thousand-acre estate that had belonged to their family for the last two hundred years.

"So who is the chit?" Clayton asked after a moment of silence.

"The chit?"

"The lucky bride to be."

"Ah! Well, naturally, I thought it better to settle for someone out of the usual gossip vine; someone unfamiliar with my lifestyle or my friends, someone who would be perfectly happy to live out her life ensconced at one of my country homes, away from the life I live in London and abroad. Someone—"

"Ignorant of your supreme decadence."

"Hmm," the duke said softly and thoughtfully. "Yes, I suppose that would be the most delicate way of phrasing it, though I rush to add there is absolutely nothing stupid about the lass—far from it."

"Where did you find her?"

"It was quite by accident. Never intended such a scam. There I was, sailing my yacht, the *Lady Lover*, with several of my friends around the south coast of the isle when a storm roared in, catching our mainsail in a tug of war and casting us onto that damned Rocken End Race."

"Please," Clayton encouraged, "the girl . . ."

"The girl . . . oh yes; the last thing I remember was the *Lady Lover* bashing her hull upon that long, wicked ledge of rocks stretching out into the sea. Then I woke up spitting seawater from my mouth, and there she appeared, sitting on a boulder that dripped seaweed and crabs. I am lying there, halfway drowned, and all she can say is, 'How do you do?' "

Clayton regarded the duke's profile. "How do you do?"

Trey replied with a short nod. "Just that. Then she proceeded to nudge a sand crab with her bare toe, giving me a generous glance of her naked leg, all the way up to here." He pointed to the top of his thigh, flashed Clayton the devastating smile for which the brothers were so famous, and asked, "Intrigued yet?"

"Possibly," Clayton muttered, narrowing his eyes. "Very well, you've described her naked toe and leg up to there. What else was she revealing?"

"She had the most glorious red hair down to the backs of her knees. Her face was white as dove down except for a sprinkling of freckles across the bridge of her nose. She dressed like a hoyden. A lot of rags sewn simply together and I vow to this day she wore nothing—I repeat, nothing—underneath. Her nipples were most prominent, possibly because she was cold. I should hate to think they remain like that all the time," Trey said with a flash of wit in his eyes. "However, she didn't seem to care a whit. When she left her rock to fall to her knees beside me in the sand, instead of crossing her arms over her round little breasts, she had the audacity to draw back her shoulders and gaze like some mermaid out to sea. I don't mind telling you, I was mesmerized."

"You? Mesmerized by a woman of lowly birth?"

Clearing his throat, turning away from the door, and staring off into space, the duke took a long, fond study of his surroundings, relishing the splendor of his grandmother's drawing room, from the lush carpets on the floor to the magnificent tapestries on the wall. "We'll get to that. But first things first. The girl crosses her long legs, props her elbows on her knees, and proceeds to stare at me. I'm shaking to my boots; teeth chattering, gut churning with water and squid. She bends near me and says, 'I trust I was sent here to save you.' I said, 'I beg your pardon?' I'm thinking, *The chit is allowing me to freeze to death and she's fantasizing about saving me*?"

"Did she?" Clayton grinned. "Save you?"

"I think not," the duke proclaimed. "What she *did* do was disappear into the spray and fog and return with a donkey with long, gray shaggy hair that bared his yellow teeth at me and brayed loudly enough to rouse Saint Peter, which didn't do my water occluded brain a mite of good. Somehow she managed to fling me onto the ass's back and with my friends stumbling along behind, escorted us up to some tumbledown old structure that was part chapel and part lighthouse that didn't spit out enough light to see a yard away, much less a mile away. The place was more than a little chilling. Obviously, the old chapel is submerged during high tides and whoever is keeping the pitiful torch lit in the crumbling octagonal structure is stranded some thirty-five feet above the rampaging waves."

Turning his gaze to Clayton's, regarding his clenched jaw and pale face, he hurried to add, "Sorry. I occasionally forget your aversion to water."

Clayton moved restlessly about the room, eventually ending up at the liquor cabinet, where he poured himself a potent brandy. Trey remained quiet until his brother had sufficiently fortified himself, then he continued. "Which brings us back to my proposition."

"I'm not certain I like the sound of that word—*proposition*." Clayton drank down the brandy and put his glass aside, one side of his mouth turning up in a manner that shouted obstinacy.

"I trust you'll hear me out completely before coming to any hasty conclusions," stated the duke.

Clayton remained silent, the soft morning light spilling through the nearby window casting shadows across his features. It was all coming to him now, why Trey had brought him here. While his brother might be wily and desperate enough to marry some commoner and get her with child in hopes that their grandmother would cough up a portion of his future inheritance, he would not stoop so low as to court her. Imagine the duke of Salterdon prostrating himself before some plebeian. Unthinkable.

"She's really very charming, Clay."

"No."

"But—"

"Absolutely not."

"*You* might even find her appealing. And interesting. I would go so far as to call her . . . fascinating!"

Clayton turned toward the door.

"Clay," the duke called. "I beg you . . ."

Clayton Hawthorne, Lord Basingstoke, Hawcroft, Winchfield, Bishopstoke, and Tichfield, among others, paused in his escape and looked back. His brother stood stiffly before the French doors, sunlight spilling over his shoulders, his demeanor rigid, his brow slightly sweating.

"I'm in trouble," the duke confessed.

"How much?" Clayton demanded with little inflection.

"What difference does it make? You've already loaned me more than most men realize in three lifetimes; I refuse to plead a loan from you again."

"Brilliant of you, considering you haven't repaid the thirty thousand you already owe me. Have you considered altering your lifestyle a bit, or is it inappropriate of me to call that to Your Grace's attention?"

Trey raised both eyebrows.

Clayton continued to regard his brother impassively, the old, familiar temper flaring to life somewhere deep in his belly. Though he did his best to conceal it, the emotion must have shown.

Trey's hands clenched, his eyes narrowed, and he laughed dryly. "Really, Clay, we've grown too old for these silly inclinations toward resentfulness of my birth advantage. I can hardly be held accountable for the fact that I was born first, and was therefore in the position of inheriting our father's title."

"And his fortune."

"You've not done so badly, Clay—"

"Correct. While you squandered away our family's fine name, reputation, and wealth, I was securing my future: plowing the ground, planting crops, and turning Basingstoke into one of the finest houses in England—all while you stood back with your nose in the air and condemned my plebeian traits. But who, may I ask you, is now begging for help?"

For an instant, Salterdon lowered his eyes and shifted his shoulders within the exceedingly fine cutaway coat before bringing his eyes back to Clay's. Clayton shook his head. "This time, I have no intention of fighting back the wolves for you, Your Grace."

"Clayton, I made bad investments—"

Clayton turned his back on his brother, strode gracefully and deliberately down the immense, marble-floored gallery toward the front doors where the majordomo stood like a sentinel, prepared to spring to his assistance.

"Dammit, Clayton, listen to me!" the duke shouted, bringing Clayton to an abrupt halt. He pivoted to face his own likeness.

Clay had seen that look before—not simply in his brother's eyes, but in the face of every fool who had ever been overly infatuated with the power and prestige their station in life could give them. They would sacrifice anything to keep it: honor, pride, dignity. In the end, they usually lost it all anyway with a single throw of the dice. Clay should know. He had won Basingstoke Hall in the same manner.

Finally, the duke of Salterdon wearily covered his face with his hands. His shoulders sank as he said more softly, "I have no place else to turn, Clay. The banks refuse to advance me any more loans. There are certain . . . gentlemen who are threatening to confront grandmother if I don't pay up soon. We both know grandmother refuses to grant me any further loans until I marry and produce an heir."

Silence.

Clayton took a long breath and slowly released it. Behind him, the majordomo's quiet footsteps retreated down the hall, and a door shut gently in the distance.

"What do you want me to do, exactly?" Clayton asked.

"Court the lass. Make her fall in love with the duke—agree to marry the duke. Bring her back to London for the wedding at which time I, the duke, will stand before the vicar and pledge my vows. She'll never be the wiser; we're identical, after all. If the duchess has a difficult time telling us apart, the girl certainly shall. Once the child has been conceived, I'll simply send the girl away to live in my country home in York."

"And if the chit doesn't care for the duke?" Clay asked pointedly.

"Don't be ridiculous. There hasn't been a woman whom you've set out to seduce who hasn't fallen heels over head for you."

Silence again. The seconds ticked by like tiny eternities; the air between them seemed charged with electricity.

Finally: "Grandmother will never accept it, Trey. The moment she learns that you've married a commoner she'll have the marriage annulled and pay the girl off—"

"But that's the beauty of it, you see. She's not a commoner. She's *Lady* Cavendish—the daughter of some deceased lord with a penchant for old castles—"

"No." Clayton shook his head. "I don't care if she is the bloody queen of England—"

"Dammit!" Trey swore through his teeth, "You owe me, Clay."

Clayton did not move. He didn't so much as blink but regarded his brother with a cold passivity that made Trey take a step back before catching himself and planting his feet.

"You owe me," Salterdon said in a quieter, more tentative voice. "If it wasn't for me, you would be dead now, and we both know it. In your gratitude that day, you vowed to me that you would someday make it up to me, that I wouldn't regret having risked my life to save yours."

"You bastard," Clayton growled. He turned toward the massive front doors, threw them open, and stalked down the curving stairwell toward his horse and groom.

Behind him, Trey yelled, "I take that as an agreement, Clayton."

Snatching the reins from the groom's hands, with the horse snorting and prancing in place, Clay flashed his brother a dark and malignant glare.

The duke of Salterdon broke into a relieved smile, and cupping his hands around his mouth, he shouted, "I swear you won't regret it, Clay. You may fall in love with her yourself!"

"The hell you say," Clayton returned, and gracefully mounted the high-spirited steed, adeptly lacing his fingers through the reins, little caring that his gloves were still tucked inside the waistband of his tight black breeches. The wind caught his dark hair as he drove his heels into his stallion's heaving sides and he muttered under his breath: "For me to fall in love with any girl, my black-hearted brother, would take a miracle."

Each had his past shut in him like the leaves of a book known to him by heart; and his friends could only read the title.

VIRGINIA WOOLF

Chapter Two

The Isle of Wight

Wind whipped up the bleak, staggered faces of Rocken End Race and slammed like a cold, gusty fist against the walls of the lighthouse. Shutters rattled. The stack of wood piled against the clammy stone wall shifted and collapsed to the floor. Miracle cast it a grieved glance, repositioned her tottering acorns, and closed her eyes again, muttering the old Druid love spell, ignoring the howl of the wind.

The ancient wood groaned. The building swayed. Tears of seawater crept through the ever widening crevices between the lichen-covered stones and formed glassy little pools on the rotting plank floor.

Miracle Cavendish was the only daughter of Lord Dexter Cavendish, deceased eight years. She had lived her entire life in the once spectacular but now ruined Cavisbrooke Castle, never having left the isle even briefly. Her father was little more than a vague memory—a stranger who had come and gone in her life so infrequently she would not have known him had she met him away from Cavisbrooke. Her mother had always assured her that he loved her devotedly, and it was that thought that had comforted her those years after her mother had tired of her secluded and solitary life and run away to Paris, leaving Miracle in the care of Jonathan Hoyt, a devoted servant and groom. The island folk referred to her as "that peculiar lass who haunts Saint Catherine's Lighthouse on the Chapel." Johnny called her simply . . . Mira.

Frankly, Miracle didn't care what the island folk called her. They were odd in their own ways, strict to their routines, their humdrum little existences. They awoke in the mornings to their daily drudgeries like everyone else in the world, except herself.

Oh yes, she was strange, very strange, and she relished it. Long ago she had decided that she would rather die than find herself shackled to the mediocrity of sameness and routine. Besides, her destiny had been planned long ago—twenty years ago, to be precise—the moment that turbulent Christmas morning when she was born during the most terrifying and destructive storm to hit the isle in centuries. According to her mother and Johnny, the winds had died, the clouds had parted, and the sun had shone brightly the very instant she took her first breath. Therefore, her mother had christened her Miracle and vowed she was destined to accomplish much greatness in the world.

Well, she wasn't so certain about accomplishing greatness, but with a name such as Miracle, she had long since reckoned that she was preordained to achieve *something* marvelous; the opportunity just hadn't presented itself to her yet. It would, though. She was certain of it!

Carefully, she finished piercing the last of nine acorns and placed it aside, next to the long cotton string she had earlier pulled from her leather pouch of medicinals—herbs, stones, feathers, chalk, and ash—then laid the twig of a hawthorn next to it. Positioned on her knees, her hands resting lightly on her thighs, she closed her eyes and rehearsed her chant:

May love and marriage be the theme
To visit me in this night's dream:
Fire and moon and sacred oak
Your threefold power we thus invoke;
Be all three my faithful friend
The image of my lover send;
Let me see his form and face
And his occupation trace
By a symbol or a sign;
Cupid, forward my design.

The wind slammed again, harder this time, causing the acorns to roll like marbles to every wall within the lighthouse. Miracle spilled onto her backside, and out of frustration, muttered a mild curse and dove to save her collection of spell-casters before they disappeared through the cracks in the floors. That is when she heard the voice—or thought she did.

Frozen, her eyes wide, her senses attuned to the thunderous song of the wind and tides that slid closer and closer to the base of Saint Catherine's Chapel beneath her, she tried her best to still the loud beating of her heart long enough to think rationally. The hag of a wise woman who had given her the bag of charms years ago had warned her against casting spells during the time of the Morrigan, the Nights of Morgana when no moon was visible in the heavens. Especially love charms!

"Nought but woe will come to the maiden who chants in darkness!" the mysterious old Ceridwen had proclaimed.

Biting her lip, stuffing the acorns and strings back into her leather pouch, Miracle convinced herself that the incantations and charms had never worked for her during the light of the moon, so why should they work against her now? Besides, the love spells were nothing more than folklore and superstition—a way to pass the dreary hours during her watch of Rocken End Race. If she truly allowed herself to believe in such silly—

A sound again. A voice.

Miracle leapt to her feet and peered through the sea-sprayed glass. Like some vanishing ghost on the horizon, the sails of a ship slipped into the fog and disappeared. For a long moment, Miracle forgot to breathe; her eyes burned from searching the swirling water and clouds, dread creeping through her breast like a hot ember. If some hapless seafarer had blundered his way onto the rocks while she was dallying with the supernatural, she would never forgive herself.

At first she thought the movement on the rock-strewn shore was nothing more than the occasionally eerie formations of wind-whipped rain and fog—the same formations that inspired tales of ghosts and goblins. Then the figure moved, if only slightly, emerging through the dense fog from the end of the Race that faced the sea. It stumbled over stones and mire until falling against the outcropping, skeletal ruins of an old ship that had washed ashore more than a half century before.

There, the figure became still. The wind billowed its black clothes like the sails of the retreating ship, and only then was Miracle assured that the figure was human. A man, by the looks of it, who stared out to sea, unmoving. Lost and wretched. Sea drenched. Cold. Possibly in need of help. *Certainly* in need of help. No one in his right mind would attempt landing at Rocken End Race during weather like this.

Forcing open the door, she carefully eased out onto the precarious perch that, in erstwhile times, had functioned as a crow's landing, a place for the lighthouse keeper to monitor the watery horizon with his spyglass. Now, however, the entire landing sagged dangerously, shook and groaned with the slightest weight, and swung from side to side with the simplest gust of wind.

With a cry, she grabbed the crumbling bannister for support, and finding little but the splintered, rotted handrail that virtually disintegrated in her hands, she flung herself back against the stone wall of the lighthouse and held her breath until the wind subsided. Only then did she cautiously ease to the edge again, and finding the figure still slightly slumped against the deteriorating, upthrusting rib of the old ship, she called, "Hello! Have you been flung overboard? Should I rescue you?"

Almost wearily, the figure turned and searched the shore as if he expected some banshee to come sailing at him from behind the outcropping of towering boulders and heaps of seaweed-littered sand. Miracle noticed then that aside from the sea spray, his clothes were not sodden, which brought her some relief. If, perchance, she had been expected to rescue this particular fellow, she would be hard-pressed to clamor down from her perch without first breaking her neck in the process.

"Up here!" she cried, waving her arms over her head and making the wobbly old walk moan again.

Finally, the figure looked up, and up. He stood with his cloak clutched around him, gloved hands gripping it fiercely. He staggered toward the building, stride lengthening as the tide rushed around his boots and frothed around his pants legs. He might have cursed. She couldn't be certain. The wind did odd things to the sounds of people's voices, especially from this distance.

Stopping at the base of the lighthouse, he stared at the open door of the old chapel, then looked back out to sea.

"You're welcome to come up!" she called.

She thought he responded.

"I cannot hear you—" she began, just as he turned up his face and rolled back the collar of his cloak. The wind caught his mass of dark hair and whipped it about his familiar features.

"Bloody hell," she cried, "not you again!"

Clayton blinked the salty spray from his eyes and did his best to focus on the siren far above him—for siren the wench certainly must be, looking as she did, flaming hair flying like brassy webs away from her head, the bodice of her brown gown molded to her body as snugly as a pair of well-fitted gloves. Clayton had anticipated a great many greetings: swoons of surprise, giddy pleasure—all the typical female reactions women employed when the man of their dreams suddenly appeared to sweep them off their feet. After all, the duke had insinuated that the chit would be more than happy to receive his attentions. He had also prepared him for her with terms like "exceptional, outrageously beautiful—beautiful enough to make a grown man weep with desire," were the man cursed with a taste for the socially or economically inferior classes, which Clayton obviously was, the duke had reminded him. Therefore, the last thing Clayton had anticipated was the look of outraged exasperation as she recognized him just before she flung herself back into the questionable security of the horrifyingly hazardous old lighthouse and slammed the door behind her.

The last thing he had anticipated was to be greeted by a she-devil wench with the appearance of some drab from a child's fairy story.

The idea that he had somehow misunderstood his brother simply wasn't plausible. No doubt about it, the duke of Salterdon had pledged on the dowager duchess's health that the "fascinating creature" would be ecstatic over the prospect of his courting her—and that she was more than passably attractive.

That should have been the clue, of course. Trey Hawthorne didn't give a flying frog about the dowager's health.

"My lord!" came the breathless cry behind him, and slowly Clayton turned to regard his valet, Benjamin, struggling out of the fog, hefting carpet bags the best he could over the rocks and rising water. Joining Clayton at last, breathing hard, the gray-haired, slightly paunchy manservant dropped the valises at his feet and stiffly straightened. He did not speak, but stared, as did Clayton, at the collapsing structure that had once been a chapel erected by Walter de Godyton, now a mere relic of the hermitage that had housed priests centuries before.

"By Jove," Benjamin breathed, his words forming vapor puffs in the chilly air. "I wager the old place is rather of a wild nature, my lord. Are you certain we've come to the correct venue? I cannot imagine anyone or anything aside from specters who might dwell in such a ghastly looking domicile."

"Concurred, Ben. However, the only goblin to haunt this old place is the one I've come here to see, I'm afraid. I fear I just saw her standing there, on that precarious little perch. She had flaming red hair that stretched straight out from her head."

"Specters," the valet grumbled under his breath, then shuddered. "You know how I feel about ghouls, my lord. Best to keep them at a favorable distance. Until you've witnessed yourself the havoc such a soul can play on a man's sanity, you simply cannot understand. I saw a man's hair turn white overnight because he came face to face with a wraith."

Clayton frowned. Benjamin Hughes had big, dark, drooping eyes that reminded Clayton of a hunting hound's, giving the old servant the perpetual look of being in the doldrums. His face was long, his jowls hanging. His nose was red—due to cold, the old man vowed, but everyone knew it was caused by his particular cravings for a "tot o' medicament," necessary to keep away the influenza that would surely strike him the moment he forgot to swallow his hourly spot. His tot was brandy, of course, and no doubt his ghouls were brought on by too many tots.

Ben had served Clayton's family for forty years, and for forty years he had jumped at every bump in the night and reported to his employers numerous sightings of ghosts, ghouls, and goblins. The dowager duchess or Clayton had found themselves occupied for hours in an attempt to convince him that no such things existed, that the apparitions the servant witnessed were nothing more than drying sheets on the line or the occasional shimmering gases that spewed from the mucky ground during certain times of the year.

On that particular afternoon, however, Clayton found himself wishing he believed in ghosts, that the image who had shrieked at him from the lighthouse had been some phantom from the afterlife and not the "fascinating angel" his brother had sent him here to seduce into marriage.

The sudden surge of icy water around his ankles slammed him back to reality. Bowing his head against the wind, he made for the sheer ledge that rose up from the beach to climb toward the misty clouds. When reaching the summit, he would contemplate his next move, whether to approach the lighthouse again or search out Cavisbrooke Castle and pray that the girl on the ledge had been a figment of his imagination.

Surely even the misguided and ill-reputed duke of Salterdon would not deceive his brother about the circumstances of his impending—albeit questionable—marriage to the daughter of Lord Cavendish.

The summit of Saint Catherine's Down rose eight hundred feet above the sea. With lungs burning, fingers freezing, and numbed feet aching from the treacherous trek up the crude steps hewn into the stone wall of the cliff, Clayton, having removed the bags from his manservant's possession, flung them to the ground and sank against a rock wall, while Benjamin clamored over the precipice and staggered up beside him. Silent, breathing hard, they peered through the descending darkness, down at the lighthouse which, during the hour-long ascension to the summit had become surrounded by roiling, driving waves that virtually climbed the sides of the building. Most of the chapel had disappeared. All that remained above water was the eroded stone crucifix, which rose up from the roof, waves licking at the feet of the dying savior.

Dizzy and nauseous, Clayton fell back against the wall again.

"Don't look," the valet gasped. Then clutching his cloak closed at the neck, Ben peered harder at the scene below and huffed. "Sacrilege, I say. Who in their right mind would submit their souls to such a fiendish place?"

"My thoughts exactly," Clayton said through his teeth. Turning from the precipice, he walked to the footpath, blotted the sweat from his face with his coat sleeve, and cursed his brother under his breath.

It had taken hours to convince a farmer to cart Clayton and his manservant to Cavisbrooke Castle. When they eventually reached the intimidating abode just after midnight, Benjamin took one glance at the ancient structure tottering on an outcropping of rock some five hundred feet above the thundering ocean, turned on his heel, and proclaimed the fog-entombed relic to be swarming with the souls of dead warriors who no doubt skulked about the halls at night brandishing bloody swords.

The fact that the farmer had taken such great pleasure in educating them both on the "lunatics" who resided in the "creepy old place" hadn't helped.

"Them folk at Cavisbrooke is as crazy as they come!" the farmer had proclaimed with such earnestness that Benjamin had groaned. "Since the day that crazy young Lord Cavendish showed up and ensconced his strange wife and her groom in that rat-infested old place, rumors started flyin'. Yes, sir, the Lady Lorraina Cavendish lived up there alone, except for that equally crazy groom, for years, with her husband callin' no more than a handful of times. I reckon all that loneliness was enough to drive anyone batty. She used to ensconce herself in that lighthouse, stare out to sea, and wait for him to return. Then she just up and disappeared one night. Vanished like a flame in the wind. Some say she's dead, that she haunts that damn lighthouse, still waitin' for him to come take her away. There sure ain't no denyin' there's somethin' strange out there. We've all seen it: the unicorn and angel flyin' through the dawn mist. Don't none of us go there no more, no siree. Not to the Undercliff. We leave the Rock to the dead who thrive there."

Clayton and Benjamin stood shoulder to shoulder on the rickety drawbridge, shivering from the cold mist, the farmer's ridiculous tirade about ghosts and unicorns nagging at their subconscious as they stared up and up the climbing turrets and walls that disappeared into the night and watched the last stars in the black sky disappear behind a cloak of fog.

"Well," Clayton eventually said to his manservant, "I think it's about time that you summon our host. We can hardly sleep here all night, can we?"

"Speak for yourself," Benjamin replied, still staring up the formidable wall.

Clayton cleared his throat and recalled again the wild, red-haired wraith who had shrieked at him from the lighthouse. Obviously it was a damn good thing Benjamin hadn't witnessed her, or they might never have made it this far.

"Benjamin—" he began.

"I won't do it . . . sir. You cannot make me. There are probably demons residing behind that door. The sort with snouts and long teeth and—"

"Benjamin—"

"Horns sprouting behind pointy ears and—"

"Don't force me to pull rank on you. I will, you know."

"You wouldn't, sir."

"Yes. I will. I'll dismiss you if you don't do something quickly. I'm freezing . . . and besides, God knows what sort of beast is living in the squalid water beneath this bridge—"

"I see your point," the valet snapped. Righting his shoulders, he shuffled hesitantly to the door, searched the barrier a long moment, then grabbed at a rope and gave it a yank.

Somewhere, the deep, hollow sound of a bell rang out.

Turning on his heels, Benjamin blinked his droopy eyes and muttered, "Positively macabre, Basingstoke. Once again I must protest this lurid and deceitful deed that, if you will allow me to pontificate without seeming redundant, will return like a backlash—"

"Benjamin."

"Yes, sir."

"Shut up."

Pursing his lips, the valet raised both eyebrows before adding in a voice like a scolded child who intended to get in the last word, "No one answers. They are probably out dancing around spewing cauldrons."

In that very moment came a scraping, squeaking grind of wood and metal as the massive door began to open. Benjamin leapt to Clayton's side, shied behind him, and uttered, "Not to fear, my lord. I'll protect you. Just give me a moment to work up my courage—"

"Not to mention your loyalty," Clayton said in a matter-of-fact tone that brought a "Hmph" from his manservant just before Benjamin, having spied a smudge of mud on Clayton's coat, frantically attempted to brush it away—no doubt an effort to focus on something other than what might or might not lurk behind Cavisbrooke's door.

At last, the door creaked open, if only slightly. An older man's round, mustached, ashen face with spectacled eyes that were as circular as moons peered at Clayton quizzically.

"Oh," came the greeting. "It's you again."

For an instant, Clayton frantically searched his memory, recalling his brother's obviously abbreviated history of his time spent at Cavisbrooke. "Hoyt, ol' man," he finally replied tentatively. "It's good to see you again."

The old man blinked ponderously, then peered at Clayton curiously, narrowing his eyes so they were little more than slits beneath his heavy gray brows, then he jumped as if he'd been goosed, and demanded in a less than authoritative voice, "What brings you back to Cavisbrooke . . . Your Grace?"

"I've returned to see Lady Cavendish, of course."

"Took you long enough," the old man grumbled, but opened the door no further.

"I say," Ben whispered near Clayton's ear. "Do you think he intends to let us in?"

In that moment, another voice sounded secretively from somewhere behind the gray-haired sentry. "Is it him? Of course it is. Who would be crass enough to show up at someone's door at midnight and expect to be invited in? Tell him to go away, Johnny. We don't want him here."

Hoyt pursed his lips, drawing his silver mustache into a bristly thatch resembling hedgehog spines. Finally, he said, "Lady Cavendish says to tell you that she ain't at home. Come back tomorrow."

"No!" came another excited whisper. "He's not to come back at all. Tell him, Johnny. I wish to never set eyes on his arrogant, rude, disrespectful face again."

"Lady Cavendish ain't up to visitors," Hoyt supplied, then muttered over his shoulder, "Shall I have 'em return to Niton, lass? It's the only place they'll find board, ya know. Course it'll take 'em the better part of the mornin' to get there . . . and they could become lost on the roads, might even walk right off the Undercliff in this bloody fog—"

"I cannot conceive of why you feel I should simply allow Duke What's-His-Name back into my home, knowing how I feel about him and his boorish friends."

"Aye, but you've never turned a beggar from yer door before. Imagine how yer conscience would bother ya knowing that the pitiable creatures were stranded somewhere on the down. Ya know what they say, lass. The aristocracy ain't got the brain to wipe their own—"

"Beggar!" Benjamin huffed.

"Ooo!" came the feminine exclamation and what sounded like the stomp of a small foot on the floor. "I grow damnably weary coping with your unfailing sense of decency, Johnny."

Suddenly the massive door was flung open, revealing the plump, spectacled servant with wiry gray hair and disheveled clothes, and behind him stood the wraith who had greeted Clayton from the lighthouse that afternoon. Adorned in the same worn and somewhat tattered dress she had been wearing earlier, her hair a mass of tumbled curls that looked flaming and alive in the meager lamplight, she planted her hands on her hips and fixed Clayton with wide, aggravated eyes.

"How dare you," she stated, and tapped her sandy, slippered foot on the floor. "I have known arrogance in my life but none quite so outrageous as yours, Salterdon. As memory serves me, I called out good riddance as you and your less-than-delightful companions quit my home weeks ago. I may have even threatened you if you ever considered returning to Carisbrooke—I don't rightly recall—but if I didn't, I should have. Now you show up on my threshold looking like a bedraggled pup—"

"Pup!" Benjamin gasped. "My lord, I shouldn't stand for—"

"Let the lady finish," Clayton interrupted, offering the lass a thin, dry smile that made her eyebrows draw together—whether in a frown or simply contemplation, he could not tell. She stood there, speechless, for a moment, suddenly uncertain, obviously formulating her next tirade, no doubt an engraved invitation to jump headfirst off the Undercliff.

Perhaps that wasn't such a bad idea after all.

Righting his shoulders, his eyes never leaving hers, which were shadowed by darkness as was her face, Clayton moved toward her, watched her chin raise and her jaw set while a sudden gust of cold, wet wind fingered through her long hair and billowed the limp skirt of her dress. Most women would have shivered, tittered about the cold, pleaded for a wrap; then again, most women of her particular class wouldn't have stood up to a duke and virtually told him to go to hell.

He reached for her hand.

She grabbed it back.

He reached again, patiently, still bestowing on her his *I'll win you over yet* smile that had melted the hearts of many stony maidens who had thought to play coy in his company. This time he caught her small hand in his cold fingers and raised it to his lips. His eyes still holding hers, which were now round as pennies, he said in as sensual a voice as his freezing body would allow, "My apologies for my previous behavior. Obviously, I was an ass, and recognizing the error of my ways, I've returned to Carisbrooke to make amends. Surely, a . . . genteel lady such as yourself will forgive my arrogance and allow me the opportunity to make up for my previous regrettable behavior."

He kissed her hand lightly; breathed warm breath on her pale skin. For an instant, she seemed mesmerized, but still she was as cautious as a bird.

He thought, *By now her knees are trembling—just slightly—enough to make her question her ability to withstand my charm*. She would reconsider her opinion of him. She would wonder if perhaps she had judged him too severely. After all, he was a duke, a very good-looking duke, at that. She should be grateful that such a catch would show her the least amount of attention.

"Your Grace," she said in a breathy voice, and gently removed her hand, took a step backward into the castle, and finished, "the way back to Niton is treacherous, even in the best of weather. You should be careful not to walk off the Undercliff in this fog."

Then she slammed the door in his face.

It began to rain. Not the typical drizzle, but a downpour, as if God, intent on taking the termagant's side in this most indelicate matter, decided to exact his special form of punishment. Water poured in a sheet from the clouds, spattered off Clayton's shoulders, and ran in rivulets down his face. Within seconds, his cloak was sodden and pools had formed around his feet.

"My lord," came Ben's drowned voice through the torrent, "shall I fetch you a cab?"

"Very funny," he snapped back, and continued to stare at the door, his teeth clenched and starting to chatter.

"Might I suggest that you discontinue your attempts at failed charisma and simply kick in the door, as any self-respecting duke would do when met with such blatant coarseness from an inferior."

Storm the stronghold. Right. He stared at the ancient barricade through the rain and darkness and cursed through his teeth.

Then the door opened again. Just slightly.

"Is he still there?" came her barely comprehensible voice from within.

Hoyt stared out at him, his spectacles becoming speckled by rain. "Aye," he replied. "Standin' there stiff as a corpse. And he ain't too happy, by the looks of 'im. Not that I can blame 'im. The weather ain't fit for a goose, much less a duke. Shall I invite him in, m'lady?"

"Oh, very well. If we must. But I warn you, Johnny, I shan't have a thing to do with him . . ."

Hoyt swung the door open and took an unsteady step backward, resting his weight on the crooked staff of a gnarled cane. Clayton glared at him through the downpour, his hands in fists at his sides, his clothes sodden through, then his gaze slid beyond the old man to the girl standing back from the door, hidden mostly in shadow, her arms clamped stubbornly across her breasts.

Finally, forcing a tight smile, Clayton stepped over the threshold into the bleak, dimly lit and cavernous foyer of gray stone and mortar that rose to Goliath heights above his head. He had hoped for light, of which there was little. He had prayed for warmth, of which there was none. He could almost see his breath as he exhaled with relief.

No sooner had Hoyt closed the door behind Benjamin, who, with a grunt of effort, dropped their saturated bags onto the floor, when the lady said, "I don't operate an establishment for the lost and wayward—not for you—again. This time, your dukeship, you will pay for your food and board, unlike last time when you and your misbegotten companions feasted upon our generosity not unlike a lot of leeches." Smugly, she added, "You may see yourself to your quarters. I believe you know the way."

Calmly, Clayton looked at Benjamin. Benjamin looked back, rain beading on his pink nose as his hound's eyes reflected his exact thoughts.

They didn't know the way to their quarters.

Finally, raising an eyebrow, Clayton said, "When I pay for my food and board, I expect service. That service includes the handling of my baggage."

She gasped and momentarily fumed. Then, with a huff of exasperation, she grabbed up the wet cases, struggled a moment until Hoyt lent a hand, and the two of them staggered off into the dark, laden with luggage. Clayton, with Ben at his side, followed a few paces behind.

"I shan't marry him, I tell you," the lass muttered to her companion, but just loudly enough that Clayton could hear. "Not for all his titles or wealth. I don't like him, Johnny."

"Give him a chance, lass. He seems much nicer this go 'round. Besides, I've never known you to turn away a being in need, even if he does look drowned as a piece of kelp."

The girl shifted the burdensome bag from one hand to the other and sighed. "If mama were here—"

"She wouldn't have hesitated to take the beggar in," Hoyt said, cutting her off. "You're just like her, you know. Beautiful, spirited, and stubborn. But there was never a truly mean bone in her lovely body. She had a way of makin' the poorest and most desperate traveler feel welcome. Aye, back then this old place didn't seem quite so dark and cold. Least not when she was present. In that way you are not like your mother—at least not tonight. I fear, m'lady, that you've grown too willful and hermetic for your own good. I cannot blame your mother, but myself. I was wrong to occupy your idle hours discussing Socrates and Plato, and encouraging this growing obsession for—"

"Hush!" she said, and cast a cautious glance over her shoulder. Clayton rewarded her with a complacent smile that conveyed his enjoyment watching her struggle with his baggage. In truth, he was more than fascinated by the conversation, and by the way her curtain of hair swayed like a willow branch from side to side each time she moved—as did her shapely backside. Perhaps in a moment, when his conscience dictated that he must, he would offer to help.

"I should have convinced your mother to send you away to a proper school," Hoyt announced with a touch of exasperation.

"Where I might have learned to pluck the strings of a harp or tickle the keys of a harpsichord. I think not, sir. My life is here, at Cavisbrooke, where I'm free to be myself . . . and to cherish those things I love most."

At last, after trudging forever, it seemed, through dark tunnel after drafty hall of bleak stone, upon watching their hosts labor up narrow twisting stairwells, dragging the baggage behind them, they finally arrived at a suite of vast, cold, and mostly unfurnished chambers. Their hostess flung Clayton's valise onto the floor, and breathing hard, she faced him and declared, "I won't bring you tea, nor will I serve you breakfast in bed. Should you desire hot water for your bloody scented baths, you may fetch it and heat it yourself. I will not supply you with a cart and ass so you might jaunt into Niton for a binge at the pub so you and your infantile inebriates can later storm through my home like a lot of mush-brained sots with the mentality of lads in knickers. You will not refer to me again as a 'comely little wench' or a 'sassy piece of stuff,' nor will you call me 'Red.' I am Lady Cavendish to you, sir, and I will reiterate that I have no desire to invite your attentions in the matter of matrimony or anything else. I don't like you, duke. Nor do I like your friends or your way of living. I don't care how many estates you own, nor do I care that you dine regularly with King George. You and your friends are arrogant boors, and if I could relive any action in my life, it would be the day I found you and your cockeyed companions washed up on shore like a lot of kelp-drenched pickled herrings. This time I would leave you there for crab bait. On second thought, the damn crabs wouldn't have you, either."

With that, Lady Cavendish gracefully stepped around Clayton and exited the room, leaving Hoyt to lean upon his staff and peer with a bemused expression at Benjamin, whose jaw had dropped at his first glance of their barren apartment, and then at Clayton. "I reckon I ain't ever seen her take such a dislike to a person," he announced with a tone of perplexity. Then, with a shake of his head and a tap of his cane on the floor, the man followed his mistress into the dark.

A tight smile still on his lips, Clayton stared at the empty threshold.

"Sir," Ben said behind him, "what would you like to do now?"

"Truly?" The smile slid from Clayton's lips. "Murder my brother."

Upon slamming the heavy door behind her, Miracle, breathing hard to catch her breath, leaned against it, slid her hand in her pocket, and closed her fingers around the bag of acorns she had earlier used in her ridiculous attempt to toy with moon gods.

Certainly, the fact that the odious duke had shown up at the precise moment she had asked Cupid to reveal the face of her future husband had only been coincidence.

She loathed the pontifical blue blood! Besides, she didn't believe in Ceridwen's charms. They were nothing more than jottings in an ancient black book whose pages were turning to dust—soon to be forgotten tales conjured up by "daft old biddies who couldn't nab a husband with quicksand," as Johnny termed the wisewomen.

She lit a candle and moved to a trunk against the wall, carefully withdrew Ceridwen's bible, and stared at it fiercely. Outside, the wind whistled around the crumbling turret—one of the first strongholds Walter de Godyton had built when constructing the castle.

An owl hooted.

Miracle jumped, spilling the candle and book to the floor. High above her, on a rafter near the ceiling, the round-faced bird peered down at her, its wide eyes unblinking in its white-feathered face.

It hooted again.

Grabbing up the book, Miracle carefully fingered through the dusty, thin pages until finding The Owl Love Spell.

> To hear the owl call in the time of the Morrigan, when there is no moon, is a disturbing sign; for it presages a tide of events haunted by troubles and sorrow, and struggle must be entered upon to ensure that all things should work together for good.

Sinking onto the floor, gripping the book in her hands, Miracle sighed. "I knew it. That infuriating buffoon of a duke is going to be trouble."

I ne'er was struck before that hour
With love so sudden and so sweet,
Her face it bloomed like a sweet flower
And stole my heart away complete.
JOHN CLARE

Chapter Three

Clayton had slept little. For hours after the foul-tempered, pugnacious ogress and her companion Hoyt—a surprisingly likable but peculiar man—had shown them to their quarters, he had paced the frigid confines of the drafty chamber, nagged by thoughts of ending this questionable escapade before it began. One could carry brotherly duties only so far, after all. Especially since Trey had lied about the circumstances of his relationship with the dislikable chit. Obviously, this was simply another one of the duke's waggeries intended to reward his companions in debauchery with a bit of humor. No doubt at this very minute they were nursing their hangovers and chuckling over this despicable farce.

Then again, it was a well-known fact that his brother was hurting financially, and the duchess, over the last months, had been vocal about her displeasure over Trey refusing to marry and produce heirs.

Clayton had a good mind to go through with the idiotic scheme. Might teach Trey a lesson. Might teach his iron-willed, meddlesome grandmother a thing or two, as well. Trey would wind up with a wife he didn't want, and the duchess would suddenly find herself having to explain to her peers that her grandson, the duke, had married a lunatic pauper.

What Trey really needed was a swift kick of reality. He should have to earn his keep by the sweat of his brow, the way Clayton had been forced to do when first striking out on his own. Clayton had asked for and received nothing from the dowager duchess. He had simply thrown himself into the restoration of the abandoned Basingstoke Hall in Salisbury, had plowed the fields himself until his hands bled and, eventually, harvested some of the finest crops in the area. He'd taken that money, invested, gambled, and made his own fortune. He still had the scars on his hands to prove it.

He did owe Trey. He could hardly deny it. Obviously, Trey must be treading deep water for him to call in his marker now.

Still, there had to be some other way. After all, Trey had obviously lied about his relationship with the young woman. Before Clayton had left England for France, where his mistress resided, his brother had informed him that he and Lady Cavendish had parted on friendly terms. She had supposedly mentioned that she would look forward to seeing him again, even hinted that she would be sensitive to his courting her. Dupe that he was, Clayton had fallen for it. Surely, he must be slipping. It had been a very, very long time since anyone had managed to bluff him successfully.

Clayton frowned and moved to the open door of the adjoining room. Within the dim interior, Benjamin lay sleeping on a rickety cot, a thin blanket pulled up to his chin. He snored softly in the quiet.

Hard to believe that a mere four nights ago Clayton had been sleeping in his mistress's arms. Warm. Dry. Satiated and a little drunk. He'd convinced her that he was venturing to the Isle of Wight on business for his brother. Hardly a lie.

Still, there had been a time in the not too distant past when he might have reconsidered leaving the Countess Blanche Delarue-Madras unoccupied for so long. Of all his lovers, she had come closest to tempting him to marriage. She didn't need his money, after all. She had plenty of her own. At seventeen, her parents had married her off to a shriveled-up, bantam cock of a count with short legs, a limp, a gorilla chest, and a face like a fox cub, who was thirty years her senior. Soon after the birth of their only child, the count had dropped dead in the arms of one of his many mistresses. His family had rewarded Blanche amply for her endurance and set her off on her own, their well wishes singing in her ears.

Ah, yes. The Countess Delarue-Madras was exquisite: always willing, eager, voluptuous. Their times in bed had been hot and fierce.

Clayton had eventually grown bored, even with her. In truth, he had grown bored with nearly everything in his life. Wealth and success offered him little challenge any longer. Why else would he have agreed to come here, to the edge of this most inhospitable world, away from his predictable escapades at the gaming tables or clubs? While Basingstoke Hall offered the sanctuary of comfort and home, in the last years it had grown unbearably lonely. One could only throw so many soirees, so many hunts. Christ, his disregardful friends had blasted away every fox within three counties.

Stepping from the room, closing the door behind him, Clayton glanced up and down the immense corridor, acknowledging the primitive little candles sputtering in the badly corroded brass sconces on the wall. No carpets here, only stone. The dampness seemed to creep up through the soles of his boots. No paintings hung on the walls, only an occasional spider's web fluttering from the low oaken beamed ceiling.

What woman in her right mind wouldn't jump at any opportunity to escape these surroundings? he mused as he carefully picked his way down the shadowy hall. *What woman in her right mind would live here?* The year was

1800, for God's sake, yet the castle was not much more modern than something Henry the Eighth might have lived in, and that was being generous, he decided. If he could believe what the old farmer had told him, Cavisbrooke Castle had been erected in the days of William the Conqueror.

Mostly, why the blazes would his brother choose this particular, obviously insane hoyden to marry . . . even if he did simply wish to spite the duchess?

Clayton stopped and listened. He had heard a noise behind him.

He glanced around, into the dark from which he had just come.

There was a movement there. A scurrying. Perhaps a rat. No doubt the place was crawling with them.

Pulling his watch from his coat, he flipped it open and strained hard to make out the time.

Eight in the morning. Perhaps it was too early yet for the lady of the manse to be about. He wandered on, down the maze of corridors, eventually becoming totally lost in the vast maze of sprawling, empty rooms and galleries that virtually echoed with their own silence. Clayton rehearsed the excuses he would make to his hosts—reasons why he would be forced to leave on such short notice—not that he needed an excuse, of course. The Lady Cavendish would be more than happy to escort him right off the perilous lip of the Undercliff.

What was her name? He tried to remember.

Trey had only referred to her as Lady Cavendish, but had, in passing, called her . . . Marianne? Margaret?

Damn. Was there not one blasted servant in the wretched place? A soul could starve for lack of food and heat . . . for even a slender thread of daylight to warm him. . . .

At last, he passed through an entry leading to a narrow, arched corridor that glowed with occasional shafts of yellow light spilling through a scattering of paltry embrasures. The sound of voices touched his ear, and cautiously, he moved toward them, pausing at the entrance of a generous cell. It was not a commodious apartment, certainly, but in the matter of light and air, at least it had the advantage over the black closet of rooms he had previously passed through.

Instead, it was a garden, lush and riot, its walls offering sanctuary to the plant and animal life abiding there. The garden was full of wonderful wall fruit, Indian corn, Caroline beans, and watermelons. Glowing in the sun were pyramids of hollyhocks and masses of China asters, cloves, mignonettes, and geraniums.

Even in its present ruined and roofless state, the great gray mass of the donjon rose to a height of a hundred feet above the ground. The floors were all gone, certainly, long since having fallen to complete collapse under the onslaught of centuries and the constant bombardment of wind and rain. Still, an outside stair led to a doorway on the second floor, formerly probably reached only by ladder. There, he noted what must have once been a small oratory, a chapel of sorts, since the altar could still be seen. Some traces of red and yellow frescoes clung to the ruined wall.

Yet it was not the sad mystery of a bygone era that captured his eye but the girl.

The red-haired girl who, with the sun washing profusely over her head and shoulders as she stooped among the verdantly growing flowers and vegetables, conversed in a musical voice with her companion.

"I would much prefer to debate Don Francisco Salva's discovery of galvanic electricity than the distasteful topic of our visitor . . . Duke What's-His-Name."

"Salterdon," Hoyt reminded her with an air of amused disgruntlement.

For a while she remained silent, immersed in her pleasant task of turning the dark soil around the roots of the plants. Her cheeks appeared rosy from her exertion, her countenance thoughtful. Odd how these cloisterlike surroundings enhanced the serenity of the moment, and the strange, surprising, and discomfiting realization pricked him that the lass yonder (no siren, wraith, or wretch—far from it) might soon belong to his brother, should Clayton decide to go through with the implausible ruse.

"I found him rude," she finally said, plucking a weed from a clump of peonies. "And arrogant. You know how I feel about arrogance, Johnny."

"He's a duke. He has a right to be arrogant."

"Nay. No man has the right to hold himself above another. You and mama taught me that yourselves."

"Aye, damn me. I never realized my own sense of morality would bare its teeth and bite me. Still, he's a guest. Did your mother not teach you the blessings of cordiality? For if she did not—"

"His hands are cold."

Clayton raised one eyebrow, crossed his arms over his chest, and leaned against the wall.

"Cold!" she reiterated and poked at the ground with her trowel. "And his eyes are . . . are mean-spirited. Yes, mean-spirited. A woman should be made to feel—"

"Pretty!" Johnny exclaimed. "Desirable! By granny, lass, you're more like your mother than I thought. She who crows about disliking arrogance. What about vanity? Eh?"

Her laughter rang in the ceilingless chamber like bells, the music echoing off the walls, floating like sun motes onto the brilliant, top-heavy flowers. Silence lingered as she sat back on her heels with her face turned into the light that drifted from the roofless height. She remained that way, her features growing flushed and slightly moist. The profound quiet was broken only by the cries of the rooks circling and swooping in black flocks above the summit where, across the deep blue square of sky, white clouds drove in quick succession.

Transfixed, Clayton could do little but stare. Even when something made her turn her head and her enormous aqua eyes met his, he could not move.

"Oh," her soft lips whispered. "He's here."

Johnny looked around from his cushioned perch on a lichen-covered stone chair whose base resembled burdened cherubs. His round face broke into a smile, and his blue eyes twinkled. "Your Grace! Please join us."

Rewarding the man with a dry smile, Clayton said, "Dare I? Is she dangerous?"

"Ho ho! I would not put it past her this morn. Seems her mood is a trifle sore, though I cannot imagine why."

Finally, the young woman regained her feet, stood uncertainly among the bowing geraniums, her fawn-colored skirt brushing her legs just above her ankles. She wore brown kid slippers and ribbed worsted stockings. She clutched a basket of onions and cabbages in one hand, pruning shears in the other. "Your Grace," she said. "Duke—"

"What's-His-Name," Clayton quipped.

Lifting her chin, flashing Hoyt a look, she set her shoulders in a stubborn angle and chewed her lower lip.

"Join us, Your Grace. Please." Hoyt motioned toward another chair, partially buried in a tangle of honeysuckle.

"Only if my arrogance and rudeness doesn't offend you."

Hoyt guffawed and chuckled under his breath. Lady Cavendish lowered her eyes briefly, then she gazed at Clayton from beneath her heavy lashes, her scrutiny of him intense and cautious, as if she had been caught unprepared.

Clayton stepped into the garden, hesitated long enough to enjoy the feel of the sun on his shoulders, then took his place beside Johnny, releasing a spray of perfume from the pollen-laden blooms.

"Miracle," said the old man. "It isn't polite to stare at your guest."

Miracle. So that was her name. Unusual. Like her. It suited her, Clayton decided, then mentally did his best to bury the thought. He had prepared himself not to like her, to thumb his nose at any attempt to woo her (for his brother's sake), to accept her invitation to leave as soon as possible. After all, he'd tried—and that was all he owed Trey. Then again, he had not been prepared for her, poised amid peonies, sunshine splashing across her perfect features.

Miracle turned away, carefully threaded her way through the flowers, fetching up another basket of turnips and carrots she had earlier placed against a far wall that was festooned in maidenhair ferns, delicate trailing vines, and velvety moss. She looked, he thought, like a fairy nymph, and she was just as elusive. He suddenly understood why his brother had chosen her as his duchess. Her naïveté radiated from her features in a way that was breathtaking. There was no hypocrisy in that face, no envy, no jealousy, certainly no cynicism. And she was surely no lunatic. The lunacy was in her being here, residing in this medieval dungeon when there was an entire world out there starving for her sort of innocence.

"Did you rest well?" Johnny asked him.

"Never better," Clayton lied, his gaze still on the girl.

"I'll see that more peat is delivered to your room. Can't have you freezing on us. Agreed, Mira?"

"Perhaps his dukeship won't be staying," she said pointedly, her fine dark brows drawing slightly together as she continued to regard Clayton.

"Poppycock! His Grace has traveled all this way to see you again. Why shouldn't he be staying? Right, Salterdon?"

Clayton crossed his legs, reason thumping him on the back of his head. He had made up his mind not to become involved in Trey's caper. He had rehearsed his reasons for bidding his hosts a fond farewell—right up until the moment he had stepped up to that door and set eyes on a . . . Miracle.

"Yes," he responded thoughtfully. "You're absolutely right."

A stilted moment, then Miracle turned back to her work, going to her knees again in the rich dirt. Her hair flowed in fiery silken streams over her shoulders and pooled on the ground near her hands where she dug.

"Mira told me you landed at the Race," Johnny said. "After your initial bout with those bloody rocks, I might have assumed you would opt for the ferry this time."

"My first bout?" Clayton frowned, his thoughts occupied on the girl's hands, dusty, long-fingered, and delicate. For an instant he forgot his brother's flirtation with death and why he, Lord Basingstoke—no, the duke—was there in the first place.

Where the blazes is my head? he wondered, narrowing his eyes and regarding Miracle even harder, his sense of annoyance growing that she could so easily ignore him, in light of the circumstances. "I had business in France," he finally replied. "It seemed a waste of time to sail all the way around the island just to catch the ferry."

"Where are your friends?" Miracle said without looking at him.

"I beg your pardon?"

"I said—"

"I can't hear you, my lady."

Exasperated, Miracle jabbed her trowel into the dirt and turned to face him. "Are you deaf?" she demanded.

"Quite the contrary. I'm simply accustomed to people looking at me when we converse."

"My apologies, Your Highness."

"Your Grace," he corrected her with a dry smile.

"Your Grace," she returned, the tone so condescendingly sweet it might have stung like a slap had he not found the flash of belligerence in her outrageous eyes so mesmerizing.

"Where are your companions?" she repeated.

"Yet snoring away, I presume," Clayton replied.

"I don't mean *that* companion. I mean *the others*." She wrinkled her sparsely freckled nose. "Those detestable men who followed you about like adoring puppies."

"Mira!" scolded Johnny.

"You thought them odd yourself, Johnny. Don't deny it. You thought the duke rather odd as well."

Blustering and turning five shades of pink, Johnny squirmed on his chair and grabbed for his cane, a gnarled stick of driftwood with a handle carved into the likeness of a horse head.

"In what way?" Clayton asked.

Her countenance coming to life, Miracle leapt gracefully to her feet. "After you were coughed up from the sea, we brought you into the bosom of our family, offered you all the comforts of our home, and you treated us as if we were little more than your servants, barking orders, whining about your 'less than agreeable accommodations.' And when you and your thoroughly detestable friends departed, you didn't so much as offer a shilling for our troubles. If you, sir, are any indication of what aristocracy has come to, I thank God that I was fortunate to be brought up here, a world away from such flagrant pretension."

"Are you finished?" Clayton said, his eyes narrowed slightly, a sardonic curl on his lips.

"No, actually." Grabbing up her skirt, she stepped over a row of frilly carrot tops, allowing Clayton a generous display of stockinged leg, and planted herself before him. She wagged one dirt-encrusted finger in his face. "I cannot conceive of how you would have the audacity to return here and think that I would harbor the least inclination for you. I don't care if you *are* a duke. There is much to be said for humility, not to mention civility. The most gallant hero is made all the more valiant by his ability to offer a simple thank-you to his inferiors. You, sir, are gauche."

"Great goose!" gasped Hoyt, and swooned in his chair, legs flung open, his cane falling to the ground with a thump.

"Johnny!" Miracle cried, and jumped to his aid.

Clayton quit his chair in one fluid movement, grabbed the old man, as did Miracle, and righted him on his cushion. Upon digging in her skirt pocket, Miracle withdrew a tiny vial of liquid, and once removing the cork stopper, proceeded to wave it beneath the beleaguered servant's nose. He sputtered and coughed. His eyes watered. Frantically, he shoved it away with a snort. "Good goose, gal, you'll kill me yet with that disgusting medicament."

"Are you all right?" Miracle asked him softly, the anger on her face now replaced by deep concern for her friend and companion.

"Hardly," he snapped rubbing the stench from his nose with the back of his liver-spotted hand. "How should I act when you insult the only man who has shown any inclination toward courting you? Good grief, I swore to your mother that I would see that you were taken care of and kept as happy as possible, considering the circumstances, but you are obviously intent on thwarting my every intent to do just that."

She blinked her enormous aquamarine eyes and set her jaw, rocked back on her heels, and frowned.

"Don't give me that look, miss. You know it's the truth. And don't deny that you've not grown a little moon-eyed over the possibility of winding up a spinster. I've heard you chanting to those bleeding acorns of yours, casting ridiculous love spells taught to you by some old witch named Ceridwen."

"She's a wisewoman, Johnny."

"Horse hockey! If she were so wise, she'd have found her own self a husband. Give me my cane."

"Why?"

"I'm off to the lighthouse."

"I'll fetch you the cart."

"I'll walk."

"Don't be daft."

"Need I remind you about civility, or does that not apply when addressing your elders?"

Her cheeks went bright red, and Miracle fixed her attentions again on Clayton. "Now see what you've done."

"What *I've* done?" he replied.

"You've been here only a few short hours and already you've brought dissension to this place."

"Basingstoke!" came the unexpected cry from the door.

All heads turned as Benjamin stumbled into the garden, his face bloodless, his knees wobbly as clotted cream. "My lord!" he croaked as the strength melted from his legs and he sat down with a painful grunt.

"Good God," Clayton and Johnny said in unison.

Clayton and Miracle reached the manservant at the same time. His white hair sticking out from his head like ruffled feathers, he clutched at Clayton's suit coat with trembling hands. His eyes were wide and wild.

"For the love of God, man, speak up and tell me what's happened," Clayton demanded.

"I saw it with my own eyes, sir."

"What?"

"The beast. It was there beyond my door, its cloven hooves clattering on the stones like bones in the wind."

"A beast." It wasn't a question.

"Huge it was, and white as a dozen ghosts, its black eyes flashing with fire and smoke rushing from its nostrils. It were awful, my lord. Wretched. Leering at me from the darkness. And the sound it made . . ." The manservant shuddered. "A roaring, blowing sound. A growl deep in its throat. And if that weren't enough—"

"Don't tell me there's more," Clayton said.

"A specter with black skin and half a face. A man draped in robes that dragged the ground. He babbled at me in tongues."

Miracle gasped and covered her lips with her fingertips. She glanced up at Johnny, who peered at Benjamin, wide-eyed, over Clayton's shoulder, all evidence of his own seizure having miraculously vanished.

"He babbled, did you say?" Hoyt queried.

Benjamin frantically nodded.

"In tongues?" Miracle ventured.

"You've seen them?" Benjamin said, his voice rising with fresh trepidation.

"No!" Johnny exclaimed.

"Certainly not!" Miracle agreed.

Clayton allowed his manservant a compassionate smile and a slap on the back. "Relax, Ben. No doubt you were only dreaming again. I'm certain our kind hosts will attest to the fact that Cavisbrooke Castle is without ghosts."

"I wouldn't go so far as to promise that," Miracle declared under her breath, causing Benjamin's gray brows to shoot up again, and Clayton to briefly close his eyes in frustration. "Rumor is, that the previous gentry who resided here, having determined to investigate every secret dungeon and passageway in the castle, happened upon a heavy iron door securely fastened. He forced it, passed through a narrow passage hewn out of solid rock, forced another door, and found himself in a small, dim room, at the opposite extremity of which he made out the figure of a man of gigantic stature, seated on a stone and holding his head between his hands; at his feet was a small wooden coffer. The gentleman made a step forward, but as the outer air came in contact with the body, it crumbled into dust, and the secret of its identity perished." Lowering her voice slightly, she added effectively, "Ever since, unwelcome guests have sworn they heard the poor departed wretch banging on the walls and wailing for release."

Lips pressed, jaw locked, Clayton snatched the vial of foul-smelling oil from Miracle's hand, and as Benjamin's eyes rolled back in his head, Clayton growled, "Thank you."

"You're welcome." Miracle smiled.

Experience teaches us that love does not consist of two people looking at each other, but of looking together in the same direction.

ANTOINE DE SAINT-EXUPERY

Chapter Four

Often she had anathematized her own susceptibility. She had been cursed with the inability to remain angry at anyone who showed the least amount of contrition for their dirty deeds, a trait she had obviously inherited from her mother, considering the dear woman had forgiven Miracle's father for virtually abandoning them to Cavisbrooke Castle. But she wasn't about to forgive his dukeship, no matter that he had shown such concern over Johnny (a mere groom) that morning in the wall garden. No matter that he had spoken to her in a far less offensive and abasing tone. No matter that his gray eyes, so cold and reprehending before when he had looked at her, now reminded her of smoldering peat ash. No matter that his hands were no longer cold.

She couldn't be certain, of course. He had only touched her briefly, first the evening before at her threshold (when they had definitely been cold), then his hand on hers when he seized her vial of eel bile oil in hopes of recovering his manservant from a dead swoon.

How dare he make her feel guilty for frightening his ridiculously gullible valet! She tore the crust from a round of stale bread and tossed it out the window to the pigeons that perched on the windowsill, cooing and hungrily watching with tiny black eyes.

"I was simply telling the truth," she said aloud to the birds, yanking out the spongy center of the bread and flinging it the way of the crust.

Snatching up a ladle, she dipped it into the simmering pot of curried mulligatawny soup swimming with turnips and carrots and peas, spooned the stew into the hollowed bread, then piled it high with yellow cheese. She shoved the lot into the stone oven, where the heat from the hearth beside it puffed the cheese and toasted it to a gold brown, sealing the heat and soup within the hollowed loaf of bread.

Miracle wrapped the bread in a warmed cloth and tucked it into a basket. She left the castle at a quick pace, swinging the basket at her side, humming to herself, and trying her best not to think about Duke . . . What's-His-Name. Salterdon. Something Hawthorne.

He'd told her once, soon after she'd fished him out of the waves. He and his companions, who'd made no bones about the fact that they hadn't cared for the attention the duke had paid her.

Not that he had paid her a great deal of attention, other than to point out her shortcomings. Her hair was too curly and too long. She should learn how to properly fashion it or she would be looked down upon by the gentry of London.

She'd informed him that she had no intention of moving to London or any place in its proximity.

He had gone on to complain that the food was too sparse, her home was too cold, and the castle's furnishings were uncomfortable and appallingly primitive. He said that her clothes were hardly fit for a bone grubber.

That had made her cry—to herself, of course. She had just finished sewing the dress the evening before. Her fingertips had still been sore from the grueling effort of manipulating the dull needle.

"Miracle!" came *his* deep voice from somewhere behind her.

Speak of the devil . . . Blazes! she thought, and picked up her stride, headed for the shortcut that slashed minutes off her trek to the lighthouse. She didn't like taking it; the steep, narrow path was dangerous; she only used it in a pinch, when a sudden storm or fog would blanket the dangerous Race and jeopardize any ship that might have ventured too close in the weather. By the looks of the sky, however, and the dark clouds building along the horizon, they shouldn't expect rain until nightfall. Until then, she had hoped to enjoy her dinner as far away from Duke What's-His-Name as she could get.

"Miracle!" the duke repeated.

"I don't recall giving you permission to use my given name," she told him as he moved up behind her. "Or perhaps manners don't apply to dukes when they address their inferiors."

He strolled up beside her, his long legs in high boots easily keeping pace. He had shucked his suit coat. His blousy shirt and silk ascot looked very white against his sun-kissed face.

Tall, she thought, and noted the top of her head barely reached his shoulder.

Odd that she hadn't noticed on his previous stay. Then again, she hadn't noticed much of anything other than his arrogance and bent for tomfoolery.

"It wasn't nice what you did to Benjamin," he said.

"*You* are not nice," she retorted, and shifted her basket to the hand between them, forcing him to switch sides.

He said nothing.

Miracle glanced at his hands and the thought struck her that they didn't seem nearly so white as they had been before—as if they had never known a moment's honest labor.

Coming to the top of the path at last, Miracle hesitated briefly before plunging ahead, carefully picking her way down the steep, rutted track, making certain to keep well away from the wicked ledge that dropped straight down to the ocean, hundreds of feet below. A moment passed before she realized that the duke had not joined her.

Miracle stopped. She looked back. Shielding her eyes against the sun, she regarded Salterdon where he stood, somewhat frozen, upon the precipice. The wind, always gusting briskly up the sides of the Undercliff, fluttered his shirt and hair, giving him a wild look.

"You don't look like a duke," she mused aloud.

"No?" he replied, raising his voice to be heard over the groan of the wind. "What *do* I look like, Lady Cavendish?"

"A farmer."

"Ah," she thought he said, and imagined that he smiled—just a flash of white teeth, then it was gone. Was he laughing at her? No doubt he found her observation silly, if not outright foolish. And perhaps it was, she thought. What would a duke know about farming? Especially *this* duke.

She turned back down the path, sending a dozen small stones scattering over the cliff and plunging to the sea below. She walked on, more slowly, listening for the sound of his step, and once realizing that he had not joined her, paused and glanced back again.

"Are you coming?" she called up where he remained, hands clenched at his sides, his features set in a most curious fashion.

"Should I take that as an invitation?" he called back.

"You may take that as simple impatience," she returned. "My meal is growing cold."

A moment passed, then another. The duke stared down at her with his intense gray eyes and his jaw working. Growing weary of his apparent inability to make a decision, Miracle turned on her heel, and with fresh determination began her descent down the steep, winding slope, stones and tussocks of grass providing a foothold. Her heart jumped and raced when the sounds of skipping pebbles touched her ear—he had joined her after all—but as she set her chin at an obstinate angle and glanced over her shoulder, prepared to reward him with an *I might have known you would chose to tag along* expression, the odd look in his eyes stopped her; he wasn't looking at her, but at the roaring, crashing sea far below. His face appeared shockingly pale.

She paused in her step and skidded on pebbles, the disturbance frightening a covey of gulls nesting near the ledge. They exploded into the air around her and him, wings flapping and snapping as the birds shrieked in alarm. Like a flash, the duke grabbed her arm in a fierce, protective grip that unsettled her more than the prospect of tumbling off the grievous ledge. Far from feeling cold, his fingers burned through her sleeve like coals.

"How very gallant," she declared, and yanked her arm away. "Is that how you intend to win me over, your dukeship? Become my hero? My lionhearted knight in shining armor intent on slaying dragons?"

"My apologies," he snapped in a tight voice, and released her, his gaze yet directed down toward the distant waves. "I only thought—"

"To save me from those monstrous birds?" She laughed lightly and smugly. "By the look on your face, duke, I should be rescuing you."

At last, his gaze came back to hers. It was hard and penetrating, causing the smile to slide from her lips. She bumped her basket against her leg, once, twice while she chewed her lower lip and pondered the unnerving sensation fluttering in the vicinity of her heart. She had never been one to make light of anyone's shortcoming or fears, yet, with the arrival of this unwelcome caller and his companion, she apparently had been intent on doing just that. It was his fault, of course. For some unexplained reason, his presence bothered her—unlike his previous stay at Cavisbrooke when she had laughed away his idiotic behavior like one would an amusing if not annoying stray pup.

More gently, she said, "I'm in no need of gallantry. I'm very capable of taking care of myself. I have for twenty years. Besides, you're really not the sort I would choose to marry even if I were to take this outrageous interest in me seriously."

"No?" he replied in an annoyed tone. "What, pray tell, is wrong with me, m'lady? Am I not handsome enough?"

Her eyebrows went up, then she frowned and toed a stone with her foot. Once again, she started down the path, treading more carefully and more slowly as he stubbornly pursued her.

"Well?" he demanded.

"I find no fault in the way you look," she finally replied, more to herself than to him.

"Then perhaps you think I'm not moneyed enough."

"I have no doubts of your wealth, Your Grace. Anyone can tell by looking at your clothes that you are hardly a spendthrift. Your manners are impeccable, when you use them. Your way of speaking is dignified and refined, obvious evidence of your education. I'm certain your lineage runs with the bluest of blood. Your closets are no doubt rattling with the bones of royal kinsmen."

Reaching an outcropping ledge of rock no larger than a table, Miracle shielded her eyes from the sun and gazed out over the span of white-tipped water and pale blue sky before dropping to her knees and throwing back the napkin covering her bread-bowl of soup. “In short,” she said, casting a curious glance back at the duke, who remained on the path with his back pressed against the wall of the Undercliff, “ ’Tis not looks, nor wealth, nor lineage that will ultimately win my heart, but humbleness, kindness, consideration . . . those are traits I most admire, Your Grace. Would you choose to join me in my meal, sir? Or don’t you care for plowman’s fare?”

He did not move, nor did he respond, just continued to stand there, back braced against the wall, the wind whipping his dark hair and white shirt while his gray-as-stone eyes regarded her without blinking.

Miracle tore away a bit of bread, contemplating it a moment, then lifted it high and held it in her fingertips. In a matter of seconds a threesome of gulls swept down from the sky. One snatched the treasure, and to a chorus of belligerent squawking from his companions, soared off into the heavens. “You and I, Your Grace, are incompatible. This is how I enjoy spending my idle hours, ascending the clouds with my friends there. The man I marry must know how to fly.

“I have little patience for the sort of amusement found in drink,” she said, and offered more bread to the crying, greedy gulls. “Such frivolity is normally followed by guilt or regret. How can one truly enjoy this false, bottled happiness, knowing ’tis only momentary and will, eventually, offer little more than misery the morrow after?”

“For God’s sake,” he finally replied, leaning harder against the stone wall as a sudden brief rush of wind whipped around his shoulders and threatened to unbalance him. “You desire a bloody saint, madam. Must he also be chaste?”

“Preferably.” She nodded and turned her face into the wind.

“Then I beg your pardon, m’lady. It is you who should be draped in nun’s clothes and locked away in a convent. Obviously you expect a bloody miracle.”

“I shall expect my husband to be faithful, sir, and cherish me above all others.” Her voice grew tight with emotion, and raising her chin and setting her shoulders, she added with fresh determination, “He’ll be proud of me, of course, and unafraid to present me to the world, unashamed of my ability to stand alone and without peer in my way of behavior and thinking. He would lay down his life for my right to be free of the strictures with which society would burden us.” Facing Salterdon again, her frustration growing as the salty bite of tears stung her eyes, she declared, “Yes, Your Grace, perhaps I do expect a ‘bloody miracle.’ But such miracles are possible if we simply believe, and have the patience to endure the wait. Are you a patient man, Salterdon?”

"No."

"I thought not. Your kind expects results instantly, with the snap of your fingers." She flung a bit of bread into the air and watched a bird streak in to catch it. "I'm certain you haven't the foggiest idea of what hunger really is, or emotional deprivation. Your world overflows with self-indulgence. Your larders are full. When you wish companionship, your power and titles will furnish you with any woman you desire."

"Obviously not *any* woman," he pointed out.

She raised one eyebrow. "Your Grace, I don't for a moment believe your reasons for returning to Cavisbrooke are to win me over to matrimony. And even if I did wish to believe it—which I don't—there is much that you would have to accomplish to win me over."

"Like walk on water and fly." A gull fluttered down and landed on his shoulder, cocked it's streaked head, and peered at him, eye to eye. "I'm sorry to say," he spoke to the bird, "that I can do neither."

The storm hit around midnight, as did the cold, driven by howling winds that whipped in drafts through the hallways of the castle like invisible spirits. Clayton slouched in a chair of carved, worm pitted oak with a worn, frayed tapestry upholstery that must have been one hundred years old if it was a day. Dust had risen in a cloud from its sagging seat when he had wearily dropped into it.

He wanted a drink—a stiff one. Preferably brandy. In his somewhat clandestine search of the premises, Benjamin had turned up nothing remotely resembling a distilled grog, which hadn't surprised Clayton, not after Miracle's ledge-top lecture earlier that afternoon. He ached from cold. Even the heavy woolen cloak he sat buried within did little to warm him. His jaws hurt from clenching his teeth to keep them from chattering. His toes were numb; his ears burned.

Before him, at a table piled high with neatly folded stacks of white linen shirts, Lady Miracle Cavendish slept with her head nestled upon a stack of partially sewn garments, her hair like shiny polished copper in the meager light of the oil lamp sitting on the table.

For the last two hours, Clayton had frozen in this place, watching her sleep, the needle and thread still pressed between her fingertips. What was she doing here, cloistered in the top of the old turret, away from what little comfort the lower chambers of the castle had to offer?

She seemed so small to him, even in this tiny chamber. Undoubtedly, she was a handsome young woman, with the kind of facial characteristics that would compliment her into her later years. Certainly, she was not like most of society's fashion-conscious femmes fatales whose youthful yet pretty plumpness would begin to sag by the end of their first year of marriage (once they had bagged a husband with a title), then slide completely into their swollen ankles with the birth of their first baby (by then hoping the husband with the title would vent his baser needs on his many mistresses, which he would happily do once he had successfully produced the necessary heirs).

Miracle would be different.

He imagined her slender and healthy, with wind-kissed cheeks and bright blue-green eyes, even after she'd birthed a half dozen astoundingly beautiful children—all of whom would look just like her.

That wouldn't happen, of course. How could he forget? The duke of Salterdon was interested in only one child—a boy. The fruit of his loins that would make Trey Hawthorne, the former duke of Salterdon's first-born son, one of the wealthiest men in England.

The wind beat upon the turret shutters, and thunder rumbled. The storm's force rolled onto the mainland and boiled around the castle, lightning brightening the room intermittently as the fierce spears erupted across the sky. Miracle stirred and drowsily forced open her heavy-lidded eyes. For a long moment she continued to rest there, her head on the pillow of soft white linen, while she appeared to make sense of her soundings. Then she saw him. She sat upright, her eyes wide, her breasts rising and falling rapidly.

"What are you doing here?" came her breathless voice.

"Watching you, obviously."

"How did you find this room?"

"I couldn't sleep—"

"So you invade the privacy of your host's home and wander about at will. How like you. Tell me where you went and what you found there. Confess, sir! What did you discover?"

"Rooms. Mostly empty. No wailing ghosts or tombs. Why? Are you hiding something here, Lady Cavendish, that you don't care for the world to see?"

The turret shook, as did the floor. The lamp on the table cast shivering light on the bare stone walls.

Frowning, the agitation on Miracle's features turning into sudden, chilling concern as her mind registered the tumult at last, she jumped from her chair and flew to the window, flinging the shutters wide, softly crying aloud as the frigid wind and rain washed over her.

"Damn fool, what was I thinking?" she called into darkness.

In three long quick strides, Clayton reached the window and grabbed for the shutter. Miracle caught his arm with surprising strength and pushed him away. Leaning against the window ledge, her face and shoulders fast becoming drenched by the icy deluge, she stared hard through the blackness, repeating, "What was I thinking?"

More forcefully, Clayton stepped between her and the window, narrowed his eyes, and caught his breath as he took the full brunt of the driving wind and rain. He grabbed the shutters, struggled with them momentarily, and finally slammed them closed.

"For the love of Christ," he said through his teeth, and turned to face her. She stood with her arms pressed to her breasts, hands clenched so tightly her knuckles shone white. Her hair clung to her head and shoulders in long, sodden strands. Her dress was wet through. "What the devil do you think you're doing? You'll catch your death."

Quickly, he removed his cloak and attempted to fling it around her. As quickly, she moved away, back to the table near the light, her eyes frantically searching the room as thunder shook the cell again. "I should be there—at the lighthouse. How could I have done this, fallen asleep that way?"

She stared down at the stack of sewing as if it might reveal an answer to her question.

"Please," Clayton said softly, taking a cautious step toward her and extending the cloak in one hand. "You're trembling, lass."

"No!" she shouted, her eyes wide and her cheeks red with anger. "Don't you think I know what you're doing? You don't give a leap whether I'm trembling, *Your Grace*. You simply want something from me—the same as all the others just like you—the well-heeled high stockings who converge on this island in your fine contraptions and your silk purses bulging with coins. You look at us as if we're specimens under glass. Curiosities. You murmur among yourselves that it's a shame that the island folk live so primitively and ignorantly. Yet you come here to buy our goods: our sheep that are the finest in England, our cattle, our wheat, you purchase our lace for your wives and mistresses, buttons and gloves for a pittance of what they're worth, then boast to your peers back in London how you bartered with 'the plebeians' until you 'practically stole' the merchandise from beneath them. Now, for some reason, you've come here and want me, but please be informed, *Your Grace,* the price one would have to pay for my heart is so far beyond your scale to imagine, you could not even begin to comprehend."

"And what price would that be, my lady? I'm a very wealthy man, rest assured, so there is little that is beyond my ability to pay."

"Love," she said with a lift of her small chin and a flash of her eyes. "Nothing more, sir, and nothing less."

Thunder cracked again, more loudly this time, causing mortar to rain from the ceiling. Miracle ran from the room. Clayton struck out after her, his ability to catch up hampered by the fact that he was unfamiliar with the narrow, spiraling stone steps that were now blanketed mostly in darkness since the meager candles had sputtered out.

She was headed for the lighthouse. He didn't need a gypsy to tell him that. And instinct told him she would take the quickest course, the trail she had taken just that morning: that wretched, narrow, winding little strip of sand and rock that balanced so precariously five hundred feet above the sea. One slip of her foot on the muddy path, and—

He burst through the doorway she had used before him, stumbled momentarily through the dark and rain, gasping for air, dizzied by the play of lightning in the clouds—giant, jagged streaks of white, yellow, and blue that danced about the towering turrets and donjon walls as if displaying some perverse ballet.

He called her name, "Miracle!" again and again, forcing his feet to move, cursing under his breath, first his brother, then her, then himself, his damnable weakness.

Ahead of him, she struck down the path, a barely visible apparition that was there one second, gone the next. Clayton slid to a stop at the crest of the trail and strained to catch a glimpse of her through the darkness and rain. His gut clenched. His legs froze. His heart climbed up into his throat and he couldn't swallow.

"Miracle!" he shouted again, hearing his words drowned in the downpour.

Far, far below him, he could hear the water writhe and roar like some flailing monster, and as the sky brightened again, casting arrows of electricity at the turbid sea, he saw Miracle on the path, fallen, clutching at a clump of tussock grass, her face turned up toward his and her wide eyes glassy with fear.

Clenching his fists, he took one step, then another, his boots sinking in the mud while the howling wind drove against him, battering his shoulders, shoving him toward the black abyss.

Finally, he reached her, braced himself against the wall, and grabbed her, locked his slippery fingers around her muddy wrists and dragged her to her feet. Miracle fell against him, clutching him, small body shaking uncontrollably, then she stumbled away again, back down the path. He caught her, spun her around, and shook her, shouting through the rain, "Little idiot! What the blazes do you think you're doing?"

"I have to go! There could be ships out there depending on me!"

"Listen to me. The tide is in, Miracle. It's impossible to get to the lighthouse—"

"There's a boat—"

"Dammit, lass, listen to this wind. To the waves. You wouldn't last ten seconds in a boat in this weather. Goddammit, I won't let you!"

With that, he tore off his cloak and flung it around her, wrapped her in it like a cocoon and swept her up into his arms, dug his boots into the mire, and plowed his way back up the path and through the rain, led back to the castle by the tiny yellow light flickering in a solitary window of the keep.

Upon kicking open the door, he strode purposefully down the maze of corridors, Miracle gripped in his arms, her face buried in his shoulder, their clothes dripping rain on the floor. Benjamin appeared from the darkness.

"Basingstoke!" came his gasp of surprise.

"Hot water," Clayton snapped. "And lots of it. And toweling. And blankets. And for the love of God, ferret out some peat and stoke the fires before the lass catches her death."

"Have done, sir, in the drawing room, as well as in our chambers," the valet added with a tone of righteous accomplishment.

The drawing room was one of the few comfortable chambers in Cavisbrooke. Walnut paneling glowed rosily from the fire in the hearth and the scattering of oil lamps around the room. There were carpets and oilcloths on the floor. A half dozen rush-bottomed chairs with backs and rails bright with wax and rubbing were scattered through the room, and a pair of overstuffed chairs had been placed before the fire. A handsome clock in a mahogany case ticked off the remaining minutes until half past midnight, and paintings of Jesus and his brethren hung on the walls.

Standing before the cheery fire, Miracle in his arms and breathing evenly, Clayton stared into the flames and allowed the room's silence and warmth to envelop him. Hard to believe that outside these massive walls a war of weather was exploding around them. Hard to believe he had challenged those elements to snatch the girl back from death's door. Very hard to believe, considering . . .

Easily, he lowered himself into a chair and continued to hold her, until the trembling in her body subsided little by little.

"I had to go," she said against his shoulder.

"Of course you did. I'm certain every seaman in King George's Navy depends on your light to show them the way home in a storm." He glanced down into her damp face and offered her a dry smile. The fire snapped, sending a spray of embers onto the hearth.

She frowned and pouted so adorably he almost smiled again. Almost . . .

"This is *your* fault, of course," she pointed out. "I'm normally not so rash and emotional. Had you not occupied my thoughts earlier I would have long since remembered to go to St. Catherine's, thereby avoiding the shortcut."

He looked thoughtful and toyed with a coil of her hair. "Encouraging, I think, that I've succeeded in bothering you so."

She regarded him intensely with her wide aqua eyes. Little by little her body relaxed, gently molding against his. Her lashes lowered.

"You saved my life," she whispered, nestling.

Clayton said nothing, just continued to hold her tightly—more tightly than he should, a voice in his head softly reprimanded. But she felt surprisingly good: soft, warm, holdable. Considering the coldness of the inclement night, a pliable, warm body felt damn nice.

Besides, he had a role to play, a seduction to accomplish. She had challenged him that afternoon on the hostile precipice, whether she realized it or not. He had never been a man to back away from a challenge.

Benjamin bustled in, his arms full of blankets. "I helped myself to the linen closet," he announced, then proceeded to fling the blankets over a chair. He quit the room hurriedly and returned as swiftly with a tray laden with a steaming pot of tea. "This should warm the young lady up, sir. I guarantee it."

Clayton glanced down into her watchful, gem-colored eyes and alabaster face. Her drying hair formed a wispy cloud of curls that enhanced the sculptured perfection of her features. Her lips were red, moist, soft.

He smiled. A real smile, not the typical sardonic curl of his lips.

Her brows drew together. "I've never seen you do that before," she said.

"Do what?"

"Smile."

"No?" He smiled again. "I suppose I don't do it very often."

"You really should. You're very severe, you know. Perhaps people would find you more likable if you smiled more."

"What makes you think people don't like me, Lady Cavendish?"

"Well . . . I was speaking generally, of course."

"Meaning yourself, possibly?"

She did not reply nor did she move, but she continued to watch him carefully from beneath her long black lashes in that way she had that reminded him of an enchanting angel: alluring, tempting, innocent.

"Sir," Benjamin spoke gently behind them. "The lady's tea is ready."

With little effort, Clayton stood and carried Miracle to the chair, tucked her within a blanket, then stepped back as Benjamin retrieved a wrap he had laid before the fire to warm, and snuggled it around her. He handed her the teacup, and she wrapped her fingers around it, briefly closing her eyes, relishing the warmth.

"See that she's taken care of properly," Clayton told his valet, hating the sound of his voice that was low and husky even to his own ears, then he turned for the door.

"Your Grace," Miracle called.

He paused, but did not look back.

"Thank you," she said softly.

Clayton sat before the pitiful excuse of a fire, drenched to the skin, chilled to the marrow, elbows on his knees and his head buried in his hands. He stared without seeing at the stone floor between his feet.

"This place is a veritable tomb," Benjamin announced as he poured a splash of hot, weak tea into a chipped china cup. Withdrawing a flask from his coat and removing the stopper, he poured a finger of brandy into it, then added a finger more. "I wager this'll warm the ice from your blood, my lord."

His head coming up, Clayton stared wearily at the steaming brew. "Where the blazes did you find that?"

"The brandy? Certainly not here, sir. I searched the cupboards half the day looking for a spot. Finally, deciding there wasn't a cask or keg to be found, I was forced to dip into my own . . . or your own. We brought it from Basingstoke, my lord."

"We?"

"I knew you enjoyed a nip every now and again. You know how you get occasionally, a bit on the morose side."

"I've never been morose in my life," he snapped.

"Ah! Very well, sir. Whatever you say." Benjamin slid the flask back into his coat and grabbed the heavy covering from the bed. He flung it around Clayton's shoulders.

Steam from the cup rose in an aromatic cloud into Clayton's face. "My front is roasting and my backside is freezing," he said through his teeth.

"Yes, sir."

"Where I'm from, we have fireplaces on each end of the room so our butts stay as warm as our—"

"Yes, sir."

"Tell me something, Benjamin."

"If I can, sir."

"What the hell am I doing here?"

"Let me see . . ." Carefully turning back the sheets on the bed, folding them precisely, then smoothing the pillow so not a solitary wrinkle marred its surface, the manservant contemplated the question. He straightened, standing very stiff and erect, and replied, "To the best of my knowledge sir, we have come to this most inhospitable place—that is, I vow, no matter what you choose to believe, swimming in departed spirits, not to mention cloven-footed demons—with the express purpose of luring the young woman, Lady Cavendish, into marriage with your brother. You, of course, are passing yourself off as His Grace, and—"

"Shut up," Clayton growled.

"Yes, sir."

"I take it from your tone that you don't approve."

"It is not my place to approve or disapprove, sir."

"Dammit, Ben, you've been like a father to me the last twenty years so don't start with this servantile poppycock now." Turning his head, Clayton glared up into his valet's eyes. "What do you think of the girl?"

"I think she is rather—"

"Do you like her?"

"Yes, I do."

"Do you think she'll be happy married to my brother?"

A look of concern turned down the corners of Benjamin's mouth.

"Don't bother to answer that. We both know there's not a woman alive who would tolerate his idiosyncrasies for long. Especially not her, and she clearly has no interest in him. Doesn't seem to have ever had."

"No? What sort would she tolerate?" Benjamin asked, pouring himself a cup of tea.

"A monk," he replied. "Better yet, a saint."

"Hardly terminology to adequately describe your brother . . . or yourself, for that matter."

Clayton relaxed back into his chair and stretched his long legs out toward the fire. In his mind, he saw her again, perched on that precarious ledge, feeding her meal to hungry birds, sunlight radiating from her face. "She desires a husband who can fly, Benjamin. How do you propose I manage that?"

Benjamin sipped his tea and looked ponderous. "I spent a good deal of time with Mr. Hoyt while you were out scaling cliffs and plundering birds' nests. It is my understanding that the Lady Lorraina was virtually abandoned here only days after her marriage to the now deceased Lord Cavendish. He returned to the castle only twice a year, and each time he promised his young wife that next time he would take her with him back to the mainland. He never did. From the time the lady came here until the night she kissed her daughter farewell and disappeared, she never left the island. For ten years, Lady Cavendish spent her days and nights in this formidable place and in the lighthouse, watching for her husband's return."

"Bastard," Clayton murmured into his tea.

"Indeed," Ben said, and put down his cup. "Yet you would submit the lass to the same fate. Ah, you look at me angrily, sir, but you cannot deny it. Your brother would marry her to appease your grandmother, then bury her away in some distant country house—"

"You forget yourself," Clayton snapped.

His voice growing softer, his shoulders relaxing, Benjamin said, "You could always leave here, sir. Return to London. Explain to your brother that the lass would have none of it. Better yet, tell him that she has already married. . . . Then again, that would be dishonest—"

"And I am not a dishonest man, am I, Benjamin?"

The servant drew back his shoulders and replied proudly, "No sir." A moment of silence, then, "Will that be all, my lord?"

Clayton drank down the hot tea, squeezing closed his eyes as the diluted brandy hit his stomach. "Yes," he replied hoarsely. As Benjamin turned for the door, he added, "And by the way, don't call me Basingstoke in front of the girl. Remember who I am and what I'm doing here . . . to win the lady's heart for my brother."

"Very well, sir." Benjamin walked to the door and paused. He watched Clayton intently for a moment before saying, "I suggest that you do the same, sir. Good night, sir."

"Good night," Clayton whispered, and sank back in his chair.

"What ideas have they been filling your head with, you young girls of to-day?"

Berthe replied: "But marriage is sacred, grandmamma."

The grandmother's heart, which had its birth in the great age of gallantry, gave a sudden leap. "It is love that is sacred," she said. "Listen, child, to an old woman . . . We marry only once, my child, because the world requires us to do so, but we may love twenty times in one lifetime because nature has so made us . . . If we did not perfume life with love, as much love as possible, darling, as we put sugar into medicines for children nobody would care to take it just as it is."

Berthe opened her eyes widely in astonishment. She murmured: "Oh! grandmamma, we can only love once."

from *A Grandmother's Advice*
by GUY DE MAUPASSANT

Chapter Five

Miracle placed a bowl of hot porridge onto the table before Jonathan Hoyt, then a saucer of scones. The table, the bench chairs, the iron-hooped harvest bottles, pewter, and stoneware utensils had furnished Cavisbrooke's kitchen for three hundred years.

"She's a worrier," Johnny stated while staring with some disappointment into his thick cereal, squinting one eye in order to more easily discern the conglomeration of grains and fruit swimming in a froth of rich cream and a slab of butter. "Has been since she was a child, always flutterin' about like a mother hen. . . . If I've told her once, I've told her a hundred times: There comes a time when the ignorant folk of this world must take care of themselves. If the damn fools ain't got the sense to make for port in a storm, they deserve to be smashed against the bloody Race."

Miracle cleared her throat, as if to remind him that Salterdon had been one of those "ignorant folk" not so long ago, then cast a glance at his dukeship, only to discover that the remark appeared to have fallen on deaf ears. Salterdon, like John, only stared down into his mash with contemplation.

Well, she thought, as least he had yet to complain about the spartan meal, as he had done on his first visit. In truth, he had said little at all that morning. Then again, neither had she, she realized. She supposed she should thank him again for his rather daring rescue the night before. Perhaps she would, she decided, at a more appropriate time.

Raising his eyebrows, fixing the sleepy-eyed duke sitting across the table with a speculative stare, Johnny said, "She says she cares about me health—"

"I do," Miracle interjected, and rewarded him with a brilliant smile and a pot of honey she fetched from the mahogany corner cupboard stacked untidily with blocks of cheeses, baskets of herbs, and bunches of brightly colored yarn.

"Sheep's fleas if you do. A woman who truly cares for a man's well bein' would feed him meat occasionally. This is a mornin' for rashers and black puddin'. She's constantly feedin' me as if I were a cow with the mulligrubs, Your Grace. Warm mash for breakfast, applesauce for me mid-meal, and potato pie and carrot fritters before bed, when what I'm *wantin'* is a slab of mutton this thick." He held up his fingers two inches apart, and his eyes looked dreamy.

"Too much meat will give you gout," she stated firmly and delivered the duke his porridge, bracing herself for his typical grunt of disapproval and a curl of his lips, at which time she would happily invite him to take a leisurely leap off the Undercliff, or else walk into Niton and partake at the Hound and Hare as he and his cohorts had done before.

Salterdon did not look up, but continued to stare somewhat bleary-eyed into his black coffee. He had not shaved so his jaw appeared very dark. No farmer today, she thought, but a gypsy whose hair was a trifle too long; it spilled over his noble brow and touched the bridge of his nose. He did, however, as his custom must dictate, wear a splendid cutaway coat to the table—not the midnight blue coat he had spoiled during last night's heroic escapade on the Undercliff, but an elegant forest green wool that made his eyes look dark as slate—*when* he looked at her. He'd barely acknowledged her all morning, however.

Not that she was bothered, of course.

The anxiousness swirling around in her stomach had more to do with the fact that she might certainly be dead now had it not been for him—and *not* because she thought he might be reconsidering his curious interest in her.

Not at all! Heaven forbid.

The sooner she saw the back of him, the better.

"Thank you," he muttered in a gravelly voice.

Her eyebrows raising, she replied, "You're welcome," then turned to Benjamin who stood near the door, ready to comply with his employer's directives. "Benjamin," she said, "You'll join us, of course."

The man, whose eyes were weary as well—no doubt from searching out specters all night—looked startled.

"Come, come, sir. Surely you're hungry."

"Famished, miss, but—"

"Then be seated, and quickly, before the porridge grows cold. There. Beside His Grace." She pointed to an empty place at the table.

"Lady Cavendish," the valet began, still obviously ill at ease with this unexpected turn. He glanced nervously at the duke, who shrugged and nodded before focusing his attention again on his fruited porridge.

"We don't stand on ceremony at Cavisbrooke," Miracle stated. "Isn't that right, Johnny?"

"Right!" Hoyt replied and dove with relish into his breakfast. "Though I could certainly do with standing on a strip of pork. Aye, I would. Did you know, Your Grace, that the Lady Cavendish refuses to cook me flesh but once a week? And then she buys it from the bleedin' butcher in Niton. We've got sheep and cattle and pigs, not to mention enough chickens, pigeons, and rabbits to feed King George's army and she won't have me wringin' a one of them's necks. My mistake was allowin' her to name them. Once she christened the damnable beasts they became part of the family."

Putting down his spoon and wiping his mouth with a napkin, His Grace raised his gaze to Miracle. "And what, pray tell, does one name a pig?"

"Samuel," she replied without hesitation. "And Claude. And Charles."

"Calls him Chuck," Johnny said, then belched. "By sausage, but the ugly boar answers to his confounded name. 'Chuck!' she calls to him and he comes flyin' as quick as his runty little legs will carry him."

Miracle wiped her damp hands on a cloth, her lips smiling and her voice quivering with humor. "I ask you, Your Grace: How does one eat something that is intelligent enough to know his own name?"

"How do you know he's not responding simply to the sound of your voice?" Salterdon asked, his own eyes beginning to twinkle and one side of his handsome mouth curling in amusement. The effect felt somewhat startling, and she almost dropped her dishcloth.

Brow slightly furrowing, her countenance taking on intense seriousness, she replied, "Because he doesn't come when I call Samuel, of course."

"By Jove," Benjamin declared as he stared with round eyes at His Grace. "What a shocking and frightening possibility. Would it not be consternating to discover that the pitiable beasts we've been devouring are intelligent enough to be eating *us* were they fortunate to have been born with hands instead of hooves? I shan't look at a boar again without imagining myself on a skewer."

Miracle laughed. "And speaking of names . . ." Centering the duke with a curious look, she asked, "why did Ben call you Basingstoke?"

The master and his servant stared at her. They looked at one another. Then Salterdon said, "He worked for my brother . . . at Basingstoke—"

"For years!" Ben chimed in.

"Old habits, you see, are difficult to break," Salterdon declared, and nodded at the servant.

"Dreadful nuisance," Ben declared.

Miracle tossed her damp cloth onto the washbasin, then swept up the kindling bag from near the ovens. The remainder of the morning would be spent baking enough bread to last them the next three days. Therefore the ovens must be stoked as hot as possible.

Stepping from the room and into the morning that had dawned cold and gray, a white layer of mist pressing upon the wet land in a vaporlike blanket, she let the door swing closed behind her. Miracle gazed out over the countryside, her eyes feasting on the undulating green pastures and distant forests that looked pale and ghostly, sheep dotting the land that dropped off suddenly into somber gray cliffs overlooking the sea. Birds flew there: rooks and screaming gulls, black and white, as much a dichotomy as the verdant, peaceful land and the turbid waters beyond. As great a dichotomy as the emotions swirling around inside her . . . this disenchantment and curiosity over her guest. Her mind did its best to rationalize this odd turn of events.

At that moment, her friend and lifelong companion, Johnny Hoyt, was sitting at their table talking to a duke as if he were the dairy man come to swap tales. The duke was eating her porridge and drinking their coffee as if it were the most natural thing in the world to break stale bread with a lighthouse keeper and a groom.

On his former stay, His Grace had requested venison and partridge and lobster. He had declined her invitation to join them at the kitchen table. Instead, he and his friends had dined in the drawing room and complained that they had no Marsalas and Madeiras to imbibe during the partaking of their "plowman's fare."

For a long while, Miracle wandered about the garden, kindling forgotten, as she wove through the hedges and rock walls, her mind going back to the previous night and those moments she had nestled in Salterdon's arms before the fire. Only once had she stood so close to a man—or rather a boy—when they had pressed together beneath a shelf of rock to escape the rain. That had been half a year ago, and she hadn't seen him since.

Joe Cobbett, however, had not looked, felt, and smelled like Salterdon. This man was a gypsy king, whose chest and arms were like stone. He smelled of soap and leather and sandalwood.

"I don't believe you," came the voice behind her. *His* voice. Her heart leaped, and she spun around, causing her skirt to swirl and her kindling bag to slide from her shoulder and down her arm.

Salterdon poised on the pathway, resplendent in his green woolen double-breasted tailcoat, which was open and displayed his green and gold striped waistcoat, buff nankin trousers, and glistening Hessian boots that nearly reached his knees. No doubt Benjamin had spent hours on the spit and polish. She could imagine his dukeship watching over his manservant's efforts with a kind of hubristic air. She tried to breathe and think what to say.

"I said I don't believe you," he repeated very solemnly.

"Believe what? And why do you continue to sneak up on me that way?"

"About the pigs; and I don't sneak. I called your name twice. Obviously," he slowly blinked and shrugged one broad shoulder, "you were occupied with your thoughts. Are you always so contemplative, Miss Cavendish, or is something troubling you? Or perhaps you simply find inordinate pleasure in reverie . . . ?"

She did not reply, but turned and walked away, toward the roost where the cackling of hens heralded the arrival of morning eggs.

Salterdon said nothing, just leaned against the door of the coop, and with his arms crossed over his chest, he watched as she unseated several hens that squawked and filled the air with the batting of wings and a flurry of feathers. With her apron, she made a pouch for the eggs—several of them, brown and speckled, and a scattering of white ones.

"So tell me," the duke said as she stepped from the coop. "Why do you do it?"

"Collect eggs?" she replied with amusement and a dismissive glance back over her shoulder.

"The shirts." He plucked a feather from her hair and twirled it in his fingers. "Why do you hide up there"—he pointed with the feather toward the fog-shrouded turret above—"and sew them?"

"Have you mentioned it to Jonathan?" she demanded in panic.

Raising both dark eyebrows and tilting his head, he said, "I saw no reason to."

Miracle allowed herself the privilege of meeting his gray eyes with her own. His gaze was penetrating and dark, somehow disturbing and revealing—revealing not himself, however, but her. The intensity of it sluiced like liquid sun through her.

Miracle stepped back, allowing for more space between them. His closeness bothered her, made her feel oddly unnerved and confused. This time, she did not meet his eyes, but focused on the pigs in the distance that were rooting in the mud and squabbling among themselves.

"I sell the shirts," she told him cautiously, "to a merchant in Niton. Mr.

Turner is his name. His patrons come from all over, but mostly from London. John . . . wouldn't like the idea of my laboring for money. He vowed to my mother that he would see that I was well taken care of during her absence; that I would want for nothing. And I haven't."

She admired the garden surrounding the dilapidated castle, and smiled with pleasure. "A person's heaven is where they make it, Your Grace. I have everything I want right here. Besides," lowering her voice slightly, she added more gently, "like any good and noble man, Jonathan has his pride, sir, and does the best that he can. But I suppose you wouldn't know about that, would you, Your Grace? To work your fingers to the bone for something you truly desire."

The duke said nothing for a long moment, just regarded her home with a distant look, as if his mind were contemplating . . . or remembering. She thought it a very strange look—unfamiliar. On his previous stay, the duke of Salterdon hadn't appeared to give a moment's reflection about his future, much less his past. Finally, he asked, "And with this money you get from sewing, you purchase meat once a week?"

"And tallow for candles and lye for soap and cotton for sewing, and . . ."

"And?"

"I manage to save a few pence occasionally."

"To purchase . . . ?"

Suddenly feeling very foolish, Miracle turned away. "I fear you would laugh."

"I doubt it," he said in a softer voice.

She shook her head and moved away, down the twisting pathway that meandered through a wild-growing patch of peonies. Her hands had begun to tremble. If she wasn't careful, she would surely drop her eggs, and—

Gently, the duke caught her arm, and when she clutched at her apron full of eggs, he swiftly took several in his hands in an attempt to help. She would not look up at him, but made a concerted effort to keep her attention centered on anything aside from the unnerving notions going on in her head.

How very odd that she would want to confide in this man. To reveal her hopes, her dreams, her fantasies. After all, aside from Johnny, her long days and nights were spent only in the company of her animals, her garden, and Ceridwen's ridiculous bible of love spells. She wasn't even certain she knew how to converse with a stranger . . . or why he would even desire to. Could she have been so wrong about him before?

"Please," she said softly, casting him a sideways glance, "my eggs."

"When you've confessed," he replied, and teasingly drew away, balancing the fragile shells in his open palms.

"You'll laugh," she told him, finding herself slightly amused by his almost childish way of behaving. He looked, she thought, like a mischievous boy, his eyes twinkling and his mouth smiling.

"You're odd, sir," she said, and made a grab for the eggs. One flew from his hand and smashed upon the path.

"Oops," he said, and raised one eyebrow. "Would you like to try again?"

Raising her chin, she did just that.

Another egg splattered on the ground.

He laughed smugly. "Keep this up and I wager you'll have no eggs for your bread. Imagine that."

"Oh very well. If you must know, I intend to renovate Cavisbrooke," she announced with a degree of angry justification. "Are you happy now? Does that amuse you, Your Grace? Imagine my wanting to rebuild this dreary old place. *Give me my eggs!* Imagine my accomplishing such a scheme, even if I tried. I'm well aware that the entire isle is rolling in humor with the very idea. Go ahead. Tell me how impossible it would be. That I would do better to tear it all down to the ground and begin again. Remind me that I'm merely a woman with little more than a pot of pennies and a head full of illusionary rainbows. 'Tis nothing I haven't heard before, Your Grace. And while you're at it, tell me again that even if I had the financial means, there isn't a carpenter or stone layer on this island who would work for me. I'm crazy, after all, just like my mother!"

She spun on her heels, causing her skirt to fly, and dashed toward the house. Dear God, she was going to cry. Hadn't she just made a big enough fool of herself?

Suddenly, Salterdon stepped around her. She plowed into him, stumbling back before catching herself. Raising her chin and setting her shoulders, she glared up into his calm visage.

"You see," she heard herself declaring in a tight voice, "if the house were brighter, and newer, and . . . grander, then perhaps my mother would come home. Perhaps she would choose to live with us again . . . to be a family . . . again."

"I see," came his soft reply. Carefully, he returned her eggs, gently placing them into the pouch of her apron. "And perhaps with this money you're saving, you'll attempt to find her."

"Yes," she said determinedly. "I shall go to Paris and find her. Perhaps while I'm there, I'll discover what it is that would draw her away from us . . . from . . . me. Perhaps while I'm there, I, too, shall become a . . .

sophisticate. That's what my mother most desired, sir. To belong to your world."

"Paris. You don't strike me as the sort of young woman who would pine for the opportunity to rub elbows with Parisian patriciates or haunt the Palais Royale or the Rue Saint Honore. The back roads of Canterbury perhaps, or the byways of Exmouth. But not Paris, love."

"Do you make light of me, sir?" Miracle demanded angrily.

"Certainly not."

"Then what makes you such an authority on me?"

He said nothing, just gazed down into her face until she felt the indignation drain from her, leaving her feeling abashed by her fit of temper—red-cheeked, inexplicably vulnerable, like a favorite child caught in a lie by a parent and wishing to make amends.

"My mother is there," she rushed to explain. "In Paris. If I could only travel there, I'm certain I could convince her to come home. She *would* come home if Cavisbrooke were . . . different."

"And why has she traveled to Paris?"

"The lights, of course! The people! The throng of activity! She had often heard that Paris was the most beautiful city in the world. What woman wouldn't love to go there? She longed to stroll the corridors of the vast museums, and she craved to study with the great virtuosos of music and art. She did so love music and would spend hours playing her pianoforte." Growing uncomfortable with the topic, as she always did when she discussed her mother, Miracle walked away to a copse of wild strawberry plants that were spangled with tiny white flowers and beads of dew. "You know," she said thoughtfully, "I find it very odd that you seem so curious about my family when before . . ."

"Before what?"

"You cared for little more than your own comforts. If this interest or curiosity is simply some ploy to win my trust and affections, then I fear you will be sorely disappointed."

They stood without speaking for a long moment, both watching the dance of gulls, dipping, diving, and swirling out over the channel. At last she looked up and found him regarding her intently, though not fiercely. His dark eyes looked soft and sleepy. She said, "Will you vow an oath not to tell Jonathan of my plans? For whatever reason, he grows despondent, almost angry, when I talk of her. Please don't tell him about the shirts, I mean."

"Yes," he replied after a moment. "I swear."

She gave him a look. "I want to believe you, but I don't think that I do. Not after last time . . . ."

He frowned. "Last time?"

"When you happened upon Joe Cobbett and me walking together near the Undercliff. I asked you not to speak of seeing us to anyone, but you did, to Joe's father, who owns the Hound and Hare. Joe was never allowed to see me after that." Her voice trailed off before she added, more to herself than to him, "Perhaps that's just as well. He's married now and happy . . ."

"This Joe . . . Did you love him?"

"I . . ." She looked away, off over the misty countryside to where a dozen sheep had huddled together and turned their backsides into the rising wind. "Once, briefly, I thought . . . perhaps . . . but no." She shook her head. "I know now that I did not love him." Quiet filled up the space between them. They stood side by side, Miracle with her clutch of eggs and His Grace with his hands in his trouser pockets, staring out over the undulating gray horizon, his face strangely blank of emotion.

The silence grew too long and heavy to remain comfortable. Miracle said, "I'm sorry about your clothes that were ruined last evening. Benjamin fetched them for me this morning and I did my best to rectify the damage. I've stitched your coat. There was a tear on the sleeve just there." She touched his coat sleeve tentatively with her finger that was slightly smudged with chicken dung and a dusting of flour. "And your shirt . . . I'm not certain the stains will remove—"

"Not to worry. There are plenty more where that one came from."

"No doubt."

At last, she turned back to the house and took several steps along the well-trod path before his voice came to her again. "I still don't believe you. About the pigs, I mean."

She smiled to herself, just a little, as her previous anger and tension seemed to slide from her shoulders. Then she looked in the direction of the swine that were grunting and nosing the ground and each other. "Claude!" she called, and a red, bristly boar raised its head and peered at her with its bright, beady eyes. "Claude!" she called again, and this time the pig came running and squealing, tail sticking up straight in the air.

"Samuel! Chuck! His Grace would like to make your acquaintance!"

The swine stampeded toward them. Tilting her head, peering back at Salterdon who, with his hands in his trouser pockets, casually regarded the ponderous animals as they scurried over and splashed through their mud pits in their attempts to join them, Miracle said, "Have a grand day, Your Grace, and enjoy your company."

Then she ambled back into the castle, pausing only long enough to glance back. Partially hidden behind the door frame, she watched as the duke of Salterdon, surrounded by the prancing, dancing, shrilling hogs, stared gravely out over the distant, thrumming ocean.

Loneliness is the first thing which God's eye named not good.

JOHN MILTON

Chapter Six

Niton was a rustic little village consisting of three muddy streets of stone cottages—most of them thatched—a handful of shops, a church, and a single-room schoolhouse. The church was a building of considerable antiquity and stood by a farmyard in a lane just west of the village. The lane, a wagon-rutted track that wove its way toward the black cliffs of the Race, offered little for the weary traveler but the White Lion Hostel and the Hound and Hare Tavern, both of which were well lit, warm, and crowded as Clayton sidled up next to the bar, nursed his tankard of warm ale, and contemplated his circumstances.

Alas, he had often been rendered by his peers as too sensible; he took life too seriously, immersing himself in the drudgery of overachievement, which was an intolerable bore to his friends, considering the duchess would have rewarded him with the moon, if he so desired, strictly because he had managed to keep his name clean of scandal. But here he stood, slowly but surely becoming more inebriated by the minute as he recalled his last days spent at Cavisbrooke Castle with a crazy lady who communicated with pigs. And pigeons. And sea gulls. A woman whose ultimate requirement for a husband was that he could fly.

She did not want a husband who was infamous for his zealous, amorous pursuit of the opposite sex, which described the duke of Salterdon nicely.

She did not want to live in a world that would expect and demand that she conform to the strict rigors of habitual social behavior evaluated according to a conventional standard of propriety. The first time she was seen conversing with hogs, the black plague of society would come crashing down on her beautiful . . .

Oh, yes, she was definitely beautiful, in a perverse way: obstinately self-willed in refusing to concur, conform, or submit to the norm.

The duke of Salterdon would simply marry Miracle, bed her, breed her, then ensconce her in some country house to waste out the rest of her life immersed in dissatisfaction and tedium. There would be no teas, no soirees, no long lines of society peers trooping in and out her door. To the ton, Lady Salterdon would not exist . . . not even to her wayward husband.

No doubt about it, Clayton mused as he quaffed the last of his ale, he should march back to Cavisbrooke, pack his bags and valet, bid Lady Miracle Cavendish and her stale, mossy, haunted abode a farewell, and go home to Basingstoke. Get on with his own life and let Trey sink like a stone in his own mire of debt. Yes. That's definitely what he would do . . . just as soon as he imbibed one more ale.

He drank until the sun crept over the Medina River and reflected off the Kingston Downs, then he tossed a handful of coins onto the bar and quit the tavern. He stood in the bracing wind, drinking in the air and hoping to blazes it cleared his head.

Clayton walked into the village. He wasn't ready to return to Cavisbrooke yet. There was too much on his mind, too much ale. He had a tendency to get a little crazy when he drank too much, which is why he rarely did it; which is why, when he did, his head felt as if a horse had kicked him . . . or in this case, a unicorn.

He stared into the window of a shop for a long while, not really seeing, his thoughts still bothered by this unanticipated war of conscience. He was torn between helping his brother and watching out for the welfare of a virtual stranger . . . a stranger with a pretty face, a naive young girl who believed in miracles.

"You," came the voice from inside, dragging Clayton back to the present. He focused on the man in the store, who tapped his knuckles on the window and bestowed upon Clayton a yellow-toothed smile as he declared in a voice that was muted by the window, "I've the best ready-mades y'll find owtsi' London, sir. Come in, if ya please, and I'll wager y'll return home as strutting' proud and fine as a cock."

Clayton stared at him through the mud-spattered glass, his hands and face growing numb with cold.

The shopkeeper moved toward the door, flinging it open to a chorus of tinkling bells, as Clayton stepped in. "Welcome!" Turner declared and swept his beefy hand out toward his cluttered collection of ready-made wearables. A film of sweaty anticipation shimmered on his ruddy complexion as he fancied the size of Clayton's purse. "I can tell by the fine cut of yer coat yer a gentlemen of em'nence and wisdom."

Clayton looked around the tiny, cramped shop, noted the collection of women's silk bonnets, two stuffed mannequins sporting men's cutaways, and shelves stacked with an array of men's shirts, waistcoats, and bicorn and tall-crowned beaver hats. His eyes, however, returned to the shirts.

Turner grinned. "Y'll be noticin' me blouses, I see. Smart man. An eye fer quality." He caught Clayton's arm and tugged him to the shelf. Peering up at Clayton with rummy eyes and a grin, he said as he swept up the shirt and presented it with a flourish, "Y'll not argue that few are as well made as this. Feel that material. *India* cotton, sir. Fine and strong as it comes. And the seams." He yanked hard on the shirt. "These'll last years, sir."

"Where do you get them?"

The shopkeeper glanced around for effect, then smirked. "Ya buy these shirts, sir, and ya can tell yer friends at home that yer wearin' the weavin's of the deranged. Sits up in her tower, she does, spinnin' the cotton into thread, and the thread into material, and—"

"It must take her hours," Clayton said.

"Days!"

"What will you charge me?"

"One pound."

"Good God, I don't pay that much on Fleet Street. That's highway robbery."

"Yer Fleet Street finery ain't this well made, and the cotton ain't India. Besides, folk buy 'em just so's they can tell their friends that the lunatic made it."

"The lunatic?"

"I see you ain't been here long, not if you ain't heard about *her*—the lass who walks the End searchin' for her mother. Daft, she is. Crazy as they come. Lives alone up there at the castle, except for her companion, that cripple of a groom who's as daft as she is. Well? Do ya want the shirt or what?"

"How many are there?"

"Three. But more's comin'. She's due here today. At any time."

"I'll buy them all."

"All?" The man's eyes lit up, first with shock and then with pleasure.

"The ones here and those coming. All," Clayton stressed. "But on one condition."

"Condition?" He licked his lips.

"That you pay the lass what they're worth."

"They're worth?"

"One pound each, of course."

"Bloody hell if—"

Clayton moved so swiftly the shopkeeper had no time to react. Twisting his hands into the man's collar, Clayton flung him back against the wall so hard the building shook. His flabby jaw slack and his eyes bulging, Ned Turner gaped into Clayton's eyes and swallowed.

"Listen to me carefully," Clayton said in a low, threatening tone. "I'm drunk and spoiling for a fight, so don't test my patience. You've grown fat and comfortable off the lady's talent, not to mention her reputation. Therefore, you will reward her for her troubles. If you feel the merchandise is worth a bloody pound, then you will pay her that. If you don't, I shall report you to the proper officials who will be most interested in the taxes you are paying—or not paying—on your trade. Do I make myself clear?"

"Sure." He nodded. "Right. Here she comes now."

Clayton looked around, out the window, noted the cart, pulled by a long-eared, shaggy gray donkey, lumbering down the road, Miracle driving.

"Yer as crazy as she is," Turner declared, his protuberant eyes still locked on Clayton.

"Agreed. Therefore, if you know what's good for you, old boy, you had better do as I've asked you. And just to make certain, I'll be standing back there, watching from behind that curtain."

Turner nodded and managed to close his mouth at last as Clayton released him, smoothed the wrinkles from his coat, and rewarded him with a flat smile. Clayton slid behind the curtained door in the back of the room just as Miracle entered and greeted the still shaken and shocked shopkeeper.

"Good afternoon, Mr. Turner," came her lyrical voice, and Clayton sensed the anger slide from him. He closed his eyes and felt a smile lift one corner of his mouth. Odd that she would have such an effect on him. "Why, sir, you look positively ashen," she remarked, her tone one of sincere concern for the greedy parasite who no doubt had been robbing her blind of profit. "Is something wrong?"

"Aught that a stiff ale wouldn't cure," Turner grumbled. "Don't know what this bleedin' world is comin' to these days . . . what with all the nefarious and unscrupulous villains wanderin' about who would do an honest man out of his proper wages."

"I see." A pause. "Have you a need for shirts today?" she finally asked.

Another pause. "I . . . right. Sure, I'll take all y've brought. Just give 'em to me and be gone. Quickly! I've some place to be."

"I've brought you twelve—"

"Right! Good. Give 'em over. There. Put 'em there. Here's yer damned money."

"Oh!" she cried. "But, Mr. Turner, this is—"

"One pound per shirt."

"Oh! But—"

"Don't ask no questions, just leave. Get the hell away from here before I come to my bloody senses and reconsider."

"God bless you, sir," she cried. The door opened and closed and silence filled the shop.

Clayton stepped out from behind the curtain. Turner stood at the shelf, his arms clutching the stack of beautifully made garments, his fat lower lip protruded in a pout that might have brought Clayton pleasure, had he not remembered Miracle, bone-weary and sleeping in the cold, dim turret.

"That'll be fifteen pounds," the shopkeeper asserted with a sniff.

Clayton withdrew his money and placed the small fortune on the table. "I'll have my man pick them up tomorrow." He moved to the window and watched as Miracle twirled around in the middle of the street, her face radiant even in the failing daylight. Then she planted a kiss on the braying donkey's nose. Bystanders paused, watched, their countenances speaking their disapproval louder than words. Miracle danced her way toward the butcher's (Hoyt would have his mutton tonight), her simple skirts whirling and her hair floating, oblivious of the villagers regarding her with open speculation.

"I don't know who you are," the man said behind him, "or what the girl means to you, but ever'one in Niton knows she's witless, just like her mother was. The former Lady Cavendish disappeared over ten year ago. The girl should be locked up in Saint Luke's, if ya ask me."

"I didn't," Clayton replied.

Clayton took a room at the hostel because he was drunk and tired and the road back to Cavisbrooke was too damn long for a man on foot at night. He hadn't intended to stay over. No doubt Benjamin would worry himself into a froth. But his head hurt. So did his body. In truth, there wasn't a square inch of him that wasn't bothered by something. What a shame that the Countess Delarue-Madras wasn't here. She was very good at allowing him to work out his energy and frustration on her . . . or in her . . . or around her. She simply held on for the ride and encouraged him with her experienced body, her sultry voice, her warm, wet mouth.

Except tonight, the memory of her didn't make him smile, didn't even make him hard with desire. In truth, the only emotion the recollections evoked was irritation and disgust because she had done the same thing with more of his friends than he could count on two hands.

Continually, his mind went back to Miracle. As ridiculous as it was, he continued to plot ways to win her over . . . for his brother, of course. She wanted respect, understanding, and acceptance. And love.

Hell, what was he thinking?

After pacing his tiny room for an hour and feeling no less drunk, he returned to the Hound and Hare, ordered more ale, and listened to the occasionally raucous conversation in the tavern. They were farmers, mostly, with ruddy faces and burly physiques, all men who, after a long day's toil in the dirt, filled their bellies with their wives' meals of cabbage and lamb and spoon bread, and then sought out the company of their peers at the tavern. There were seamen scattered throughout the room as well whose lewd stares followed the amply endowed but less than comely wench delivering trenchers of bread and cheese to their tables.

The group gathered around him, though, were apparently from the mainland, and they appeared to be of comfortable means. Their splendidly cut coats spoke of their wealth. Their women, all of whom were clustered together like little hens in a corner, were bedecked in their trained, high-waisted, clinging muslin dresses that were all the rage now on the Continent, their hair arranged in curls and coils and ringlets hanging down their backs. The women tittered among themselves and occasionally peered toward their spouses as the gentlemen surrounded the muddled lad who appeared to be warming to the idea that he was the center of the moneyed fellows' attention.

"I'm tellin' ya," declared the young man. "They're crazy up there—them folk on the cliff. Loony as they come. Some folk say they seen the girl chanting to the moon. Some say she ain't nothin' more than a spook."

The men chuckled and murmured among themselves. A stout, white-haired popinjay with a big nose and lantern jaw flipped the storyteller a coin and blustered, "Don't stop now, boyo, tell us more."

"Oh sure, I'll tell ya more," the boy declared and puffed out his scrawny chest. "Some folk say the Lady Lorraina killed herself."

Clayton stared down into his tankard, barely noticing he had long since emptied it, not even noticing as the taverner replaced it with a fresh one. He felt sick. He felt suspended. He wanted to drive his fist into the pompous ass's face, yet, for the last fifteen minutes, he had been as drawn by the idiotic tales as the moronic gentlemen who fed the lad's bravado with coins and brew.

"Lady Lorraina Cavendish was the most beautiful woman in England, some says. And the randiest," he added with a smirk that brought a burst of laughter from his audience. "She liked the men, she did. Used to wander down from that creepy old castle on the nights when she wasn't tower watchin'. Use to sit right over in that corner there—" The boy motioned to a table in a dark corner of the room, where a shadowed figure sat with its back to the crowd. Clayton could just make out the image from where he stood.

The lad continued. "She let seamen buy her drinks until the wee hours, then she'd conveniently plead helpless and ask her admirer to see her home, if ya get my meanin'. Lovely, she were, with hair as red as a sunset and down to her arse, certainly not the sort a man would consider throwin' over for another, no sir. Not like that young buck Cavendish did. Pleaded with him, she did, to take her away from here, but he wouldn't have it. So she killed herself. Flung herself off the ledge of the lighthouse and onto the rocks below, leavin' her wee daughter who grew up to be daft as her mother. She still lives there in the moldy ol' place. Folk swear the castle is haunted—that Lorraina haunts it. I've seen her meself."

"No!"

"You expect us to believe—"

"Believe what you want! But I'm tellin' ya, when the dawns are so misty you can cut the air with a knife, y'll see her, at the foot of the Undercliff. She comes ridin' out of the gray soup on a unicorn."

"A unicorn!"

"Aye, a unicorn: a white monster of a beast that flies over the sand and water breathin' smoke and fire and with eyes like burnin' embers. And there's Lorraina, her red hair flyin out behind her like a silk flag from hell. Some says she rides them waves and rocks lookin' for her husband to return and—"

Clayton drew his gaze from the solitary figure in the corner. "Do you honestly believe that ridiculous cesspool of fabrications?" he asked, his deep, refined voice cutting through the palpable quiet, causing the storyteller to snap shut his mouth and look around while clumsily attempting to stand upright.

"Who the devil do you think you are?" the boy stuttered. "And what the devil do you know about it?"

"Enough to know you're full of—"

"You ask any one of us who live in Niton. We've all seen her, and once we saw her, I vow our lives ain't ever been the same. Ain't that right, Harry?"

The bartender, in the process of scrubbing the surface of the pitted bar, paused and nodded, not bothering to raise his eyes. "Aye, we've seen her," he grumbled. "Some of us closer than we should've, I reckon." Squinting one eye, he glowered at a lad near the back of the room, hidden behind a cloud of smoke. The youth, barely older than a boy, was a younger version of Harry. Ignoring his father, the boy went about his business of collecting empty tankards from the tables, then shuffled as quick as he could into the back of the building.

The storyteller, full of himself, not to mention too much ale, elbowed his way through the gathering of onlookers until standing toe to toe with Clayton, who continued to lean against the bar in an imperturbable manner, mentally thanking Benjamin for insisting that he wear his "ruffian" clothes, as the valet called them: doeskin breeches and a peacoat that had seen much wear and tear during Clayton's jaunts with Dutch. He wasn't certain how he would explain ruining a second set of clothes to his manservant, should the little pissant before him decide to further try his patience.

"Truth is," the boy began, and hitched up his pantaloons with an air of importance, "I happen to know the present Lady Cavendish, shall we say . . . intimately?"

The bystanders whooped and raised their ales and meads in toast, sloshing the brews onto their hands and sleeves as they pressed closer, hoping for a row, their drunken grins encouraging the growing tension.

"You're a liar," Clayton said, his gaze riveting the smaller lad, who continued to smirk while finding himself unable to force his eyes from Clayton's. Little by little, the noise died throughout the cramped room.

"A liar," the boy repeated, and laughed in a choked sound. "Yer callin' me a liar?"

"Pete," someone whispered. Then a young man moved up beside his friend, clamped a hand on the braggart's shoulder, and slightly shook him. "Give it up, Pete. He's bigger'n you, and by the looks of him, a wee bit wiser and not near so caught in his cups. Come on, lad. We'll race down to Godshill and take a pint. I'll buy."

After taking a quick look around and finding his audience had begun to disperse, Pete sneered and backed away. "Right then. But let's make it to Week Down. I know a pretty little redhead there what knows how to make me good and hard."

The group shuffled out, leaving the tavern mostly empty. Clayton drank—first ale and then mead, then he slapped coins on the bar and moved toward the back of the room, to the figure who sat at the table, candle doused, smoke swirling around her shoulders.

He stared over Miracle's shoulder a long moment. Her trencher of food had barely been touched. Beside it sat an empty tankard. She seemed to sense his presence. Her shoulders looked very square and tense. Her fingers gripped the handle of her tankard fiercely. Her sudden voice, sounding sharp-edged and tight, startled him.

"It seems you've spoiled their fun, Your Grace. A shame. The boy's stories were just getting good, if not a trifle fanciful. I especially enjoyed the part about my mother, myself, and Jonathan being lunatics." She picked up her tankard, and finding it empty, slammed it back down on the table. "Of course, the idea that my mother was a whore is most intriguing. If they only knew how much she loved my father . . ."

Hesitantly, he reached his hand out and placed it on her small shoulder. She flinched.

"I thought you didn't approve of drinking," he said, finding the attempt to keep emotion from his voice an effort.

"None of us are perfect, sir. Least of all me, There are times when the occasion calls for a tipple. Joe!" she called, causing the scattering of tipsy patrons to peer at her quizzically, then bow their heads together and mumble. Joe Cobbett hurried from the rear of the tavern, a damp white cloth hung over his shoulder. There was a thin strip of moisture over his fuzzy upper lip as he paused some distance from the table and gaped at Miracle as if she were a ghost. "Another ale, please," she said, "and bring one for His Grace. It's the least I can do for the man who so conscientiously stood up for my reputation. Please, Your Grace. Join me."

She had yet to even look at him. As he eased into the chair across from her, she continued to stare down at her nibbled pieces of cheese and bread. Her hands rested on the table in tightly balled fists. Her normally rosy cheeks appeared pale. The almost nonexistent light in the room caused her face to look overly gaunt.

"I suppose this is where you inform me that you have had second thoughts about coming here—to Cavisbrooke, I mean. Perhaps you stayed a mite too caught in your cups on your previous visit, and forgot all the particulars concerning my family's reputation. Therefore, after much consideration—"

"Stop putting words in my mouth," he told her in a deep, stern voice.

"Do you deny you've not considered the possibility that you made a mistake in returning here?" At last, her dark lashes raised. She pierced him with eyes that were big and soulful, angry and anxious . . . and wanting.

He swallowed. "No," he replied softly. "I won't deny it."

She didn't so much as blink but continued to regard him fixedly, even as Joe plunked the full tankards onto the table, sloshing dark ale over his hand. He then hurried away.

"Then why do you remain?" she demanded. "You're fully aware that I don't want you here."

"Don't you?"

Her eyes flashed. She reached for her ale, tipped it up, and drank deeply, leaving a frothy residue across her upper lip. She swept it away with the back of one hand.

Clayton relaxed against the back of his chair. "Perhaps I would've believed you more had I not discovered you here. A woman who craves companionship enough to subject herself to the company of these morons, knowing she'll be the topic of conversation, is undoubtedly desperate to be around people. You may not care for me as a person, m'lady, but you can hardly deny that my company at Cavisbrooke has been welcome. You haven't, after all, insisted that I leave."

"And would you leave if I insisted?" she demanded hotly, her cheeks becoming kissed by intense feeling.

He took a moment to respond. "Yes. Of course. My time is too valuable to waste it on a woman who has no desire whatever for me. Will you sit there and tell me that you've no interest in me, Miss Cavendish?"

"Yes!" she returned frantically, and snatched up her ale. "But I don't for a moment believe I am anything more than a dalliance, perhaps an experimentation to test your virility on someone who proves to be a greater challenge than the 'weak, tittering, witless little ninnies' you and your companions crowed about conquering during your previous stay. Oh, yes, Your Grace, I heard it all, you and your malicious friends bragging about your conquests, comparing women as if they were horses on a track. *Yes,* I want you to leave before . . ."

Leaning forward, he wrapped his fingers around her wrist, steadying her hand that had begun to shake violently. "Before what, Miracle?"

Trembling, shaking her head, and doing her best to extract her arm from his fingers, Miracle closed her eyes and tried to breathe. "Before I convince myself to believe you. Before I come to like you. To depend on you. I don't understand why you're trying so hard this time to make it so. I shan't end up like my mother, I tell you. Go away, Salterdon, I beg you. Just go away and leave me alone!"

With that, she jumped from her chair, spilling it back onto the floor and toppling her ale into Clayton's lap. For an instant, she looked mortified. Then, without another utterance, she fled the tavern.

Ale seeped into Clayton's trousers, crept down his thighs, then down, into the tops of his boots. Joe Cobbett came running, his white cloth waving like a war banner. The young man stumbled clumsily before he dove to the task of mopping up the brew from Clayton's crotch.

Snatching the cloth from Joe's hand, Clayton snapped, "For God's sake, be careful before you emasculate me completely."

"Sorry, Your Grace. Only meant to help. I seen what you done for Lady Cavendish, and . . ." The young man's Adam's apple slid up and down his throat, then he lowered his voice. "She ain't crazy, m'lord. Far from it. In fact, she's 'bout the smartest lass I ever knew. She'd make any man a faithful and useful wife. Aye, she would. Just be patient. She'll trust ya eventually. Once she trusts, there ain't nothin' she wouldn't do for ya. She'll be yer best friend, sir, I swear it."

"Quite the expert where she's concerned, aren't you, Mr. Cobbett?" Clayton proceeded to blot the wetness from his lap. "Tell me something, Mr. Cobbett. Were you in love with Miss Cavendish?"

Joe glanced back at his father, who eyed them like a rabid bulldog.

"Did she love you?" Clayton demanded. "Answer me, dammit, and quit shaking like a mouse."

Joe's face suddenly flushed, and his eyes became flustered and furious. "It's 'cause of you that I ain't with her now. You and your waggin' tongue, tellin' me father that you seen me with her. I coulda been married to Miracle instead of the silly bitch I live with now. I'da taken her away from here so these lot a talesayers couldn't talk about her no more. But you ruined it all—"

"Joe!" barked the boy's father. "Wot the blazes is goin' on back there?"

"Nothin', da," Joe shouted back, then giving Clayton one last go-to-hell glance, he spun on his heel and shuffled away.

Clayton stared after him. "Bastard you may be," he muttered to his absent brother, "but at least you had the common decency to save her from the likes of him."

The room spun as he forced himself to stand, to move toward the door, to descend the two narrow steps outside the tavern. The night was cold and clear and bright with starlight. He could see his breath as he exhaled and gazed up at the sky, wishing he had thought to bring his overcoat.

Where was Miracle?

On her way back to Cavisbrooke, of course.

He had humiliated her. He shouldn't have acknowledged her presence there, in the back of the room. Then she could have silently slipped away like a wisp of air, and no one but Joe Cobbett would have been the wiser.

Why the blazes should he care about what or how she felt? She had invited him to get the hell out of her life . . . before she got hurt. Before, like her mother, she wasted her youth—indeed, her life—loving some son of a bitch who looked upon their union as little more than a grueling necessity.

He was trying to convince her that it wouldn't happen. Damnation. When had he become such a bloody liar?

With flowing tail and flying mane,
Wide nostrils, never stretched by pain,
Mouths bloodless to the bit or rein,
And feet that iron never shod,
And flanks unscar'd by spur or rod
A thousand horses—the wild—the free—
Like waves that follow o'er the sea,
Came thickly thundering on.

LORD BYRON
from "Marzeppa"

Chapter Seven

Clayton opened his eyes to blackness, cold, and wet. His face hurt. His back ached. Where the hell was he? And what the hell had happened?

He couldn't think. There were a thousand angry bees buzzing inside his head—or so it felt. He thought he might vomit, if he didn't die first.

Flashes of faces streaked through his mind's eye, as briefly as lightning and grieving him as painfully. Vaguely familiar faces belonging to vaguely familiar voices.

"Don't no man call me a liar."

Closing his eyes, Clayton rolled to his stomach and groaned. The ground began to undulate beneath him, like water . . . rolling . . . rolling . . . each slow swell lifting him then dropping him while the voice of the water seemed to growl up from the deep, dark belly of the ocean and threaten to drag him under.

Where was he?

Not Africa. Not the ship—the sinking ship, with its jib and staysails ablaze and the masts a towering torch against the pitch-black sky. The voices clattering about in his head were not those of a doomed ship's crew, nor the sounds of his parents' cries as they screamed out his name.

"Clayton, darling! Jump, Clayton. Jump!"

So many bodies, thrashing and splashing, screaming and burning, drowning, praying, dying. Sinking to the bottom of the fathomless water with its squadron of shimmery jellyfish and scavenging sharks.

He wasn't ten years old again.

Focus on something pleasant.

Blue-green eyes that twinkled in mirth. A soft red mouth that was forever ready with a smile. A saucy disposition. A naive seductiveness that would tempt a saint, much less a lord who was simply attempting to help his brother achieve his contemptible and questionable objectives. Oh, no. He wasn't about to become overly fond of her. He was here on a mission, and besides, she would soon be his sister by marriage.

She was crazy. Had to be. Who in God's name would continue to wait for the return of a loved one for ten years?

Had the damned pigs actually responded to their names?

He could carry responsibility only so far. So what if his brother had saved his life—kept him from sliding back down into that frothing green sea a third time?

Why in hell had he shelled out a small fortune for shirts he could have purchased for a fraction of the price from his tailor in London?

Why had he bullied a tavern full of ruffians in an attempt to so valiantly defend the girl's reputation?

"Don't hit 'im again, Pete!"

"Ya don't kill 'is kind. Just take 'is damn purse and let's get out of here."

"I'm gonna teach 'im a lesson, by crackers. I'll show 'em 'is kind don't come 'ere and—"

"Hush! Someone's comin'."

"I told ya we shouldn't 'ave come here. It's too bleedin' close to that creepy ol' castle. Ya know wot they say about—"

"Shh! Wot's that?"

"There! It's comin' this way. Gore, but I don't believe me bleedin' eyes. We're dead. Pete. We're dead!"

Clayton pushed himself to his knees, forced open his eyes. The blackness had turned to gray as dawn worked its way through the thick mist and fog. Gritting his teeth, he gradually stood, slowly straightened, briefly closed his eyes again until the world ceased spinning.

Surely he had imagined it all, too much grog and mead. His damn conscience had nagged at him incessantly as he paid the hostel keeper for a room he'd barely used. It nagged and nagged about his idiotic temper. He'd allowed it to get the best of him again, never giving a thought to how the whole damn affair would have upset her. Best to have simply slid away from the pub without acknowledging her. Then they both could have pretended that the disgusting fracas had never happened, that he had never even been there, as mesmerized by their stupidity as the others.

All the rest that followed: Had he imagined it? The figures appearing out of nowhere, racing at him from the downs, the starlight making their animated faces look ghoulish, the cries of alarm, the sounds of running feet diminished by the thundering, rolling explosions of . . . What?

Through the darkness there had come a being with no face—only eyes, his body draped in flowing robes, a streak of fire flashing in his black hand as he raced up out of the night on a . . . What? The specter had babbled in tongues.

Christ. He was getting as bad as Benjamin.

There were no cloven-hooved dragons breathing smoke and belching fire, no faceless entities with lightning streaking from their fingertips, only a lot of wet-behind-the-ear delinquents who were by now counting out the few remaining coins they'd lifted from his pockets.

Clayton looked around, unable to see anything but a wall of fog. Somewhere beyond that wall, the ocean thundered. The sound seemed to surround him, to drown him, like water.

He swallowed. When the devil had this fog moved in? How long had he lain there, unconscious and bleeding?

The water could be anywhere, in front of him, in back. One wrong move and he could step off the Undercliff and plunge to his death on the rocks or waves below. It would serve him right, he supposed.

God, his head hurt. If he survived to return to Cavisbrooke, he would have Benjamin pack their belongings; he would bid his peculiar hosts adieu, he would return to London and inform his brother that his dukeship could carry on his dirty deeds without his brother's help.

Clayton wanted no part of the girl; none whatsoever. Not if he knew what was good for him.

A breeze touched his cheek, then another. Slowly, the mist began to move, to swirl. A single beam of sunlight cut through the gray, a shaft of butter yellow that dissipated the clouds with its warmth. Little by little, the world revealed itself, took form and shape and pale color. Clayton looked down. He stood on the ledge of a precipice some fifty feet above a stony, shell-studded expanse of sand.

Before him stretched the ocean, glistening and white-topped, reflecting the blood-red sun that balanced on the watery horizon, filling the sky with streaks of crimson and yellow. On the beach, emerging from the mist, was . . .

He closed his eyes. He kept them closed while pain thumped inside his temples.

It was that damnable grog again. He simply could not imbibe without it doing odd things to his mind.

Clayton eased open his eyes; he stopped breathing.

The silver-white beast pranced at the edge of the frothing green water, haunches and shoulders rippling, massive neck arched, and magnificent chiseled head turned into the wind. It seemed as if Clayton could feel each thunderous footfall, could hear the short, sporadic snorts emanating from its distended nostrils, each breath a billow of smoke in the frigid dawn air. But it was the woman on the beast's back that captured his attention.

Exquisite. Her long red hair a banner, blowing in the wind. Breathtaking. Her face aflame with the color of the fiery sun. Heart-stopping. Oh, God, she was an angel, for nothing that wild and free and beautiful could possibly be human. Her long, pale legs, revealed by the scanty garment she wore, clung to the animal's sides as it moved fluidly through the rushing waves. She wore no shoes. She sat upon no saddle. Gripped no reins with her white hands, but clung gently to the creature's smoke-gray mane, as if she and the snorting steed were one.

They danced, she and beast, as if to some magical music audible only to their ears. The dragon . . . the unicorn . . . the mythological Pegasus trotted in place, long, perfectly shaped legs pumping up and down while its hooves flashed like gold in the warming sunlight.

Clayton turned away. He stumbled over a clump of brushwood and a scattering of heather and spiny wildflowers before stopping abruptly. He covered his face with his gloved hands, then ran his hands through his hair, stared down at the trampled grass, and took a deep breath.

Slowly, he turned back toward the sun, squinted his eyes against the intensifying light, and shielded the rays from his face with one hand as he cautiously moved to the precipice again and focused on the beach below.

The sea rushed and ebbed, foamed and hissed. Gulls and auks and other sea birds dove toward the torpid surface of the water. The angel and unicorn had vanished—if they had ever been there at all.

"Can you imagine, Benjamin, that very soon now, our civilization may well see man traveling underwater? That we all might well be journeying from continent to continent by way of a submarine vessel?"

"A lot of balderdash, miss. Had God intended man to swim underwater like a lot of fish, he would have given us gills."

"Oh, but imagine the possibilities! Surely you were aware that in 1775 David Bushnell of the American Colonies recorded in the *Transactions of the American Philosophical Society* a letter stating that he had all but succeeded at his attempts to manufacture the perfect underwater sailing vessel. It wasn't until 1785, however, that a gentleman scientist, Robert Fulton, expanded Bushnell's research to an extent that Napoleon himself has invited Fulton to France in hopes that Fulton might build him a fleet of underwater battleships for his navy."

"Good God," the manservant muttered. "I shudder to imagine the consequences of such a machine. The next thing you know, we'll be flying through the skies in the belly of some iron monster."

"And I suppose if God had intended us to fly—"

"He would have given us wings, m'lady."

Miracle watched the valet do his best to clean the mud and damp grass from Salterdon's clothes. For the first time in an hour, she felt drained of energy, unable to dredge up the necessary small talk that would, perhaps, alleviate the manservant's concern over his employer.

Carefully, she placed a warm, damp cloth on Salterdon's forehead, allowed her fingertips to hesitantly toy with the fringe of dark hair spilling over his brow. She wasn't certain she wanted to acknowledge the worry she had experienced when Salterdon had not returned from Niton by midnight. After all, for the entire ride home to the castle after their confrontation at the tavern, she had fumed and fussed aloud about his arrogance and his ability to disturb her emotional well-being. She had ordered him to get out—to leave Cavisbrooke—and she had meant it . . . at the moment. Now, however . . .

Unbelievable, when just days before she would have proclaimed good riddance and tossed his belongings after him in the dirt.

She shouldn't have stormed out of the tavern and left him to find his own way back to the castle. The countryside wasn't nearly so peaceful as it appeared. There were village folk who looked on anyone with ties to Cavisbrooke as an oddity, if not an outright threat. And, of course, there were the cliffs, always threatening to slide into the ocean with no warning. Only a few short months before, an entire section of the Undercliff had given way, burying a family who had only thought to frolic there in the sunshine.

His eyelids fluttered. "He awakes," she announced softly and urgently. Benjamin, who had paced the floor since arriving back at Cavisbrooke with his employer, unconscious, in the bottom of a cart, leapt to His Grace's aid.

"There, there, sir. You'll be fine in no time. Try to breathe deeply. Yes. That's right. In and out. By Jove, I knew I shouldn't have allowed you to walk into Niton alone. The moment I suspected something might be amiss, I should have come looking for you. Can you tell us, sir, who did this to you?"

His lips moved.

Miracle leaned forward, as did Ben. They waited for him to speak again.

"It doesn't matter," Salterdon finally said and closed his eyes again.

Miracle sat back and studied His Grace's face. "The fire is dying, Benjamin. Will you fetch us more peat?"

"Right away, miss."

She waited until the servant quit the room, then, sinking deep into a worn and comfortable chair, Miracle continued to regard her patient closely, as she had for the last hour while he slept. She noted that the lines of his angular and chiseled face, normally so rigid, seemed not so hard and far less cynical during sleep. Yet, he was not without that ruthless air that was always so apparent in men of his station.

At last, he opened his eyes, stared at the ceiling, breathed quietly without moving. Finally, he said, "I dreamt I was flying."

Miracle smiled, albeit reluctantly, and leaned forward, propping her elbows on her knees, her chin in her hands. "Where were you flying?" she asked.

"Above the sea. I could feel the wind beneath me and the sun on my face. I wanted to go higher, but I was afraid."

"Afraid of what, Your Grace?"

"Of falling."

She tilted her head. "Had we never conquered our fears of falling we would never have learned to walk."

"Touché. How long have I been here?"

"Since mid-morning. Benjamin grew worried and traveled to Niton. He found you near the cliffs."

He raised his head and winced, touched his swollen eye with his fingertips, then focused on her. The study was intense. She felt vulnerable and exposed.

Leaving her chair, Miracle moved to the window and centered her attention on the gray horizon. "I should have warned you at the tavern that there could be trouble. The young men of this island may, on the surface, find pleasure in entertaining the gentry who holiday here, but they also hold a great deal of resentment for the upper classes. The down, sir, can prove to be a treacherous place after dark for anyone with a full purse."

"I suspect you were too busy mentally murdering me yourself."

"Perhaps. I suppose I should thank you for your rather gallant defense of me, although I must confess, most of what they say is true. I have to wonder, though: Would you have displayed such bravado had you not known it was I sitting in the distance?"

"Meaning?"

"Mayhap your valiancy was only a ploy to win my admiration."

He offered no response but lay quietly on the settee and stared at the ceiling. There was a deep cut on his lip. Miracle found herself watching it, and his lips that looked firm and soft, too. She had never really noticed a man's lips before—and certainly not this man's—nor had she ever pondered the idea of those lips kissing her . . . until now. She suddenly wanted to take back the hateful words she had shouted at him the night before—demanding that he leave. She took an unsteady breath and gripped her hands together.

"Their stories—the lads at the Hound—have they yet convinced you that Johnny and I are lunatics?"

"I haven't yet come to that conclusion . . . totally."

She looked at him hard: his face, his penetrating eyes, the dark, untamed hair that tumbled over his forehead and down his neck in a confusion of upturned ends. There were abrasions on one cheek that appeared red and angry. She could not think of what to say, whether to again defend her peculiar lifestyle or acknowledge it because, in a flash of insight she realized that she had come to care what he thought.

"I've never been one to defend my philosophies," she declared in a rushed, slightly panicked tone. " 'Tis no one's business how we live or think or feel. Not their's . . . or yours."

Salterdon lay back and closed his eyes. His cheeks looked suddenly ashen. Miracle hurried to him, went to her knees beside him, ever so carefully touched her fingertips to his slightly swollen forehead.

With no warning, he grabbed her wrist. She fell against him, her face near his. "I'm beginning to wonder who, exactly, is the insane one here," he said in a low whisper. "You . . . or me. Surely it must be me, because I'm beginning to not give a damn about what they say or what I see or hear. But that's not what bothers me most."

Pulling her closer, so close she could feel the rise and fall of his chest against hers and the warm brush of his breath against her mouth, he murmured, "You bother me. What are you? An angel? A witch? A savant or a lunatic? Have you cast some spell on me, Lady Cavendish, so I see spiritual beings astride flying horses, and faceless crusaders riding dragons? Who are you? Answer me, dammit, or—"

"Or what, Your Grace? Will you finally leave Cavisbrooke?"

For a long moment, he said nothing; yet, when she attempted to pull away, he braced the back of her head with his free hand and twisted his fingers in her hair. "Be still," he ordered her. "Be very still and I'll release you. Good. Just relax. I won't hurt you. I only want . . ."

"What do you want?" she demanded. "You come to my home uninvited. You invade my privacy. You seem to think that I'm yours for the taking. Rest assured, sir, that I am not."

He released her wrist, allowed his fingers to relax in her hair. "What are you afraid of?" he asked more gently, tentatively stroking her cheek while he searched her face with his hypnotic gray eyes. She felt, suddenly, a warming within her, a softening, melting invasion of her senses. In an instant, her world focused to a pinpoint: his lips that were slightly parted and breathing lightly on her cheek. And while the instinct to flee became an overwhelming urge, a part of her could only lie there, pressed against him, while her world filled with the sight, sound, and smell of him. She began to tremble.

"Answer me, Miracle. What are you afraid of, Meri Mine? That I might seduce you away from this cold, wet, and bleak place? That I might lure you away from your illusionary rainbows? What is this obsession for remaining here, waiting for some ghost from your past to come home? For burdening yourself with caring for some dilapidated old lighthouse and a cripple—"

"Johnny sacrificed his life for my mother and me. He's the only friend . . . the only family I have, sir. And as far as my mother is concerned—"

"She's gone, for God's sake. How can you expect that she'll return after ten years? Listen to me, love. All the staring out to sea and believing is not going to bring her back. You're wasting your life—"

Struggling free, Miracle stumbled back and stood with her hands at her sides, breathing hard. "She loves me. She tells me so in her letters. Would you like to see them? The words sing of the excitement, Salterdon, the beauty of the world beyond Cavisbrooke. They take me on a journey of wonderment; arouse me with tales of the strange and incomprehensible and awe-inspiring. There are cities of shining marble, of glistening cathedrals, warm and friendly people who welcome strangers and don't give a bloody leap if you're . . . different. When she's ready, she'll return. Then the lot of you naysayers can go to hell."

She ran from the room and fled down the dark corridors to the winding stairs of the turret. Breathing harshly, Miracle scaled the slick, crumbling stone steps to the circular room and stood for long minutes doing her best to control the upheaval of emotions roiling inside her.

How dare he presume to pass judgment on her life, her ideal, her dreams? How dare he make her question her own resolve?

Dropping to her knees beside the old leather trunk shoved against the wall, Miracle carefully opened it, cautiously reached for the tidy bound stack of yellowed letters, all postmarked from France, and clutched them fiercely to her breast.

"Silly girl, getting so emotional. What does he know about my life? My desires? My dreams? Any more than my father understood my mother."

There was another stack of letters; some much older, all postmarked from London, most addressed to her mother, the most recent ones addressed to her, though they weren't recent at all. They had stopped arriving after her father's death two years after her mother's disappearance. He'd been killed in a fall from a horse, cracked his head open on a rock, and bled to death before anyone found him. He'd left her a decent bequest—enough to get by on until she turned twenty-five years of age.

Try as she might, she could not recall his face, only his rigid demeanor, his cold blue eyes, and his unsmiling mouth. He'd been young, handsome, and brash. He'd promised her mother each time he called twice a year that he would, eventually, take her away from Cavisbrooke.

But he hadn't.

Miracle could never recall Lord Cavendish even addressing his daughter directly. The only thing she could remember was his gasp of astonishment when, after an extremely long period of absence, he'd returned to Cavisbrooke to discover Miracle had grown into a young lady. "Good God," he'd declared with a sneer on his lips, "she looks exactly like her mother."

Naive, innocent, ignorant little Miracle had burst into a smile, jumped up and down for joy, believing her beloved, aloof father had meant the comment as a compliment. After all, her mother had assured her over the years that her father loved her devotedly. He loved them both. He said so repeatedly in the many letters he wrote from London. He was simply a very busy man . . . and, like most men, he had trouble showing his affections in person.

Miracle had believed that lie as well . . . until she discovered his letters after her mother abandoned her, and Johnny, and Cavisbrooke. There had been no outpouring of love and devotion. Not even a solitary mention of Miracle's name. Only curt scribbles demanding that Lorraina cease her melodramatic temper tantrums . . . and, yes . . . he still wanted a divorce.

Miracle flung open the window shutters and turned her face into the wind. The cold brought tears to her eyes as she released a ragged sigh and forced the memories aside. She would focus on the present—as always. Live each day as if it were the beginning of forever, as her mother had taught her.

Oh, but sometimes it was so damn hard . . .

She shivered and ran the heel of her hand across her forehead; a voice whispered softly in her ear, *You want to believe him. You want to trust him. You want to teach him how to fly.*

"But I'm afraid. I'm so very afraid."

Miracle touched her fingers to her wrist, then her cheek, where Salterdon had caressed her ever so lightly, and she thought aloud, "His hands were not cold after all."

I want
someone to laugh with me,
someone to be grave with me,
someone to please me and help my
discrimination with his or her own
remark, and at times, no doubt, to admire
my acuteness and penetration.

ROBERT BURNS

Chapter Eight

"I am confident, sir, that you have made the wisest decision. There is much to be said for loyalty toward one's own flesh and blood. After all, where would we all be without that singular thread of adherence for our kin? However, the price one pays for chicanery, even when perpetrated out of loyalty, is ofttimes of too much consequence to be tolerable for a man with conscience. Oh, yes, sir. The sooner we can leave this dreadful old place the better. I shall have our bags ready within the hour."

Clayton stood outside his bedroom door, listened to and watched his manservant scurry about the chambers, grabbing up his personal belongings and flinging them into a pile on the bed; Clayton wondered what, exactly, truly impelled his valet to move so hurriedly: his trumpeted sense of honor or the fear of coming face to face with his "demon beast" again.

Leaving Benjamin to his chore, Clayton moved down the corridors, listened to the echo of his footfalls upon the stones, and visualized Basingstoke—his home—warm, welcoming, full of light and color. He would dash off a note to Blanche and invite her to join him. He would take her to bed and keep her there until all thoughts of Cavisbrooke and Miracle Cavendish were sweated from his memory.

He would inform his brother the duke that if Trey wanted a wife, he could get her himself because he, Clayton, lord Basingstoke, normally an honorable rakehell, wanted no part of robbing this young woman of what little dignity she maintained.

He would simply explain to Lady Cavendish that he had made a mistake in coming here. He had discovered that she would not be happy as duchess of Salterdon (which wasn't a lie). She simply would not fit in with his lifestyle, his friends, his family. The pompous aristocracy would break her spirit, not to mention her heart. Clearly, she was not interested, in any case.

During one of Benjamin's explorations of the castle, the manservant had discovered a long corridor of rooms which, he presumed, belonged to Miracle and Mr. Hoyt. Clayton wound his way to the vast gallery and stood for a moment at the threshold of the passageway while the cold and damp settled within every seam of his clothing. Meager light shone from the scattering of sconces on the walls; tiny candles dipped by Miracle's hands formed yellow halos on crudely framed pictures hanging from iron hooks pounded into the stone. There were likenesses of horses flying, rearing, pawing; all with flaring nostrils and strangely dished heads, their muzzles small enough to fit in a child's hand.

"Your Grace," came Hoyt's voice from the darkness. The man materialized from the shadows of the corridor, his round face smiling, the cane in his hand making a *tap tap tap* on the floor. He seemed not at all surprised or discomposed to discover a guest mousing about his lady's private chambers.

Joining Clayton, Johnny gazed up at the charcoal sketch of a prancing horse. "Miracle's work," the man announced, unable to stem his rush of pleasure and pride as he looked at the lifelike portraits. His eyes shone as he focused on Clayton. "One of her many talents. Are they not extraordinary, Your Grace?"

"Yes," Clayton replied. "And somewhat disturbing."

"Mira is very passionate about her loves. Where one person feels an inkling of fondness, Miracle experiences a universe of sensitivities. I'm not certain if that is a curse or a blessing. What do you think, Your Grace?"

Clayton said nothing, just studied the likeness of the powerful white steed and recalled the ghostly vision he had witnessed that morning near the sea.

"You've searched me out for a reason," John declared. "Perhaps you've reconsidered your reasons for returning to Cavisbrooke? Please, Your Grace, say nothing yet. Come and join me in my chambers. It's warmer there, and comfortable."

Johnny ambled down the corridor, leaning his weight slightly on his walking stick until pausing at the threshold of his apartment. "Please," he called out, then disappeared into the room.

Clayton did not join him immediately, but continued to stand where the old man had left him, his hands in his trouser pockets, his gaze fixed on the dark at the far end of the corridor.

He did his best to focus his thoughts again on Basingstoke and how wonderful it would feel to sleep in his massive, comfortable bed with its piles and piles of down counterpanes and satin-covered pillows. He even imagined, albeit briefly, Blanche sprawled out across the bed, her arms and legs thrown wide in invitation, her blacker-than-night hair tumbled over his white sheets.

But the image was far too elusive, like trying to clutch water in the palm of his hand. No matter how fiercely he struggled to hold it, it slid through his fingers and vanished, leaving him with the disturbing mental picture of Miracle on his bed, her lush sunset-colored hair like a fire spread over his sheets, her slender pale legs open, and—

"Coming, Your Grace?" Hoyt called.

"Depraved bastard," Clayton muttered to himself, of himself. No doubt about it, he should get out of this damnable domicile of inveiglement before he did something he would find impossible to live with.

Surprisingly, John's private apartment was truly comfortable, if not crowded, with its Gothic architecture and once fine furnishings of mahogany, walnut, and rosewood. There were threadbare Oriental carpets on the floor, and china figures cluttered about the occasional tables. Paintings in gilded frames, no doubt once belonging to the residence's previous owners, hung on the walls near the overburdened shelves of leather-bound books—enough, Clayton decided, to stock the smallest library at Basingstoke.

"Sit down," Johnny invited. "There. Before the fire. I fear you've frozen since you arrived at Cavisbrooke. You must understand: Mira can be too frugal for her own good . . . and mine, occasionally. I see you're admiring my collection of books. Extraordinary, wouldn't you say? Do you know that Mira has read them all? Yes! Every one of them. Most of them more than once. Her favorites are those in there, bound in green leather. *The Wonders of Science in Modern Life.* There is little of science that modern man has written upon paper that she has not read. She's fascinated in what we, as human beings, are becoming."

"Yet she lives in a fantasy," Clayton said, holding his hands palm up toward the cheery fire.

John moved up beside him, stared down into the fire, then handed him a drink. "Port," he announced. "I recall from your last visit that it was your favorite."

Raising one eyebrow, Clayton accepted the glass. He detested port. However, it was the duke's favorite.

"Enjoy, Your Grace. It'll be our little secret. Miracle has no idea I've stashed meself a bit here and there. She doesn't approve, you know. Says 'When the wine is in, the wit is out.' "

"I fear she may be right, but thank you, anyway." Clayton turned the glass up, swallowed, then shuddered.

John dropped into a chair and regarded Clayton with a weary smile. "The first time you came here, Your Grace, I wasn't certain I liked you.

Thought, actually, that you were a self-centered, arrogant ass and not good enough for Mira. I haven't totally changed my mind."

Clayton flashed him a smile and reluctantly drank again.

"I'm not even certain that I trust you or your reasons for being here. And if I thought for a moment that Mira despised you as much as she says she does, I would have long since sent you packing. She's very special to me, understand. There is nothing I wouldn't do to keep her happy."

The man sighed, and his eyes took on a sleepy look. "I sense in you, Your Grace, a thread of goodness. A man of compassion. A gentleman of compunction. While I question your motives for choosing Mira to, possibly, take her place at your side, I do not question my desire to see her rescued from this future her parents have provided for her. I do not relish the fact that she is looked upon as an oddity. I do not relish the fact that her mother and I have instilled in her the unrealistic fantasies of two people who cannot accept the cruel hand fate has dealt them."

Clayton stared down into his glass of port and watched the fire reflect on its amber surface. The liquor and warmth from the hearth made him drowsy, or perhaps it was simply capitulation that drained his resolution from him. Sinking back into the chair, he again turned the glass up to his lips and imbibed deeply.

John's eyes shone with fondness and delight as he smiled and reminisced. "Her mother and I knew she was special from the day Mira was born. Most babes cry with their first breath. Mira laughed. From that moment on, our lives were filled with her indomitable spirit and insuperable sense of dignity. She has taught me much, Your Grace, of gentleness, of patience, and of faith. I have not always been a benevolent or attentive man. Children have a way of doing that, sir. Of forcing aside our less than desirable traits for those more redeeming . . . if we choose to save our loved ones from the mistakes we make of our own lives. Do you care for children, Your Grace?"

His gaze fixed on the dancing flames, Clayton allowed a faint smile to turn up the corners of his lips. "I've never given the possibility a great deal of thought. Perhaps because I've never met a woman who I could visualize as mother of my children."

"Never?"

Clayton looked at Hoyt and was struck by the intensity of the old man's stare. Those eyes, pale as a cloud-swept sky, seemed all-knowing, and at the same time, desperate.

"Never?" John repeated, his tone sharp as an arrow.

Clayton waited a moment before downing the remaining port, then he put aside his glass and left the chair.

"Miracle is watching the tower tonight. Says we're likely to have a storm, which means we will. She can tell at a glance when trouble is brewing," John told him pointedly and with a touch of humor in his voice. "You might find her at the bottom of Black Bluff near Saint Catherine's. She digs clams there and swims while she waits for nightfall."

"Thank you," Clayton said, then started for the door.

"Your Grace?"

He looked around.

"The damned lighthouse is little more than dust and rotten timbers. Perhaps she will listen to you if you convince her that her being there is far too dangerous—"

"What gives you the idea that she would ever listen to my advice?"

"Because she likes you. Oh, don't look so skeptical, Salterdon. I've known her much longer than you have, you know."

"You love her very much, Mr. Hoyt."

The old man looked thoughtful, his eyes distant, well-grooved lines of concern forming between his brows. Before Johnny could answer, Clayton slipped from the room.

Clayton made his way to the foot of the Undercliff and walked the stretch of craggy beach toward Saint Catherine's Lighthouse. Time and again he slowed and glanced back, watched the waves lap at the prints his feet had etched in the damp sand. He was in no danger of being cut off by the encroaching tide, as there was always that wickedly steep staircase grooved into the Undercliff's face that rose like a monolith above the chapel. Still, the hour was growing late, the light dim, the wind stronger and colder. He buttoned his cloak.

He wasn't certain what had driven him to come here. Perhaps because he felt he owed her the explanation of why he had decided to leave Cavisbrooke. She would be relieved, no doubt. After all, only last evening she had demanded that he go.

He found her footprints first. Tiny indentations of her bare feet in the sand. They ribboned up and down the narrow stretch of sand, first toward the water, then back again, as if she were dancing with the waves. Then, at last, his gaze sought for and found her. Miracle sat upon the ground, her back braced against the rib of the decaying ship where he had first landed on the isle. The girl appeared abnormally interested in one of her feet.

"I fear I've hurt my foot," she announced to him as he joined her and bent to one knee beside her. The wind toyed with her long red hair and had kissed bright color onto her cheeks. Yet, she did not look up at him, but focused on the bleeding injury on the sole of her foot.

Clayton yanked the linen stock from around his neck and proceeded to bind it tightly around the injury. "That's what comes from frolicking barefoot amid a lot of broken shells and stones, Meri Mine."

Miracle said nothing while he wrapped and tucked. He sat back on his heels. Leaning against the boat, she regarded him at last with her big eyes that looked as deep and green as the water beyond her. "You sound like my father," she told him. "Or how I always fancied him sounding, had he ever shown any interest in my welfare . . . had he even spoken to me at all." She laughed and moistened her lips with her tongue.

"I don't feel like your father," he said.

"What do you feel like?"

He stared into her eyes, her face, her lips that were red and slightly dry from the cold wind. The scattering of little freckles on her nose gave her the appearance of an imp, a child full of mischief. There was something intensely innocent and yet sensual in the way she regarded him, as if he were some fascinating curiosity she had found washed up on her beloved Black Bluff sand.

"I'm not certain," he finally admitted, then forced his gaze away, to a pair of curlews that were fluttering out over the water in search of food.

"I've been sitting here these last minutes trying to decide whether I like you," she confessed. "I suppose if I like you, then I would have to trust you. And if I trusted you . . ."

"What would you do, Meri Mine?"

From the corner of his eye, he saw her tip her head, as if she were regarding his profile intensely, perhaps waiting until he looked at her again. But he didn't.

At last, she raised one hand from her lap and caught his chin in a deliberately firm hold with her cold fingertips, and turned his face back toward hers. "Then I suppose I would share my secrets with you."

"What sort of secrets?"

"Miracles. Do you believe in miracles, Your Grace?"

Her fingers trailed over his cheek, to the cut on his forehead that she touched with incredible tenderness. In her eyes came a look of despair and guilt, as if she somehow blamed herself for his misfortune.

"Do you?" she asked again. "Believe in miracles?"

"I . . . don't know." He shook his head. "No. I suppose I don't."

"Why?"

"Perhaps because I've never witnessed one."

"Perhaps you simply don't know what to look for."

With no warning, Miracle leapt to her feet and struck out at a run toward the lighthouse and chapel. Slowly, Clayton stood, and with the wind whipping the tail of his cloak around his shins, watched her pause at the door of the ancient stone chapel and look back. "Come on!" she called, then disappeared into the building. Still, he remained where she had left him, the skin of his face warm and tingling where she had touched him.

Water rushed around his booted ankles. Coming to his senses, Clayton followed Miracle's tracks up the strand, to the doorless threshold of the chapel, then stopped. Darkness loomed back at him, as did the smell of dampness, rotting kelp, and fish. "Miracle," he whispered into the chamber. "Come out where I can see you."

There came a scratching sound. Then, from the farthest corner of the small chamber, a scant light flickered to life. With candle in hand, Miracle turned back to Clayton, her face little more than an apparition in the dim, wavering illumination. Her eyes looked liquid.

" 'Tis bad luck to tarry in the threshold of a church," she told him, and her voice in the cold chamber sounded hollow. "Mayhap God will question your piety."

The ocean surged and hissed behind him.

Clayton took a cautious step into the chamber, his gaze fixed on Miracle's face, her gentle eyes and tolerant smile. She lifted her hand toward him. "Quickly," came the encouragement. "Our time is short. The tide will be in soon."

"Then perhaps we should leave," he hurriedly offered.

Appearing to float across the floor, Miracle moved along the far wall of the chapel, the candle raised and illuminating the enclosure which, Clayton noted, had apparently been chiseled from the Undercliff itself. There were no seams, no mortar, no signs that the chapel had been constructed from anything other than solid stone. He might well have been standing in the mouth of a cave.

"Have you never seen anything so inspiring, Your Grace?" She held the candle up to the frescoes and figures cut into the stone: images of the Virgin Mary cradling her infant Jesus. Around her feet bowed a multitude of robed and armored soldiers, their bloodied swords cast upon the ground. But it was Mary that captured his attention. Her eyes, reflecting the candlelight, looked alive and weeping tears.

Her countenance radiating awe, her voice slightly breathless, Miracle said, " 'Tis said that buried beneath this floor is a saint. That as long as he sleeps peacefully, no harm will come to those who live near the Undercliff."

"And if he's disturbed?" Clayton asked.

"Then the face of these monoliths will crumble into the sea."

Clayton looked beyond Miracle to the distant dark doorway. Miracle moved toward it. "The stairway to the lighthouse," she explained. "Since the outside staircase has fallen to ruin, 'tis the only way in or out. Would you like to see the tower for yourself, Your Grace?"

There was challenge in the invitation. Why, he couldn't guess. Perhaps because she thought he wouldn't care to delve too deeply into the wet, stinking tomb. Or simply . . . perhaps she *was* a little crazy. This odd behavior could be nothing more than her innate ability to flaunt her unpredictability.

Finally, he moved toward her, felt his boots sink in the quicksandlike floor, a rush of consternation sluicing through him as the muck sucked at his ankles and gripped him hard. His heart was beating fast as he joined her at the foot of the steps.

"Careful," she called back as she ascended before him. "The steps are very narrow and steep. And extremely slippery." Then she disappeared up the dark bend above him.

"Just what the hell am I doing here?" he muttered to himself, then cursed through his teeth as his foot slipped on something slimy and he fell against the wall.

By the time he joined Miracle in the lighthouse, she had perched upon the wide windowsill that was no less than four feet thick. She swung her bare, sandy feet and regarded him with such intensity that he felt as if he had gone before a magistrate.

"So tell me," she said. "What do you think of my world?"

He glanced around the small chamber, noted the mechanics of the lighthouse, an unsafe pit of a furnace full of wood ash, then the simple cot shoved against the wall. There were stacks of books, sketches on linen canvases of birds and boats. A pair of kid slippers. A shawl. "It is rather . . . sparse," he replied, and glanced again at her bare feet. "You're bleeding, love."

"I've never brought anyone here," she said, ignoring his observation. "Not even Joe Cobbett, though he wanted me to. I wouldn't of course. 'Twouldn't have been proper."

"It isn't proper to bring me here, either," he told her pointedly and smiled.

"Aye. But then, you're a gentleman. Aren't you? Joe Cobbett wasn't a gentleman. Besides, 'tis my decision who I choose to be my friends."

"*Am* I your friend, Miracle?"

She lowered her eyes and chewed her lower lip.

Clayton moved toward her.

"No," she commanded, bringing him to an abrupt stop. "You'll stay away from me until I tell you otherwise. 'Tis *my* heart. *I* will choose to whom I wish to give it."

Gracefully, she dropped to the floor, and keeping a cautious and attentive eye on him, she moved to the far side of the room, glanced toward the sea, and frowned. Daylight was quickly disappearing, and with the encroachment of darkness, an intense chill had set in. Still, she did not seem to be bothered, though her clothing was ill suited to the cold. Her dress consisted of a single layer of cotton that had been dyed fawn brown. Its long sleeves were overly full and open about her wrists. There were no frills, no lace, no ruches. Only a delicately braided belt of ropelike material cinched around her tiny waist.

She looked, he thought, like a child, and the idea occurred to him that she no doubt knew little or nothing about the ways of a man, how the sight of her small naked foot peeking from beneath her skirt hem could set a man's blood to racing, or how a simple flash of her arm up her sleeve could make his body go hard as stone. Oh, yes. She obviously knew nothing about a man's baser instincts, or she wouldn't be looking at him now, all timidity and innocence, with wide aqua eyes that were so large they seemed to take up her entire face; she wouldn't part her lips like that, just enough so he could see the tip of her pink tongue toy with the edge of her pearl-white teeth. And she certainly wouldn't allow her gloriously blazing hair to fall so sensually and softly around her face and over her shoulders to blanket her full, pointed breasts. A woman with any worldly common sense would recognize him for what he was, a jaded womanizer who, when it came to women, had the morals of a tomcat.

Then again, a man of his experience should acknowledge her ignorance, and get the hell out.

"John's late with my dinner," came her words as she continued to gaze down the distant beach. "It's not like him. Did he seem well when you last saw him?" she asked, her mind obviously not on Clayton any longer.

He tried to respond but couldn't. He couldn't seem to do anything but allow his eyes to wander up and down her slender form as she leaned, with her back to him, against the window ledge while searching for her friend. He noted how her skirt clung to her gently rounded hips and buttocks, and he could see her ankles. It was then that he noticed her stockings, discarded in a filmy pile near her cot.

At last, she turned to face him, her countenance a melee of emotion that he was beginning to recognize any time she grew concerned. Yet, whatever fears for Johnny she had thought to voice were silenced as her eyes met his. A richer pink now suffused her cheeks—a blush not of the wind and cold, but discomposure. It was as if she had allowed herself to play the temptress but suddenly, like a poorly rehearsed thespian who found himself on a stage before critics, she discovered the folly of her misjudgment and became frightened.

"What are you thinking?" she demanded pointedly.

"That you are . . . very beautiful," he replied honestly.

She narrowed her eyes. "I'm not beautiful. I'm . . . unusual. Johnny calls me . . . exotic. And I'm not intelligent, I'm simply eccentric. And I don't like hypocrisy nor indecisiveness. You, Your Grace, are both. Oh, no . . ." She circled him. "I don't believe you. How can I believe you when before, you could find nothing positive to say about me and my home. Now, because you want something from me, you flower me with compliments. Beautiful now when before I was tatty and tacky and unfit for the company of sensitive townsfolk."

"I was blind," he said, not bothering to follow her with his eyes as she paced about him like a vixen scrutinizing a trap.

"You think because you speak kindly now to me, that you break bread at my table, and treat Johnny as your equal, that I should forgive your previous ill humor—"

"I apologize," he announced in a deep, clear voice that seemed to reverberate his growing irritation in the stone chamber. "A thousand times I beg your tolerance and forgiveness—"

"And if I don't forgive you?"

"Then you, mademoiselle, can go to hell."

She stopped suddenly.

He slowly turned to face her. "I've grown far too weary of this game, Meri Mine. I'm not a man of extreme patience when it comes to dealing with coy women. I've no reason to be. There are a thousand other women out there, all of whom are as beautiful, or exotic, or intelligent, or eccentric. And a damn sight easier to get along with."

He moved past her toward the stairwell. A candle burned halfway down the flight, painting the spiraling stone steps in shadows and wavering light. He descended the stairs almost recklessly, cursing the recurring image of her feminine stockings tossed so carelessly near her cot.

Yes, better to get the hell away from the bloody island as fast as he could, before this dangerous game he was playing for his brother became real . . . before he fell in love with her himself.

What had the vicar once preached? Thou shalt not covet thy brother's wife?

Reaching the chapel, he froze. Water lapped at the bottom step, frothed and hissed and appeared to lick long green tongues up at his boots. He stumbled back two steps, then Miracle's small, firm hand on his shoulder stopped him.

She slid by him, paused at the water's edge and looked back up at him. He stared down at her for a few hurtling moments, his heart beating in his ears, the closeness of the quarters and the rising water seeming to suck the air from his lungs. Her eyes regarded him intensely as Miracle leaned against the wall of the stairwell. In the gloomy confines of the stifling tower she seemed small, yet there was nothing in her expression that denoted weakness. He sensed that if he attempted to escape her company and his damnable circumstance, she would stop him at whatever cost.

"What is it?" he snapped. "Say it and get it over with. The goddamn tide is coming in." He glanced beyond her to the rising water.

"I've made you angry," she said.

Releasing a sharp breath, Clayton took another backward step up the tower, leaned against the wall, and closed his eyes. He tried to swallow, to ignore that sense of rising and falling that made his head dizzy and his stomach sick.

"I apologize," came her voice through his fog. "You've been most kind since you've returned to Cavisbrooke. Perhaps my mistrust stems from the fact that I'm constantly scrutinized and criticized by the village folk. I've been forced to question any act of kindness or consideration because too often there have been obscured motives for their courtesy. But at some point, one must trust, mustn't one? And the truth is, Your Grace, I've begun to like you . . . a little. Therefore, when one deems to like someone, even if it is just a little, there are certain responsibilities that go along with it . . . such as trust. Your Grace . . . is something wrong?"

Forcing open his eyes, Clayton focused on the water that, in the past eternal seconds, had climbed yet another step up the tower. It flirted now with the hem of Miracle's threadbare little dress of rough cloth, and in a disjointed instant, he forgot the wretched tidewaters and could see nothing but the way the damp material clung in an almost immodest fashion over her rounded bosom—and there were those nipples his brother had waxed on about—*his brother*, for God's sake—they thrust out the material of her dress like tiny rosebuds. Could she not see that? Didn't she know how flagrantly arousing she looked, poised there above the mystical chapel with its ancient, weeping Virgin, looking like some seductive Madonna herself?

Passing one hand over his eyes, he said through his teeth, "Wrong? Yes, something is wrong. I want to get the hell out of this place before I do something I'll regret for the rest of my life."

She thought he meant to quit the tower. He didn't. He wanted away from Cavisbrooke, from Saint Catherine's, from her. Definitely from her.

Miracle lifted her white hand to him, and the sleeve of her gown slid back, exposing her slender wrist and forearm. The pale hair on her arm shimmered like spun gold in the wavering candlelight. "Are you afraid?" she asked softly. "The water isn't so deep. I'll help you through it. Please, Your Grace. Take my hand."

"I'm not an invalid!" he shouted, only in the cavernous tower it sounded more like an angry, wounded roar that made the girl flinch and move away, down into the water. "I am not afraid," he said in a more controlled tone. "I—am—not—afraid, damn you." Then he knocked her hand away, and stumbling down the steps, grabbed her around her waist and heaved her up, flinging her over his shoulder as she cried aloud in surprise and kicked and pounded on his back.

"Put me down! Barbarian! What are you doing?"

Swatting her derriere, he growled, "Shut up and allow me to be a gentleman for once."

"Pray, sir, a gentleman would not treat a lady as if she were a sack of grain!"

The driving water surged around his ankles, then his shins as he struggled toward the door of the chapel, his gaze focused on the distant, watery horizon that seemed to surge higher with every beat of the ocean's heart. He slid once and nearly fell, fumbled for his footing while the sand beneath his feet was sucked away by the current's undertow. At last, he burst from the building, staggered as the rising night wind thrust into his face, and as the waves climbed higher up his legs, he forced himself toward the Undercliff where the steep steps offered certain sanctuary from the water.

He took the steps two at a time, until his legs and lungs began to burn with exertion and realization struck him that he continued to hoist Miracle on his shoulder. At last, he stopped, slid her down his chest, his arms clutching her to him, her body pressed against his, while her feet danced in midair above the rock landing and her glorious hair, spirited by the rising wind, floated around their faces like a wispy copper cloud.

Eye to eye, lips but a breath apart, they poised there, breathing in unison, the beating of their hearts an echo of the other's, as the wind and sea roared around and below them. He was going to kiss her, God help him. He knew it, and yet he couldn't stop it, any more than he could stop his heart from pounding in his chest. He was going to kiss his brother's future wife and he would then be forced to live with that thought every time he looked Trey in the eye.

"No," came her voice through the roar of the wind, yet she didn't struggle, but clung to him, her hands twisted into his heavy damp cloak, anchoring her every curve against his as her skirt whipped and billowed like a leaf in a windstorm. "I don't want you to kiss me," she cried. "I won't let you!"

"No?" he heard himself yell back, even as he lowered his head, even as he watched her lips part and her eyes grow drowsy and her body limp. His lips brushed hers—oh, Christ they were soft and warm, heating him while the wind and the salty sea spray stung his face with cold. For an eternal instant he could not move, but poised there, lips barely touching hers while the feel and smell of her embedded in his memory so he knew he would never forget.

Burying his hands in her soft hair, he clutched her and pulled her hard to his face, opened his mouth and covered hers, filled her up with his tongue—like he had kissed a hundred women before her—experienced women who knew what to expect from a man like him. She floundered, struggled, and kissed him back, in her own inexperienced way: no tongue, a bit dry, a bit clumsily, uncomfortably, bashfully. He didn't want to stop.

"P-please," she finally stammered and gasped for breath.

He raised his head, just barely.

Limply, she lay in his arms, head fallen back, arms flung almost lifelessly out from her sides; her eyes closed. The wind danced with her hair, spraying it like a flaming Chinese fan around her head. He thought she had fainted; then she murmured words that were virtually lost in the gale:

"I—I did not give you permission to kiss me, sir. Therefore y-you should release me promptly before—"

"Before what?" he replied, allowing his gaze to follow the pale curve of her throat to the soft white hollow at the base of her neck. A pulse fluttered there, rapidly as a fairy's wing.

"Before I-I-I demand that you do it again."

With that, she sprang to life, became, once again, all arms and legs that kicked and flittered, her face flushed, eyes wide, mouth slightly swollen and abraded by the kiss.

At last, Clayton allowed Miracle to drop gently to the rock, and he withdrew his hands, fell back against the face of the Undercliff, and wished like hell that his brother had let him drown.

One day I wrote her name upon the strand,
But came the waves and washed it away:
Again I wrote it with a second hand,
But came the tide, and made my pains his prey.
EDMUND SPENSER

Chapter Nine

He had *kissed* her!

She had *allowed* it! She had even *enjoyed* it! For an instant, she had experienced a new form of flying. Her blood sang. Her body vibrated like a stroked harp string.

This odd, confusing, *fascinating* man had kissed her, making her forget for the moment that if she didn't hurry, there would be no hope of returning to the lighthouse—not with the waves and tides as turbulent as they were tonight. *As turbulent as her insides.*

Oh, Lord, he had kissed her. What would Ceridwen's bible say about this? Was the moon right? The stars aligned? Was he, after all, her destiny?

Who was he, anyway? *What* was he? A hero one moment, almost child-like the next. A farmer one day, a true aristocrat later, with all the airs and arrogance that went along with it. It was in his walk, his stance, the elegant, well-cut clothes he wore, not to mention the way he had of looking down his nose at anything he found objectionable. Aristocrats, especially dukes, were notorious for that, regarding their less-than-distinguished world with a tendentious eye.

It wasn't a trait that she found appealing in the least . . . normally. *This* duke, however, had a way of making it seem just a little alluring, a bit exciting. More than once—even before the kiss—he had made her heart skip a beat (she could hardly deny it any longer)—like now, as he walked at her side, offering her his arm in a gentlemanly manner each time they were forced to leap a creek bed or a cluster of brushwood on their journey back to Cavisbrooke.

Miracle had decided that his unfathomable eyes—gray as channel fog—were more than a little disturbing. They were full of secrets, cynicism, and guilt. It was the way he had of avoiding her eyes when she attempted to look into his soul, for the eyes *were* windows to the soul, and repeatedly the duke of Salterdon shuttered those windows against her, not only on his first stay at Cavisbrooke, but during this visit as well. She wanted to trust him, but dare she? After her mother left, she had trusted only one person in her life, and that had been Johnny. He had taught her the value of honesty, of truth, of forbearance, and forgiveness.

Perhaps it was time to forgive His Grace.

Miracle ran down the path ahead of Salterdon, her knowledge of the track enabling her to skip effortlessly over jutting roots and outcropping stones even though darkness had descended. She felt safer here, with yards of distance to separate them.

What if he tried to kiss her again? Would she allow it? Would she play coy and bashful? Why hadn't he spoken to her since she had allowed him such a shocking liberty? What went on in a man's mind after such an intimate occurrence? Why had he looked so pained, so angered, so frustrated when he had at last released her? Why had he appeared as if he wanted to hurl himself off the Undercliff?

Had she disappointed him?

It wasn't as if she *knew* what to do. Joe Cobbett had only kissed her once, and it had certainly been nothing like Salterdon's. Joe's kiss had been little more than a dry brief peck that left her wondering what all the fuss was about between men and women. But Salterdon's . . .

Ceridwen's bible had said nothing about open mouths and tongues, of burning eyes and pounding hearts that robbed her of breath and all physical strength. This was certainly something new. She felt confused, a little out of focus and out of control, and that wasn't good. She suspected that a man like Salterdon would shy from such a weakness.

Blazes! She had even begun to care what he thought!

Topping a rise and breathing rapidly, she stopped suddenly and focused on the distant view. At the bottom of the hill she could just make out Johnny's cart and donkey. The terrified animal was braying loudly as a half dozen boys on shire horses thundered in a circle around her friend, all whooping and shouting as he flailed at them with his cane.

"Away with you," came his voice. "Hooligans! Ruffians! Be gone and leave me in peace!"

Striking off at a run, taking no notice of the stones slashing the bottoms of her feet or His Grace's linen stock flapping from her instep like a tattered flag, she flew toward the ambushers. "Stop it!" she cried. "Leave him alone!"

Plowing into the midst of the fray, she fell to her knees and grabbed Johnny where he huddled on the ground near the cart.

"Witch!" a lad hooted.

"Lunatic!" another crowed.

"Why don't the two of ya leave this isle to normal folk?" still another boy shouted.

"Go away!" Miracle yelled. "Why can you not leave us in peace?"

Someone flung a stone. Miracle cried out as it glanced off her cheek. Another followed. Wrapping herself around Johnny, she hugged him close and whispered in his ear, "It's all right. I won't let them hurt you."

"Come 'ere, luvie. If ya want to wrap yer arms around a man, ya might as well make it count."

A hand twisted into her hair and flung her aside. She hit the ground hard, skidded, felt the skin abraded from her arms and hands as Johnny howled out his distress.

"Son of a bitch," came the sound of Salterdon's fierce and threatening voice through the melee. Through her haze of shock, she watched Salterdon swing with Johnny's cane at her attacker, cracking it against the villain's head, sending him sprawling with a groan. Then he spun on his heel as a mounted rider bore down upon him; he swung again, driving the chiseled horse head into the boy's rib once, twice, while the massive, terrified horse the boy rode shied and whinnied and took off into the dark at a dead run.

Then there was quiet but for the sound of her own breathing and the thudding of the horses' hooves as the attackers fled into the night.

"Mira, Mira," cried Johnny.

"Meri Mine," Salterdon said softly, and fell to one knee beside her, his gentle hands brushing the hair back from her face. She did her best to focus, to swallow the lump of emotion in her throat as his fingers tenderly caressed her face, her hands, and arms, cautiously checking to see if the ruffians had broken more than her spirit.

At last, she managed to gather her wits enough to sit up. Seeing Johnny, collapsed and leaning back against the cart, his face white, Miracle tried her best to stand, only to sway into Salterdon's arms. "Help him," she pleaded up into his concerned eyes. "Because I fear I might faint."

With that, she found herself swept up in Salterdon's arms and carefully deposited into the cart. Miracle took several deep breaths, closed her eyes, and kept them closed until Salterdon appeared again, and with teeth clenched and body straining, hoisted Johnny into the cart. Miracle opened her arms, and as her one and only friend sank down against her, she cradled his head on her shoulder, and whispered, "There, there, Johnny. I swear I won't let them hurt you again."

Miracle sat at Johnny's side until he slept. She held his hand. She soothed him with words. She read to him from a book of poems until his eyelids grew heavy, his breathing less laborious, and slight color returned to his cheeks. Still, he struggled with Morpheus, gripped her hand fiercely, and whispered, "Sweet Mira, forget an old man and see to yourself."

"I'm fine, Johnny. I promise."

"Your face is bleeding. Your dress is torn. Merciful God, strike me dead for bringing this fate upon you. I should have insisted that your mother send you away from this place. We were both too bloody selfish. You brought us such joy. We loved you so much . . ."

"And I love you," she replied softly. "Now sleep. By tomorrow this terrible affair will be nothing but an irritating inconvenience."

Gripping her hand, he pleaded, "Don't go back to the lighthouse tonight. Promise me. Those young hooligans—"

"Would never come to Saint Catherine's."

"It isn't safe, I tell you. Another storm and the dreadful place will topple into the sea."

"Nonsense. Saint Catherine's Lighthouse has withstood two hundred years of storms. It's steady as the Rock of Gibraltar."

"Mira—"

"Oh, very well, sir. If it will make you rest easier, I promise not to return to the chapel tonight. Although I'm warning you, if a ship breaks up on the Race during my absence, I shall never forgive either one of us."

Johnny relaxed. After moments of silence, he drifted. Only then did Miracle press a soft kiss to forehead and tuck the blanket around his shoulders. "Why?" she asked quietly to herself. "Why must they continue to taunt us?"

"Because people are afraid of diversity," came Salterdon's voice behind her, and Miracle looked around, somewhat startled, to find him standing at John's chamber door. He had removed his cutaway and held a blue and white basin of steaming water. There was a cloth flung across one shoulder. In a rush, the memory of his body pressed against hers made her feel lightheaded.

Perhaps it was only the last horrible hour that made her experience this breathlessness and faintness. Could it be that the incident was God's punishment for her questionable behavior with Salterdon?

"They look upon difference as some kind of disease," he continued, an edge of bitterness in his tone. "As if the difference were contagious and threatening. Human beings are rather odd about that, perhaps arrogant in their beliefs that only their own sense of values and convictions are right and acceptable. If we were as moral and righteous as we profess to be, we wouldn't have annihilated our brothers since the beginning of time with war."

"I don't recall having invited you here," she said, forcing her old belligerence back into her voice. How very frustrating that she should struggle so hard to work up her combativeness in his company. She didn't want to like this man. She had responsibilities, after all. Had she not allowed him to occupy her time at the lighthouse, she would have gone sooner to discover why Johnny was late delivering her dinner. Perhaps this entire ugly incident could have been avoided.

"I don't recall having asked you to," he returned with a cryptic smile, then placed the basin on a table and proceeded to roll up his sleeves. For a moment, Miracle stared at his hands that were somewhat abraded. He had long, strong fingers and well-manicured nails. His forearms were muscular and tanned, with a sprinkling of soft black hair. Occasionally, during her outings on the downs, she had witnessed the local farmers bathing their upper bodies in a stock trough. Their forearms had been tanned as well, right up to the place where their shirt sleeves had begun; the remainder of their torsos had been white as fish bellies—an image that had repelled her.

Odd, however, that she would look at this man, who had probably never known a day's hard toil in his life, and fancifully imagine that his shoulders and chest would be as sun-browned as his hands and forearms. Odd that his hands had not been so brown on his first stay at Cavisbrooke. Perhaps they had been, and she hadn't noticed. No, she thought. She would definitely have noticed.

Salterdon pulled up a chair and dropped into it, then he dipped the cloth into the steaming water and wrung it out.

"What are you doing?" she demanded.

"Relax," he told her, then catching her chin in his fingers, gently touched the warm cloth to the cut on her cheek. "I'm simply returning a favor, Meri Mine."

"Ouch! The water's hot—"

"Will help to kill infection—"

"Cobwebs would suffice. Careful! You have the finesse of a blacksmith."

"I've often heard that healers make the worst patients."

"I'm hardly a healer, Your Grace." She looked him in the eye for the first time. "Will it scar, do you think?"

A smile twitched his lips, then he appeared very solemn again. "I think not. Now hush and let me nurse you."

Setting her chin, uncertain if she liked the sense of control his resolute voice seemed to have over her, Miracle did her best to relax as Salterdon lightly bathed her forehead, her cheeks, her chin, then eased the soft, warm towel over her eyes, forcing her to briefly close them, then to her mouth, her lips, that were slightly parted. His touch was soft as a breath, and just as warm, causing her to feel . . . How, exactly, did she feel?

"Meri Mine," he said softly. "Why are you crying?"

"Am I?" She swallowed and forced open her eyes, spilling tears down her cheeks. "No one except my mother has ever touched me with such kindness, Your Grace . . . and that was so very long ago." Swiping the discomfiting tears aside with the back of one hand, she tried to laugh. "It is I who should be washing *your* feet. You're our guest, after all, and twice you've come to my rescue. If I'm not careful, I might come to believe in fairy tales—of heroes rescuing fair maidens in distress."

"And what's wrong with believing in fairy tales?"

"Like hope, they can vanish like smoke when confronted by reality."

"Is that why you remain here, cloistered in this fortress? Because you're afraid of reality?"

"Reality is what happened tonight, Your Grace. It is prejudice and bigotry. It demands that we conform to the strictures of what is customary. I think I would rather die than fossilize in a society that dictates what I can or cannot do or say or think. What are rules, sir, but limitations we thrust upon ourselves or others?"

He said nothing, just bent his head and proceeded to wash her foot.

With her body relaxed against the back of her chair, her eyelids heavy, Miracle studied the top of his head, his glorious dark hair that, having been tousled by the wind, was a mass of unruly loose curls. There, too, was a light dusting of sand, a sliver of grass. Without thinking, she reached for it, her fingertips brushing the rich spray of chocolate brown strands that sprang to life at her touch.

His movement stopped. His face came slowly up. His eyes met hers.

"You're beautiful," she whispered. "Odd that I never noticed before. But then again, I didn't like you then. Do you mind if I touch you, Your Grace? I suppose in your world it's wrong. But in my world, I cannot help but worship that which I find comely." Allowing her lips to smile, she touched her fingers to his noble forehead, to the bruise she had tended only that morning. Closing her eyes, she allowed herself to explore him: his brows—heavy, soft; his nose—strong and aristocratic. And his high cheeks, his jaw, lightly studded with a day's growth of beard. His lips, full, warm, slightly moist, slightly parted . . . How very bold she had become!

His tongue touched her fingertip, and she gasped, and her eyes flew open. As swiftly, he caught her wrist with his wet hand and turned his mouth into her palm, breathed upon her sensitive flesh, then kissed her, there upon the delicate skin between her thumb and forefinger, and she shivered.

"Oh, sir," she murmured. "I fear you forget yourself. Johnny—"

"Is asleep," he whispered against her hand, and touched her again with his tongue.

Gasping again, she withdrew her hand quickly and leaned toward him, so their faces were but inches apart, her gaze fixed on his eyes that looked smoky with desire. "You're quite shameless, you know."

"I know."

"I never gave you permission to kiss me, much less to do *that* with your tongue. Do you forget who you are, sir? And who I am?"

For a long moment, he said nothing, just poised there, rocked back on his heels, one elbow resting on one black-clad thigh while he regarded her face, his dark eyes appearing to register her every feature. Little by little, the intensity of his countenance turned into something else, a disconcertion shadowed by an odd, disturbing resignation, anger, and disgust. The turn was enough to make her sit back and grip the chair arms in confused anticipation.

"Apparently so," he finally replied in an acid tone that brought her as much consternation as had the wicked teasing of his tongue. In a blink, his composure had turned from flirtatious to animal. She felt as if she were staring into a wolf's eyes that were hungry and fierce and dangerous. In an instant they had gone from fire to ice.

The cloth sliding from his fingers and into the basin of tepid water, Salterdon slowly stood, his gaze never leaving hers as he clenched his fists at his sides. "Damn your eyes," he said in a husky voice. "Damn your innocence. Damn your lips and damn your ability to make me forget who I am . . . and who you are, or who you may become if I allow myself to remain here."

"Your Grace?"

"Stop calling me that, dammit. My name is Hawthorne, not duke, not duke What's-His-Name, not your dukeship, not Your Grace . . . just . . . Hawthorne. Say my name, Miracle. *Say* it."

"Hawthorne," she responded softly, bemused by his apparent anger and frustration, equally surprised by the ease with which his name floated from her tongue. "Hawthorne. 'Tis a very nice name, Your Grace."

Silence.

Miracle felt warm color suffuse her cheeks as he continued to stand before her, regarding her with a look bordering on murder and laughter.

At last, he turned on his heel and moved toward the door, paused at the threshold, and gripped the doorjamb with one hand while the other massaged the tense nape of his neck. Finally, he said without turning, "Try to get some sleep, love. I'm certain Johnny will be fine in the morning." Then he was gone, leaving silence and an unnerving emptiness in his wake.

Benjamin sat in a chair before the dwindling fire, head fallen forward, snores emanating from his mouth. He wore his cloak. His flask of brandy tipped precariously on his lap. Clayton paced the room ten minutes before the manservant blinked his eyes and clumsily sat up. He stared at Clayton, his eyes shadowed by fatigue, his brow furrowed with worry. A moment passed before the circumstances set in.

"Good gosh," he declared, and grabbing his flask, stumbled to his feet. "I beg your pardon, my lord. I must have tottered off. Can't think of what could have caused me to act so carelessly."

"No?" Clayton plucked the flask from the valet's hand. "You're drunk, Ben. Intoxicated. Muddled. Cockeyed." Removing the cork stopper, he turned up the flask and drank deeply, until the brandy hit his stomach with a burning punch, then he hissed through his teeth. "Slopped. Blind. Stiff. Tight. Wet."

"By Jove," the servant muttered. "So I am. Can't think of when I last weltered in the grape to such an extreme. Let me think . . . must have been the time that little wench who worked for your grandmother up and married some quick-fingered Cockney with one eye and a peg leg. I quite fancied her until that."

"Really, Ben, you could do much better."

"Yes, sir. So you said at the time, sir." Rousing somewhat from his stupor, Benjamin frowned and withdrew his timepiece from his waistcoat pocket. "Must have been a bit more caught in the old cups than I realized. It's grown quite late. It'll be midnight before we reach Niton."

Clayton walked to the window and looked out, drank again, then wiped the brandy from his lips with his wrist.

"We *are* still leaving, sir? Aren't we?"

It was a rare night that one could count the stars in the sky, but they were there, twinkling against the black, scattered like diamonds around the sickle-shaped yellow moon, which floated above the reflective sea. Clayton focused on his reflection in the windowpane and wished like hell that he was already there, in Niton, with its ruddy-faced farmers and seamen who smelled like fish.

"Sir," Benjamin said near his ear. "Our bags are packed. Ready to go."

"Then unpack them."

"Oh, but, sir . . . my lord, 'twould be folly to remain here, and besides, I saw them again, sir. We simply cannot remain here any longer. It isn't safe."

"Saw what, Benjamin?"

"The beast. And the dark specter babbling in tongues."

Imbibing the last of the brandy from the bottom of the flask, Clayton turned to stand face to face with his ashen cheeked companion. Benjamin's eyes were round as saucers, his breath rich enough to ignite peat.

"You think me mad," Benjamin muttered.

"Not at all," Clayton replied.

Ben's eyebrows shot up. He swayed a little from side to side, then hiccoughed.

"I saw them myself," Clayton confessed.

Benjamin swallowed.

"And the angel and the unicorn, too."

"You . . . don't say."

Clayton clamped one hand on the man's shoulder, squeezed him comfortingly. "I think we're both a little mad, my friend. Rephrase. I am a great deal mad or I wouldn't still be here. Don't get me wrong, Ben; I want like hell to leave this musty, damp old place with its cobwebs and ghosts and goddamn unicorns and dragons. But I promised my brother . . ."

He laughed shortly, cynically, then shoved the servant away. "Who the bloody blazes am I kidding? I'm not here any longer for Trey. I'm here for me. Because she mesmerizes me, Ben. She fascinates me. I want to learn if she's for real. It's not demons or faceless marauders who terrify me. It's her. What she is. What she may or may not be."

"She's to *become* your brother's wife," Benjamin declared.

"Yes," he said softly. "My brother's wife. My brother who has been given everything: a respected title, a dozen estates, a fortune once my grandmother dies . . . not to mention my parents' undivided attention. After all, Trey was the firstborn, the heir apparent—"

"My lord," Ben interrupted, catching Clayton's shoulders in his hands. "Your parents loved you."

"But not like they loved Trey. Can you comprehend what it was like for me? I was nothing more than Trey's shadow, Ben. A mirror image that stood aside from the reality while the reality was lavished with attention. Trey; he makes a bloody mess of his life and what does he care? There will always be someone there to set him straight, to get his life in order. Namely me."

Taking Clayton's face firmly in his hands, Benjamin regarded him intensely. "And here you are, Clay, helping him again—hoping to win the lass over so the union might reward His Grace with the respect and comfort only your grandmother's money can buy him. Let's leave this place before this perverse interest you have in the girl grows beyond your means to control it, unless, of course, you wish to marry her yourself."

Clayton laughed, a harsh and abrupt sound, and turned away from his friend. He shook the empty flask, then tossed it away, paced the room, his eyes taking in the barren chamber as he said cholerically, "Don't be ridiculous. I have no desire whatsoever to marry Miracle Cavendish. The idea is absurd."

"Then why are we here, my lord? Or more to the point, why do we *remain* here?"

"I don't know," Clayton said wearily. "Perhaps I'm simply fascinated by unicorns."

My horse with a mane made of short rainbows.
My horse with ears made of round corn.
My horse with eyes made of big stars.
My horse with a head made of mixed waters.
My horse with teeth made of white shell.
The long rainbow is in his mouth for a bridle
and with it I guide him.
When my horse neighs,
different-colored horses follow.
When my horse neighs,
different-colored sheep follow.
I am wealthy because of him
Before me peaceful
Behind me peaceful
Over me peaceful—
Peaceful voice when he neighs.
I am everlasting and peaceful
I stand for my horse.

from Louis Watchman's version of
the Navajo "Horse Story"

Chapter Ten

The moon and starlight were bright enough to spill through the embrasures and dimly light the vast corridors that stretched out like a maze before Clayton.

Basingstoke. Basingstoke. Basingstoke. He repeated the name in his head as he moved as silently as possible across the stone floor, occasionally reaching out with one hand to finger the wall, hoping the contact of cold stone would steady him in his intrusive exploration of his host's home.

Basingstoke. Hawthorne. Clayton. Not the duke of Salterdon. That was his brother. He was becoming too caught up in this despicable role he'd been playing, forgetting that he had come here to win Miracle Cavendish for his brother.

Once, while in Paris, lying in his mistress's arms, he had mentally compared the ruse to the spinning of a spider's web. The silken, transparent labyrinth of his lies would lure Miracle in, and once captured, he would wrap her up with his charm and deliver her to his brother. He had looked at it as a game, like the games of switched identity he and Trey had played on their friends and family during their childhood. But, until arriving on the isle, Miracle Cavendish had only been a faceless entity whom his brother had tossed off as some backward country bumpkin who was, apparently, slightly light in intelligence—or so his brother had insinuated.

Another lie.

Now, however, he was beginning to feel as if he were the one caught in the web. The harder he struggled to remove himself emotionally, the more fiercely he felt bagged. This immense and abnormal preoccupation with the girl was beginning to bother him. Yet, here he was, stealing through the corridors of her home in hopes of unraveling her mysteries. Perhaps then he could put this "perverse interest," as Ben had called it, to rest. Perhaps then he could leave this place and return home, leave the girl and his guilt to molder away in this dark passage of cells.

Coming to John's room, he slid inside. The dying peat in the fireplace lent a reddish gold gloom to the interior. The empty port glass from which he had earlier imbibed still sat on the table near a chair. Hoyt's lap blanket lay on the floor in an untidy heap. His bed was empty.

This was ridiculous, creeping about the old man's chamber in the middle of the night like some common thief. He wasn't even certain why he had come here, to this room. There was very little here of Miracle, aside from the books that she had supposedly read. But there was something nagging at him—bothering him about the situation with Miracle and Hoyt and her mother's disappearance.

A sudden draft through the door scattered papers from a stack on a desk. One landed near his foot. Clayton retrieved the page, tilted it toward the light from the hearth, and allowed his eyes to peruse it: the script was written by an obviously unsteady hand.

At last, his gaze went to the hearth ash, watched the yellow heat pulsate and wink like little glowing eyes as he continued to hold the paper and its writings in his fingertips that were growing numb with cold. "Christ," he said after a long moment.

Another wind, colder this time, bringing him back to his senses. Carefully folding the paper, he then slid it into his trouser pocket and wished like hell that he had put on his cloak, his cutaway at the very least, but he hadn't wanted to wake Benjamin. The poor sod was having enough trouble dealing with the fact that he was going to be forced to remain at Cavisbrooke a while longer—or at least until Clayton "came to his senses."

A noise. Clayton moved to the door, paused, looked first one way up the corridor, then the other. Nothing, then a figure materialized from the shadows and stopped in the distance, too far to make out who or what it was. His mind raced with a dozen excuses he would make for nosing around Hoyt's private chamber, should he be discovered. But then the apparition moved, not toward him, but away, dissolving back into the obscurity of the black gallery.

Clayton followed, keeping to the wall, farther and farther, until the walls grew older, mustier, and damper, until no light shone at all through the embrasures and no candles cast meager light to help his passage. Perhaps he had just imagined the phantom, he must surely have done that morning on the beach. There were no angels and unicorns. No babbling specters riding dragons and brandishing swords.

He moved ahead. There came a scraping, grinding groan, and, for an instant, a sliver of light appeared, then disappeared in the distance. A door opening and closing?

At last, he came face to face with a wall. He heard voices, muffled, sounding like Hoyt barking orders and . . . the drumming, thundering, like . . . a horse running.

Clayton slid his hand over the stone wall and brushed against the cold steel of a heavy latch. He closed his fingers around it and shoved. The wall gave and easily slid open.

The bright flash of firelight and color assaulted his eyes, and he winced, squinted, and focused on the activity before him. *Our unicorns and dragons, Benjamin, my friend*, he thought. And, of course, the angel.

Miracle, astride a high-cantering bay stallion of unquestionable spirit and beauty, circled Jonathan Hoyt, who stood near a campfire, issuing orders like a seasoned soldier.

"You must ride with your legs and seat, Mira. Listen to me. You are to become one with the horse. Your movements must be fluid and you must force the stubborn beast up under you. Yes! That's my girl. Feel the animal's power surge up through you. You must be in control. You are the master, Mira. Never for a moment allow him to think he is or he may well kill you."

"Hasan would never kill me!" she shot back, and dug her bare heels into the stallion's lathered sides, demanding more speed and collection.

"You must demand his respect, Mira!"

"I have his respect!" she cried back, and with that, she spun the snorting horse toward a barricade of tumbled stone, and then drove him forward at a fierce speed.

"Mira!" John shouted. "I beg you—"

With a graceful leap, the horse and rider left the ground and flew over the wall, disappearing into the dark.

Flinging his cane to the ground, John cursed and shook his fist, hobbled toward the wall, and falling against it, stared off into the night. "Blasted gel," Clayton heard him mutter. "She'll kill herself yet on these unpredictable beasts. Ismail!" he shouted.

From a brightly colored tent erected beyond the dancing firelight, Benjamin's specter appeared draped in the recognizable abbah of a desert Bedouin, dark face partially covered. "Find the lady and bring her back," John barked. "And she damn well better be in one piece or I'm havin' yer skinny arse for me dinner, ya bleedin' barbarian. No doubt you've been encouragin' this unhealthy behavior . . ."

The slightly built man deftly scrambled over the wall, despite the encumbrance of his trailing robes, and vanished into the night.

From his place in the shadows, Clayton watched John wearily drop onto a pile of stones and run his hands through his thinning hair. Only then did Clayton allow himself to study his surroundings: the Bedouin tent and its colored filjans, mijdims, and amuds, a well-worn carpet positioned near the fire on which pots of coffee were steeping. There was even a hadhira built around the front of the tent to keep out the cold wind.

There were a score of acres enclosed within the perimeters of this apparently secretive oasis—an oasis that was obviously erected for the comfort of the Arabian horsekeeper, and his collection of, by Clayton's estimation, at least a dozen horses that were scattered over the walled-in grounds, all grazing peacefully in lush, ankle-deep grass—until the sudden, trumpeted call of alarm erupted from someplace in the dark. Within a blink, the animals moved as one, heads flying up, nostrils wide and ears erect, as they swung their heads in Clayton's direction and pranced nervously, as if waiting to be told what to do next.

Then came the familiar, eerie blowing and roaring, the thunder vibrating the ground, shivering up Clayton's spine and riveting his eyes on the ghostly form materializing from the dark.

The dragon. The unicorn.

No illusion this time, no specter brought on by too much grog—no bad dream—no dream at all.

It came, scattering the other horses to the far corners of the encampment, its forelegs prancing chest high, white hooves flashing in the firelight, silver white tail arched up over his haunches and flying out behind him like a banner. Massive but graceful neck arched. Challenging black eyes flashing. Fiery red nostrils stretched and open and blowing steam into the cold night air.

John's cautious voice called from the distance, "Your Grace, please don't attempt to flee—"

"I'm not accustomed to running from horses," he responded calmly, although the stallion continued coming, now baring its teeth, its entire muscular body appearing to grow with each reverberating footfall.

"He'll challenge you," John called, then he stumbled to the tumbled barricade and shouted into the night, "Ismail! Ismail! Where the devil have ya disappeared to?"

Clayton planted his feet.

The stallion planted his, sliding to a stop no more than ten feet from Clayton, close enough that when the animal blew again, the hot moisture of his breath felt like steam on Clayton's face. The animal reared, then pawed the ground, sending turf flying into the air like little missiles.

"Napitov!" came Miracle's cry, and suddenly she appeared, sliding from her bay horse while her odd companion scrambled to collect the reins and hurry the lathered animal away. Features set, her red hair a wild spray around her face and shoulders, she marched, with whip in hand, toward Clayton and his agitated challenger. "Napitov!" she stated again more firmly. "Away! Napitov, no!"

The horse roared and tossed its head, causing its flowing, steel-gray mane to fly furiously. As Miracle neared, the horse spun, danced, kicked, then pranced in place between Miracle and Clayton, blocking her way, shielding her from Clayton with his body.

"Away," she ordered again, not the least intimidated by the animal's odd, aggressive behavior. Then she offered her hand, and as she lightly touched the horse's muzzle, the transformation was immediate. The uncontrollable dragon-beast lowered its noble head and nickered softly, almost seductively, like a man crooning amorous words to his beloved. The animal lipped her fingers, her jaw, her ear, nuzzled her hair and made soft, low sounds in its throat.

"Away," Miracle murmured more gently, and slid her hand down the horse's strong neck, her hand small against the flexing, bulging muscles working beneath her palm. Only then did the stallion move away, and Miracle turned her attention to Clayton. In a blink, the almost drowsy look of pleasure that had marked her features while stroking the horse became, once again, a look of fiery anger.

"I should have allowed him to kill you," she said, moving toward him, the whip gripped in her fist as if she might strike him. "How dare you invade the secrecy of this place? You've no business here, Salterdon. You've no business at Cavisbrooke. On the island, for that matter. Why the bloody hell don't you go back to where you belong?"

Clayton slid his hands into his pockets, never taking his eyes from hers. "What the devil are you doing here?" he asked.

"I told you—"

"That it's none of my business." He glanced around. "As a young man I traveled a great deal with my parents. Our last journey together took us to the Far East, to the cities and deserts of Arabia; my father had business there. I've seen Bedouins who live similarly, and the horses—"

"Get out," she snapped.

"Are Arabians, of course. I should have realized it when I saw the two of you riding on the beach at dawn, but I hardly expected to see the horses here. What, may I ask, are they doing here? Specifically, what are you doing with them, I mean, aside from hiding them from the rest of the world? And who is your friend there? I mean aside from being a specter babbling in tongues and frightening my manservant out of his wits? Come, come, Meri Mine. A young lady shouldn't harbor such secrets from her suitor."

"You are not my suitor, and I don't owe you any explanations."

Having retrieved his walking stick, Johnny limped up behind Miracle and scowled. "Calm down, Mira. If you won't discuss the situation rationally, then I will—"

"You won't!" she cried furiously. "I haven't worked feverishly to keep these horses a secret the last years to have this—this arrogant, high-stocking buffoon dash home and announce to the entire world that I'm caching away royal horses."

"It was bound to come out eventually," John argued. "You cannot keep them hidden away here forever. I'm surprised that you've managed it this long, considering your appetite for riding over this island like a bleedin' bat out of hell. I'm tellin' ya, Salterdon, the gel will be the death of me yet the way she rides these damn devils. That's how I damaged me leg, ya know, by climbin' onto that beast there—Napitov. Bah! Me thinkin' I could tame and train him. I've been a groom and trainer all me life, sir, but I ain't ever dealt with animals like this. They're too damn smart for their own good. Too damn human, if ya ask me—"

"They simply will not allow you to break their spirit," Miracle snapped back. "And they are far from dangerous if you will simply take the time to understand them. They are more loyal than most people I know." She glared at Clayton.

He smiled back, bringing hotter color to her cheeks, if that were possible.

Snapping the crop against her leg, Miracle stepped around Clayton and moved to the door, struggled to shove it back, then disappeared into the castle's dark corridor.

"You've done it now, Your Grace," John said. "You've just breached the sanctuary of her most prized possessions. She'll be forced to deal with you now, not just patronize you. A wise man would know how to use the situation to his best advantage."

"Blackmail," Clayton stated, still staring after Miracle.

"Precisely."

Somewhere in the distance, perhaps by his campfire or from within his tent, Ismail sat on his carpet and played his flute and burned his incense while Miracle tossed and turned in her bed. The sheer curtains draped from the tester gave the firelit room a hazy glow—almost cheery, certainly comforting. This was her world, as unusual as it might appear to outsiders, with Oriental tapestries depicting horses in flight across sandy stretches of desert, Bedouin warriors upon their backs. Across the stone floor was scattered mounds of fragrant hay. A cat lay curled before the fire, purring loudly enough that Miracle could hear, and near the window her noble, gallant horse dozed with his head lowered and eyes partially closed. This, too, was customary, even for kings, to bring their most prized horse into their private chamber where it would be protected and pampered even before his own children. The prized one was never for sale, at any cost. Wars had been waged and battles won and lost over a solitary horse.

It seemed that the whole world rested, while Miracle was, at last, forced to leave her bed and pace.

The storm moved in at just after midnight. Tumbling clouds obliterated the moon and stars. Miracle listened to the wind and rain slash against her bedroom window and watched the lightning flash over the distant black rooks of the Undercliff. Normally, she would have been there, in the lighthouse, stoking the fire and straining to make out any speck of light on the turbulent watery horizon. But thanks to his dukeship and his ability to rattle her judgment with a look, a touch, a kiss, she wasn't there. And thanks to his dukeship, her secret was out, her horses discovered, her crime revealed.

So where was the panic? Why were her knees weak from the memory of his kiss that afternoon on the bluff, and not from the fact that she should be frantic with worry over the prospect that there would be no beacon to help a ship in distress? Why did she not quake from the possibility that she might well spend the rest of her life in prison, now that her Arabian herd had been discovered?

A nudge from behind. Miracle smiled and turned. Napitov nickered and lowered his velvety muzzle into her hand then he swung toward the door, ears pricked. He pranced toward the door, hooves clashing against the floor as he exited the chamber. Miracle listened. The music stopped.

Napitov snorted his alarm.

Miracle hurried to the corridor and stopped, her heart suddenly climbing her throat. Her houseguest stood in the distance, his obvious intrusion into her private chambers thwarted by the stallion's alertness. Once again, Napitov stood between her and Salterdon, his stance challenging.

"He considers you a threat," she said loudly enough that His Grace could hear her. "Stallions are like that. They guard their property at all cost—even with their lives if they must."

"I'm well aware of a herd sire's behavior. I just find it a little odd that he would consider you his property. Normally, it's the other way around."

Miracle leaned against the wall. "You continue to astonish me, Your Grace."

"Good. Now will you call off your guard dog?"

"You're very bold to come here, to my chambers. Not a very gentlemanly way to behave."

"I couldn't sleep."

"Afraid of storms, your dukeship?"

"If I say yes, will you hold my hand?"

"No."

Miracle returned to her room and stood before the fire, hoping it would warm her. She was shivering suddenly and couldn't stop. She wanted to hurry back to the door and discover if he had retreated. Perhaps he had; she'd heard no footsteps. Napitov remained quiet. Ismail still played his flute. The melody of it lent a melancholy tone to the still chamber, causing a tightness in Miracle's throat that confused and annoyed her.

With a silent curse, she spun back toward the door and stopped. "What do you think you're doing?" she demanded. "If you don't leave these premises now, I shall call Ismail. Bedouins don't look highly on women in their care being bothered by outsiders."

"All right. Call him." Salterdon moved into the room, his hands in his pockets. The linen stock hung untied around his throat; his shirt lay partially unlaced. He looked as if he'd spent the last hours tossing in his bed. "Fascinating." He studied his surroundings. "But not surprising. I don't think anything could surprise me now—not after discovering your little harem tucked away in the belly of a deteriorating old castle. It all makes sense now, why you encourage the rumors of goblins that supposedly haunt the old place, perhaps why you often go to such lengths to foster the stories of your eccentricity. The more people fear you, the less likely they'll be to come snooping around Cavisbrooke."

He laughed softly; the sound was warm, but menacing, too, making her stomach quiver, her knees shake. With his dark face made bronze by firelight, his hair a tousled mess, he could have passed as a Bedouin himself—a wandering desert warrior capable of driving fear into kings.

"What do you want here?" she demanded.

"You, of course."

Her eyes flashed. She grabbed for her riding crop.

"Come, come, Meri Mine. You're not the violent sort." His hands still in his pockets, he moved toward her, backing her toward the fire so the heat became more and more uncomfortable on the backs of her legs. "I've decided it's time to negotiate like two reasonably rational adults. You can be rational on occasion, can't you?"

She swung with her crop, lashing him across his shoulder. He didn't so much as flinch, not even as a thin seam of blood began to soak the white cloth. A sickness sank in her belly at the sight, and dropping the crop, she tried to flee. He caught her in two strides, wrapped one arm around her waist, and hauled her from her feet.

She kicked and flailed.

He flung her onto the bed where she sank into the deep, feather mattress and scattering of tasseled pillows. He joined her, spread his body out on hers, his long, strong fingers imprisoning her wrists to the bed, his legs pinning hers against the tumbled sheets. She stubbornly stared up at him —his mouth that had so tortured her earlier, his unshaven jaw, his pirate's eyes that were fierce and sharp as a predator's. "I'll scream," she threatened and gasped for air.

"Will you?" he replied, breathing as heavily. "I've been lying in my bed for the last hour arguing with my reasoning. The logical part of me says I should continue to win you over with gallantry—hell, I practically got myself killed defending your reputation, and that got me nowhere—not really. Then it occurred to me that you're not the sort of woman to be won over with pretty phrases. You're too damned bullheaded for that. Too distrustful. You expect every bastard to be like your father, I think. You won't let yourself care for a man who may end up leaving you . . . like your father left your mother. Be still, dammit, and listen to me." He tussled with her again, pressed his body harder upon hers, until she could feel the length of him, from his stomach to his feet, wrap around her, mold into her. The leather of his boots cut into her calves that had become exposed in the fracas.

"Do you intend to rape me?" she demanded, her breath coming hard and fast against his lips that were so close to hers she could feel the warm whisper of his breathing.

"I don't rape women, Meri Mine. I don't have to."

"Arrogant bastard—"

"I'm going to tell you a story, Lady Cavendish. A legend, actually, about a ship that left Russia some five years ago for England. That ship was loaded with a priceless treasure for King George—horses. Arabian horses. Some of the finest mares and yearling colts ever bred in Russia. But the ship was lost—no survivors. A wealth of horseflesh sank to the bottom of the ocean. What a loss! Oh, there have been rumors, from time to time, of travelers coming across horses running wild on some deserted island—mostly greedy sea captains who would like to get their hands on the reward money being offered for the animals' return—but after five years, all parties have long since given up hope . . ."

Miracle turned her face away, buried her profile into the soft blanket beneath her. Weakness stole through her. She couldn't concentrate. All feeling seemed to be centered on the hard thumping of his heart against hers, his body—her body—warming against the other's, skin pressing became damp where they touched. He had just informed her that he knew about her horses—where they came from—that they had belonged to a potentate—that they had been a gift for the king. Yet the anger and fear that should have consumed her was being eclipsed by her body's response to his.

Oh, God, it hurt—there, where his knee pressed between her legs. "Please," she murmured.

"Please what, Meri Mine? Please don't leave at dawn and return to London and inform good cousin George that you're harboring his trove of priceless horseflesh? Please what, Meri Mine?"

"What do you want from me?" she cried.

"We both know what I want—"

"Then take it, damn you. I can't bear this another minute."

He stared down at her with his wolf eyes, his fingers digging into the soft flesh of her arms, his knee turning her insides to hot liquid, then, with no warning, he rolled, dragged her atop him, and buried his fingers in her hair that spread across his neck and bleeding shoulder. He gripped her painfully, forcing her head back, exposing her throat to his lips. "You disappoint me, m'lady. Where is your fight and fire? Will you capitulate so easily? Do you love those damn animals so much? Would you sacrifice your innocence to keep them?"

Her eyes closed, she groaned, shook her head, unable to reason beyond the feel of his body against hers. "Kiss me," she heard someone plead, then to her shame realized it was herself. "Kiss me again, like you did on the cliff. Here, on my mouth—I want to taste you again, with my tongue this time. Kiss me, Your Grace, or I shall—"

She lowered her mouth to his, felt his lips stiffen, then part, become hot and supple and wet, allowing her entry, meeting her tongue with his own and drawing it deep inside him while his hands left her hair and twisted into her clothes, grasping, tearing, running up and down her back, then cupping her buttocks through the thin material of her sleeping gown and pulling her fiercely against his moving hips while he made sounds of pleasure and pain deep in his throat.

Ah, yes, this was flying, this freedom, this abandonment to the senses. She wanted to experience his hands on her breasts, thrill to the feel of his rough fingers squeezing then releasing the sensitive flesh and their tingling nipples. She arched her back and offered them to his mouth, and he breathed hot, quick, panting breaths through her gown and closed his teeth gently on the nubs that were little hard points that felt on fire when he licked them.

She felt . . . consumed. Abandoned.

Opening her legs, she straddled him. The sudden infinite pleasure of her private body brushing upon the coarse, taut material covering his made her gasp and quiver and ache. It was a moment before she realized he had become perfectly still—not so much as breathing. She opened her eyes.

His gray eyes were fire-bright, his face flushed and sweating, his lips pulled back slightly as if he were in pain. His fingers gripped her arms fiercely. He said, "For God's sake, don't move. Don't even breathe." He swallowed—or tried to. His body felt rigid beneath her—dense and hard as stone.

"But I don't want to stop," she replied honestly, then added in a husky whisper, "I like what I feel. Nay, Your Grace, I don't care to stop."

"Yes you do. Oh, yes you do. Ah, God, what the hell am I doing here? No! Don't move or I'm going to forget that I'm supposed to be a gentleman and . . . Mori Mine, there is a certain etiquette to proper love-making—steps a man goes through to seduce a woman—proper responses a woman enacts so the whole affair doesn't become so . . . torrid."

"Torrid is bad?"

"Torrid is . . . stevedores and tavern wenches."

"Proper ladies don't experience these feelings?"

His body relaxed somewhat, and his fingers gripped her less fiercely. Salterdon grinned. "A proper lady wouldn't acknowledge torrid, even if she wanted to."

"Then I'm glad I'm not a proper lady, Your Grace, because these feelings you've aroused are quite extraordinary, if not disarming. I've thought of nothing but your kiss since this afternoon—"

"And you're too bloody honest for your own good."

He rolled her away and sat up, shoulders sagging, his loose stock draping down his back, his dark hair a mussed cloud of waves and curls. His shirttail had pulled free from his breeches, exposing a small triangle of his back. Miracle noted the skin looked as dark as his face and hands, and she smiled.

Salterdon cleared his throat and stood up, smoothed back his hair, straightened his stock, all without looking at her. At last, he said, "Cover your legs, please."

Raising one eyebrow, Miracle tugged her gown hem down over her ankles. "Your Grace, I fear you're priggish."

"Hardly," he replied, and moved toward the fire, continuing to comb his hair with his fingers. "I'm simply attempting to remind you who we are—"

"And who are we, sir? I shall tell you now, that you are not the same man who graced Cavisbrooke before."

He suddenly turned and looked at her with so fixed a stare she forgot to speak for a moment. Sliding from the bed, gripping a tapestried pillow to her stomach, hoping it would somehow give her the strength to confess what had been plaguing her mind the last hours, Miracle walked toward him, watched as the intensity of his stare grew. Indeed, his entire countenance took on a most unusual unease and cautiousness.

"Meaning?" he demanded in a dry voice.

"That you've changed. I cared not a whit for you before. I despised your callousness, your crassness, your arrogance. But while you've been here these last days, I've seen none of that, and I've asked myself why. How can a man simply change his personality—indeed, his heart and manner of living? And I've come to only one conclusion."

"And that is?"

"Mayhap you acted the way you did because of your friends. Perhaps while in their company you're forced to act out your pretentiousness—"

He laughed mirthlessly, closed his eyes, and shook his head. "My God, you are naive, aren't you?" he said softly. "Don't you realize I'm standing here now because I had every intention of blackmailing you? Agree to marry me, or I'll tell the entire goddamned world about your beloved horses . . ."

Withdrawing a crumpled paper from his pocket, he stared down at it a confused moment, then, with an inward curse, wadded it up and flung it as hard as he could into the fire.

"Do you love me?" she asked gently, and placed a hand on his arm. He moved away, leaving her standing before the fire, alone, gripping her pillow that reflected the fire in red and gold prisms. "If not, then why would you choose to marry me?"

"Because you're . . . extraordinary. And rare. And the most beautiful woman I've ever known," he responded, his back still to her as he stood at the window and watched rain spill down the panes in runnels. "Your innocence enthralls me. Your naïveté astounds me. I . . . like your freckles. I . . . like your bare feet covered with sand. I admire your dedication and your loyalty. I think you're a little bit insane . . . and that excites me. Your unpredictability fires my enthusiasm. I awake in the middle of the night and count the hours until I can see you again because each time we come together, I feel born again, like the world is fresh and clean and you're going to introduce me to yet another new experience. I . . . want to save you from this lunacy."

Opening his arms to indicate his surroundings, he turned to face her again. Arms still extended, his hands in fists, he added through his teeth, "And then I realize that the lunacy isn't here, but out there, where I come from, and I think that you could somehow rectify it. Make my world a little less . . . empty."

"You do love me," she told him, and smiled.

He shook his head. "No. I . . . need you."

"Is that not a part of love? Perhaps the most important part?"

"I know what the hell love is. I've been in love at least a dozen times!"

"Obviously they didn't fulfill your needs or they would be at your side now. Wouldn't they?"

He lowered his arms. "I should never have come here," he said aloud to himself. Then he stepped around her, and without so much as a backward glance, he quit the room.

Clayton slammed the bedroom door as hard as he could, which wasn't easy. The five-hundred-year-old medieval portal had obviously been hewn from one solid slab of oak and weighed as much as an entire goddamned tree. He kicked it once, then again for good measure. Hitting it with his fist was out of the question, though he wanted to, oh how he wanted to. He wanted to hurt something, preferably not himself.

Didn't Miracle Cavendish know a young lady such as herself should never allow a man into her private chamber? Didn't she realize that a young lady in her nightdress never received a male caller? Didn't she realize that when she stood before the fire dressed in her nightdress that the light from the fire would silhouette her body in a way that could make a bloody monk get hard? Hard enough to hurt . . . hard enough to obliterate a grown man's (who should know better) willpower . . .

Hadn't she been taught that a young woman should never allow her base desires to run rampant? For God's sake, she wasn't supposed to outwardly acknowledge her feelings. She wasn't supposed to seduce him! What happened to playing coy and hard to get? What happened to modesty? To the coquettish fluttering of lashes and the becoming blushes of discomposure—even if it was all a lot of balderdash.

Damn. How would he explain to his brother that he had tumbled in the sheets with Trey's intended? How would he ever look at the future duchess of Salterdon without the image of her straddling his hips and offering up her nipples to his greedy mouth? How would he ever sleep again without the mental vision of her making her kind of passionate, unfettered, unashamed love to another man—his own brother—haunting him?

What the blazes made her think he'd fallen in love with her?

"Damn!" He kicked the door again . . . and again . . . and again.

First love is only a little foolishness and a lot of curiosity: no really self-respecting woman would take advantage of it.
GEORGE BERNARD SHAW

Chapter Eleven

"His name is Ismail," Miracle explained, "and he is from the Anazeh tribe of the Nejd. As a young man, he guarded, cared for, and trained his chieftain's horses for battle. Many years ago, his tribe was raided by another, and his chief's best mares were taken. It's custom that the animals' guardian must be given over as well in order that the horses remain happy, healthy, and one with Allah. Ismail was forced to leave his tribe and family and wander as a slave with his captors. Many times he was forced to accompany the horses into new sands, taken by new tribes until finally he and the horses became the possession of the empress of Russia. In a rare but noble show of friendship, she decided to present our king with the royal gift of some of her finest horses, but, as you say, the ship disappeared before it ever reached England—or so everyone thought. It broke up on those rocks—there—at the very end of the Race, during a particularly fearsome storm. The vessel sank like a stone. All but one man was killed, drowned by the awful currents or crushed against the rocks." She remained silent for a while as she watched auks skim over the sea, dip and dive, then soar toward the gray sky. "John and I buried them in the chapel. It seemed only fitting, don't you agree?"

She got no response, but continued nevertheless. "I discovered Ismail clinging to the ship's mast that can still be seen jutting out of the sea upon occasion, when the tides are very low. The horses were scattered up and down the strand, wet and freezing, but due to their extreme loyalty to their handler, they would not leave. I daresay they would have remained there and starved, had I not rowed my boat out to Ismail and saved him. Because I saved him and the horses and therefore set him free of his enforced imprisonment, he feels that I was sent to him by Allah, who obviously wishes me to own the animals—and him, of course. I've no desire to own Ismail; I can't seem to make him understand, however. So you see, I didn't steal the horses. Actually—"

"Allah plunked them into your lap, as a gift," Salterdon said. "And who are we to argue with Allah?"

Miracle laughed, causing several auks flying in a group to scatter and flap away. Swinging her legs, her brown skirt billowed nearly to her knees as the wind swept up the Undercliff to where she and her tense and quiet companion perched on a tussock-littered precipice far over the ocean. A half-eaten apple lay in her lap, along with a crust of bread she had brought for the birds.

Leaning against Salterdon's shoulder, she regarded his immobile profile before saying, "You may kiss me if you like."

"Here?" He raised one eyebrow and glanced down.

"Here." She pointed to her lips. "I've thought of nothing else all morning. Are kisses generally so wet and warm? Is the tongue always involved? I think that's the part I like most. And here I thought tongues were good only for benefiting mastication and speaking."

"For God's sake," he muttered and turned his face into the chilly wind. The damp air made his hair curl and wave in a boyish manner around his temples and over his forehead. He had turned the collar of his cutaway up around his nape.

She blew in his ear. He grunted in annoyance and scrambled to his feet, sending stone and dirt drifting off the ledge to the white-capped waves far below.

"I suppose a lady wouldn't do that, either," she called after him, doing her best to muffle her laughter.

"No, she wouldn't," he declared and continued walking.

With a sigh, Miracle followed, running to catch up. Looping her arm through his, she offered up her apple. " 'Tis very sweet, Your Grace, and delicious."

"Thank you, Eve, but no thank you. Just because Adam fell for that trick, don't think that I will, too."

"Only a bite, then I'll leave you alone to brood, if that's your desire."

"I don't brood. You're beginning to sound like Benjamin."

"You do brood. You're brooding now, though I can't imagine why. A bite, Your Grace? 'Tis said that the apple is magic. Its nectar will bring you health, happiness, and riches beyond your wildest dreams."

"Oh very well, if that will make you happy." He stopped walking and reached for the apple.

She snatched it away and danced backward, her cloud of hair rising in the gusty wind. Then, very slowly, she lifted the apple to her own mouth and took a bite, held the crisp red and white fraction between her teeth, and tossed the core away.

"For heaven's sake," Salterdon muttered as Miracle advanced, her eyes twinkling. "Stop this, Miracle. What's got into you? You're acting like some kind of . . . of . . . Quit looking at me that way. You have juice dripping from your chin. Now it's running down your neck—" He grabbed a linen square from his pocket, then did nothing but stand, hands at his sides, the white, embroidered kerchief flapping in the wind, his hair spilling over his eyes, his jaw tensing, flexing, his sensual mouth flattening into a line of emotional strain the nearer she came.

Standing so closely her body brushed his, Miracle eased up on her toes and offered him the apple, still held with her teeth. His body felt rigid as stone. He didn't so much as breathe.

Finally, he said in a deep, dry, and husky voice, "You smell like apple. And rosewater. Your hair is like a soft fire that I want to bury my face in. Dammit, Meri Mine, don't tease me this way or—"

"Or what, Your Grace?"

"I'm trying my best to be a gentleman."

"I like you better when you're not. The apple, sir."

"Meri—"

"Why do you call me that? Meri Mine?"

He watched her eyes a long minute as little by little his shoulders relaxed. His countenance softened. Taking her face in his hands and holding her gently, he said, "Because you make me merry. You make me happy. You make me laugh." Bending his head, he took the sliver of fruit into his mouth, allowed his lips to linger an eternal moment before kissing her. As before, the blood surged, the heart quickened. The familiar lethargy that stole through her the day before made her grow weak at the knees, dizzy in her mind. No, she hadn't imagined it—no fantasy of her deepest dreams. She knew it now for what it was.

He kissed her harder, his body rigid, his fingers digging into her arm as he pulled her roughly up against him. She could feel his passion building, as it had the night before, and the idea that she could trigger his desire so easily made her bold. She leaned into him, kissed him as fiercely, and allowed a low, pleasurable moan to escape her throat. She clung to him when he pushed her away and stared down at her eyes that were as turbulent as the building clouds on the horizon.

"You're playing with me," he growled. "Not wise, Meri Mine. Teasing can become dangerous if you don't know what you're doing."

"Teach me," she replied, her lids slumberous, her body lethargic with a weakness she was only beginning to understand.

"I'd like to. God, how I'd like to," he said under his breath. "But I didn't come here to seduce you. I came here to take you back with me, Miracle. To see that you become the future duchess of Salterdon. There will be plenty of time for all this once you're married. Listen to me!" He shook her. "Agree to marry . . . me . . . and I'll spend the rest of my life making love to you."

Feeling slightly unbalanced by his terseness, Miracle smiled unsteadily into his intense, unreadable eyes and placed her hand upon his cheek.

"My, but you *are* an honorable man, sir. And here I thought men of such nobility cared little for a woman's virtue." Wiggling free, dancing backward, her cheeks warm with desire and her heart throbbing with the new and unexpected emotions he stirred inside her, she took a moment to catch her breath. "You constantly surprise me, Your Grace; you who crowed about your countless conquests on your previous stay—"

"Forget my previous stay, dammit. I'm not the same man . . ." He turned away and took a moment to collect himself. "Will you marry the duke or not?" he finally demanded in so angry and frustrated a tone that Miracle sobered.

"Perhaps, if I thought the duke truly loved me," she replied as hotly. "Perhaps, if I understood why he would choose me of all the women who must desire him, love him—no doubt some of the most beautiful women in England, whose wealth must exceed mine to extremes. Why me, Salterdon? Tell me, damn you. Make me believe, and mayhap I would consider the marriage . . . now that I've come to care for you."

For a long while, he stood with his back to her, his dark hair ruffled by the rising and falling wind, his silhouette tall against the backdrop of sky and sea. At last, growing weary of his silence and frustrated by his odd manner, Miracle turned on her heel and stormed away.

It had been a long while since Miracle had last visited Alum Bay. The ride up the rugged coast was a long one, but Napitov's smooth and trusty gait always made the jaunt pleasant.

She reached the bay's shore by way of a deep and ragged ravine. Before her, the sea rolled into the cliffs with great impetuosity, sending a spray of misty fog climbing far up the looming faces of chalk of so pure a white they were almost blinding in the late afternoon sunlight.

For a long while, Miracle sat astride Napitov and watched the local village folk lower themselves down the cliff face by ropes, baskets strapped to their waists, as they cautiously collected the eggs and feathers from the nests of various sea birds, which flocked in amazing numbers on the ledges and crevices of the cliffs. Then she and her patient, obliging stallion continued their journey down the narrowing, rocky path, through a break in the cliff wall that was all but obscured by the abundant growth of samphire and ferns cascading over the opening like a verdant waterfall.

"Easy," she consoled her suddenly nervous horse. Napitov pranced in place, snorted, and shook his head, for a moment refusing to proceed into the dim, misty lair. Once Miracle had felt the same, the one and only time her mother had brought her here to meet Ceridwen. As a child, she had thought the place frighteningly magical. The tints of the spiraling cliffs were so bright and varied that they had not the appearance of anything natural. Deep purplish red, dusky blue, bright ocherous yellow, gray, and black succeeded one another as sharply defined as the stripes in silk. Occasionally, the braver children who lived near Alum Bay would venture into the chasm to collect the various colored sands, which they arranged fancifully in phials or made into little ornamental articles and sold to visitors. But the children didn't come often; their parents wouldn't allow it . . . not as long as Ceridwen lived yonder in the ancient stone hut.

To reach the hut, one was forced to wade a broad expanse of shallow, transparent water. His head down, Napitov grudgingly carried Miracle through the pool while strange and exotic fish of every color darted around his hooves. Finally reaching the blue shoal, she slid from the stallion's back and soothed him with words, rewarded him with a carrot she took from her pocket, then approached Ceridwen's den, parting the lush vegetation that curtained the entrance.

As always, the door stood open. Miracle waited on the threshold, allowing her vision to become accustomed to the dark interior while the odd scents of spices and perfumes wafted around her.

"Come in, m'lady Cavendish," came the scratchy voice from inside. "I've been expecting you."

Miracle smiled, as always, amazed. There had been times when, as a younger girl, Miracle had approached the hut as quietly and secretly as a cat, thinking to trick her old friend. It had never worked. Having been born blind one hundred five years ago, Ceridwen's hearing was still as sharp as a nail—or perhaps her acute senses had nothing at all to do with her hearing, but, as the suspicious villagers vowed, to her magical abilities.

Stooped at the shoulders, her hair a gray silken mat that spilled to the floor at the foot of her rocking chair, Ceridwen stared with white, pupilless eyes out a window. Miracle sat on a milk stool at her side. They remained silent a long while, the only sound the occasional creaking of the chair as it rocked back and forth.

"It's been three months and seven days since you last came to see me," Ceridwen finally said. "Then you were despondent over a man—an intruder, you called him. You wished to know how you could expel him from your home. You didn't care for him much, as I recall. I told you then that he had two faces, that he would eventually reveal the good side of himself—"

"The duke wishes to marry me," Miracle announced.

Ceridwen nodded and continued rocking.

Leaving the stool, Miracle paced, occasionally stopping to study the curious collection of drying herbs and flowers, the conglomeration of stones, and the trove of feathers, animal bones, and pulverized bird shells, all of which were stored in tiny reed baskets Ceridwen had woven herself.

"Damned aggravating, vacillating man. One moment he's attempting to seduce me, the next he's as stony as the bloody Undercliff," she said. "He denies that he loves me. He says that he simply needs me, yet he wishes to marry me. He kisses me passionately one day, the next scolds me for kissing him. He is as inconstant as the weather."

Returning to Ceridwen's side, taking the old woman's fragile hand, Miracle went to her knees and searched her companion's face. "Is this what love is? Does it crash upon you, then withdraw like the tides? For if it is, I don't think I like it much and cannot understand why all of humankind would pine so to experience the emotion. If this is truly love, Ceridwen, then love is an enemy to us all."

Again, Ceridwen said nothing, just stared out the window with her white eyes and rocked in her chair.

" 'Tis times like this that I miss my mother most. Perhaps she could explain how she could love a man who obviously didn't love us."

"Would you settle for the life your mother lived?" Ceridwen asked.

"No."

"Then I trust you'll make the proper choice. You'll marry the one who truly loves you, m'lady."

"Does he love me?" Miracle asked, stunned by the urgency in her own voice.

" 'Tis not my way to say, child. You must discover your destiny on your own—"

"But I must know, Ceridwen. I would rather live the remainder of my life alone than waste it loving a man who cares nothing for me . . . like my mother did." When Ceridwen still refused to respond, Miracle stood. She wasn't surprised that her friend had refused to answer. The times her mother had come here to plead a recourse for her predicament, Ceridwen merely forced Lorraina to face her own demons and find a solution. Ceridwen had treated Miracle no differently, even when she had pleaded for Ceridwen to help her find her mother.

At last, Miracle moved to the door, but stopped as the old woman said, "Be cautious, m'lady, and trust your instincts. They have rarely let you down before."

" 'Tis my instincts that fail me, madam. There is a part of me that still dwells on the man he was, while the other grows more and more fond of the man he has become."

"Trust your instincts," she repeated, then commenced rocking again.

Miracle ran down the corridor to Salterdon's room, her slippered feet barely making a sound on the cold cobblestone floor. She skipped occasionally, not unlike an excited child, swallowed back the giggle tickling her throat, and cast a disapproving glance at the miserable candles sputtering at the shadows. Tomorrow she would spend the day dipping candles, but tonight she would celebrate.

Benjamin started as she flew into the chamber. Gripping a stack of clothing against his chest, he stared at her with houndlike eyes and pursed lips.

"Where is His Grace?" she asked, and danced toward the passageway into Benjamin's quarters.

"Imbibing a spot with Mr. Hoyt, I believe," he replied, then snapped closed his mouth in consternation.

Miracle laughed. "Relax, Benjamin. I'm well aware that John has an occasional tipple. I also know exactly where he hides his stashes." Regarding the neatly folded laundry in his arms, Miracle advanced, ran her fingers over the pristine white shirts. "Where did you get these?" she asked, counting a dozen or so shirts before the valet proceeded to stack them tidily into the wardrobe.

"Purchased them in Niton, miss, though I cannot imagine why. He must have a hundred blouses at home, all just as new as these. Basingsto—er—ah—His Grace doesn't usually have much use for a lot of finery, not with his penchant for labor."

"Indeed," Miracle said thoughtfully as Benjamin closed the wardrobe door with a bang. An impish smile crossed her lips. "You may tell His Grace that such a costly sacrifice for my benefit wasn't necessary. Never mind, I shall tell him myself, I think."

Twirling on her toes, she hurried from the room and down one corridor after another, finally arriving at John's apartments. Jonathan sat in a chair before the fire, his bad leg propped upon a pillowed stool. Salterdon poised by the hearth, a cordial in one hand, the other tucked into his coat pocket. She recognized the shirt he was wearing was one of her own, and the thought occurred to her that another time she would have been angry; she would have informed him that she didn't need or want his charity—if indeed that had been his idea in purchasing the garments.

But she could think of nothing but the image he made, so dapper and elegantly dressed, but with the distinct air of a wild animal confident of his prowess. Those gray eyes, dark and warm as the ignited coals near his feet, left her momentarily speechless, forgetting why she had searched him and John out in the first place.

"My, don't the two of you make a distinguished pair," she finally greeted him, skipping to John's side and planting a kiss on his cheek. Then she offered His Grace a quick curtsy, causing him to flash his heart stopping, mocking grin and raise one eyebrow. He and Hoyt exchanged amused glances.

"M'lady is in fine fettle this evening," John declared.

"I have wonderful news," she announced. "I couldn't wait to share it with the both of you." She produced the letter from her skirt pocket and waved it in the air. "A letter from my mother!"

"Ah," John replied, then removed the spectacles from his nose and carefully folded in the stems.

"It seems she's spent the last eight months in Rome. She describes the villages and cathedrals in glorious detail—and the people—she lived for a month with a countess in her chateau overlooking the Tiber River. Imagine spending your days basking in the sun on a veranda overlooking the river, then dancing until dawn in the arms of some handsome count."

She pirouetted, causing her skirt to twirl around her ankles, then laughed breathlessly. "She sounds deliriously happy, though occasionally her thoughts seem a bit confused. And her handwriting grows somewhat unsteady. But none of that matters, does it? What's important is that she wrote. After nearly a year, she finally wrote!"

Falling to her knees beside John, who continued to stare into the fire, she gently laid the letter in his lap and waited for him to shift his gaze to hers. "The letter was postmarked only three weeks ago in Versailles. We could go there, John—"

"No."

She clutched his arm and did her best to continue to smile. "I have money, if that concerns you. I've saved up enough—"

"Leave it alone, Mira. I'll not allow ya to go traipsin' off to God knows where, lookin' for a ghost. Nothin' you could ever say or do could or would bring Lorraina back to this miserable pile of rocks."

Struggling from the chair, grabbing up his cane, John said, "Let it alone, lass. Be happy with what you have there—"

"They are naught but words on a paper," she argued. "How could I ever be satisfied with only that?"

"She loves you enough to care to write—"

"But she doesn't love me enough to come home or to bother with letting me know where I might find her." Standing, allowing the letter to drift like a leaf to the floor, Miracle moved to the window and did her best to focus her thoughts on something other than the tight band of emotion closing off her throat. Dusk had fallen, tinting the countryside a bleak, colorless gray. Lightning flashed in the distant clouds, and rising winds whipped up the sea waves into frothy caps.

"Well." She tried not to blink, tried not to acknowledge the hurt and anger choking off her breath. "It seems we're in for another storm tonight. I'll have Ismail bring Hasan around. I should get to the lighthouse as soon as possible."

"Miracle," John called as she moved toward the door. "I beg you, lass; don't go. You'll find no solace there from yer distress. Leave that wretched place to the damn wind and waves, Mira!"

Still standing at the hearth, his drink in hand, Clayton watched Miracle quit the room, her shoulders back and chin thrust stubbornly, if not proudly, despite Hoyt's attempts to stop her. As Jonathan followed her into the hallway, Clayton bent and retrieved the letter and was still regarding it carefully when Hoyt reentered the room, brow sweating, his jaw flexed by the discomfort in his leg. He hobbled unsteadily to his chair and flung himself into it, gritted his teeth, and rubbed his leg before cursing explosively. Only then did he lift his eyes to Clay's, then to the paper in his hand. Dark color crept into the old man's cheeks, and he sank back into his chair.

Clayton folded the letter and tossed it into the fire. He watched it dance momentarily with the swirling, rising heat before it burst into tiny flames. Only when it lay in scattered ashes amid the coals did Clayton turn to John again. "When the hell do you intend to tell her that you wrote it?" he demanded in a soft, stern voice.

"I don't know what you mean," John snapped.

"I think you do. When the hell do you intend to tell her?" he said again, this time in a voice as steely as a lance.

Defeatedly, John let out his breath and closed his eyes. "Soon," he finally said. "When I know the time is right."

There are two tragedies in life. One is to lose your heart's desire. The other is to gain it.

GEORGE BERNARD SHAW

Chapter Twelve

He found her standing upon the rickety old lighthouse perch, pale hands clasped to the deteriorating balustrade, her white face turned into the wind that battered the surroundings with a ferocity that was startling. Yet Miracle's stance was challenging, as if the upheaval of anger boiling inside her could match the savagery of the impending storm.

Clayton called to her twice before she turned her head and saw him, standing near the foot of the chapel, his exposed flesh stinging from the bite of the driven sand. While her long hair danced around her head and shoulders, she stared down at him with an emotionless smile, empty eyes; a stone statue void of the passion and happiness she had exuded earlier.

The platform on which she stood undulated in the wind like a boat on waves. It creaked and groaned and sprayed mortar to the ground; a sliver of wood spiraled downward, bounced off the upthrusting stone cross atop the chapel, then fell near Clayton's feet, and for the first time he experienced the same fear as John Hoyt. Little by little the old lighthouse was crumbling to pieces.

"Miracle!" he called. "Come down from there!"

"Go away," she replied. "I don't want you here!" Then she disappeared into the house.

The tide rolled in. It slunk around his ankles and hissed like a snake across the sand beneath his boots. Clayton shivered, stumbled back, unable to breathe until the water had slithered back out to sea, only to roll like some frothing green monster into a configuration that came rushing toward him with the speed of a horse out of control. He stood frozen, incapable of movement, anticipating the beast swallowing him, yet it didn't. Just feet away it deliquesced into rushing fingers that wrapped even higher around his legs—cold, clammy, insisting and taunting.

Clayton moved through the chapel door, refusing to look back as the sea scurried in after him and lapped at the feet of the painted Virgin. The first step leading up to the lighthouse was already underwater. Halfway up the spiraling stairwell, he paused and looked back; nothing so far, but there would be. It would climb up the narrow tunnel like water rushing into the bowels of a sinking ship.

At last, reaching the summit, Clayton leaned against the wall and tried to breathe; he mopped his sweating forehead with his coat sleeve and wondered if he were suffocating.

"I don't want you here," came Miracle's voice.

Clayton tried to focus his eyes. It wasn't easy. The room looked alive with light and shadows. The fire in the pit was only beginning to glow. It cast yellow spears through the windows toward the turbid sea, doing little to dispel the darkness.

At last, he found Miracle.

She perched upon the wide windowsill, her legs drawn up, arms hooked over her knees, head resting back against the wall. The fire's glow made a yellow slash across her face. Her eyes looked anguished.

At once he was struck with how truly beautiful she was, and how sad.

"He writes the letters himself, doesn't he?" came her small voice. "I've known for some time, or at least suspected. I wanted to believe, don't you see? I needed to believe. Just like when my mother used to read me letters from my father. Oh, how the words proclaimed his love for me. How he missed me. How he would someday take us away from this miserable, horrible place. Then, during one of his last visits, I heard them arguing. She said she was weary of the lying. What sort of man was he that he would simply abandon a child—as if she never existed? I didn't stay to hear his answer, of course. I loved him . . .

"Then my mother left." She wiped her nose with the back of her hand. " 'Twas on a night like this. A fierce storm had rolled across the channel and I was frightened. Mummy tucked me into bed and kissed me. She said she loved me. That she would never leave me."

Clayton braced himself as the wind howled and the building shook. He glanced back, down the stairwell, watched the glow from the sconces on the wall gyrate upon the stones the way light reflected off waves. He smelled the sea, dank and musty, like stagnant water in the bottom of a well, and as calmly as possible, he tugged loose the stock around his neck so he could better swallow.

"Meri Mine," he said in a dry whisper. "Come with me. This place isn't safe. This light isn't going to help anyone—it's too damn dim. So I want you to take my hand, and we're going to leave before it's too late."

She looked away, out into the dark, where lightning danced upon the distant, disturbed horizon. "I was frightened of storms, and always mummy was there to reassure me . . . but she didn't come that night. No matter how loudly I cried for her. Odd how those memories seem so obscure. I want desperately to remember that night. Can you understand that, Your Grace?"

He nodded and moved farther into the room. Had the floor really shifted? Had the walls swayed? He was *not* on a ship again. He *wasn't* sinking. Water wasn't going to pour into this cabin and suck him under. Rationalize, for God's sake. He was a grown man, not ten years old again.

"I come here," Miracle said, still staring out to sea, "because this is where *she* used to come. Always watching out there, dreaming of other places, hoping against hope that my father would return as he'd promised and take us away from here. She would stand there, on the platform, with her face in the wind and pretend that, if she willed it strongly enough, the wind would lift her up and carry her away. Occasionally she allowed me to join her, and we would both dream of—"

"Flying," he said softly.

Finally, she turned her big eyes back to his. "Would you fly with me now, Your Grace?"

"Where?"

"To wherever my mother is." Sliding from the sill, she moved as if floating across the floor, and raised up her hand to him. "Take my hand, sir."

Clayton stared at it before meeting her gaze again. Her eyes were luminous and distant, like one living a dream. "Do you intend to kill us both?" he demanded. "Pitch us off the walk or some such nonsense?"

"Trust me." She smiled and he suddenly felt unbearably touched, beset by a maze of conflicting emotions. He thought her insane. He thought her capable of killing them both, and with disturbing mental imagery, he saw them both plunging headfirst into the hungry sea.

Yet, like some helpless automaton, he took her hand, so fragile and cool, into his own, which seemed to him to be clumsily big, trembling, and sweating.

As she moved toward the door, he hesitated. She gave him a swift sideways and upward glance from her blue-green eyes that somehow made his reluctance crumble. He followed her through the threshold, onto the wobbly platform, into the wind, amid the rain and dancing spears of light and rumbling thunder.

Helpless. Helpless. Helpless. That's all he could feel.

Since the moment he had seen her standing in that verdant garden with her basket of flowers and vegetables, her ankles peeking at him from beneath her fawn skirt, that scattering of pale freckles across her nose, he had become helpless, unable to resist her. A man with so little willpower against her unusual magic that he had committed the grievous sin of falling in love with the woman who was to become his brother's wife.

She pressed close, her shoulder to his, her arm looped around his, her fingers entwined with his, and offered her face to the wind god. The yellow light through the panes illuminated her in a halo, set fire to her hair that, even as it became wet from the rain, whipped out behind her as if it had life of its own.

He saw no fear in her face, only peace—escape. Was she flying? Had she left him here, afraid, clutching the balustrade so fiercely he could, albeit remotely, feel the splinters of rotten wood digging into his flesh?

Relax. Breathe. Trust her.

The erratic light glowing from the pit reached as far as the immediate sea below him, and the water and waves were climbing up the sides of the lighthouse; only the very tip of the stone crucifix atop the chapel could be seen, and even as he stared down through the dim light and rain, he could see the waves swallow the cross into its turbulent depths.

Too late for escape. No way out.

The wind howled more loudly. The rain drove more determinedly.

"Your Grace," came Miracle's voice through the roar. "Your Grace, please . . ."

He forced his gaze away from the water, back to her face.

"My hand," her lips said. "You're hurting my hand."

He gripped it fiercely, so fiercely he wondered if he might have shattered it. Still, he could not seem to release it. He might fall. He might slide under.

"Clayton, darling, give me your hand!"

"Come with me. *Quickly!* This way, my lord. Careful. There. Stand there. I'll secure the door. There, there, Your Grace. Safe now. You're safe now. I've shut out the storm—"

"No you haven't," he snapped in a tight voice. His body pressed against the wall within the dry sanctuary of the lighthouse. He forced open his eyes, feeling the rage of the storm pound against the structure at his back.

"You're frightened of the storm?"

"The water. The goddamn water."

Her cool hands cradled his face. Her fingers brushed aside the wet hair clinging to his brow. "Shh," she consoled him. "The water can't reach you here." She stroked his face, his brows, his lips. Going up on her toes, she pressed her cheek to his, and his arms came up to clutch her almost painfully to him. He buried his face in her hair, allowed the smell of rain, of rosewater, of sweet, warm, feminine flesh to sluice through him, and suddenly the storm seemed neither fierce nor loud, but faded into a drone that was eclipsed by the softness of the gentle, willing body in his arms.

"I was ten," he heard himself saying. "My brother and I had traveled to the Far East with my parents. We were on our way home when there was an explosion on the ship—a fire. It opened up the belly of the ship and it sank like a stone. There were so many passengers . . . so few skiffs. So many hurt, burned by the fire. There were bodies strewn over the water like so much flotsam. Those of us who survived the fire clung to anything that floated . . . for days. Few rations. No water to drink. People were dying . . .

"Then the sharks came.

"They took my father first. Then eventually my mother . . . when she grew too weak to fight, too despondent over my father . . . Sometime during the night while my brother and I were sleeping, she slid into the black water and disappeared. They were everywhere, the sharks, bumping the bottoms of the skiffs or whatever driftwood the survivors clung to. At some point I lost consciousness. I awoke with water in my face and my brother crying my name. All around me there were gray bodies, dorsal fins that seemed to hang suspended with each swell of the water. My brother . . . jumped in and swam for me—swam right through the bloody sharks —I remember him kicking the cursed monsters, all the while yelling at the top of his voice for me not to give up. He saved my life, Meri Mine."

Miracle looked into his eyes. "I won't let you drown, sir." Going to her toes, she pressed a timid kiss to his lips, lingered, her warm breath soft upon his mouth. He closed his eyes.

"Meri," he heard himself murmur. "Meri. Meri. I . . . can't. I shouldn't. I . . . have a confession."

She kissed him again. Her hands came up and tugged away his stock while her warm tongue teased his lips, his teeth, until he allowed her sweet invasion. The breath left him. The chill of his wet clothes and the trembling of fear vaporized into a warmth that began in his chest and flowed outward. Burying his hands in her hair, he forced back her head. Her eyes were slumberous, her lips red and slightly parted. "I have a confession . . ." he repeated.

"Tell me, my lord. Quickly, so I might kiss you again."

"I . . . I love you."

A smile. A tear. Wrapping her arms around his neck, she brought down his head and kissed him fiercely, then hugged him with a strength that seemed too great for her slender body. It left him breathless and aching.

"You tremble, sir. Are you still so frightened? I promised you that I would keep you safe, and I will." She slid his coat off his shoulders; it spilled to his feet. She tugged his shirttail from his breeches, and when it hung loose to his hips, she ran her warm hands beneath it, slid them up over his belly, making him catch his breath. He flinched, listened to the voice of warning screaming in his head, and then he ignored it.

She removed his shirt and stood before him as if mesmerized. "Nay, you're not like those farmers at all, Your Grace. You are . . . bronze and beautiful. I'm not certain I have ever seen anything so perfect. Is it wrong of me to say so?"

"Perhaps. I . . . don't know. I don't know anything, anymore, Meri Mine. If I did, I wouldn't be here now, I think."

Standing still as a statue, he watched as she removed her dress. She stood before him naked, except for the stockings, which reached only to her pale thighs. He could not take his eyes away from the downy nest at the juncture of her legs—a silken shadow of copper red, like the blaze of hair on her head.

She walked to him, paused, her upthrusting white breasts with their pointed pink nipples lightly brushing his chest. He took them in his hands, closed his fingers over the soft-firm globes, and allowed his lids to drift shut. A great many lovers had come and gone through his life, most of them with little scruples about revealing their assets, certain that one feel, one taste of their flesh would drive him wild with desire. His grin had mocked them. His often sarcastic remarks had cut them, infuriated them, caused them to slap his arrogant face.

But they hadn't been Miracle. Their innocence hadn't enthralled him. The use of their bodies hadn't been a gift from the heart, but a means to their own ends.

Even now, as he gently ran one hand down her soft, slender belly and found that place between her legs that felt warm and wet and inviting, he got the impression that he was taking nothing from her, that this surrender was no surrender at all, but an awakening, a flower opening, loving and embracing the sun after a lifetime of dark solitude.

They drifted to the floor, lay amid the pool of her clothes and a scattering of acorns and strings that spilled from the pocket of her skirt. For a long while, they didn't move, just lay wrapped in each other's arms, bodies pressed so tightly they could not tell where one ended and the other began, flesh pressed against flesh, hot, sweating.

Then her hands were on him again, exploring, searching, tracing each defined contour on his chest and stomach, then inching down, into the waistband of his breeches . . .

He clumsily clawed at the buttons, releasing himself into her hand.

A pause.

A swift intake of breath.

An escalating of her heart beating against his.

Ah, how easy. How gentle her touch. A worshiping caress that sent shivers vibrating throughout him.

He floated with the sweet, surging ecstasy. Cool fingertips against his taut, pounding skin. He felt on fire, there, where she stroked him, learning the shape, the dimension, then farther, low between his legs, causing him to bow his back, to raise his hips, to thrust hard into her cupped palm.

Kisses, light as the flutter of a butterfly, scattered over his stomach, his arms, the tense cord in his throat, around his ear. Upon his closed eyelids. Onto his mouth. She breathed into his mouth, in and out, while he could only roll his head from side to side on the cushion of her disposed clothing and imagine how good it would feel inside her.

She straddled him, as she had before, poised there, her eyes meeting his as she waited.

And he complied.

Her face looked sublime with the intimate pain, radiant with the glow of light behind her and the fire of visceral discovery. Her head thrown back, her glorious hair flowing over her shoulders, her breasts, brushing the tops of her thighs and pooling over his loins, she offered herself as if she were some virginal sacrifice to a god of passion.

His blood roared. His body shook. The air in the small chamber became impossible to breathe. His lungs were bursting, and suddenly he was drowning in a tide of incredible heat, in her eyes, her smell. Twisting his hands into the clothing beneath him, he tried to surface, to think—*oh futility*— How could he think when he wanted to possess her? To burn his body into hers. He wanted to conquer her indomitable spirit, absorb it, make it his own. He wanted to fly with her. He wanted to show her how magical this could be.

Yet, it was she who was showing him; he had bedded a hundred women, but it had never been like this. He felt like the virgin, experiencing for the first time, not just the sublimity of the body, but of the heart. It was a . . .

Miracle.

At last, she lay down against him, body to body, heart to heart. Wrapping his arms around her, crushing her small form to his, he rolled. Lying on their sides, one of her legs over his hip, loins still joined, each gazed into the other's face. Her eyes appeared dazed, her cheeks were flushed and still moist from the rain. Then her small red mouth turned up, and she whispered, "Now, when you think of water, you'll remember me. Perhaps then you won't feel so afraid."

He laughed. "Remember you? Meri Mine, how could I ever forget you?"

Their mouths met with a wild violence. They rolled and twisted. Their arms and legs struggled for dominance, while he thrust his body into and out of hers with a savagery he had never thought was in him.

She moaned and gasped. She clutched at his shoulders and cried, "Oh, please. This pain, this pain—"

"No pain," he breathed into her ear. "Pleasure. Only that. Hold on, Meri Mine, and let *me* teach *you* how to fly."

* * *

Clayton awoke lying facedown and naked on the floor, the sun pouring through the window burning uncomfortably into his back. A moment passed before he could think of where he was.

Back on the ship? Wood creaking and groaning around him. Water hissing and roaring in the distance.

Slowly, he opened his eyes. His shirt lay in a limp heap near the door. His breeches and boots had been tossed randomly; his stock was draped across the back of a chair, resembling a dead ferret.

Groaning, he rolled over and sat up, his gaze going immediately to the delicate feminine stocking cascading off the windowsill.

"Damn," he said.

His head hurt. His body ached. He smelled like Miracle. She was burned into his nostrils, his chest, his hands, between his legs. In his mouth. Oh, the things he'd taught her. He should be mortified.

"Damn."

He stood. "Meri?" he called.

Silence.

Clayton moved to the window, focused his bleary vision on the shore below. *GOOD MORNING, YOUR GRACE* was scrawled in big letters into the sand. A grin crept across his lips, and once again, the night's memories tumbled through his mind, causing his body to react, to grow turgid and restless.

He dressed quickly, not bothering to tie his stock or put on his coat, nor did he bother with his boots. With his clothes clutched in his arms, he ran down the beach barefoot, following Miracle's small footsteps, and took the shortcut to the castle so he reached Cavisbrooke in half an hour. He found Benjamin steeping tea and toasting crumpets.

The servant eyed him with a slightly horrified expression. "Good gosh," Ben said. "You look as if you've tumbled through the night with a doxy." Leaning nearer Clayton, Ben sniffed and frowned. "Good gosh, you *have* tumbled through the night with a doxy."

"Hardly," Clayton snapped. "Have you seen Miracle?"

In a wink, Ben's expression became concerned. "I'm afraid to ask—"

"Then don't." He moved to the back entry and looked off down the path. She wasn't conversing with her pigs. No sign of her at the henhouse.

"I believe this calls for something stronger than tea," Ben declared and pulled his flask from his coat pocket and proceeded to uncork it. He took a deep drink, closed his eyes, shuddered his shoulders, then grimaced.

"Agreed." Clayton snatched the bottle from Ben's hand and turned it up to his own mouth. The brandy hit his gut with a punch.

"Perhaps this is none of my business," Ben said, eyeing the flask, "but may I ask what the blazes you thought you were doing? You'll have to tell him, you know—His Grace, I mean—else he'll be expecting a . . . how shall I say this?"

"A virgin on his wedding night?"

Ben cleared his throat. "The moment she begins to whisper sweet—"

Clayton grabbed Ben by his coat and said through his teeth, "I don't want to hear about it. Understand? I don't wish to discuss it. I don't need reminding that I've made a muck out of this entire fiasco and that it serves me right for attempting such a farce in the first place. Now, draw me a bloody bath so I can drown myself in it."

Ben nodded, extricated himself from Clayton's grip, then hurried from the room. No sooner had the valet quit the room, than Clayton turned to discover Hoyt at the threshold of the back door, an ax in one hand, a headless chicken in the other.

"Well, now," Hoyt said, his eyes blurry behind his spectacles, his mouth set in a grim line. "I'd say yer lookin' like a man with a weighty problem, Yer Grace."

"Do I?"

"Aye." John moved into the room, his limp exaggerated without the use of his cane. He slammed the fowl onto the chopping block and proceeded to whack off one crooked, yellow foot, which he flung to the cat that meowed and circled his legs. "I felt like a bit of meat today," he announced. Or maybe I was just in the mood to kill somethin'. What do you think, Yer Grace?"

"If you have something to say, Hoyt, then say it."

Whack went the cleaver again. "I suspect you'll be marryin' the girl for certain now. I mean, now that you've spent the night with her and come home lookin' ragged as a tomcat. Not that she looked any better, though I venture to say she appeared a bit happier about her sorry state. Not like you. You look like a man with a noose around his neck." *Whack!* "Is there aught you'd like to tell me, Your Grace?" *Whack! Whack!* He tossed the cat another foot.

"Yes." Clayton took another drink from the flask, hissed as the brandy burned down his throat, then said through his teeth, "She knows it was you writing the letters, Johnny, my man."

Stupid thing to say. He took another drink, but didn't look away. If the old man was spoiling for a fight, he was in the mood to give him one. Clayton wasn't going to be the only one dealing with a conscience in flux.

The cleaver poised in the air momentarily before John slowly lowered it to the block. He said nothing for a long while, just stared down at the chicken, his heavy breathing slightly ruffling the white and brown feathers. "Just tell me this," he finally said, his voice weary. "Do you love her? Truly love her? That's all she wants, ya know, is someone to love her." His head turned. He regarded Clayton with faded eyes. "I've never quite understood why ya come back, m'lord. If I thought for a flea's wink that yer reason was nothin' more than to beguile her for some insidious reason, I'd kill ya right here and now with me own two hands. But I've seen the way ya watch her. I hear the way ya speak to her. I loved a woman meself, once. Aye, I did. I know what love can do to a man. 'Specially lovin' a woman like Miracle. One look in their dreamy eyes and a man can loose himself. He can become a little insane himself, I vow. Aye, damn me, but love can make a man into a fool that fast." He snapped his fingers. "And once it's there, mate, it'll always be there. Imprinted on yer damn heart. You can try to fool yerself, tell yerself that there will be others, but there won't be no others like her. 'Til yer dyin' day ya won't ever forget the look in her eyes when she laughs, or cries, or flares up in anger."

His throat growing tight, Hoyt stared down at the chicken. "Damn me, but I've gone and butchered Agatha. I don't rightly know what come over me."

"Love makes fools of us all," Clayton said softly.

"I'll have to dispose of the corpse, I reckon."

"I reckon."

"This'll be our little secret, Your Grace? She'll think Agatha wandered off and got plucked by a mutt or someaught."

Clayton nodded.

Hoyt moved toward the door, the limp, footless fowl drooping from one hand. As he disappeared over the threshold, Clayton took another drink from the flask, then wiped his mouth with the back of his hand.

Were his feelings for Miracle so obvious?

Did the same emotions fill up his face the way John's did when he thought of Miracle's mother?

Oh, yes, those eyes could drive any man insane.

He went to his room. Ben was adding one last bucket of hot water to the washtub, a great fixture on wheels hand-painted with pictures of flowers and butterflies and bunnies peeking up from copses of grass. Ben helped him remove his clothes, then, without relinquishing the brandy flask, Clayton stepped into the tub, wincing as the hot water bit at his thighs that were slightly smeared with Miracle's blood and his own semen.

He slid down into the steaming water and lay back his head, felt his skin swell and his scalp prickle with the heat while the memory of John's face, weathered and wrinkled, had illuminated with as much pain as bliss when recalling Lorraina Cavendish.

Would he, Clayton Hawthorne, Lord Basingstoke, look similarly twenty years from now when he recalled those moments of passion in Miracle's arms? Would his eyes reveal the pain he experienced each time he thought of her loving another man—as Lorraina had loved her husband?

Because there was no way around it. Lovely, dreamy, childlike Miracle, who talked to animals and stole royal horses, would someday become the duchess Salterdon, his brother's wife, if he, Clayton, persisted in continuing this grievous game of switched identities. He could reveal himself now for who and what he was, why he was here, and have her toss him out on his ear, never to see her again, or he could continue the ruse and be forced to spend the rest of his life desiring her from afar.

Christ, anything was better than living his life with no Miracle at all.

She moved silently up behind him, slid her arms over his shoulders, plunged her hands into the hot water, and spread it across his chest. "My lord," she whispered against his ear. "I've missed you."

His eyes closed, and Clayton smiled.

"I've sent Benjamin for tea, and I've told him to take his merry time."

"You'll have people talking, Meri Mine."

She laughed gaily and sat on the edge of the tub. The rising steam made her cheeks flush; it turned the snug bodice of her light brown gown transparent. Her nipples looked like pert coins pressed into the worn material.

"I was wondering," she said. "Will every time we make love be that glorious? Is it always that wonderful?"

"That depends on the people, I suppose."

"I'm talking between us, of course. You and I."

He wrapped his fingers around her wrist. It felt brittle as a bird's. "Only if you agree to become the duchess of Salterdon."

Sliding from the tub and going to her knees, Miracle took the soap from Clayton's hand and slid it over his shoulder. He easily recognized the stubborn tilt of her head, the set of her chin. Frustration mounting, he grabbed hold of her arm, his fingers painting wet splotches on her sleeve. "What the blazes is wrong with you? Most women would sell their soul to marry into that sort of wealth and position."

"I'm not most women," she replied, and batted her lashes. "Or so you said last night."

"This isn't a laughing matter, Miracle."

Miracle pulled away, rolled the soap over and over in her hand until lather bubbled up through her fingers. Her small white teeth nibbled at her lower lip. She looked, he thought, like a scolded child.

"If I leave here again without you, Meri, I won't come back. Ever. And think of this . . . you may well be pregnant—ah, Christ, I hadn't even thought of that." He covered his face with his hot, wet hands, dragged them through his hair that was fast becoming saturated by sweat and steam. "Pregnant. Now wouldn't that be a hell of a mess. What the devil was I thinking?"

"Pregnant," she said softly, with a touch of wonderment in her voice; her entire face began to glow; her eyes shone. Leaning nearer, her freckled nose almost touching his, she said, "Do you think so? Would it please you? Would you like for me to give you a child, m'lord?"

Looking into her radiant face, Clayton tried to swallow. "Yes," he answered as softly, though even as he said it, he inwardly cursed himself for the absurdity of even thinking it—of admitting it to her and to himself. "Yes," he repeated. "I would like nothing better than to see you with child. *My* child."

She smiled and her eyes twinkled. In a flash she was suddenly on her feet, tiptoeing like a dancer, exposing her ankles and slippered feet, toward the cheval mirror, doing her best to pooch out her concave stomach. When that didn't work, she grabbed up a pillow, and before Clayton's bemused eyes, shoved the pillow up under her skirt.

Offering her profile to the mirror, she regarded it first one way, then the other. "Would you think me still comely?" she asked, chewing on one finger. "Would you still make love to me? What, do you think, would you like to name him? Your Grace?"

Like a breath, she was back beside him, her nearness warming him, her scent, like fresh roses, surrounding him, filling up his senses so he felt dizzy. His eyes closed, he lay his head back against the tub, shivering as she ran her fingertips over his face and through his hair. "Your Grace," she murmured, "why do you look so sad? Mayhap the idea of my having your child isn't as pleasant as you would have me believe."

With a low growl, he took her in his arms, forgetting the pillow, and pulled her atop him, into the water, and she did little more than gasp and giggle, then settle onto him, her skirt floating in the water around her thighs. The passion rose inside him. Made him hard. Made his heart pound in his chest, only this time the fierce, erratic beating felt like a knife twisting.

Burying his dripping hands in her hair, he kissed her open mouth, ravaged it with his lips and tongue until she melted against him, arms clinging to his slick shoulders, while he grew bigger and harder between her legs, until she parted her thighs and he pushed his body into hers so fiercely she whimpered in her throat, and struggled, and dug her little nails into the skin of his back.

She wanted pleasure. Instead, *he* took pleasure. He found it on her wet breasts confined in her blouse. In the tiny, sensitive nub between her legs. He thrust wildly, until the water and pillow feathers roiled onto the floor, until she was clinging to the tub and gritting her teeth, her eyes clamped shut and her fiery hair streaming over her face in limp silken cords.

He climaxed with an intensity that made him cry out, as much with anger as with relief. When he fell back against the tub, spent and winded, Miracle lay upon his chest, her head nestled under his chin, her arms and legs wrapped around him, her wet skirt twisted around her waist. A scattering of tiny white feathers clung to her bare pink buttocks. Only then did he realize the water had grown cold—what little water there was remaining in the tub.

"Does that answer your question?" he asked, finding his throat dry as dust.

Raising her head, she regarded him with her big, blue-green eyes before struggling from the tub and walking gracefully from the room, leaving a trail of water and soaked goose feathers behind her.

I never knew how to worship until I knew how to love.

HENRY WARD BEECHER

Chapter Thirteen

"Men are odd. Most confusing. They sniff about a woman's skirts with the appetite of a famished hound, and once assuaged grow lethargic with indifference. I wonder if they truly know what it's like to love. I mean, with the entire body and soul. Until it hurts. Do you think so, Chuck? Does he think of me when he's out there, alone, walking? He could have invited me, couldn't he, instead of sneaking away in the middle of the day?"

Chuck the boar wiggled his red snout and grunted for more corn. Miracle hardly noticed. She was too busy staring out over the rolling downs. "And such a beautiful day," she said softly. "A day for picnics. A day for picking flowers. A day for strolling hand in hand with a lover . . ."

Daft girl. She had never been one to dwell on such things. There were candles to be dipped. Soap to be skimmed. Rugs to be beaten. Eggs to be gathered. Where was Agatha?

Such pathetic mooning. Such silly daydreaming. She was acting like a child.

"Mira."

She spilled her bucket of corn to the ground. Chuck pounced on it, tail wringing and hoofed feet scrambling. With a frown, Miracle snatched up the pail and started down the path toward the henhouse.

"Mira," John called after her.

Miracle walked faster, her skirt brushing aside flowers that released a spray of perfume into the air.

"You'll have to speak to me eventually," John called, limping after her. "We live in the same house, ya know."

"Don't be reminding me, Mr. Hoyt."

Flinging open the henhouse door, Miracle stepped into the coop with so little warning that a half dozen birds exploded into the air, sending a shower of feathers raining over her shoulders. She waved them away and did her best to focus on the line of straw-stuffed crates. Only when the birds had settled down did he call to her softly again.

"If you were aware I was writin' the bleedin' letters, why didn't ya say aught?"

Miracle shoved her hands into the egg pouch on her apron and stared fixedly at Agatha's empty nest. Her eyes burned. She wondered if it were because she was now forced to face the reality that those letters, few as there had been, had not really been from her mother, that Jonathan, her one and only friend, had duped her, or because the man who had, at last, won her heart, would suddenly avoid her like the plague.

"Go away," she croaked, then stomped her foot.

"Would ya not have hurt worse had there been nothin' at all for the last ten damn years? Why won't ya give it up, lass? Let her go."

She sniffed and blew a feather off her nose. "Agatha seems to be missing. Would you know anything about that, too?"

Silence, then some grumbling about a stray, perhaps a fox.

"You've bloody butchered her, haven't you?" she demanded. "Every time you get upset, one of my girls disappears. Agatha was—"

"A bleedin' pest. She come peckin' after me gonads anytime I come within five feet of her. But, hell, I didn't come here to discuss demented birds with a hate for men."

"Mayhap Agatha had the right idea," Miracle muttered, then stepped from the coop, out into the light and fresh air. John gazed at her with so forlorn an expression, she felt her anger cool. Another time and the grief might have consumed her, left her feeling totally abandoned and disconsolate.

"Tell me this," she said. "Were all of the letters written by you? The early ones, too?"

John opened and closed his mouth, saying nothing.

"Never mind." Stepping around him, she moved up the path, back to the house.

"Will ya be takin' yer ridin' lesson on Napitov?" he asked.

"You may tell Ismail that I will not be riding Nap this morning."

The candles wouldn't dip. No matter how many crushed flower petals she added to the soap, it came out smelling like hog fat. She burned the bread. Discovered one of her pet rabbits had escaped its hutch and devoured the cabbage she had marked for supper.

She couldn't concentrate, but found herself staring off into space, her mind vacillating between Salterdon and her mother.

Would he turn out to be another lord Cavendish—a seducer of innocence who, with his caddish charm and good looks had corrupted a squire's daughter, then, forced to marry her because of a child, had deposited his naive wife off in some rambling old castle as far away from his family and peers as he could get? Oh, yes, she knew the story. Johnny had already confessed the entire fiasco, but that had been a mere few years ago, back when she still adored her deceased father's memory. She supposed Johnny had felt that her obsession with one ghost, meaning her mother, was enough to deal with. Well, at least he had been honest about that.

She wandered the castle, rooms she had not frequented in years. There was her mother's favorite, a cavernous chamber that had once been the great hall. The towering ceilings and stone walls had offered Lorraina the perfect setting for her music. For hours, Miracle would sit on a little pillow on the floor (Lorraina would allow no other furniture in the room) and listen to her mother play the pianoforte. The notes would reverberate hauntingly off the old stone and polished mahogany floor. With her beautiful white face uplifted toward the ceiling, her red hair spilling down her back, she was the most beautiful woman Miracle had ever seen; she prayed every night that she would grow up to become half as lovely, as kind, as forgiving . . .

The pianoforte, silent since her mother's disappearance, still stood in the center of the room, covered with a dusty cloth, and in the far corner near the window overlooking the sea was a child's pillow.

Miracle turned from the room, slamming the door behind her. She moved hurriedly down the corridor, past closed doors entombing childhood memories that she refused to liberate. Faster and faster she went, fleeing the silence and emptiness.

Odd how the silence and emptiness had not felt so looming and suffocating until the last few days—all because of him, because he had filled up a place in her days and nights, made himself necessary to her existence. She had not wanted to fall in love with him—oh, no!—because everyone she had ever loved had abandoned her. Love was an emptiness—a loneliness—a treasured possession that, once lost, left a wound in one's heart that never healed. *Never.*

Ismail ran from his tent as she entered the courtyard. She ignored him, but walked fast to Napitov, who nickered softly upon seeing her. She mounted, dug her heels into his sides, and within minutes they were flying down the beach, his steel-silver mane whipping her face, his nostrils blowing, his breath roaring. They splashed through the waves; exploded through a gathering of gulls on the ground.

She searched everywhere for Salterdon, little caring that a scattering of village folk stopped to watch her in her maddened rush across the down. They thought her insane anyway, and it no longer mattered if they saw her horses, because Salterdon had already discovered them. Her secret was out.

At dusk, they arrived at Saint Catherine's Hill.

Salterdon stood far out on the rocks, his back to her, the water churning around the boulders beneath his feet. Her heart pounded with relief. It raced with anticipation.

She slid from her horse and ran the perilous distance, leaping from stone to stone, boulder to boulder, her dress hem becoming wet with sea spray. "Hello!" she called, but he didn't turn. Perhaps the wind had cast her voice asunder. "Hello!" she called more loudly, cupping her hands around her mouth.

His head moved slightly, but only his cloak shifted, rose and fell, danced around his legs that were planted firmly apart.

Reaching him at last, breathing hard, Miracle stepped around him, smiling. He still did not acknowledge her. Just stared ahead, his eyes like cold flint; his whole face was as colorless as rock. His aloofness stung her like a slap. He was the same man she had saved those months ago: cold, distant, repellent.

"I . . . was frightened," she forced herself to say. "When you didn't return to Cavisbrooke after a few hours and Benjamin had not seen you, I feared you might've met with some disaster."

At last, his eyes met hers. A smile touched one corner of his mouth as he searched her face. "No," he said, sounding weary. "No disaster, Meri Mine. None so obvious as to be visually noted, that is." Taking a deep breath, he again looked at the sea. "Have you noticed? I'm surrounded by water, before me, beside me, soon to be behind me. It laps at my boots, and yet—"

"You are an island, sir."

"I think of you—"

"Instead of death."

He laughed mirthlessly. "Today they are one and the same."

"I don't understand."

"Of course not. I wouldn't expect you to."

Turning, Salterdon started back to the shore, leaving Miracle to stare after him, her back to the wind, her hair waving around her face. She hurried to follow and caught him as he reached the shoal.

Throwing her arms around his waist, she pressed her face into his back. "Why are you so cold, sir? Why do you avoid me? Tell me what I've done so I might undo it."

"Let me go," he said in a tight voice.

Squeezing closed her eyes, clutching him fiercely, she cried, "I won't! Don't ask me to. What crime have I committed other than loving you?"

Silence. Then, "Do you love me, Meri Mine?"

With that, she released him, stumbled back while he slowly turned to face her. Her body trembled as it had never trembled to thunder.

"Do you love me, Meri Mine?"

She flung herself against him, arms around his neck as she pressed her lips to the salty skin of his throat, the curve of his hard, unshaven jaw. He stood stiff and tense, ignoring her lips, her ploys to move him. Even as she ran her hand down over the bulging ridge in his trousers, he did nothing.

Falling to her knees, she grappled at the straining buttons on his breeches.

He grabbed her wrists, and she struggled. He lurched her to her feet. Fingers biting into her arms, he dragged her into the chapel and flung her up against the wall.

"Is this love to you, Meri?" he grated through his teeth, dragging up her skirt, sliding his hands beneath her buttocks and between her thighs, spreading her legs as he easily lifted her and slammed her body back against the Virgin fresco. Then he drove his body into hers, while he shut his eyes and turned his face aside—drove and drove, each thrust driving her back into the stone wall that sent splinters of pain through her. Yet, she could only clutch at his shoulders, his hair, try vainly to wrap her legs around his pumping hips.

When it seemed his body would explode, he withdrew from her and climaxed, allowed his seed to pulsate across her lower belly and down her legs. Then he released her, suddenly, and stepped away.

Miracle slid to the ground, lay stunned in the wet sand and streamers of seaweed. She could do nothing but stare up into his flushed features as he adjusted himself in his trousers.

Finally, he said, "Is that love to you, Meri? Because if it is, you can get that from any randy sailor at any port in this or any other country." Then he spun on his heel and left the chapel.

Miracle stared after him before clawing her way to her feet. She ran after him. "Bastard!" she screamed. "You're a bloody animal, and I wish I had let you drown!"

He continued to walk, head down, cloak billowing.

"I despise you! Did you hear me? Answer me, damn you!"

He stopped, and slowly turned. The sun setting behind him turned his image into a silhouette, stark and black against the horizon. "No you don't," came his calm voice. "And we both know it. Therefore, you have a decision to make, Meri Mine. I'm leaving for London tomorrow, with or without you."

She shook her head and wrung her hands together, approached him cautiously. "We could remain here. We'll live at Cavisbrooke—"

"Do you think I haven't thought of that? For the last twenty-four hours I've imagined myself giving up family, friends, home, wealth—everything—and moving here, to live out my life with you. Only you. But I need people, Miracle. I need to hold on to some thread of sanity in your insane world. Aside from that, I have . . . certain obligations. Certain debts I'm forced to repay. I can't allow this penchant toward emotionalism to get in the way."

"So that's it? I marry you or never see you again?"

He said nothing, just turned again and moved off down the shoal, toward the blazing sun, ignoring the tide sweeping in around his feet.

She found John with Ismail, sitting cross-legged on his frash. The smell of strong coffee and incense hovered in the air.

Ismail scrambled to care for Napitov, to carefully bathe his lathered body, to dry him with toweling, to prepare him a great pail of warm mash once he had cooled sufficiently. The stallion nickered softly to Miracle before obliging his groom. Miracle watched the pair walk off into the night, and she blinked back her tears, then turned to leave the courtyard.

"Mira," John called.

"I don't wish to talk," she replied.

"But you've always talked to me, Mira."

"I thought you were my friend then."

"I was and am."

Staying her step, staring at the door, and clenching her fists, she declared, "He's leaving. Tomorrow. He's demanded that I make a choice: Cavisbrooke or him. I leave with him or never see him again."

For an eternal moment, John said nothing. Only the sounds of the distant horses interrupted the silence. Since she had found them on the beach, they had been a big part of her world, filling up her emptiness with the pleasure of their existence and odd but special friendship. She awoke in the morning, eager for her misty dawn rides on Napitov's back. The scent of horseflesh, the companionable nickering they made upon seeing her, had lent a certain magic to her days.

"I . . . cannot leave," she announced, hating the emotion she heard in the words, despising the awful pain in her chest.

"Why?" he replied solemnly.

She faced him at last. He seemed so small to her now, sitting there on the ground by the fire, his bad leg stretched out before him, his cane (which she had carved for him herself) placed at his side. "This is my home, sir. All that I have ever known. Not once in my twenty years have I left this island. What would I do there? How would I act? Nay, I shan't leave—not for him."

"Do you love him?"

Lowering her eyes, she didn't bother to fight the tears any longer, but allowed them to rise up and flow down her cheeks. "Yes. But there is much here that I love as well."

" 'Tis no greater choice than any other maid is forced to make when deciding to marry. Do you think it easy for any girl to leave her home? She goes on and builds a new life, a new home, with her husband. And someday she will encourage her own children to fly the nest. 'Tis the way of nature, Mira."

"But who would take care of you, John? Who would prepare your meals? Darn your clothes? Dip your candles and make the soap? And the horses—who would love them like I do? What would happen to them after you're gone? And there are the rabbits, and the chickens, and the hogs. I fear they would become stew before I reached London."

"Will you be satisfied to spend the remainder of your life chanting to acorns and the moon in hopes Ceridwen's bible will plop some local sheep farmer into your lap to marry? At last you have this opportunity to find happiness. Take it, Mira."

She shook her head almost angrily and turned away again.

"Where will you run now?" John barked. "Back to that damn, bloody lighthouse like yer mother did? To stand on that perch and stare out to sea, allowin' yer fantasies to swallow you up?"

"I don't wish to discuss my mother—"

"It's time we did, Mira," he said in so sharp and harsh a voice that Miracle stopped in her tracks.

Behind her, John struggled to stand. She could imagine him, leaning heavily on the cane, stiffly straightening. Then came the scrape of his bad foot on the ground and the thump and tap of his cane on the stones. "I think yer reasons for not wantin' to leave have got little to do with yer devotion to this bleedin' mausoleum of a house, or even these animals. Yer still waitin' on her, on Lorraina. After all this time, ya think she'll still come home.

"Yer just like her, ya know. Wantin' to believe in the impossible. She waited ten damn years for yer good-for-nothin' father to come take her away from this place, and he never did. And he never would have, because ya know why?"

She covered her ears with her hands, pressed them painfully against her head.

"Because he had a goddamn wife and family already, Mira."

She stared at the ground.

John moved up behind her. "It took yer blessed mother ten years to learn the truth. But learn it she did. After one of Cavendish's infrequent visits, she followed him back to London. Imagine her surprise when she discovered another Lady Cavendish—"

"I don't believe you!"

"Yer mother didn't confront him then; she was wise enough to think the situation through; she'd sacrificed ten years of her life, after all . . . and there was you to think about."

Miracle started for the door. John grabbed her.

"Eventually, she wrote him—"

"You're lying, John."

"She told him what she knew and demanded an audience with him here at Cavisbrooke. She threatened that if he didn't come, she'd reveal to all of England that he was a bigamist. He came, of course. Do ya remember that night, Mira?"

She shook her head frantically.

"You were there for the most of it. I found ya standing in the hallway, yer little face white and streaked with tears. Ya weren't no bigger than a minute then, scrawny as a little bean pole with eyes so big and sad it broke me heart to see them. It was about that time that yer mother and Cavisbrooke come stormin' from the room; they didn't see us, standin' there, me holdin' ya in me arms and trying to shield yer eyes and ears from the ugliness."

"Stop. Please stop," she wept, feeling like that child again, watching the two people she loved most in the world destroy one another.

"Cavisbrooke left the house, and yer mother followed him. I think she would've followed all the way to hell that night, and that night seemed like hell. All the lightnin' and thunder, the wind howlin' like a banshee, drivin' the rain so fierce it stung the eyes. I went after yer mother, for you, 'cause I knew the only thing that would bring Lorraina back was you. I finally come up on 'em at Saint Catherine's. By then, it was all over. Lorraina lay dead at the bottom of the Undercliff, and Cavisbrooke stood there in the rain still as a stone, his face frozen in a look of terror. He said it was an accident, that Lorraina had slipped. I wanted to kill him with me bare hands, and would have, had it not been for you. All I could think of was you waitin' back at Cavisbrooke, alone. So I allowed the bastard to go on his way, Mira, on one condition. That he continue the financial support he'd provided for you and yer mother the last ten years. And he did, for a while, then the money stopped comin'. By then I was tired of the lies, tired of ya holdin' on to the belief that the man loved ya, so I told ya he was dead."

She turned to face John. His visage looked ashen and tormented. He could not meet her eyes.

"I buried Lorraina at the foot of the Undercliff," he said, and his voice cracked. "So ya see, Mira, she ain't ever comin' back. You can stop yer dreamin' and believin' in miracles."

"All lies," she said.

"Aye. Ever'one of them, lass."

"Is there anything else you'd like to confess?"

At last, he raised his eyes to hers. "I only did what I thought was best. You were my life, Mira. I loved you as devotedly and deeply as I . . . loved yer mother . . . but the time has come for change. I want out, Mira. Away. I want a life of me own while I've still got a few years to enjoy it. I'll never have the opportunity unless yer gone from here and married."

"Oh, now you confess that I'm a burden? That I've ruined your life? That you actually *want* me gone?"

No reply.

Miracle turned and walked away, left the courtyard, ambled down one corridor after another, until finding herself in the piano room again. She flung back the sheet and, after a moment's hesitation, slid onto the dusty bench, ran her fingers over the keys, closed her eyes, and allowed her fingers to lightly touch the ivories, filling the chamber with the simple tune her mother had once taught her.

The two of them, sitting together on the bench, Lorraina's cool hands atop hers, stroking out the music, rewarding her with a hug and kiss when she finally got it right.

"Meri," Salterdon said from the door.

She looked up, regarded his tall form in the entry, then carefully placed the sheet across the instrument again and stood up.

He walked to her, into the light of the solitary candle. His face looked haggard.

"Sir," she said, "I've given your proposal some thought, and . . ."

"And?"

"I'll leave with you tomorrow, if you like."

"Yes, I'd like that very much," he replied in a thick voice and opened his arms.

After a second's hesitation, she slid into them, buried her face into his chest, and clung to him fiercely.

Whom we love best, to them we can say least.
Proverb

Chapter Fourteen

London

Miracle awoke feeling miserably stiff, cramped, and overheated. The immense noise outside the chaise seemed overwhelming, as were the smells of burning coal and sulfur and miscellaneous other unpleasant odors that made her feel unbearably ill.

Salterdon sat beside her, staring out the coach window, apparently lost in thought. He'd spoken little to her since they left Cavisbrooke—only the occasional chitchat as he provided her with what little information he thought necessary to alleviate her curiosity.

It struck her as she watched him, how little she really knew of him. What had his childhood been like? Like her, he had lost his parents at a young age, although he had mentioned a brother. He and his brother had been raised by the duchess of Salterdon, whom, Miracle supposed, she would be forced to meet very soon.

Miracle yawned, rubbed her eyes, and cleared her throat. Salterdon ignored her.

"Will she like me, do you think?" Miracle asked.

"Who?" he replied, still watching the activity out the window. How relaxed he appeared, spine conforming to the plush leather seat, long legs splayed slightly, and his body swaying with each jounce of the coach. Then again, this was *his* world. No doubt he'd found the quiet and isolation of her world as foreign.

"The duchess, of course."

His mouth curled in a derisive manner, and he laughed shortly. "I doubt it," he replied. "But then, my dear grandmother likes very few people and tolerates even fewer. You'll get used to her eventually. You might even begin to like her, once you've forgiven her for her rather peculiar idiosyncrasies."

"Does she know about me?"

At last, he turned his head and looked at her. "No."

"Then I shall come as quite a surprise to her."

A look of thoughtful amusement came and went in his slate eyes. Then he became somber again. "She'll be livid at first. She will have had something else in mind for the mother of her great-grandchildren: someone all wrapped up in pretty ruches and lumbering about under the weight of jewels and affectation, not to mention her father's long and impressive list of titles. The duchess does love to crow, you understand. To her peers. There is an unspoken rule among my class that everyone outranking a clerk or tradesman should exhibit a form of pomposity over their much ballyhooed lineage. No one could possibly come close to rivaling the duchess's ability to boast."

Sidling closer, nestling against his arm, she smiled and said, "She sounds marvelous. I love a challenge."

"Of course you do, Meri Mine. You won me over, didn't you?"

She grew warm with pleasure. "Tell me more about your family."

"Must I?"

"Why do you avoid it?"

"Do I?" He grinned.

Miracle sat back and studied his profile. "Tell me about your brother. What's his name?"

He looked out the window again and frowned. "Clayton."

"Older or younger?"

"Younger."

"How much younger?"

"Not much."

"Are you close?"

"Unbearably so."

"I always wished for a brother."

"I can't imagine why."

"To champion me, of course."

"Champion? Most likely he would humiliate you publicly, despoil the family fortune, not to mention the name . . . Shall I go on?"

"What, pray tell, does your brother do to occupy himself, when he's not humiliating or despoiling you?"

"He . . . gambles; he's won and lost fortunes at Crockford's, Roxborough's, and Brooks. He simply cannot leave the green hazard table alone, despite his abhorrence of his fellow gamblers—a group of repugnant individuals who make a mockery of their well-born position in life; you'll meet them all, in time," he added with an air of contempt. "The out and outers, as they're called. The handsome, titled young men who are up to everything, down as a nail, a trump, a Trojan, snobs who can patter flash, floor a charley, mill a coal-heaver, come coachey in prime style up to every rig and row in London. They all will illuminate a nauseating disregard for the feelings of every man, woman, and child with whom they come in contact. That, Meri Mine, is the one true hallmark of the 'blood.' " He took a deep breath and slowly released it, clenched and unclenched his hands as they lay in his lap.

"My brother . . . is a liar," he confessed in a belligerent tone. "And he falls in love with women he has no right to fall in love with. He secludes himself in some falling down old country house and . . . broods because he's . . . lonely."

"Why is he lonely?" she asked softly.

"Because he's alone. Because he's amassed a fortune, succeeded in establishing one of the greatest homes in England, and has yet to fill it with wife and children." He shook his head. "Do you know he won't even live in the manse? Instead, he occupies some vine-covered carriage house out back of the stables—"

"Stables?"

He glanced at her. "Yes, stables. He shares our father's love of horses, you see."

The rise of hurt in her throat made Miracle sit back. "Tell me more," she pleaded, desperate to remove her mind from the horses she was forced to leave at Cavisbrooke. She didn't want to think of Napitov, and she didn't want to think of John or the fact that she had refused to see or speak to him again before leaving the isle.

Why did it feel as if her heart was breaking each time she thought of him? Why had her heart ached so to forgive him? After all the lies . . .

Salterdon watched her face for a long moment, then again focused on the activity outside the coach. "He's vowed that he won't live in the house until he finds the perfect woman to share it with. Mind you, I said perfect. Since restoration of the estate has been complete, he's paraded mistresses and/or lovers through its halls, thinking eventually he'll find one who suits the place . . . and him."

"But there are no perfect women," she pointed out.

"I'm not so sure about that, Meri Mine."

He reached across the seat and took her hand and gave it a squeeze, laced his fingers through hers, and raised it to his mouth, pressed his lips gently to the pale, sensitive skin on the inside of her wrist.

Warming, Miracle leaned into him again and stroked his cheek with her nose. She whispered in his ear, "Sir, you haven't graced me with a kiss in ages."

"No?" He allowed his lips to linger along hers, lightly touching but not kissing. It seemed he gave the idea great thought before gently but firmly pushing her away. Then he regarded her with an odd, half-rueful expression.

"Lesson one," he said. "This isn't the isle or Cavisbrooke. As the future wife of the duke of Salterdon, you must adhere to a certain decorum. The freedom to come and go and do as you please, with whomever you please, is against the rules of polite society. While you're in London, be aware that you're under constant scrutiny. One mistake could cost you much."

"Polite society can go to blazes," she said angrily. "I'm not marrying society, sir, I'm marrying you."

"You're marrying the duke of Salterdon—same as, Meri Mine."

A discomfiting thought. Had she been so naive, in love, and crushed by John's truths that she had failed to consider such an inevitability? Had she been so naive as to think that life as the duke's partner would be carried on in the same manner as her life at Cavisbrooke?

A dark shadow seemed to pass over her, cold and bleak and frightening. Miracle stared out the window. She could feel him watching her—those eyes that were as changeable as the sky—clear and sparkling one moment, cold and gray as fog the next. She could not make out his mood. Indeed, since they had traveled from the isle the day before, Salterdon had been standoffish and . . . brooding. Oh, yes, his brother wasn't the only one who could brood.

Therefore, she did her best to concentrate on the activity outside the coach, to get her mind off the percolating fear and uncertainty of her future, and to ignore the infuriating and nagging questions that continued to loom in her mind:

Have I made a mistake? Have I left the only home I have ever known because I truly love this man, or because I wished to simply run away from the memories and pain associated with my past?

Had John not confessed to the truth of her mother's death and her father's deceptions, would she still have ultimately agreed to marry Salterdon, though she loved him desperately?

The coach emerged from Borough High Street and came upon the river. Beyond it lay a city with a straight, uniform skyline, its parapets crowned with a halo of stone belfries, almost as many, it seemed to Miracle, as there were masts on the river. Above them, the cliffs of an immense cathedral carried the eye upward to a remote golden cross and ball. The dome on which these symbols rode belonged to a different world from the houses below, which, shrouded by the smoke of the chimneys, were clustered so close to the temple's base that they seemed to be crowding into its portals.

In truth, she could not see the sky, only gray, as far as the eye could travel. Where were the clouds? The birds? The sun? How did these people survive without the occasional sun-kissed breeze blowing in their hair and faces?

The river lay below, lined with wharves, warehouses, timber yards and manufactories. Spanning it was a bridge, its dark camelback arching over steep slopes crowded with carts and pedestrians, and bowers in whose recesses old women sat selling apples and sweetmeats. Below the bridge, the river was dark with masts and almost hidden by the throng of barges and wherries.

So many people: their skin pale and their faces aged not by weather but by the strife of existing in this mélange of humanity.

The coach lumbered up the cobbled, odoriferous incline of Fish Street and burst upon the heart of the city, where it ground to a snail's pace amid the crush of people and traffic. Miracle drew back. The noise bombarded her. For an instant, she could not breathe.

"So many people," she said aloud, and did her best to laugh convincingly. "I would not have thought that this many people lived in the entirety of England. How do they survive?"

"Any way they can," came the unemotional reply.

Leaning into the window, Miracle searched beyond the sea of faces, to the unpretentious, uniform three- and four-story houses of brown and gray brick, their skylines of parapet, tile, and chimney stacks broken only by the white stone of Wren's belfries.

Before them ran the roadways of flagstone pavements guarded from the traffic by posts and wrought-iron railings before the houses. Every house had the same sober, unadorned face of freestone-bordered sash, the same neat white pillars on either side of the pedimented doors, the same stone steps over the area crowned by a lamppost. Only the beautifully molded doors and brightly polished knockers, with their lion masks, wreaths and urns, did the people's instinct for individuality bear through the all-pervading, almost monotonous framework.

Yet, it was not those facades that riveted her most, but the narrow, winding lanes and courts behind them, which she glimpsed through the archways. From there came the whiffs of laystall and stable, ragged children swarmed there in the darkness, and cobblers sat at hutches with low open doors.

How awake and bustling was the city! Hardly the quiet, sleepy atmosphere of Niton, whose main traffic was little more than donkey carts and the occasional coaches of curious tourists. Would she ever grow accustomed to these odd, discomfiting surroundings? Would she grow as indifferent to this lifestyle as those fighting to survive in it?

Deeper into the city, the throng grew. She watched postmen in scarlet coats with bells and bags going from door to door; porterhouse boys were scurrying down the walks with pewter mugs, bakers in white aprons shouted "Hot loaves!" and small chimney sweeps—lads of no greater stature than Miracle—hefted their brushes and pails from house to house.

There were hawkers with bandboxes on poles; milkmaids, with the manure of cow sheds on their feet and pails suspended from yokes across their shoulders, were crying their wares, competing with the bells of dust carts, the horns of news vendors, and the roar of iron wheels on the flagstone streets.

"You'll grow accustomed to it," Salterdon said behind her.

Swallowing, Miracle shook her head and with a rousing sense of despair, replied, "I'm not so sure."

Clayton moved restlessly about the foyer of his brother's present paramour, the spouse of some barrister who took his arthritic self off to Madrid twice a year, leaving his wife to occupy her idle time with shopping and tumbling about the bed and floor with the duke of Salterdon, when Trey could fit her in among his other half-dozen mistresses.

Obviously, Dierenda What's-Her-Name was most convenient for Trey's current purpose, considering the house she occupied was an hour's drive out of London. The duke of Salterdon had burrowed up in this obviously lavish lair since he had purportedly left London for a holiday abroad—or so the duchess had been informed.

After a thirty-minute lag, at which time Clayton mentally rehearsed his telling his brother to go to the devil, then imagining his confession to Trey that he had compromised his future wife, not to mention falling in love with her, the duke came bounding down the stairs, hair disheveled, shirt open down his chest. A woman's drunken laughter and bawdy remark followed him.

Upon seeing Clayton, standing at the bottom of the staircase, his countenance obviously radiating his feelings at the moment, the duke paused and raised both dark eyebrows.

"You're back," he announced, and flashed his white-toothed smile full of devilment. "And so quickly."

"Yes," Clay snapped. "I'm back."

Salterdon took the last landing of steps two at a time, landing on the floor with a bounce and a hearty slap on Clayton's shoulder. "You look the devil, Clay. Don't tell me the venture was unsuccessful."

"It was successful."

"Excellent!" Glancing back up the stairs, where a winsome, buxom blond woman, draped in transparent silk, leaned across the balustrade, exposing most of her ample cleavage, he said, "We'll talk in the parlor. Clive!" he called.

A servant with an indifferent demeanor appeared.

"Bring his lordship a brandy. He looks as if he could use one."

"I don't care for a brandy," Clayton said.

"Very well then, a port—"

"Nor a port. God forbid."

"Then what the blazes do you want?"

"To get the hell out of here," Clayton snarled and walked past him into the parlor.

Trey followed and closed the door. He leaned against it, arms crossed over his chest, and watched Clay pace the room. "So tell me," he finally said, "was she everything I made her out to be?"

"No. You made her out to be a mostly mindless bit of stuff who was desperate to marry the first man who showed the least bit of interest. But that is beside the point. After I was forced to sufficiently lie my way into her good graces, then succeeded in emotionally ripping her life apart, she eventually agreed to marry me . . . or rather you." Clayton planted himself by the cold hearth and propped one elbow on the marble mantel. He ran his fingers through his hair and refused to look at his brother.

"Where is she now?"

"Ensconced at your Mayfair apartment. I thought the close proximity to Hyde would alleviate some of her jumpiness. I suspect she wasn't fully prepared for London."

Trey grinned. "You look quite dapper in my clothes, you know. They suit you. You might try investing in a few well-cut threads yourself now and again. You might find yourself appealing to a better class of woman than tavern wenches and milkmaids. Then again, I suppose farmers can't be too choosy."

"You call that a better class of woman?" Clayton pointed toward the door, then he dragged off his brother's cutaway and flung it at him. "Get dressed, for God's sake. You're disgusting."

Trey laughed as he caught the coat, then he tossed it back to Clayton. "Keep it. You'll be needing it for a while."

"No." He shook his head. "I'm finished. I did what the devil you asked me to do—"

"Is she sufficiently in love with me?"

Clayton walked to the window and stared out at the garden enclosed by hedges of bramble and hawthorn. Here and there patches of old-fashioned flowers, like bright splotches of paint, broke the monotony of the verdant grass.

"I asked you a question," Trey said as he moved up behind him.

"Yes," he replied more calmly.

"And how did you accomplish such a feat? Come now, don't be shy. I have to know everything if I'm to capably step into your shoes."

"I simply . . ."

"You had a plan, of course, once you met her."

"No." He shook his head. "Not really. It all seemed to happen so . . ."

"Naturally? Good lad. No doubt you convinced her that you actually admired her for her peculiarities and her rather unique appearance—"

"Beauty. And yes, she is very unique."

"How do you think grandmother will react?"

"I shudder to imagine."

Trey moved away. "I should see her as soon as possible, don't you think? Begin the arrangements for the ceremony—something quiet—find some village away from London so the entire affair is kept as low-key as possible. Grandmother will be agreeable, of course. She wouldn't want her friends to know too much about the chit—"

"Her name is Miracle." Clayton turned to look at his brother. They stared at each other across the room.

"I'm well aware of the young lady's name, Clay. You needn't remind me."

"She's twenty years old going on ten. She talks to animals—"

"Do they talk back?"

"Yes."

Again, Trey grinned. He dropped into a chair and stretched out his long legs. The top two buttons on his trousers were undone. His shirt fell open, completely exposing his hard chest, and he waited.

"She's . . . lost," Clayton continued. "Without home or family. But then, I'm quite certain you are already aware of that. Predators have a way of sensing weakness in their prey. She's desperately afraid of being abandoned again, but she trusts me . . . you. *The duke*. And she believes me —you—when I—*you*—say you'll never desert her."

Salterdon frowned and slightly pursed his lips.

"I fully believe that London society will break her heart, not to mention her spirit. The sooner you can get her away from here, the better."

"What about children?" Trey said. "Is she healthy enough to supply me with a few?"

"I thought you were interested in only one."

"A son, of course. Then again, our first might be cursed as female. We'll simply have to keep trying until a male or two is produced."

"And once she's produced the required son, or sons, what then? When you've finished breeding her, what then?"

"I suppose we'll cross that stream when we come to it, good brother."

Clayton took a long, slow breath and held it until his head buzzed. "I wonder if we might have turned out differently had our parents not died," he said.

"My goodness, we're maudlin today. This should be a day of celebration, m'lord Basingstoke. I finally intend to be married. I'll give our dour dowager duchess exactly what she wants: an heir to the dukedom. In the meantime, it's up to you to see that our little mouse remains adequately satisfied and sufficiently hidden until the time comes to reveal her. Of course, I'll pop in now and again to acquaint myself. Simply wouldn't do for me to marry a virtual stranger, now would it? Might make our wedding night a bit awkward. Wouldn't you agree?"

Clayton said nothing, just stood before his brother with his hands fisted at his sides, anger and confusion roiling in his gut as bitter as bile.

"Anything else?" the duke said, one corner of his mouth curled so sardonically Clayton thought of smashing in his teeth. "Is there something you wish to tell me?"

At last, Clayton shook his head. He quit the room, slamming the door behind him.

Disappointment to a noble soul is what cold water is to burning metal; it strengthens, tempers, intensifies, but never destroys it.

ELIZA TABOR

Chapter Fifteen

After searching the house on Park Lane for Miracle, Clayton still posing as the duke was informed by the tittering servants, Gertrude and Ethel, that her ladyship could be located out back, where she had spent most of her time since arriving yesterday. Clayton found Miracle in the small but adequate stable, a brick structure with a cobblestone floor and three stalls. She was giving the gangly, pimple-faced groom a thorough verbal trouncing.

"These conditions are appalling, Thaddeus. Simply appalling."

"Yes, milady."

"The bedding is filthy and the poor animals look as if they've not been curried in a fortnight. Subsequently, they're obviously miserable."

The lad's Adam's apple bobbed up and down as he hunched his shoulders and shuffled his feet.

"A healthy horse is a happy horse, Thaddeus, just like us. How would *you* like to spend *your* days and nights bogged up to *your* hocks in offal?"

"Yes, milady." Thad's eyes then found Clayton, where he casually leaned one shoulder against the laystall door. He smiled thinly and raised a finger to his lips, silencing the distressed young groom. The boy's face went beet red.

"A horse is a noble creature, Thaddeus," Miracle continued as she paced, hands on her hips, brow furrowed in a frown as she stared in concentration at the floor. "Once shown care and respect, the beast's loyalty will surpass even the most devoted friend's. Give me that fork.

"Thank you. Now, our first challenge will be to remove the morass and rebed with fresh straw. Filthy stables cause weak eyes, and a running at the nose. The decomposition of vegetable matter and the urine give out stimulating and unhealthy vapors, and a strong smell of hartshorn. How can it but cause inflammation of the eyes or lung, or glanders and farcy?

"I daresay the animals' hooves will be reeking of thrush, but we'll remedy that with a bit of . . . let me think." She chewed on the tip of one finger. "A poultice with linseed meal, I believe. Yes! We shall put it on hot and let it remain twelve hours; then use a paste made of two ounces of blue vitriol, one ounce white vitriol, powdered as finely as possible, and mixed well with one pound of tar and two pounds of lard. Will you remember this, Thaddeus?"

He nodded and stared at her dumbly.

"You'll apply the mixture into the cleft of the hoof and allow it to remain twelve hours, then remove it with soap and water. Once that's accomplished, I'll speak with His Grace about refurbishing this bleak abode with a few windows. 'Tis no wonder the gelding drains so at the nostrils. The respiratory problems caused by these damp, stinking surroundings will ultimately find His Grace's steeds dead as the proverbial doornail. I simply cannot think what would motivate a man of such esteem to ignore these trusted friends."

"Perhaps because that man of such esteem is too busy courting the woman of his dreams," Clayton announced, causing Miracle to jump and drop the fork. Her beautiful eyes suddenly wide and flashing with excitement, she flew into his arms, jumping up and down on his toes.

"You're back," she cried, covering his neck and jaw in kisses, hugging him fiercely. "I've missed you dreadfully, sir! I waited up half the night for you to return—"

Planting his hands on her shoulders to stop her jigging, Clayton flashed Thaddeus a smile and a quick nod of his head. In a wink, the lad scurried from the stable, leaving them alone.

"I should be careful about flaunting your obvious unbridled affections in public. No one talks faster, longer, or louder than the help."

"Why should we care?" she asked, trying her best to plant another wet kiss on his cheek.

Laughing, Clayton shook his head. "Meri Mine, what am I going to do with you?"

"Marry me, of course. Just as soon as possible."

"In due time."

"I thought you were most eager to make an honest woman of me, sir." She tilted her head and smiled temptingly.

He grinned at her infectious merriment. "There are certain—"

"Don't tell me," she interrupted, exasperated. Stepping away, grabbing up the fork, she proceeded to stab at the rotting straw. "There is a certain etiquette dukes must follow when they intend to take a wife, which is obviously why you didn't return to Park House once depositing me here so unceremoniously last evening."

"We hardly have the privacy that we did at Cavisbrooke."

She said nothing for a while, just poked at and slung straw into a pile outside the stall. Stink and flies rose in a cloud around her shoulders; she didn't seem to notice. "Your stalls, sir, are beggarly."

"I apologize."

She stabbed the straw once more before turning on him again. There was hay in her hair and fire in her eyes. The old belligerence was there, tottering on the edge of her forbearance. Clayton didn't know whether to be relieved that after these last three days of emotional lassitude she was finally showing signs of her old self, or to be wary.

"What now?" she demanded. "Do I spend my days talking to myself out of boredom while you hop about the city with your friends? And speaking of friends, you won't subject me to *their* company again, will you?"

"Their company?"

"The witless ne'er-do-wells I helped fish out of the tide along with you."

"Ah. I hadn't thought of that." He shrugged and replied, "I suppose it won't be beyond the realm of reason that you should find yourself in their company again. I'll try to keep it brief and infrequent, however. Will that make you happy?"

" 'Twould make me happier if you saw them not at all," she pointed out seriously.

"Good God. The woman is already attempting to peck at me. The next thing I know she'll be telling me what to eat, how to dress, and at what time I'm to be home at night."

"Which is what a wife is for, sir." She rewarded him with a sunny, entrancing smile that roused a surge of tenderness and protectiveness in him—and envy, if not outright jealousy of his brother. Yes, he was finally admitting it to himself. He wanted to break Trey in two with his hands, not only for perpetrating this damnable farce, but because he would have this glorious, breathtaking face to look at for the rest of his bastardly life.

"Among other things," he added under his breath, and grinned, allowing his gaze to travel slowly up from her ankles, to her breasts, to her face. Her big eyes regarded him languidly. Her soft, pink lips carried the slightest hint of a pout. Her cheeks looked rosy from her exertion and the heat in the stifling enclosure.

"Don't look at me in that manner," he told her in a rough, urgent voice.

"What manner, Your Grace?"

"As if you want me to come over there this minute and tear off your clothes. As if you want me to make love to you here and now."

"You haven't made love to me since the chapel," she pointed out in so low and sultry a voice he barely heard her. She briefly lowered her eyes; a move that, in any other woman, would have seemed excessively coy and would have irritated him to extremes. After all, he was not, and never had been, a man whose mind, heart, and body could be manipulated by female wiles. Miracle, on the other hand . . .

Forcing himself to look away, to ignore his body's rise in heat, the not so subtle awakening of his lower extremities, he ran his finger around the high, miserably stiff collar of his shirt. Damn her for her naïveté. Damn her for being so beautiful she robbed him of all willpower. Damn her for agreeing to marry him—or rather his brother. Damn her for falling in love with Trey Hawthorne, duke of Salterdon.

"What I did to you in the chapel could hardly be termed as lovemaking," he snapped irritably.

"No?" She moved toward him. "Then what was it, Your Grace?"

"It was . . . depraved. Animal. *Criminal.* My God, I've never been driven to such a flagrant act of . . . lust."

"No? 'Tis nice to know I have that effect on you, sir."

She ran her hand up his arm, to his shoulder, his ear, and the hair curling softly around it. He moved away, if only slightly. "This is neither the time nor the place, Meri."

"For one who once boasted so about his prowess, you've certainly made a turnabout since coming to London."

"They were a lot of doxies and dollymops," he argued. "They weren't you."

"Not even a kiss?"

At last, he allowed himself to look at her again—at her mouth. "No," he said with a dry throat. "Not even that."

The days passed, and the hours, giving Miracle too much time to dwell on her circumstances, not to mention her past. Her days were filled with confusion and guilt. She missed her home. She missed Napitov and Ismail. But mostly, she missed John. Now that her emotions had sufficiently calmed and she could think more rationally, she realized why John had done what he did and said what he had. She would never have left him otherwise; her love and responsibility to him ran too deep.

Time and again, she walked to the desk secretary and thought of writing him. But what would she say? I'm sorry? I miss you? I forgive you for all the lies? I understand that you only meant to spare me pain?

Dear John, this city is overwhelming and dirty and there is no sky to see or birds to hear and I haven't seen my fiancée in four days, and I'm afraid I'm on the verge of becoming dreadfully unhappy. Help!

Her nights were filled with thoughts of Salterdon. His arms, hands, and lips. His body in hers. Crushing hers. She awoke several times clutching her pillow, her legs wrapped around it, hugging it, the pressure in her loins so full and miserable she hurt. Dear Lord, what had she become? What was this new curiosity about her own body? Why did the mere thought of him bring about this miserable, craving heat? Why did she wake up twisted in her sheets, her body sweating and aching so horribly that the only surcease she could find was by her own hands? Oh, but she was doomed to hell for certain now. She began to dread the black eternal nights as she dreaded the long, empty days.

Miracle spent her days doing her best to engage the help in conversation. She followed them from room to room, chatting until she was blue in the face, and rarely getting a response other than "Yes, milady. No, milady. Very good, milady." On occasion, she attempted to help them. They wouldn't have it, and told her so in no uncertain terms. "Whoever heard of a lady beatin' carpets? Washin' dishes? Scrubbin' floors? We'd be findin' ourselves on the streets if His Grace were to learn of it."

"There's hardly any danger of that," she announced loudly enough that Gertrude, Ethel, and the cook all stopped their chores and stared at her as if she were daft. "Well," she said, "I haven't seen the cheeky beggar in four days. Obviously, he's forgotten all about me."

Cook, an overly thin Frenchman with a lisp, sniffed and replied, "His Grace is a busy man, Lady Cavendish. He has certain responsibilities."

"You're bloody right he does," she snapped back, making the man's upper lip curl. "And I'm one of them!"

It was then they suggested that she offer her services to Thaddeus, in the stables, which is where she was when her wayward fiancé finally called again.

"So tell me, Gertrude, how is our fair lady since I last saw her?" came the familiar voice from the foyer. Only, it wasn't familiar. Not really. There was something different about the way His Grace's words flowed in a sort of stiff monotone. Without emotion. Not that she should be surprised. With each brief and sporadic visit, the man who had so dramatically altered her life had changed: grown remote, moody, argumentative.

"Farin' just fine," the maidservant replied, and chuckled in the way that had won Miracle's heart completely. In truth, had it not been for Gertrude, Ethel, and Thaddeus, the last week would have seemed much worse. Gertrude's giggle reminded her of a gurgling brook, full of air and bubbles and lilting music. "She's a right ray of sunshine, Your Grace. Me and Ethel have grown right fond of her the last days. She's right intelligent and not nearly so tetched as we first thought when you sprung her on us."

"Oo, aye," Ethel Steckal, the upstairs maid, joined in. "I ain't had to pick up after her since she's been here. Right tidy, she is. Even plumps her own pillows and empties her own bath. And not once has I been forced to lug out her chamber pot—"

"Ethel!" scolded Gertrude. "Yer speakin' to His Grace!"

"Well I ain't," Ethel said with an added "hmph."

Footsteps sounded down the hallway, then diminished into the parlor.

"So where is our little saint?" came the muffled query.

Miracle frowned.

"Out back in the stables. Or maybe she's still in the library readin'."

"Good God, whatever for?"

"Sir?"

"What is she reading?"

"Them books you brung her four days ago."

Silence. Then, "Never mind. Tell her I wish to see her as soon as possible."

"Yes, Your Grace."

Miracle was still standing in the dim corridor, staring at her feet and trying to reason why the mere sound of Salterdon's voice should so unnerve her (aside from infuriating her because she hadn't spoken to him in four days) when Ethel rounded the corner. The slightly built servant, whose wiry hair and pointy little nose and chin gave her the appearance of a hedgehog, jumped as she came face to face with Miracle hidden in the shadows.

"Milady," Ethel squeaked. "Gor, but you 'bout give me a fit of apoplexy skulkin' there." The girl clutched at her heart and sank against the wall for effect. "His Grace wants to see you."

Miracle raised one eyebrow. "Summoning me, is he?"

"That's right." Tugging a kerchief from her frilly apron, Ethel dabbed it to her nose and sniffed. "The sooner the better."

"Serves him right if I refuse to see him at all. After all, I've heard not a willie's wick from him in all these days."

Scratching her armpit, Ethel shrugged. "Best get use to it, milady, if ya don't mind me sayin'. Dukes is busy men, 'specially durin' the season. 'Specially this duke. There ain't a highborn young lady in London who wouldn't like to get her claws into him. No one's succeeded, o' course, until you. I don't mind tellin' ya, milady, the lot of nobs is gonna be fair spittin' when they find out he's brung you to London to marry. I'd watch me back if I's you." She winked and bestowed Miracle a wide, mostly toothless smile. "Now ya best be off, miss. He don't seem to be in a patient sorta mood. Let's see yer hair. Are ya certain ya won't be pullin' it up, maybe addin' a pin curl here or there?"

"He's accustomed to my hair down," she replied, patiently allowing the girl to flitter around her, fluffing her hair then stepping back to scrutinize her dress.

"Maybe I should draw up a quick bath, milady."

"I think not. He's also accustomed to seeing me dressed like a waif."

"Suit yerself, luv." With one last adjustment of Miracle's tresses, Ethel hurried from the hallway and up the stairs. Miracle watched her until the girl paused halfway up, peered down at her, and shooed her with her hands.

Still, Miracle hesitated. For the last four days she had fumed over being deposited like some empty milk pail and forgotten. But the moment Thaddeus had burst into the stable, babbling excitedly that His Grace had arrived, she'd been overcome with her usual excitement over seeing him at last. Mayhap he had a good reason for up and disappearing.

Taking a deep breath, she lightly ran down the corridor and flung open the parlor door.

Standing at the secretary, filing through a stack of correspondence, the duke looked up.

Miracle froze.

"Well, well," he said with a half-smile, and tossed down the letters. "There you are."

"Your Grace," she replied almost silently, her eyes locked on his. "I thought you had forgotten me."

"Hardly."

"After not hearing a word from you in four days—"

"Pressing business. You understand."

He moved gracefully toward her, his step slow, a curl on his lips. The gray stones that were his eyes moved at leisure down her body, to her bare feet peeking from beneath her skirt hem.

His eyebrows went up; he stopped. "What, pray tell, is that?" He pointed at her feet.

"Toes," she replied, and wiggled them.

"I was referring to the rather objectionable substance between them."

"Oh." She studied them a moment, then curled them under. "Dung," she announced quite proudly.

"Ah. I should've guessed by the smell."

Miracle clasped her hands behind her back. "I was working in the stable, helping Thad."

"Thad?"

"Your groom."

"And what were you doing with Thad in the stables?"

"Horsing around." She giggled and bit her lip, dug her toes a little harder into the floor when he only stared at her as if she were some experiment in a chemist's phial.

At last, he relaxed somewhat. "Amusing."

"I thought so."

He turned back to the room, sauntered about it with his arms crossed over his chest.

"Your mood seems contemplative, sir. Is anything wrong?"

"Why do you ask?"

"You haven't so much as offered me a hug," she told him timidly.

Leaning back against the secretary, resting his weight slightly on his hands, he said nothing for a moment. Finally, he took a deep breath, smiled, and opened his arms. "Where were my thoughts? I'm sorry, love."

Ignoring the butterflies of consternation fluttering in her stomach, she eagerly danced across the floor and melted like liquid against him. His strong arms encircled her, held her close.

"I'm sorry I've been so neglectful," he said softly near her ear, his warm breath tickling her nape, stirring awake her passion. "London has a way of exhausting every free minute. When I've settled in better, we'll go for a tour."

"You promised that four days ago," she teased in her most sultry voice, and nibbled his ear, bringing about an intake of breath, a tensing of his body. His arms closed more tightly around her.

"Kiss me," she murmured, aware of the urgency of the words. "While there's no one watching."

A slow smile curved his mouth. He took her face in his hands, lightly, gently, and tipped her head to one side. His kiss was tentative at first, just a dry brush of his lips across hers, then he slid his mouth onto hers with a boldness and hunger that made her whimper.

He closed one hand on her breast, then slid it down her side, trailed it along her thigh, his fingers tugging up her skirt while his mouth did odd things to her senses. Very odd.

Then his fingertips slid up the inside of her leg while he imprisoned her with his other arm and kissed her so forcefully she thought her neck would snap.

She wiggled and attempted to break away. She was suddenly suffocating, repelled, and she shook her head, or tried to, and attempted to wedge her arms between them. "Please," she finally managed to gasp, and turned her face away. She struggled as he gripped her more tightly, buried his face in the curve of her throat and drew the delicately thin skin there between his sharp teeth.

"Stop," she said. "Don't—you're hurting me. Please, Your Grace, not here."

"Thought you missed me," he growled in her ear. Then his hand was on her there—between her legs, and as she tried her best to pull away, he spun her around, onto the desk, knocking knickknacks and paperweights onto the floor. With one quick movement, he flung up her dress and proceeded to unbutton his breeches.

There was a knock at the door.

He froze.

Closing her eyes, Miracle whispered, "Thank God. Thank God. Thank God—"

Gazing down at her, his gray eyes amused, one eyebrow lifted, he murmured, "What a shame. Just when we were getting started."

Miracle jumped away. She backed toward the door as Salterdon straightened and righted his clothes, flicked away a speck of lint from the sleeve of his immaculate, splendidly tailored, navy blue cutaway, and retucked his stock.

Another knock.

"What is it?" he replied.

"Lord Collingwood is here to see you, Your Grace," came the announcement through the door.

"Collingwood!" Salterdon strode past Miracle to the door and whipped it open.

"Salterdon," came the greeting. "I heard you were back in London. The fellows are meeting at the Windsor at Charing Cross at half-past. Come join us."

Still standing rock still, her hand pressed to her mouth, the somehow disturbing taste of him on her lips, Miracle tried to ignore the sense of coldness and anger that sank like an anchor in the pit of her stomach.

Where were the butterflies? That exhilarating rush of thrill she'd experienced at Cavisbrooke each time he touched her? Even when he looked at her with such smoldering eyes, her heart had stopped. Where was all that pent-up desire she had harbored for him the last many days?

Why had she felt so . . . repulsed?

The voices in the foyer rose and fell in camaraderie: boisterous and hardy, occasionally vulgar, reminding her of those awful days Salterdon and his friends had occupied Cavisbrooke. Miracle tiptoed toward the entry, only to be stopped short as Salterdon appeared again, a well-dressed stranger behind him and peering curiously over his shoulder.

"Sorry to rush," the duke told her with a smug grin. "Perhaps later we'll take up where we left off. Hmm?" Then he winked and closed the door in her face.

"Who, or rather what, was that?" came the amused query as they departed the house.

"No one," came the reply. "Simply an acquaintance."

A moment passed, then the door opened a fraction. Gertrude peered around the door, her wide, round eyes as big as pennies. "Never mind, lass," she said. "His Grace is a busy man."

"Obviously."

Drawing back her shoulders, her jaw set and chin thrusting, Miracle marched by the sympathetic servant and headed for the stairs.

"Will ya be havin' yer afternoon tea, milady?"

"No, thank you," she replied, her voice cracking.

Reaching her room on the second level of the four-story townhouse, Miracle kicked open the door, then stood for a moment, counting backward from ten while the pain in her toe throbbed abominably. Limping, she paced the floor, moving first to her bed, then to the window. Below, traffic moved up and down the crowded lane, and beyond that, riders paraded through Hyde Park on high-prancing blooded horses.

She thought of Napitov and Majarre, Aziz and Salifa. She thought of Ismail, stooped over his wujar or playing his flute. She thought of the lighthouse, dark now, with no one to run it. How many ships might be lost on the Race because there would be no light to warn them during the storms? She thought of her pigs and chickens and the doves that roosted in the moss growing so lushly along Cavisbrooke's skyward parapets.

Oh, John, if you were here, you would know what to do, to say. You would assure me that everything is going to be fine; that these terrible doubts that have arisen will soon go away; that I've made the right decision, that I've fallen in love with the right man.

Dear, sweet John: who had only wanted to protect her from all the ugly truths, whose devotion to her and her mother had never faltered through the years. He had sacrificed his life for them. If he were here, he would know what to do. If he were here, mayhap she wouldn't feel so lost and lonely and suddenly so desperately frightened.

"Lass," came Gertrude's voice close behind her. "Yer toe is bleedin'. Let me fetch ya a bowl of tepid water and—"

"No, thank you."

"Milady, ya mustn't take his rudeness of manner to heart. It's the way of 'em, ya know. And what with His Grace's friends all pilin' in for the high season—"

"Did you know," she interrupted, "that until I came to London, I wasn't aware of the season? I'm certain my mother must have spoken of it. She wasn't like me, you know. She had such grand dreams. She would've felt right at home in London, with these people. She would've known what to say and do, and she would never have cloistered herself up in this house, never seeing another soul."

She sniffed and did her best to smile. "I wonder if she felt this way before she . . . married my father."

"What way, milady?"

"Frightened. Confused. Disappointed. And . . . angry."

"I reckon all lasses would feel that way. But it all comes down to lovin' him, don't it? Ya do love him, milady?"

"I did. *I do!* It's just . . ."

She turned back to the bed and threw herself across it.

"There, there," Gertrude said, "if yer worried that His Grace ain't fond, well, I seen his face when he first brung ya here. I vow I ain't certain I ever saw him so happy. There was something in his eyes—"

"But it's not there now," Miracle argued. "At least, not today." She shivered with the memory of his touching her.

"Aye. He did seem a bit more like his old self. His Grace can be a mite on the temperamental side. Then again, the trait runs in his family. His brother—"

"But you don't understand." She buried her face in a pillow. "It's *more* than that. *More* than just being temperamental."

"What is it, lass? You can talk to Gertrude."

"Oh, Gerti," she wept. "His hands were cold!"

Remorse: beholding heaven and feeling hell.
GEORGE MOORE

Chapter Sixteen

"Hear ye all members of this said establishment, Brookes' Club for distinguished noblemen and gentlemen at sixty Saint James Street, that on this night of June, in the year of our Lord, 1800, the following rules will apply in the course of business:

No gaming in the eating room, except tossing up for reckonings, on penalty of paying the whole bill of the members present."

"Tossing up the bloody food is more like it," Lord Selwyn shouted, and the patrons of the club, which included James Fox, Lord Carlisle, Sir Stepney, and Lord Robert Spencer, the duke of Marlborough's brother, let out a tremendous shout of approval.

"We're damn tired of beefsteaks, boiled fowl with oyster sauce, and apple tarts for our dinner! I expect a bit of pheasant and fish for all the money I wager and lose in this dignified establishment," Sir Stepney declared with a roaring laugh, then added, "The Salon des Etrangers provides its noblemen with leg of mutton, roasted goose or pigeon, and currant pudding at no extra cost. I say we all hoist our sails for Paris, gents. All in favor?"

"And lick Napoleon's boots? Poppycock and balderdash. I'd feast on boiled beef until my dying day before I agree to that."

Someone pounded a gavel. Another rang a bell.

"Gentlemen, gentlemen!" the club crier beseeched the rowdy gamblers and patrons until their laughter subsided somewhat. Only then did he continue.

"Every person playing at the new guinea table do keep fifty guineas before him.

"Every person playing at the twenty guinea table do not keep less than twenty guineas before him. Hear ye, hear ye, so be the established rules of this order by Sir Brooks himself. Continue with your gaming, sirs."

"Continue with our gaming," Lord Spencer declared and lifted his glass of port toward the hazard table. "As if I ever stopped. But say, one of our fine colleagues is pocketing his guineas—sorry as they may be—and bidding us a fond goodnight—or mayhap not so fond. Basingstoke! One more go at faro and macao. I'll even spot you a few shillings. You damn well need it, the way you've been losing the last few nights. What's happened, ol' boy? Lady luck finally decide to shine her golden light on someone else for a change?"

Clayton pressed a coin into the servant's palm who delivered his coat and tried his best to ignore the cajoling of his boisterous companions. Briefly, he squeezed closed his burning eyes: too much smoke, too many late night hours, too little sleep. Too much ale and French wine. And bad gin.

He should be back at Basingstoke. Home. Pouring out his energy and frustration on turning the soil, on planting, building, instead of festering and growing more agitated in these stifling surroundings. He'd lost a bloody fortune the last few days, all because he couldn't keep his mind off Miracle Cavendish.

Why, dammit? Because she believed in flying? Because she communicated with animals better than she did with people? Or simply because she belonged to his brother . . . his brother who had had everything dropped into his lap from the first minute he was born, who'd yet to learn how to appreciate the wealth and power his station in life had brought him, who didn't have the slightest notion what a woman like Miracle Cavendish could do for him, if he allowed her?

He moved unsteadily toward the exit. Someone slapped a hand on his shoulder and breathed their distilled breath against the side of his face. "One more go, ya young bastard. I'm enjoying emptying your pockets too much, Basingstoke, after all the times you've sent me home with a gouged purse. A round at the whist table. What do you say?"

Clayton looked over his shoulder and into the bloodshot eyes of Sir Fritz Drummond, who had once belonged to one of His Majesty's three regiments of foot guards and had lost the position because of his penchant for gambling on the job.

"Sir," Clayton said in so soft and threatening a tone that Fritz's eyebrows went up. "Remove your hand from my shoulder."

"And if I don't?"

"Then I'll be forced to remove it myself."

"What's wrong, Basingstoke? Poor loser?"

"I'm too damn drunk to debate the issue, Drummond."

Sir Harry Calvert, adjutant-general to the duke of York, moved up and gently took Drummond's hand from Clayton's shoulder. "You don't want to fight him, Fritz. The last man who did wound up with a rapier stripe across his lower belly, just a humbling few inches from his most prized and personal assets." He smiled at Clayton. "We all know how Basingstoke feels about our occasional lack of decorum. No need to prove him right again. Go home and sleep it off, Hawthorne, whatever it is that's eating at you. I'm quite certain you'll be back tomorrow night in fine form, plucking our purses and robbing us all of our last shilling."

Saying nothing, Clayton turned his back on his companions and exited the club. Breathing deeply of the thick night air, he watched the traffic move up and down Saint James Street coming and going from one reception to the other. Ah, the season. The glorious, stomach-churning season. When every parent paraded their daughters down the potential path of marriage, hoping that someone like himself would pluck up the tender little chickens and carry them away to live happily ever after in the land of milk and honey. He'd already received two dozen invitations by post, another dozen hand delivered by starry-eyed mamas who were inordinately interested in Basingstoke Hall.

"So tell me, my lord, is it true that you decline to live in the house, choosing instead to reside in some apartment in the stables? You're waiting for the perfect woman to share it with? Have you recently seen my daughter, my lord? It just so happens I've dropped by to present you with an invitation to join our reception. You can't attend? Oh. Well. Tell me, Basingstoke . . . how is your brother the duke faring these days?"

A group of men rounded a corner, laughing, shouting comments to the travelers on the street. Clayton gave them little notice until they practically plowed him over. His patience at an end, he turned angrily . . . and looked directly into his brother's eyes.

"By gosh," the duke said, and broke into a smile. "Look who we have here, lads and ladies. Lord Basingstoke!" Trey slapped him on the shoulder and Trey's friends pressed close, all with slightly drunken smiles, each with their arm around women of questionable reputations. The female at Salterdon's side swayed a little, then grabbed his arm for support. She hiccuped, then giggled. "Haven't heard from you since you arrived back in London," Trey said.

Paying little notice to his brother's swaggering friends, Clayton focused on the street, did his best to block out the noise, the infuriating press of people, the fact that the stink of burning coal and horse dung burned his nostrils. Where the devil were cabs when you needed them? "You were to let me know before you came back to the city," he finally said to Trey.

"Was I? Yes, perhaps I was. Oh well, it was a spur of the moment move."

"The barrister must have come home from Madrid."

"Most unexpectedly."

Clayton whistled at a hackney, then noticed it was already occupied. "I suppose this means you'll be wanting to see Meri soon," he muttered under his breath.

His smile widening, the duke sidled closer, dragging his female companion with him, and gave Clay a wink. "Have done, ol' boy."

Clayton's eyes cut to Trey's.

"Yes." Trey continued in a low tone. "Just hours ago. Curiosity got the better of me, I confess. Wanted to see exactly what I was getting myself into. I realize it was a risky move, considering we haven't discussed the details of your stay at Cavisbrooke. Then again, I do so enjoy flirting with the razor's edge; must run in the family, don't you think, Clay?"

Moving around Clayton, pressing closer, Trey said near his ear, "Her mouth is delicious, wouldn't you agree? And that place between her legs . . . my God, it drove me out of my good senses."

Clayton walked away, or tried to. He was forced to elbow his way through the duke's sycophants, only to stumble into the street, straight into the path of a barreling post chaise. Trey grabbed him by his coat and dragged him back. Spinning, Clayton knocked his hand away, then planted one hand on his brother's chest and shoved him aside. The crowd whooped; the women squealed.

Gaining his footing and straightening his coat, Trey raised one eyebrow and tugged his arm free of the woman's grip. He forced a smile. "Seems my good brother isn't in the mood tonight for camaraderie, lads. I wonder why?"

Burying his hands in the duke's coat front and twisting, Clayton dragged Trey so close he could feel Trey's breath against his face. "What's even more curious than my mood is why, or how, you could leave the company of Lady Cavendish for that little tart there."

"Tart!" the woman at Trey's side squeaked. "Just who the blazes are ya callin' a tart? Yer Grace, will ya be allowin' him to talk to me that way? I'm a lady, after all, or so ya says."

"Seems you're a mite touchy about the girl," Trey commented to Clayton. "Then again, we're all aware of your commiseration toward the downtrodden. And she is an entertaining bit of stuff, not to mention comely . . . if you peel away the layer of horse dung between her toes. In fact, I would wager to say that my wedding night will prove to be more enjoyable than I had once believed . . . if her body proves to be as soft and curvaceous in bed as it did in my arms earlier this evening."

The world turned red. His voice low and savage, Clayton hissed, "What have you done to her?"

"What do you think?"

Clayton hit him. Hard. Across the jaw.

The duke flew backward with a grunt and groan of pain. His friends caught him before he hit the ground, and hoisted him to his feet. The suddenly silent crowd then moved back, while Trey returned Clay's fixed stare and raised one hand to tenderly smear blood from his lip. "It seems I hit a rather sensitive nerve," he said. "Perhaps my brother wishes to demand satisfaction. What do you think, lads? I wonder if there has ever been a duel fought between brothers—not just *any* brothers, mind you, but identical twin brothers. Might make good conversation at the chocolate houses. What say, Clay? Shall we give it a go?" Leaning closer and lowering his voice, Trey added with a droll smile, "Is her hot, willing little body worth dying over?"

Little by little, the anger drained from Clay, replaced by the thick, drugged sluggishness of inebriation and cold reason. What the devil was he doing, flogging his brother in public, allowing Trey to get under his skin, to aggravate the envy he'd experienced since putting eyes on Miracle Cavendish for the first time.

A hackney pulled up at that moment; Clay turned away from the crowd and his brother, and climbed aboard. He fell back into the worn seat only to discover his brother had partially mounted the step behind him.

"One thing more," the duke told him. "Until I've spoken with grandmother, our little fairy is not to be seen in public. I don't want word of my betrothal to reach the duchess before I do. In fact, grandmother is not to even know of my impending marriage until after the deed is done. I've some business that takes me to York for the next few days—"

"Have you had her?" Clayton blurted, his voice sounding exaggeratedly slurred in the stifling confines of the hot hackney. Sweat ran down his temples and burned his eyes. He thought he might vomit. He was certain he would if his brother confessed to making love to Miracle. He might even kill him, so desperate did he feel in that moment.

Trey regarded him intensely before responding less snidely. "That's really none of your business, now, is it, Clay?"

A moment of reasoning passed. Clayton shook his head, sank into the less than luxurious seat, and stared straight ahead.

Trey continued. "While I'm in York I'll make the necessary arrangements for the marriage . . . post the banns, et cetera. Then I'll return to London for the girl. Until then, brother Basingstoke, enjoy her while you can . . . with my blessings."

Stepping away from the cab, Salterdon slammed the door and barked something to the driver. The conveyance lurched away. The drone of traffic, of cabbies whistling and jousting for position, of horses whinnying, and the sound of iron wheels on the cobblestone road surrounded Clayton like a womb. He felt stifled . . . hot. He wanted to jump out of the hansom, run down his brother, and hit him again.

His head fell back against the seat, he closed his eyes, and imagined Trey sauntering into Park House to be greeted by Miracle, her face alive with excitement. He imagined Trey kissing her. Imagined her response: how she would mold her body into his, part her lips, eagerly accept his tongue. She always made a soft little sound in her throat—a sound of surrender, desire, mounting passion.

Ah, yes. Her mouth was delicious. The mere thought of it had driven him to bury himself in hazard every night and to drink himself into oblivion because it was the only way he could make himself stay away from her. The only way he could take his mind off the reality that his brother was going to marry her.

Damn him. Damn him.

Damn Trey Hawthorne, the duke of Salterdon, for not realizing what he had.

"Sir? You! Asleep in me bloody box, wake up."

He opened his eyes. Where was he?

Forcing himself, he scrambled out of the hackney, stood for a moment on the curb, and tried to focus on his surroundings. The houses, with their striped awnings and flower boxes at the windows, all glowed with light. Occasionally, music drifted to him. Laughter. On the opposite side of the street stretched the dark Hyde Park. A lone rider on his high-prancing steed trotted down Rotten Row, the long strip of reddish brown earth running along the green, singing as loudly and drunkenly as he could.

Park House. How the blazes had he ended up here?

He dug for a coin in his pocket, and found nothing.

Clamoring onto the hackney, the driver called back, "His Grace done took care of it, sir."

"I see. Did His Grace also tell you to bring me here?"

"He did, sir," he replied through the dark. Then, with a snap of his whip, the horses pranced away, leaving Clayton standing on the sidewalk and staring at his brother's townhouse.

With a will not of his own, he moved through the white picket gateway with its trellis of roses, along the garden path flanked by sweet Williams and pansies, up the steps, through the unlocked entry, and into the foyer, where he came face to face with a startled Gertrude dressed in her sleeping gown and ruffled nightcap, her hands full of cheese and bread as she made her way to her own sleeping quarters.

"Lud!" she cried, and jumped back, flinging her bedtime snack to the floor where it landed with a thump on her foot. "Ya startled me, Yer Grace, comin' at me through that door with no warnin'. What's a lass to think, sir? Ya could have been some mucky man out to make mischief with me body or someaught." Squinting to better see him in the dim light, she studied his face, her own screwing into a look of consternation as her eyes traveled down, over his simple frock coat, to his leather breeches, Hessians, and spurs.

"Where is she?" he demanded in a rough voice, bringing her penny eyes flying back up to his.

"Yer . . . Grace?"

"Miracle, dammit. Are you deaf as well as dumb?"

Bosom swelling with indignation, Gertrude huffed, but before she could respond, a door opened on the above landing. Dressed in a white, floor-length cotton gown, Miracle floated partially down the flight of winding stairs before stopping stock still at the sight of him. One hand gripping the balustrade, her hair loose and wild and flowing all the way to her knees, she looked as if he had awakened her. Her eyes were dark and sleepy. Her mouth slightly pouting. She didn't smile or speak, but glared at him as she had the day he'd first arrived at Saint Catherine's Hill. All that was missing was the howling wind and a rampaging sea.

"Get out," he growled at Gertrude as she attempted to grab up her cheddar from the floor. When she didn't comply immediately, he shouted again, "Get out and stay out, unless you wish to find yourself unemployed on the morrow."

She scurried from the room. A door slammed in the distance.

His gaze still fixed on Miracle, Clayton moved to the bottom of the stairwell, one foot resting on the bottom step. "Come here," he ordered her.

"Nay. I think not."

"Come here, dammit. Now."

A moment's hesitation, then she slowly descended, stopping only when they stood face to face. "You're inebriated," she stated with no emotion.

"Yes. I am. I'm drunk. And angry. And jealous. What do you have to say about that?"

She appeared to ponder the question. Then, with no warning, she slapped his face. Not once, but twice. As fiercely as she could. So fiercely her fingers curled from the sting of fiery pain. Then she drew back her shoulders and thrust up her chin. "That's for bringing me to this detestable city. And for deserting me the last week. For disappearing for four miserable days without a word of explanation, then for showing up this afternoon with no solitary sign of contrition for your behavior—and for treating me like a barbarian, then leaving me again only moments after you arrived."

He moved up the step.

Miracle retreated a stair, stepping on her gown hem in the process. It clenched upon her neck like a noose.

"Tell me," he said softly. "Did you enjoy my kiss this afternoon, Meri Mine?"

"No. I . . . I detested you this afternoon! Everything about you. Your horrid hard eyes and that infuriating way you have of smiling as if everyone else in the world were bugs. That way you have of making the rest of us plebeians feel inferior. But I shan't feel inferior to you or anyone else in this godforsaken city.

"No! I did not enjoy your kiss this afternoon, sir. I hated the feel of your hands in my hair, on my face and—and body. I grow ill now to think of it. Stand away! Don't touch me. Not with those hands. They're cold. Horribly cold. Even now I shiver to think of them on me! Oh, go away, Salterdon, and leave me alone. I wish . . . I wish I had never come here! I wish I had never fallen in love with you. I want to go home. To Cavisbrooke. At least I was happy there!"

Miracle fled up the stairs, into the dark, tripping on her gown hem, stumbling, refusing to look back because already his dark eyes and the red imprint on his cheek were haunting her and regret was caught like a fish bone in her throat. She wanted to take back all the ugly words that had just spilled from her mouth because she had trooped down those stairs with her well-rehearsed speech anticipating coming face to face with the cold-blooded, frigid-handed, swell-headed buffoon she had grown to loathe those months ago at Cavisbrooke. There was no way this side of perdition she would marry *that* man. Instead, the moment her palm had connected with his cheek, the very instant that look of surprise, pain, and vulnerability had flashed through his eyes, she had felt herself tumbling back into that same guagmire of confusion in which she had flailed throughout the afternoon.

How could she detest the man one moment and grow weak with love for him the next?

How could she loathe the touch of his hand, and now—God help her—desire him again?

Why the blazes did love have to be so irrational and painful?

He followed her up the stairs, his footsteps thundering and vibrating the floor like an earthquake. She ran down the corridor to her room, attempted to slam the door in his face, but he kicked it open, propelling it against the wall so hard two pictures fell from the wall.

Backing toward the window, hands fisted, teeth clenched, she declared, "Get out. I don't want you here."

"My house, remember? We're not at Cavisbrooke any longer, Meri Mine. I can bloody well come and go as I please. As the duke of Salterdon, I can damn well take what, and who, I want. That's what birthrights will do for you, sunshine. Meri Mine. Come here."

"Go to blazes."

Her eyes wide, her back pressed painfully against the windowsill, Miracle reasoned feverishly. "If you touch me I'll scream. I'll jump from this window. I'll—I'll—"

"You didn't object so strenuously this afternoon, did you?" he demanded through his teeth.

"Stay away from me or I'll—"

"You'll do nothing," he said in so deep and silky a voice her heart skipped. He was little more than a shadow before her, tall, broad, looming and threatening, until he stepped into the faint light spilling through the open window at her back. Then his dark eyes turned to tiny sparks of fire.

Lifting one big hand to her face and cradling her small cheek, he murmured, "Did I say you'd do nothing? I was wrong. I know exactly what you'll do. You'll roll those big green eyes up to mine and with one coy lowering of those outlandish lashes, you'll turn me inside out. You'll make me crazy. You'll make me want you more than any woman I've ever known. You'll wrap me up in your magic and make me, for a little while, feel happier than I've felt in my life. You'll make me look forward to tomorrow, when so many bleak and lonely tomorrows have rolled past me I once thought I would rather be dead than face another one alone."

Curling his long fingers around her nape, he gently pulled her against him, pressed her head to his chest, slid his hands into her hair, and kissed the top of her head. "Meri, Meri," he breathed. "Don't be angry with me. I thought I could do without you. I tried. But I've found that I want you now more than ever, and time is running so damn short."

She started to speak.

"Don't," he told her, and tipped up her chin with one finger. "Forgive me. I never meant to hurt you, sweetheart." He saw the passion bruise on her neck—a dark shadow on her white skin—and a look that was almost terrifying crossed his anguished features. "Bastard," he murmured, then clutching her jaw in his fingers, he demanded, "Make love to me. As if we'll never hold one another again. I need you tonight, Meri Mine. Please . . ."

Forgetting her earlier anger, forgetting that just moments before she had been ready to fly out the window in an effort to escape him, Miracle closed her eyes, surrendering to the odd, confusing effect his nearness stirred inside her. *This* man's hands were warm, tender, stirring the blood in her veins with a mere brush of his fingertips upon her flushed and tingling skin. He made her want him with every fiber of her being. He made her, with a simple whispered word, ache in the very pit of her heart and deep into her soul. Ache with love. And desire. And passion. Perhaps tomorrow she would dwell again on that *other* man, the one who occasionally roused to so infuriate her, but tonight *this* was the man she loved. This was the man she would marry—no other.

His hands lifted the gown over her head, then dropped it to the floor. The cool breeze through the window made her shiver as she stood before him, nude, her hair slightly dancing across her back and shoulders and falling softly as down over her breasts.

He lowered his head, and as her eyes drifted closed, she felt his lips against her cheek, slightly moist and soft, his breath smelling faintly of sweet liquor, his clothes a little of fragrant tobacco. Then his hands slid beneath her breasts, gathering them gently in his long fingers, his thumb stroking the tight, erect nipples so gently she trembled.

"Oh, oh," she murmured, and swayed against him, all resistance lost. And to think that just moments before she actually thought that she hated him; that she hoped to never see him again; that she had actually contrived to leave Park House at dawn and return to Cavisbrooke, hoping to put him behind her forever.

"Oh," she sighed, and smiled, and quivered. The fragrance of his skin filled her senses. The steady beat of his heart beneath her hand made her whimper with a new pleasure that dissolved in a hot ecstasy that mounted until control vanished like mist. Her legs throbbed, the mound between them swelling unbearably and uncontrollably.

"Tell me you want me, Meri Mine." His voice was husky and urgent.

"Yes. I want you."

"How badly do you want me, Meri? Show me."

"But ladies don't—"

"Show me, dammit. Make me believe."

Her hands went to his breeches, tore at the buttons, releasing them one by one until his heavy splendid organ sprang into her hand, grew larger and harder and arced like a magnificent sword toward her body's opening.

He lifted her onto the windowsill and parted her legs, moved between them, sliding his body into hers little by little until she whimpered, until she clutched at his hips, until he filled her to the extreme, until she was forced to grip his shoulders, the back of his neck, to raise her hips to accept all of him.

He shuddered.

She couldn't breathe.

His arms around her, holding her fiercely, he said, "Don't move, Meri Mine. I want to stay this way forever. Would you mind?"

Swallowing, her eyes closed and her ear pressed against his chest, she shook her head. "I think not," she finally managed. "But I wonder what the good folk on the street would think tomorrow were they to look up and see us."

Laughter, like gentle thunder, sounded in his chest, and he squeezed her tightly—so tightly—just before his hips began to slowly pump, to withdraw and drive, to awaken the pain, the beautiful pain, that started like an ember in the heart of her womanhood and radiated outward, to every extremity, to her fingers and toes, to grip her heart and lungs, to sluice through every muscle until she could no longer control herself.

A moan rose from her. She grabbed the windowsill for support. Her head fell back, her body arched, offering up her breasts, which quivered with each deep thrust he made into her body. When she thought she could stand no more, he moved his hand down between her legs, there, where their hot, wet bodies were joined, and stroked the swollen apex of her desire.

The cataclysm came, rising up like swift liquid pulsating fire, turning her body to stone, incapable of movement, erupting, ripping, disintegrating. Consciousness became water—deep and dark and rushing. Roaring. Sweeping her away on a tide, and in some distant space of her mind, she wondered if she were dying, and she sobbed shamelessly.

Gently, gently, the tide ebbed. She awakened. Opened her eyes that were streaming with tears.

His face above her was pained, yet his eyes were soft and shining, his mouth faintly smiling. Then the rhythm began again, and his countenance became chiseled stone. He moved his body in and out of hers, striving for the beautiful death himself, faster and faster, nearly bruising her from the mounting, necessary frenzy, each impact lifting her hips from the windowsill, their bodies slapping together, flesh against flesh, sweat against sweat, and suddenly, the spasmodic fire sprang up inside her again unexpectedly.

The climax erupted through him, growled up from his chest, made his body into stone that shook and convulsed and exploded into her. His head thrown back, his fingers digging almost painfully into her bare buttocks, he allowed the flood of life to fill her up, even as her own body shook and quaked and quivered with its final release.

"Meri, Meri," he moaned. "My divine little girl. My . . . Miracle." He sighed and shivered and hugged her fiercely to him. "I love you."

The way to love is to realize that it might be lost.

GILBERT K. CHESTERTON

Chapter Seventeen

Miracle sat throughout the morning at the bedroom window, temple resting against the frame, the warm sun in her face, as she watched the hectic activity on the street below. Occasionally, she lifted the freshly cut rose she had found on her pillow when awakening earlier, and she twirled it beneath her nose. Its petals were soft yellow, its leaves dark, waxy green. It smelled like heaven.

She smiled drowsily.

How beautiful the world seemed this morning! Sparkling fresh. Vibrant. For the first time since arriving in the city she longed to join the hustle-bustle going on around her. This was *his* world, after all. She fully intended to accept it. To conquer it. It was the least she could do for the man she loved. Oh, how she loved him!

Her heart thrilled at the very memory of their lovemaking the night before, here, at the window. On the floor. The chair, and, last but not least, the bed, until the first streaks of red-gold sun began to paint the gray sky with dawn light. She had then slept the deep sleep of exhaustion and happiness, stirring only when he lightly kissed her cheek and whispered, "I'll be back, my love, I promise."

"Yes, but when?" she now said aloud, gazing down on the street, then laughing. She turned away from the window, hugged herself, and twirled around, just as Gertrude walked to the door. The servant regarded her with round eyes and pursed lips, causing Miracle to laugh even harder.

Dancing across the room and grabbing the startled servant in a fierce hug, Miracle said, "It's a glorious morning, Gerti! Don't you agree?"

"Yes, milady, but—"

"Of course it cannot compete with a ride on Napitov along the channel with sea spray and fog kissing my face. Nay, I shan't think of Napitov now. I refuse to feel maudlin on so wonderful a morning. By the way, did His Grace mention when he might return? I should bathe and brush my hair, perhaps change my dress. I want to look perfect when I see him again. Ethel!" she called from her doorway. "Will you draw me a bath? And use a touch of that rosewater you produced yesterday! Mayhap I'll even weave a few of these roses into my hair. I think he would like that. My dear

Gertrude, why are you standing there like a statue? Have you nothing to say?"

The maid wrung her hands and fiddled with her apron. A crease of concern marred her brow. "Milady . . . lass . . . I was wonderin' . . . just how long have ya known His Grace?"

Dragging a brush through her hair, regarding the bloom of color the mirror reflected off her cheeks, Miracle smiled sheepishly. "Four months total, I think. Three of which I deplored him. Can you imagine, Gertrude? When I first met the duke and his delinquent cohorts, I thought him indecorous. Arrogant. With a heart like a stone and a soul as black as the pit. He was rude and cold and . . . but not any longer," she pointed out to Gertrude's mirrored image. " 'Twas once said to me by my mother that true love can change the most ignorant and savage of men. 'Tis proven to be true. Yes! The man who returned to me not so long ago is of a completely different nature, my dear Gertrude. Don't you agree?"

"Oh, yes, milady," she replied under her breath. "He's most definitely a different man. Umm, has His Grace ever spoken of his family, miss?"

Tying her hair to the top of her head in preparation for her bath, Miracle nodded and grabbed a hairpin from the dressing table.

"And did he happen to mention he had a brother?"

"A farmer who lives in a stable. Can you imagine, Gertrude? Where is Ethel with my bathwater? I fear he'll return before I'm dressed."

"The brothers were quite close, milady. Ya know what they say about blood bein' thicker than water. There's probably naught they wouldn't do for one another."

Miracle ran to the open window and gazed down on the traffic in the street, the pedestrians who moved up and down the walk, the women with their parasols, the men with their top hats and walking canes. No sign yet of Salterdon. Looking back at Gertrude, she frowned.

"Oh my, Gerti, you look white as a sheet. Is something wrong?"

"Well, I . . . I . . . milady, I don't know how to say this, and I'll no doubt lose me position, but . . ." The woman chewed her lip, her worried eyes closely regarding Miracle's features. "Yer truly in love with the man, milady?"

Miracle nodded.

"And I reckon it would break yer heart if he turned out to be . . . less than what you thought him to be?"

"Miserable. I've given up everything I once had for him. I should be lost as the proverbial goose if it weren't for His Grace. Why, Gertrude? Have you something to tell me? Is there something I should know?"

Ethel appeared at the door, clutching a sloshing bowl of steaming water.

Hair spilling into her eyes from beneath her frilly cap, she announced, "Y've got a visitor, milady."

"His Grace—?"

"A Mistress Ellesemere, milady. Says she's come by orders of His Grace."

Ellesemere?

Miracle eased from the room, walked lightly on the balls of her bare feet to the top of the stairs. Below her in the foyer waited a slender, prim, gray-haired woman in a plain, high-waisted muslin gown and a frilled tucker with tiny pleats around her neck.

Ethel tapped her on the shoulder. "Yer shoes, milady."

Miracle took the slippers and slid them onto her feet. Only then did she cautiously, watchfully, make her way down the stairs.

Mistress Ellesemere regarded her closely, her brown eyes bright with curiosity . . . and humor? "Lady Cavendish?" she said, smiling. "I was sent to Park House by . . . His Grace, the duke of Salterdon . . ." Clasping her hands before her, tilting her head first one way, then the other, her gaze ran up and down Miracle, hesitating on her hair, then her dress, and finally, her somewhat tattered shoes. "Fascinating. I can see what he meant now. A diamond in the rough. A jewel in need of a bit of spit and polish."

Miracle frowned.

Mistress Ellesemere circled her, her "hmms" punctuated by an occasional "ahh."

"I feel like a bleeding horse," Miracle finally blurted. "Would you like to see my teeth as well?"

"Spoken crassly, but reflecting a certain quantum of humor. But to be witty is not enough, my dear. One must possess sufficient wit to avoid having too much of it. Especially in this day, when women are encouraged to be seen and not heard."

"Who are you?" Miracle demanded. "And why are you here?"

"How remiss of me." Mistress Ellesemere offered her hand. "I assumed he had spoken to you on the matter. Obviously, he hasn't. His Grace has employed me for your benefit. To act as your companion, to . . . smooth away a few of your rougher edges. To . . . educate you in your role as the future duchess of Salterdon."

"Oh," she mouthed, and felt the slow creep of anger rise up her neck to settle like hot torches on her cheeks.

"Obviously, His Grace feels I'm lacking in certain qualities deemed important to his family and peers," she said in a tight voice.

Mistress Ellesemere moved up behind her and gently brushed a length of hair that had tumbled from the knot on her head back over her shoulder. "He's not ashamed of you, my dear. Far from it. In truth, I've never known this particular man to care so deeply for a woman. He simply wants to assure that you're happy as the duchess. A life that such a position offers can be trying, even for the most prepared—"

Miracle moved away.

Mistress Ellesemere took a deep breath and slowly released it. "He told me there could be some resistance—"

"Then he shouldn't have sent you. I fear he's wasted your time and mine. I'm perfectly capable of carrying out my duties as the duke's wife without any sort of interference or . . . tutoring . . . or— If His Grace finds my person and manner so objectionable, I cannot imagine why he would harbor the least amount of desire whatsoever to marry me. Therefore, you may leave and inform His Grace that your services are not required."

Hands clasped again in a show of patience, her chin set as stubbornly as Miracle's, Mistress Ellesemere shook her head. "I cannot, Lady Cavendish. I'm employed by His Grace; therefore, I take my directives only from him. My personal belongings should arrive—"

"Your personal belongings?"

"Of course. I'm to live here. To companion you."

"Then *I* shall leave."

"Whatever pleases you, my dear."

They glared at one another.

Finally, Miracle turned on her heel and marched for the door, threw it open, and came face to face with three burly, whiskered men hefting trunks on their backs. She watched them parade past her into the house, then continued her belligerent descent down the steps, her stride lengthening down the path and out the gate, into the throng of citizens in high hats and neat broadcloth cutaways, smack into the middle of the beautiful women draped in their fancy silks and simpler clinging muslin gowns with scalloped hems that dragged the ground.

Bumped and jostled, swept helplessly along in an effort not to be tripped or trod upon, Miracle moved amid the crowd, her face still burning, her mind racing, paying little attention to where she was going.

Just who the blazes did he think he was, insinuating that she was less than worthy, in her current state, to represent his family in marriage?

He sure as blazes hadn't cared how she acted or what she looked like when they were on the isle—or in bed.

But this wasn't the isle. Far from it. These were no farmer's wives and daughters with shoulders stooped from labor and brows wrinkled from squinting hard to see their sewing at night in candlelight, but brightly colored, elegantly gowned women carrying parasols and shopping baskets, beaded reticules dangling from silk cords around their wrists, all with exuberant faces, laughing and discoursing with their companions.

Miracle allowed herself to be swept along, suddenly mesmerized, a little frightened, and very overwhelmed by the sights, sounds, and smells. They bombarded her from every side. On the pavements apprentices, freshly risen from their masters' counters, were taking down the shutters of bow-fronted multipaned windows, and ragged urchins were leapfrogging over the posts. Amid the wide, clean streets, there were brewers' drays, drawn slowly by draft horses; vast hooded wagons with wheels like rollers, and carts with hay for the London markets were stopped in the middle of the road, causing hackney coaches to stack up behind them, giving cause for the aged jehus waiting on their stands to jump up on their boxes to shout and shake their fists.

Little by little, she forgot her nervousness. What was there to be nervous about, after all? No one seemed to notice her. Why should they? She was no different from them. Besides, she was going to marry the duke of Salterdon very soon and once she did, there wasn't a solitary woman, no matter how refined and exquisitely dressed, who wouldn't accept her. She would be certain to explain *that* to Salterdon when she saw him again.

She walked for miles, it seemed, down one street after the other, flotsam in the rushing tide of activity. Store windows crowded the pavements, and she stopped to stare, her hands pressed against the glass windows. There were more silks, muslins, and calicoes in every color and print than she could wear in a year. China and glassware, jewels and silver all glittered with everything the heart of man and woman could ever desire.

On and on she went, deeper, little noticing as she passed from the finer district to less prosperous surroundings. Gradually, the flood of finely dressed folk dispersed into workmen in aprons and padded leather jackets, raree-show men carrying the mysteries of their trade on their backs, and women selling canaries from wicker cages on church walls. How loudly and beautifully the tiny birds sang, regardless of their sad, filthy, and overcrowded cage. Puffing out their tiny pale yellow chests, they warbled as if doing their best to be heard amid the cacophony.

Smiling, Miracle paused to listen, to coo and encourage the lyrical creatures. She stuck her finger through the wires, and giggled as a particularly scrawny bird with a crooked leg perched upon it and proceeded to sing.

"You!" the bird lady shouted. "You in the brown dress. Away with ya! Ye'll damn well find yer own corner to hustle, if ya know wot's good for ya. This is my bloody portion and I ain't givin' it up to the likes of you."

Looking around, regarding the hag with strawlike hair sprouting from beneath a crumpled velvet hat decorated with stuffed, faded canaries, Miracle said softly, "Were you speaking to me?"

"Who the blazes else would I be spakin' to? The bleedin' queen of the Nile?"

Slowly, Miracle straightened. "I was only admiring your birds." She attempted a smile, only to be greeted with a sneer and smirk as the hag of a woman moved closer, her hands on her hips. "Who buys them?" Miracle asked, hoping polite conversation would win over the sour dealer.

"You daft?" the woman barked. "Who the devil do ya think buys 'em? Miners, o' course."

"Miners? Whatever for?"

"T' take down t' bloody hole. Fer the gases." The woman tapped her temple as if mocking Miracle's intelligence. "If there's gas in the mines, the birds die first."

"Oh!" Miracle cried. "That's dreadful. Cruel. They're far too lovely to sacrifice. How could you do it? Wouldn't a crow or rook or some such pest work just as well?"

"Ya keep panderin' on me corner and I'll bloody well use you," the woman cried, and gouged Miracle in the chest with one finger. "Now bugger off, me fair little doxy, afore I start screamin' foul."

"Ouch!" Miracle cried and stumbled back. "Madam, just who do you think I am? Or rather, what do you think I am?"

One eye squinted, her fists still plunked on her scrawny hips, the bird lady leered at her. "No guesses yer one of them Spitalfields dollymops tryin' to cop a quid for yer doss tonight."

"Dollymop! My good woman, I'm Lady Cavendish—"

"Ha! *Lady?* Ain't no lady I ever saw wot dressed like that."

"What's wrong with the way I'm dressed," she demanded angrily.

"Looks like somefin retrieved by the damn bone grubbers and rag men. Lady. Bah! Eh, Barney!" she yelled at the paunchy leather-aproned butcher across the way. "This bit of fluff says she's a lady."

"Oh! How dare you," Miracle declared, then with dismay, she noted that several men in sweat-stained clothing had stopped their labors and begun to laugh and comment. Her face burning, she stared at the sneering woman, no longer comprehending her insults or wanting to. The spot on her chest where the hag had poked her throbbed abominably, and for the first time, as she glanced around, searching for an avenue that would offer her the quickest, most dignified escape, she noted that the once fine and stately houses of the West End had become a sprawl of unfinished jerry-built houses and less-than-prosperous businesses. She noted, too, the scattering of women occupying street corners, their clothes thin from wear, their shoes patched. They shouted now and again to the more finely dressed pedestrians, who ignored them, and the women even went so far as to approach the occasional coach that was forced to stop in traffic.

"Very well," she said through her teeth, and rewarding the black-toothed crone a thin little smile, she casually reached over and flung open the birdcage door. With a sudden, startling whoosh, the birds came swooping out in a flapping, twittering, yellow cloud.

"Arrch!" the drab shrieked, and made a frantic, futile attempt to grab the escaping birds in midair. "Me birds! Me bloody birds! Devil! Witch! Help! Somebody grab her! Stop her! Police!"

Miracle moved away, her stride lengthening, until she began running. She ran until the woman's shrieks diminished into the drone of activity surrounding her, until she was brought up short by the looming, gloomy facade of Saint Luke's hospital for the insane, with its Hogarthian figures of Melancholy and Raving Madness flanking the gated entrance. Her breath coming fast, she clutched the locked iron entry and stared up the black-sooted stone walls, to the equally sooted windows that were open now, revealing the white, emaciated faces of the inhabitants, all staring down at her with vacant eyes.

She turned away, frantically searched the street, the buildings, the river of blank faces moving before her—all intent on their destinations—not a one of them noticing her. She might as well have been a crack on the pavement.

Then came a flutter near her face. She looked around. The canary with the crooked leg perched on her shoulder, cocked its head, and began to sing brilliantly.

A hand slammed down on her other shoulder; she cried out in surprise and hurt. The grip felt crucifying, and she spun around.

The gate of Saint Luke's gaped open like a mouth. A dingy-coated attendant stood there, while the other, dressed similarly, but standing a foot taller, held onto her with a hand like a vise.

"Goin' somewhere?" he growled, and rewarded her with a rotten smile.

"You must understand, Your Grace. These pitiable creatures are constantly finding their way out of the buildings and onto the streets. There isn't enough staff to oversee everyone and there is precious little funds for the proper precautions. My attendants were simply going about their responsibilities as so directed. When they saw the girl, she was more than apparently confused and aggravated. She fought them tooth and nail, screaming at the top of her lungs in despair and claiming to be a lady. Not only that, but she claimed to be the future duchess of Salterdon and demanded that we contact you. She seemed so . . . adamant, Your Grace. You must understand, we at Saint Luke's must take all precautions before admitting a patient. Therefore, I thought it best to send for you. I realize what an imposition this must be—"

"Get on with it," Clayton snapped at the nervous administrator, and continued to pace, trying his best to ignore the distant noises echoing down the tunnellike chambers of the institution. Mistress Ellesemere sat in a straight-backed chair against the wall, her gaze following him, her reticule gripped with both gloved hands in her lap.

Administrator Wilkes nodded at an assistant. A door was opened, allowing the humanlike howls and wails to tumble in, along with the stench of physical and mental decay.

Clayton stared at the wall, his hands in his coat pockets, and wondered what his punishment would be for murdering his brother.

"Your Grace," Wilkes intruded. "The girl. Do you know her?"

He turned toward the door, and there was Miracle.

Each of her arms was held tightly by an attendant. She stared up at Clayton with round, glassy eyes and her stubborn little chin faintly quivering.

"Release her," he growled in so threatening a tone, Wilkes jumped in alarm.

"Your Grace," the administrator whispered. "I understand your position. If she is someone—shall we say an acquaintance you would rather not publicly acknowledge—"

"On the contrary, Mr. Wilkes. The lady is exactly who she claims to be. The future duchess of Salterdon. Now tell your bullocks there to take their goddamn hands from my fiancée before I bring charges against this establishment for kidnapping and abuse."

Once freed, Miracle swayed unsteadily. Clayton moved forward, wrapped his arms around her, and supported her slight weight against him. She trembled, though she tried not to. He could feel the emotion raging inside her, and her valiant struggle to contain it.

"Shall we go home?" he asked her softly.

Her head nodded. Her small white hands clutched at his coat front.

"Ah . . ." Wilkes intruded, his features becoming more discomfited by the moment. "There is another slight issue, Your Grace. A Miss Crabb, sir. Seems there was a slight altercation between her and Lady Cavendish."

Clayton frowned, feeling his entire body go rigid. He smelled entrapment brewing, which was just one of the many nuisances his class was forced to endure the moment men like Wilkes, who profited in human weakness and frailty, sensed there was a shilling or two to be had.

"Altercation." It wasn't a question.

A door opened then. A hag blundered into the room, lips curled, eyes wild, growing wilder upon seeing Miracle. "That's her! I'd know her anywhere. Come flyin' at me, she did, squawkin' about me canaries. The next thing I know, she's gone and released them. Ever' bleedin' one of 'em! Now I ast ya, gents, just wot the blazes am I suppose to do about me livelihood until I get new birds?"

Clayton's eyes shifted to Miracle, who continued to huddle close, her head turned from the hag, but refusing to look up at him. He felt the granite tenseness of his shoulders relax, and his features softened. "Meri," he said gently, "is this true?"

" 'Course it's true!" the woman barked. "Do I look like a bleedin' liar?"

Raising one eyebrow, he fixed the drab with a stony look that caused her mouth to snap shut.

"Meri," he said again, and this time, she pulled away, and tugged loose the ribbon beneath her chin. There came a wiggling between her breasts, then the scrawniest canary he'd ever seen, with a crooked leg, scrambled out of Miracle's blouse, hopped onto her shoulder, then onto the top of her head. It flurried its wings, and proceeded to sing.

Clayton looked around at Ellie.

Ellie covered her mouth with her gloved fingers, her cheeks growing rosy with suppressed mirth.

"We'll reimburse you, of course," he said to the hag.

"Damn right, ya will."

"What will it cost me to keep you from pressing charges?"

"I'd say at least . . ." Her mouth screwed to one side and her eyes narrowed. "Twenty quid."

"Twenty . . . ?" He took a breath. "Very well. I'll see to it. Now, if you'll excuse us, the young *lady* has had a trying afternoon."

Mistress Ellesemere preceded them from the building and was settled into the shiny, black-lacquered coach with its red and gold coat of arms on the door by the time Clayton and Miracle, with the canary still roosting on her head, exited the institution.

With his arms still around her, Clayton helped Miracle into the coach, sank into the luxurious squabs of the seat, settled her onto his lap, then rapped on the ceiling. As the conveyance rolled away from the hospital, Miracle turned her face into his chest.

"Would you like to cry?" he asked her, and nudging aside the bird, which fluttered onto her leg, kissed the top of her head.

"No," she replied in a muffled voice.

"It might make you feel better."

"I shan't cry in front of you."

"Why?"

"You'll think me weak. And so will I. I could never tolerate sniveling women. I refuse to become one."

"Very well."

They rode through the dark streets a while without talking, then Clayton pushed her away slightly and caught her chin in his fingers, forcing up her face. There were tear streaks on her cheeks. "Meri Mine," he said in a voice gruff with emotion. "Do you realize how worried I've been the last hours? When you didn't return to Park House by dark, I didn't know what to think. Had something happened to you? Had you become so angry with me you decided to return to Cavisbrooke? I imagined every sort of catastrophe that could have befallen an innocent who was unfamiliar with this city."

"I wanted to prove to you that I could fit in among these people. That I didn't require the mistress's interference."

He smiled. "Occasionally you're too stubborn for your own good."

"I'm . . . sorry."

"Don't be sorry, my love. It's one of the reasons why I . . . care for you so deeply. You're one of the strongest women I've ever known."

"Nay, not today. I was frightened. That terrible place . . . the poor lost souls forced to reside there. This city . . . I was invisible, sir. No one saw me. They looked right through me. I was as inconsequential on the street as I was in that wretched institution. I was nothing more than another featureless face staring with vacuous eyes at the humanity swimming around me. It wasn't an experience I care to repeat."

"Therefore . . . ?"

"I suppose I shall be forced to concede to your wishes. I'll work with Mistress Ellesemere, if I must. But only to satisfactorily achieve my own ultimate objective."

"Which is?" he asked her eyes that were now flashing with the lights glistening from the houses they were passing.

Offering her finger to the canary, her emotionalism obviously forgotten due to the pleasure she found in the tiny yellow pet, she replied stoically, "To make you the perfect wife, of course. That goes without saying, sir. I love you much too devotedly to humiliate you in any manner."

"You could never—"

"Hush," she said, and placed one fingertip against his lips. "Locked up in that fetid, horrible place, I had a great deal of time to think. I asked myself why an institution should be allowed to languish in such a deplorable condition, and I came to the conclusion that such circumstances can be avoided or repaired only by those people in a position of power. Who better than the wife of a duke? Don't you see, your darling grace? As duchess, I could make a difference for those lost souls."

"Such lofty ideals," he said softly, then hugged her close, rocking her gently, staring through the dark at Mistress Ellesemere's dim features. "Can you understand now, Miss Ellesemere, why this divine little brat has so enraptured me?"

"I understood the first instant I saw her, Your Grace," came the reply.

Clayton sat in the dark, alone, his eyes closed. Behind him, the parlor door opened, then quietly shut. Mistress Ellesemere moved up beside him, eased into the chair nearest him, then sat silently for a long while, back erect, hands folded properly in her lap. They listened to the occasional strains of music that danced momentarily on the breeze floating through the open window. The heavy scent of roses permeated the midnight air.

At last, she said, "The young lady is tucked safely into bed. She feels much better after her toilette."

"Is she all right?" he asked wearily.

"Oh my goodness, yes. No vapourish miss, that one. But I think you know that. Oh, there are a few bruises here and there, which is to be expected if she struggled as tigerishly as Administrator Wilkes claimed, which I suspect she did. She doesn't strike me as the sort of young woman who would play the meek mouse for any man. She loves you devotedly, you know."

"She loves the duke."

"She loves the man. You. It would make no difference to her if you were a bone-grubber, Clay. Why don't you tell her the truth?"

"My brother—"

"It's about time your brother takes care of himself. For heaven's sake! You've continually picked him up by his boot strings since you were children. You are not responsible for his mistakes, therefore it is not your responsibility to amend them. Clayton, from the day the duchess employed me as yours and Trey's nanny, I've watched him manipulate you with unbelievable finesse, just like he does everyone else. Oh, he does it charmingly enough; I've fallen victim to his mesmerizing smile myself, but not any longer."

"He saved my life, Ellie."

"How many times have you saved his, my dear boy?"

"You don't understand." Leaving the chair, Clayton moved to the window. The breeze felt bracingly cool and damp. There would be rain before daybreak, spoiling at least a dozen morning garden parties thrown by matchmaking mamas. "There are times when all I want to do is put Trey from my mind—my life. But how do I do that to a man who is such a vital part of me that when he aches a hundred miles from me I feel the pain?

When he cuts himself, dammit, I bleed. The time he fell from that horse—"

"You woke up screaming and holding your head. I remember."

"When he came down with that fever—"

"You shook in convulsions yourself for two days, until his fever broke."

"Sometimes I can hear his thoughts before he even speaks them. When I look at him, Ellie, I know the reflection looking back at me is what I could become if I allowed myself. It's in me, you know. The women. The gambling."

"Which is why you shun the city and your peers. Which is why you're so attracted to Miracle. She's the antithesis of everything your brother's life-style represents. Yet, you've come to me with this favor. You want me to change her—"

"Not change her, Ellie. Just . . . prepare her. He thinks he's going to marry her, put a baby in her, then deposit her in some distant, crumbling old country house, out of his way so he can go about his merry life doing whatever the blazes he pleases. His peers would think nothing of his settling her in the country if she's some drab, dowdy little mouse. It's done all the time, isn't it? Marriages strictly for convenience: for dowries, title, et cetera. The society sharks would feast on her—rip her apart. There wouldn't be a door opened to her, which is what he wants, Ellie."

Bending over Ellie, bracing his hands on her chair arms, he regarded her eyes and said, "By the time you and I are through with Meri Mine, there won't be a man or woman in this fair city who won't accept her, respect her, and . . . love her."

"Love her as fiercely as you?" she said, and covered one of his hands with hers.

"No," he replied after a moment. "No one could ever love her as fiercely as me."

You will find as you look back upon your life that the moments when you have really lived are the moments when you have done things in the spirit of love.

HENRY DRUMMOND

Chapter Eighteen

"Lesson one, my dear: A young lady never, under any circumstances, ventures into the city alone. Always her mama is present, even if the young lady is attended by her father. If the mother is unavailable, then she is accompanied by her companion. Therefore, such occurrences as took place yesterday will be avoided."

Miracle gazed out the coach window, noting how people stopped to stare as the duke's finely appointed conveyance wove through the crowded street. The young women's eyes grew wide with interest; their companions, too, craned to catch a glimpse of the passengers within.

"Meri," Salterdon said, "are you listening?"

"Yes," she replied absently, then brightening, she turned to him and asked, "Where shall we go first? Are you certain my hair is fine? It feels very odd being off my shoulders." She lightly ran her hands over the coiffure, fingers toying with the short ringlets at the front and sides, then back to the heavy coils of hair that had been swept up to the top of her head and tied with green ribbons, which flowed in streamers over her shoulders.

Salterdon looked past her to Ellie and nodded.

"Lesson two! It is bad form to be favorably inclined toward *everyone.* As the duchess, you'll be forced to carefully choose your associates and friends. Those choices will be based on equality of rank. There will be a great many who will, of course, try their best to negotiate their way into your good graces by whatever means they can possibly employ. Invitations to teas, soirees, hunts. They will fawn and flatter. They'll send gifts and pen you the most pretentiously florid letters you are apt to read outside of William Shakespeare. Lesson three! Never believe a word of it or you are likely to become as bone-headed as they are."

Miracle laughed brightly. "Then what should I do? How does one gracefully decline a person's requirement for friendship?"

"It's known as *the cut direct*, a social technique designed to express disapproval, reinforce superiority, and demonstrate exclusivity. You must choose the most public place available—"

"Whatever for?" Miracle asked, astonished and appalled by the blatant cruelty of such an act.

"Witnesses, of course. Were you to snub them in private, they would simply play ignorant and at some point, try again. However, once the cut is executed say, in a ballroom or the opera house, when every eye in the place immediately goes directly to the duke and his wife upon their entrance, then the cuttee has little choice but to acknowledge the slight and, as gracefully as possible, fade into the woodwork.

"First, you must make certain your intended victim sees you; establish eye contact, if possible, wait for a sign of acknowledgement—a nod, a raised hand, a smile—very important, you see, because if the victim suspects what is about to take place, she might well ignore *you*, and therefore feel she has been the cuttor and *you* the cuttee. Once you have his or her attention, you approach—and sail past, stony-faced, as if the individual were not there. Do not look back to revel in their discomfiture, however. That would be abominably rude."

Sitting back in the seat, Miracle looked from Ellie to Salterdon, who reposed in the corner of the carriage, his perusal of her sleepy-eyed, his mouth curled in amusement. "Your Grace," she said firmly. "Must I truly be so deficient in feelings? And how will I know who to cut, and when?"

"You'll know, Meri Mine. I promise you."

The etiquette lessons continued. Clayton listened to Ellie's patient tutoring with half an ear. He nodded and spoke when asked to, his gaze shifting occasionally to Miracle, who continued to struggle to keep her mind on Ellie and not the buzzing, bustling activity on the street.

He'd slept only a few short hours after Ellie had bid him good night and retired to her own room, and that had been sitting up in a chair by the window, his long legs stretched out with his boot heels propped upon the windowsill. He'd awakened to discover Miracle in the garden amid rain-kissed flowers, a cat on her lap, another lapping cream from a cup near her foot. The canary, of course, balanced on her head and warbled to the heavens. The noise of traffic beyond her seemed incongruous to the serene picture she made with her doe eyes, child's freckles, and unbound hair. Not for the first time since bringing her to the city, he was tempted to sweep her up and take her back to Cavisbrooke. To save her from her future. To save her from his brother. To save her from his own betrayal.

Their first stop was to a tiny but elite shop on Bond Street, where Clayton bid the ladies a pleasant morning with the dressmaker, and made his way down the street to the outrageously expensive Marcel Swift, "custom clothier to His Majesty and the Most Distinguished Noblemen and Gents." The duke of Salterdon and his peers did indeed shop here. Clayton didn't, choosing instead to purchase his simpler togs away from the heart of the West End, where the labor was less expensive and the tailors were more appreciative of his business.

But today, and tomorrow, and the day after that, until his brother returned to the city, he was the duke of Salterdon, and as his brother had mentioned not so long ago, it behooved Clay to dress the part, especially since he intended to introduce the future duchess to the entirety of London.

Ah, but His Grace was going to be greeted with such a pleasant surprise when he returned to London.

By the time the duke and his fiancée attended the opera three nights later, word was out, as Clayton knew it would be, of Trey's impending marriage. As the Red Sea did for Moses, the crush of nobility parted before them, allowing them access to His Grace's balcony box with its heavy red velvet curtains and swags and cushioned chairs emblazoned with the family crest.

As usual, Miracle seemed unaware of the commotion she caused, caught up as she was in the excitement of attending her first performance. While her change of hairstyle and the addition of the newest Parisian gown altered her appearance somewhat, there was no modifying the vivacity with which she tackled each new experience.

Settling into the chair behind Clayton, Ellie leaned forward and said in his ear, "Seems our Miracle has caused quite a sensation . . . Your Grace. But then, you knew she would. I suspect that word of the impending marriage should be reaching the duchess any day, if it hasn't already."

He crossed his long legs and glanced toward Miracle. Her dark red curls framing her face, she leaned slightly over the balustrade to study the elaborately carved motif decorating the outside of the box, which caused a ripple of excited conversation below.

Ellie whispered, "I thought you hated the opera, my lord."

"I do, but Trey enjoys it."

"I must admit, I never believed you would be able to pull off such a ruse in public. You're quite good at being pompous, not to mention cavalier and insolent. And you look smashing in his clothes. How much did they cost the duke?"

"A small fortune. As did Miracle's wardrobe and the ruby and sapphire necklace he purchased her as a wedding gift. There were the earrings to match, of course. And the tiara that's de rigueur for any and all self-respecting duchesses. Have I forgotten anything?"

Touching his shoulder in a concerned way, Ellie asked, "How are you holding up, darling? Are you certain you want to continue?"

His gaze again going to Miracle, where she squirmed in her chair and tapped her foot in impatience as she waited for the performance to begin, Clayton nodded. "Very certain," he finally replied.

They arrived back at Park House at just after midnight. Miracle had fallen to sleep with her head on Salterdon's shoulder. He roused her with a light kiss on her cheek.

She blinked and raised her head.

Ellie had already quit the coach and stood in the dark near the house, waiting. Salterdon, upon exiting, offered his hand, and accepting it, Miracle stepped to the ground, swaying a little.

With a soft laugh, he caught her. "Meri Mine, I've never known a woman who could fall asleep so deeply so quickly, then have such a devilish time waking up."

"I suppose you've awakened a great many women with a kiss?" she asked sleepily and rubbed her eyes.

He smiled.

Miracle turned away, moved along the picket fence, her silken pelisse lightly brushing against the top-heavy roses cascading over their trellises. Clayton watched her curiously. Her mood seemed . . . reflective. In truth, she had said very little throughout the evening. Her face during the performance had exhibited little of her previous enthusiasm. Her smile had been strained when greeting well-wishers.

Pausing, fingering a particularly large yellow bloom with her gloved fingers, she said, "I see how they watch you, you know. The women. They look at you wherever we go. I see the yearning in their eyes. And the envy when they look at me. They're wondering, Why her? What could he possibly love and admire in her? Sometimes," she said softly, tipping her head and looking at him askance, "I feel like such a fool. I feel as if I don't deserve you. I wake up in the mornings believing this will all end—that it's some sort of perverse trick; that you'll suddenly disappear from my life, like everyone else, and I'll be alone . . . again. And I become frightened."

Taking an unsteady breath, she said, "It's been a very long time since you last kissed me, Your Grace."

Clayton walked to her, took her face in his hands, and gently kissed her forehead.

"That's not what I had in mind," she murmured.

"No doubt. But it'll have to do, for now."

"Until we're married?"

"Yes."

Miracle pulled away. "My, haven't we become proper since coming to London? In truth, sir, you hardly seem like the same man who pursued me so adamantly at Cavisbrooke. Even the way you dress is different. So formal—like one of *them.* You seemed so much more natural in your shirt and breeches, with your hair wild with wind and your mood as mercurial as the weather."

"Miracle," Clayton said, "aren't you happy?"

"Oh my, yes!" she exclaimed, suddenly smiling. "How could I not be happy? I feel like a princess. I have a wealth of clothes, and my hair— Do you care for it, curled and coiled atop my head?"

"Very pretty."

"It itches a bit," she admitted as she scratched her scalp. "But as long as it pleases you." Laughing, she danced to him and kissed him on the cheek. "You must think me terrible, sir, awfully ungrateful."

"Not at all."

"I'm so very fortunate to have you. Imagine your choosing me, above all others, to be your wife. I promise to do everything in my power to make you happy, and above all, proud." Backing away, she smiled and blew him a kiss. "Good night then. Will I see you tomorrow?"

He nodded.

Turning on her toes, she hurried up the walk, passed Ellie who continued to stand near the door in the shadows, and disappeared into the house.

"Good night," Clayton called softly.

Miracle took the stairs to her room two at a time. Once inside, she slammed the door and fell back against it, covered her face with her hands and tried to breathe.

What was she going to do?

Angrily, she pulled at the ribbons and pins in her hair and flung them to the floor. Then Ethel came in.

Without a word, the maid hurried to her aid, caught her shoulders, ushered her to the chair before the dresser, and forced her to sit in it. Carefully, Ethel searched through the coils and curls, plucking out pins, uncoiling braids, while Miracle stared at her reflection in the mirror and did her best to swallow back her emotions.

"Did ya enjoy the opera, milady?" Ethel finally asked.

"No," she spurted. "I couldn't understand a bloody word they screamed. Nor could anyone else, I'm certain, but it didn't matter to them because they weren't watching the performance, anyway. They were all looking at me, or rather His Grace. I wager even the performers were more interested in what, or who, was watching them from the duke's box than they were on delivering their melodious tragedy. What shall I do, Ethel? I fear the longer I remain here, the more I realize I'm not cut out for this life. I'll be a miserable failure as the duchess. I don't like opera or tea parties or long hours spent in idle gossip."

Twisting in her chair, Miracle stared up into Ethel's mouselike features. "Do you realize it's unsuitable for a 'lady' to read? The fact that I know how would no doubt send London society into a fit of vapors. And as far as physical activity—heaven forbid. As Mistress Ellie explained it: 'The hallmark of a lady is to be idle—except for dancing, of which there can never be a sufficient amount of waltzing to make her ladyship's face glow with warmth and exercise.' Oh, I am an ungrateful miss."

She left the chair. Ethel scrambled after her, doing her best to unravel Miracle's hair as she paced the room. "Is love to be such an absolute sacrifice?" Miracle asked aloud, expecting no reply and getting none. "Is love not blind? Tolerant? Is it not to take or sustain difference without protest or repining? Would I not be just as capable to raise his children—to represent our marriage—without all of this?" She swept her hand toward the half dozen dresses that had arrived from the clothier only that morning.

Moving to the window, she looked down on the moon-drenched garden and the street, where the duke's coach still remained, where His Grace stood, his hands in his pockets as he conversed with Ellie.

What were they discussing?

Her, of course. What else? Perhaps her next lesson in etiquette. Elocution? The future duchess must certainly master the art of speaking to her public in the most eloquent and effective manner. Poise, perhaps. One should command the skill and grace of dealing with others. After all, there was a great deal of finesse to 'cutting' someone publicly.

Little by little, her quandary faded as she watched Salterdon, there in the moonlight. "Ungrateful miss," she said again, to herself, as Ethel began to brush out her long hair and hum to herself. "I have everything my dear mother dreamt of having for herself, and yet all I can do is whimper. But can I be faulted for missing my home? For missing John? For dreaming of the mornings I rode Napitov through the waves below Saint Catherine's Hill? Is a woman to be faulted for missing the only life and love and friends she has ever known until now? I was happy then, Ethel. Very happy. And when I'm with His Grace I'm happy . . . most of the time. When we're alone. When I'm not reminded who and what he is, and what I must become to be with him.

"Ungrateful miss . . . Whatever shall I do?"

Rain fell constantly for the next two days. Miracle divided her time between staring out the window, discussing with Samantha (what she had named her crippled canary, assuming it was female, Sam should it turn out to be male) the changes she would make to London were someone to suddenly die and make her queen, rereading books she had read when first arriving at Park House, and spending long hours in the stable with Thaddeus, mucking out the stalls and grooming the horses.

It was during her rummaging through the musty back room of the stable that she came across an odd four-wheeled carriagelike contraption blanketed by layers of dust.

"Racer," Thaddeus explained in his usual lazy drawl as he lounged back on a stack of hay bales and stared at the ceiling that was leaking rain into buckets on the floor. "His Grace tried his hand at the horses a time or two and lost his . . . cost him a thousand guineas, it did. He threatened to send ol' Pretender there"—he pointed to the tall, long-backed chestnut with his nose in a grain bucket—"to the butcher, but his brother bought the horse to keep him from it. His brother eventually intends to move him down to—"

"Can he run?" Miracle asked, eying the racing contraption.

"Aye. He can run all right. When he bloody well wants to. It's why His Grace bought him in the first place. Paid a right fortune for him, he did."

"Who was the groom?"

"Me."

Surprised, Miracle regarded the lanky lad where he lay on his back, chewing on a thread of hay.

"Broke me damn leg last time I rode him," Thaddeus explained and scratched his belly. "It'll be a cold day in hell 'fore I climb on him again. If ever there was a crazy horse, Pretender is it."

"Will you rig him up for me?"

"Milady?"

"Pretender. To the racer."

Shrugging, Thaddeus slowly climbed to his feet and proceeded to drag out the equipage. There were trunks of leather strappings, some covered in silk, others in velvet. For the next hour Miracle stood back, anxiously waited until the lad had at last completed the somewhat complicated task, then she stared upon it in amazement, excitement thumping in her chest.

The pole was small, but lapped with fine wire; the perch had a plate underneath, two cords went on each side, from the back carriage to the fore carriage, fastened to springs. The harness was of thin leather, covered with silk; the seat for the driver to sit on was of leather straps, and covered with velvet; the boxes of wheels were brass, and had tins of oil to drop slowly for an hour; the breechings for the horse were of whale bone; the bars were small wood, strengthened with steel springs, as were most parts of the carriage; but all was so light of weight that Thaddeus could carry the whole, even with the harness.

Spying one last trunk, Miracle dug through it, producing the groom's clothes: a white satin jacket, black velvet cap, and red silk stockings. "Tell me," she said to a disinterested Thaddeus. "Are there frequent carriage races?"

"Naw," he replied, and flopped back on the hay. Miracle felt her enthusiasm crumble. Then he added, bringing her gaze back to his, "Naught but once a month. First Sunday each month, milady. Right across the way in the park." His eyes widening, he shook his head. "I won't be climbin' in that contraption again. A lad was killed two month ago, dragged from here to perdition when the damned carriage flipped on a stone and overturned. There weren't enough left of him to bury by the time they got the horse stopped."

Biting her lip, Miracle ran her hands over the silks, then regarded the chestnut that was swishing flies with his tail. "I wasn't thinking of you driving," she told him thoughtfully, beginning to smile.

He rolled his head and stared at her, then bounced to his feet as if on springs. "Ya wouldn't, milady. Ya couldn't."

"I would. I could. I shall, Thaddeus! And you shan't breathe a word of this to anyone."

"Meri? Meri, wake up. For God's sake, what the blazes has come over you?"

Miracle forced open her eyes. His Grace gripped her shoulders and stared into her face. Behind him, Ethel and Gertrude fidgeted worriedly. Ellie wrung a kerchief and looked from her to Salterdon.

Taking her chin in his fingers, Salterdon tipped up her head and regarded her features fiercely. "When the devil have you taken to sleeping throughout the day?" he demanded. "Have you forgotten we have seats for the matinee? After which we were to take supper with Earl Fanshawe and his wife."

"Matinee? Oh, I . . . no, of course not. I haven't forgotten. How could I forget something so . . . important as the matinee?" she muttered under her breath. Spying the tub of water that had long since grown cold, Miracle frowned.

Salterdon sat back, elbows on his knees. "I'll have a word with Miracle alone, please," he announced in his most authoritarian tone.

Ethel and Gertrude gave a quick curtsy and hurried from the room. After a moment's hesitation, Ellie followed.

Leaving the bed, Salterdon paced, hands in his pockets, his exquisite cutaway of forest green wool caught behind his wrists. "I'm waiting," he said, not bothering to look at her.

Wrapped only in the dressing gown she had donned earlier, when she had fuzzily attempted to prepare for her afternoon with her fiancée and his friends, before she had sleepily thought to catch a catnap before climbing into the steaming tub, Miracle slid her legs off the bed and sat up.

"Well?" he barked.

"My apologies," she offered, and stifled a yawn behind her hand.

"Your apologies. How do you propose I explain this slight to Fanshawe? The countess Fanshawe arranged this evening specifically for you so that she might introduce you to a few of our more influential friends."

"You needn't use that tone," she retorted. "I'm not a child, sir."

"No? That's certainly not the impression I've been given the last week. Indeed, you've done nothing but act the brat, Meri. You've consistently refused your lessons with Ellie. Twice I've come to join you for dinner and you've remained abed asleep. I would like an explanation."

Returning his look with as much belligerence, she said, "I like to sleep."

"More than you care for my company, I presume."

"More than I care for the company of your peers, Your Grace, or your dreadfully boring plays. In truth," she added, coming off the bed, "I would rather plow an entire section with my own hands than drudge through another evening of listening to Madam Opera shrill at the top of her lungs."

His eyebrows went up. Both of them. She wasn't certain whether she saw amusement or outrage flicker in his gray eyes. It didn't matter, however. Her mood was as sore as his.

Rocking back on his heels slightly, clasping his hands at the small of his back, Salterdon moved to the window and collected his thoughts.

Chewing her lower lip, Miracle stared at his broad back, the dark hair so carelessly curling over his coat collar. The urge to fling herself against him was almost more than she could bear. Even in her anger, his presence could consume her. It dissipated her irritation and frustration into inconsequential vapor.

"Meri," he finally said. "Do you think I enjoy forcing these distasteful necessities on you? I only demand it for your own good. So that you might achieve the utmost respect from your peers and underlings."

"I have no underlings," she stated firmly.

"As duchess of Salterdon you will have a great many underlings, sweetheart, and they will demand hierarchy from you. They thrive on it, Meri. They all must have their leadership, and royalty and nobility supply it. If you cannot accept that responsibility, then . . . perhaps you're simply not cut out for the position. Perhaps you would like to return to that miserably gloomy old haunt you called a home and live out your existence as a dried-up old spinster whom the island looks upon as a lunatic. You can eke out your survival by sewing your fingers to the bone. You can spend your nights breathing life into some crumbling old lighthouse that no one who sails the channel gives a bloody hell about. In short, you can die miserable, lonely, and unfulfilled . . . just like your mother did. I wonder," he said, turning back to look at her with hard eyes, "had Lorraina been gifted with the same opportunity, would she have acted so damnably ungrateful?"

"You're very cruel," Miracle said, her eyes filled with hot tears.

For an instant, his stony facade appeared to soften; his shoulders sagged. Then drawing himself up again, he cleared his throat and motioned toward the wardrobe. "Be dressed in fifteen minutes, not a minute more. If we hurry, we can still make the second half of the play and we won't miss Fanshawe's dinner party in your honor."

"Is there anything else, Your Grace?" she said through her teeth.

"Yes. Wear the white gauze and silk gown that was delivered yesterday. Ellie says you look quite smashing in it. And for God's sake, do something with your hair. You look like an urchin."

He moved to the door.

"If this is how my life as duchess is to be led," she declared to his back, "being told how to speak, to act, and even to dress, not to mention being spoken to so callously by one who's professed to love me, then perhaps I would be happier a dried-up spinster living in a gloomy old haunt."

Poised in the doorway, his back still to her, he said, "Suit yourself, Meri Mine. It is your decision to make."

Clayton quit the room. He encountered Ellie at the top of the stairs.

"Must you speak to her so cruelly?" she demanded, following him down the stairs. "Surely you understand how radically different this lifestyle is to her, Clayton. You have taken a child of the earth—of spirit and freedom—and locked her in a cage. You're attempting to alter the very essence of what she is."

"If I wanted your opinion, I would ask for it," he snapped and stalked into the parlor.

Stopping short at the entry, Ellie fixed him with a telling look. "I never thought I would say it, my lord, but you're acting more like His Grace every day. Perhaps you've played the role too long, and much too convincingly. You are starting to believe it yourself."

He poured himself a drink.

"I won't let these obnoxious, pretentious sons of bitches destroy her," he declared in a surly, self-deprecating tone.

"So you'll do it yourself?"

He quaffed the brandy and poured another, his mouth pressed in a tight line, his jaw working. "I won't let Trey bury her. I won't let him breed her like a fucking horse, then put her out to pasture the moment she drops a son in his lap. He can't hide her now, Ellie, while he goes about his flagitous existence."

"Has it occurred to you that she might be much happier 'put out to pasture'?" Ellie crossed the room and removed the drink from his hand. "Confess this entire farce to her, Clay. Take her to Basingstoke. Marry her yourself. We both know it's what you want. The idea of her marrying your brother, of her having his children, is clawing at your insides. Why must you continue to be so stubborn?"

Turning away, Clayton stared at a Roubillac bust on a pedestal, his hands clenched at his sides.

Cautiously, Ellie moved up behind him. "There's still time," she said softly. "Before His Grace returns from York. Before the duchess dowager learns of the betrothal."

"Miracle would never forgive us . . . me. And Trey—"

"Will forgive you in time."

He laughed mirthlessly. "I don't think you comprehend just what sort of wealth Meri is worth to our impoverished duke. My God, Ellie, you have no idea the sort of finagling I was forced to do just to convince Trey's clothiers to advance him more credit. She represents financial security and freedom from his indebtedness. She also represents the naïveté that will allow him to continue with the lifestyle to which he's grown accustomed—that being debauchery, of course."

"What makes you think the duchess will approve of Trey's marrying the girl?"

"She won't have any choice, if he's already married her."

Ellie frowned and shook her head. "I would never have believed you to stoop to Trey's level of deceit. You're right, you know. Miracle probably wouldn't forgive you. I know I wouldn't, no matter how deeply I loved you."

Clayton retrieved his drink, glanced at the clock on the mantel, listened to it tick away the seconds. "This could all be moot, of course. The way she's been behaving lately, the decision could very well be already made, in her own mind. She's obviously been preoccupied; she's sleeping little. She's unhappy, Ellie."

" 'Tis hard to say, my lord. While her sleeping seems erratic, when I've managed to rouse her from the bed during the day there's been a certain vibrancy to her. Almost every evening before nightfall, we take a long walk in the park. She seems fascinated by a certain stretch of Rotten Row. Three days ago I found her sketching the path, every curve, bump, and stone."

"Do you think she's met someone?" he asked softly. "Another man?"

Miracle moved to the door in that moment, a vision in her white gauze and silk high-waisted gown, the cut of which emphasized the roundness of her breasts. As custom dictated, Ethel had dampened the chemise beneath so that the undergarment clung to her figure, leaving the dress itself free, as if clothing a sculptured form. And what a perfect form it was, Clayton acknowledged, each delicate curve reminding him how good her body had felt wrapped around his—once.

A cashmere shawl swagged off her shoulders. Its rich royal color and finely woven fringed border showed to great effect against the whiteness of her dress. A light veil covered her braided and coiled hair, and she wore long buff gloves that reached all the way up her arms, nearly to her short sleeves.

She stared at him a long intense moment, her big eyes full of green fire, her red mouth a soft pout. Then she curtsied. "I'm ready, Your Grace," was all she said.

Love was to his impassioned soul, not a mere part of its existence, but the whole, the very life-breath of his heart.

MOORE

Chapter Nineteen

Earl Fanshawe's house in the Tottenham district was a study of the arts and blatant ostentatiousness. The walls were cluttered with paintings by Hogarth, Gainsborough, Reynolds, Romney, and Zoffany. Cosway miniatures clustered the Adam brothers' finely crafted tables, and candlelight reflected handsomely from the glassware and silver plate scattered throughout the room.

The men clustered on one side of the parlor, each imbibing their after dinner cordials. The ladies grouped on the other, each perched on the edge of her chair like a colorful bird. Indeed, they resembled a lot of plumage fowls, what with ostrich feathers sprouting from the little hats they wore fixed at an angle to their heads so as not to hide their intricate coiffures—most being wigs, of course, which were currently the rage in Paris. Clayton noted that the countess Fanshawe's hairpiece had begun to slide precariously onto her brow. Another half hour and it would tumble right into her ample lap.

Miracle had said little throughout dinner. She had smiled, of course. Nodded. Gracefully accepted the overly eager guests' congratulations and good wishes. Cleverly, she managed to evade the questions that seemed too personal, occasionally glancing toward Ellie, who remained in the background chatting quietly with other 'companions.'

Now, as Miracle sat amid the circle of chattering women, she appeared . . . meditative, not in the least cognitive of the buzz of conversation going on around her. Her eyes looked distant, her beautiful, youthful face a curious blank.

He could not take his eyes from her now any more than he could cease watching her at dinner. This dreadful entrancement sickened him and weakened him. Frustration pounded at his temples. He wanted to toss her to the floor right here, in front of these simple-minded, soft-bodied fools and introduce them to passion—real passion. Unfettered desire.

"Lady Cavendish," the countess addressed Miracle, forcing her attention back to her present company. Smiling hugely, Lady Fanshawe said, "Lady Stanhope and I were just sharing our opinions regarding the ancient Greek way of styling hair. It seems to be all the rage this season. What are your thoughts on the matter?"

"On hair?" she replied absently, and tilted her head slightly in apparent concentration, exposing the soft, perfumed curve of her nape.

The half dozen women surrounding her nodded and leaned slightly toward her. Clayton glanced at Ellie, who had apparently been listening more closely to her "student's" conversation than he thought. He hoped to blazes that the woman had, at some point during their etiquette tutoring, informed the future duchess that whatever opinion she publicly declared regarding fashion would, by the time the sun rose in the morning over the palace, become de rigueur across the city. If the future duchess proclaimed that women's hair should be purple and adorned with birds' nests—and most importantly, that *she* planned to coif her own hair in such a way—every fashionable female from London to Paris would be gliding along the streets with baby birds cheeping on their purple heads . . . all within a fortnight.

Her back very straight, her gloved hands folded in her lap, Miracle sat quietly for a long moment, lost in contemplation. Then she raised up her eyes and stared fixedly from beneath her long black lashes directly at Clayton. A look of mischief momentarily lit the stormy green depths of her eyes; soft color kissed her cheeks.

I dare you, his raised eyebrow challenged her.

I should because I'm angry with you. What better way to declare exactly how I feel about your pompous hierarchy and your earlier brutal disregard for my feelings? her narrowed eyes replied.

She took a breath.

He held his.

"A woman should be free to wear her hair in any manner that enables her to feel good about herself . . . to wear it in the way that most suits her individuality," she finally stated.

The women stared at her blankly, then sat back in their chairs, obviously disappointed in her neutrality. Again, they lapsed into idle chatter, and Miracle's attention appeared to dwindle.

Where is she? Clayton wondered. Back at Cavisbrooke, riding her precious Napitov through the dawn fog? Sitting by Ismail's campfire and listening to him play his flute? Perched upon that precarious little balcony outside the lighthouse, staring out to sea and dreaming of flying?

He had not witnessed that look of sublime contentment in her eyes since bringing her to London.

"Earth child," Ellie had called her. "You are draining away the very spirit that makes her who and what she is," Ellie had declared.

"When will you cease this martyrdom toward your brother? 'Tis the man she loves, not the title."

"Your Grace?"

Frowning, Clayton turned to his host.

"I say, Your Grace, would you care for a port?"

"Brandy," he replied without thinking, and offered up his empty glass to a hovering servant.

Several of the men guffawed and blustered in surprise. Fanshawe exclaimed, "Damn me, you're going soft as your brother. Never thought I'd see you develop a taste for brandy. Brandy has always been Clay's drink. Don't tell me he's switched to port."

Clayton stared into Fanshawe's face.

"Speaking of your brother," Lord Cartwright joined in, "haven't seen or heard from him in a while. Has he gone off to Paris again with that countess . . . what was her name?"

"Delarue-Madras," Earl Stanhope declared, and stared, smiling at the ceiling. "Comely wench. Hot-natured. I knew her myself for a while, back before she was widowed."

The servant reappeared with Clayton's drink. He didn't notice at first, until the manservant cleared his throat.

Fanshawe leaned toward Clayton and lowered his voice. "Heard you've had a go at the gel as well, Your Grace. Back when Clay was buried up to his ankles in Basingstoke mud. What do you think Clayton would say if he knew you were humping his current mistress?"

Clayton stared down into the brandy, then slowly raised it to his lips.

Earl Fanshawe leaned forward then. "I reckon those days are finished, Your Grace. Now that you've got such a pretty piece of stuff for your own."

Mouth curving into a sinister smile, his gray eyes lifting to encompass his leering companions, Clayton replied flatly, "Gentlemen, you are speaking of the future duchess of Salterdon. My wife. I should be very, very careful, if I were you."

Their jaws snapped shut. They sat back in their seats.

"So tell us about your childhood," came the countess's voice, drawing Clayton's attention back to Miracle. Her aqua eyes pinned him; she seemed oblivious to her curious companions.

What had she heard?

Had she witnessed his idiotic blunder with the brandy?

At last, she turned her attention to their hostess. "My childhood?" she repeated.

"Were there sisters and brothers?"

"No."

"Friends? With whom did you spend your hours?"

"My mother."

"Your mother?" The women laughed among themselves. "Yes," Miracle stated more adamantly, "We played crambo and clumps. Charades and consequence. On particularly rainy days, we ofttime played slippery hog. Other times, I simply sat and listened to her play the pianoforte. If I remained very, very quiet and patient, she would allow me to sit on her lap, and she would teach me to pick out a tune. You see, she was all I had, and I was all she had, since my father . . . was so often away."

"And where are your parents now?"

Raising her chin, and with a brittle attempt at bravery, Miracle said, "My mother is dead. And my father is . . . dead as well."

"How very sad. But how very fortunate that His Grace has been so kind as to take you under his wing."

"Take me under his wing?" Color bloomed momentarily on her smooth, perfectly carved cheeks. "Yes," she supplied wearily, a little sadly. "I suppose that it is."

"Your Grace?" Lord Cartwright said.

Clayton forced his attention away from the women.

"I was saying to Lord Derby, sir, that there seems to be an escalation of highway robberies of late. Have you heard that Mr. Bowes, half brother of the earl of Strathmore, was recently robbed of a gold watch and purse containing thirty guineas at Epsom races? I fear our love of the horse and race will soon decline if we're consistently disposed to such crimes."

"Racing the beasts will never diminish," argued Derby. 'Since man first climbed onto the horse's back, his want to put spur to flesh and whip to lather has consumed him."

"Agreed," Miracle announced, causing every head in the parlor to swivel her way. The men blinked in bemusement. The women gaped.

Leaving her chair, moving to the group of men who immediately leapt from their chairs, uncertain of her motives and yet in shock that she should join in on their conversation, Miracle said, "There is a thirteenth-century romance, penned by Sir Beuys of Hampton and printed by W. Copland in 1550 that mentions their love of racing even then:

In summer in Whitsontyde,
when knights most on horseback ride
a course let they make on a day
Steeds and palfrey for to assay
which horse that best may run
three miles the course was then

who that might ride should
have one pound of ready gold.

She beamed a smile at each of the men.

Earl Fanshawe blinked and shuffled his feet, glanced, discomfited, at his guests, then at Clayton.

Clayton put down his brandy. "Lady Cavendish is quite the equestrienne," he explained.

"You ride?" Lady Derby blurted behind Miracle.

"Certainly. Doesn't everyone?" she replied.

Someone cleared their throat.

Glancing around, noting the women's astonished, obviously disapproving looks, Miracle set her chin and declared, "I also read. *Imagine that.* The English, Latin, and Italian classics are most entertaining, but it's the works of Plato, Aristotle, Demosthenes, and Thucydides that stir the contemplative sphere of the mind. While it's written that Lord Chesterfield once encouraged his son to study the great philosophers, regarding classical scholarship as proper and necessary to the character of a gentleman, he obviously failed to recognize that women are as capable of intellectual growth and stimulation as are their husbands."

Silence.

Then Lord Gooch, a pasty-faced young man with eyes as small and black as a wheatear's, stepped forward and announced unsteadlly, "Chesterfield also stated that it is the study of Greek philosophy that must distinguish a man; Latin alone will not. I, myself, prefer the works of Homer."

"I fear I made a cake of myself, didn't I?" Miracle asked as she accepted Clayton's hand and stepped from the coach, into the rain.

"Yes," he replied, "and the duke as well. But never mind. It'll take a few days to sink in, but within a fortnight we'll no doubt find women scavenging their husbands' literature, not to mention riding their horses."

Without replying, Miracle followed Ellie through the downpour, ignoring Clayton's attempts at chivalry by sheltering her beneath the tent of his cloak.

Gertrude threw open the door as they mounted the steps. Ellie and Clayton tried their best to shake water from their clothes while Miracle searched the rafters for Samantha. It had become customary the last days, for the canary to sweep down the stairs and land on Miracle's head with a chirp of greeting. Ironic that Clayton had spent a fortune of his brother's money on the finest clothes, books, toiletries—all the necessary accoutrements that normally made women content and happy—yet Miracle found her pleasure in a solitary skinny yellow bird that pooped on her shoulder at every opportunity.

Why was he surprised?

"Samantha!" Miracle called, searching up the winding flight of stairs.

Clayton exchanged amused looks with Ellie, then glanced toward a curiously perturbed Gertrude. The plump maid stood to one side of the entrance hall, wringing her hands, her eyes full of tears.

Frowning, he started to speak, then his eyes traveled down Gerti's arm, to the hand she extended to the table. A bundle lay there, wrapped in a lace hanky. A yellow feather peaked from beneath the embroidered edge. His heart stopped.

Miracle turned in that moment, caught his expression of alarm, and her gaze followed his.

Her body shaking, Gertrude gently picked up the bundle and extended it to Miracle. "She was singin' away one minute, and the next . . . I found her on the windowsill in yer room, as if she'd slipped off while peerin' out the window. I reckon she was waitin' for yer return, milady. She just weren't strong enough to hold on. Her little heart just give out."

Miracle stared at the bundle without blinking.

While Ellie stood rooted to the floor, hands clasped together, Clayton moved to Miracle's side.

Gently, Miracle took the bird from Gertrude and cradled it in her hands. "Cold," she whispered.

"Aye, miss. She departed not long after you and His Grace left this evenin'."

"She seemed so much stronger—"

"I reckon looks can be deceivin', milady."

"Meri," Clayton said. "Let me have her—"

"No!" She gave her head an emphatic shake and clutched the pet to her breast. "We'll bury her, of course. In the back, if you don't mind."

"Of course. The first thing tomorrow—"

"Tonight. Now," she stressed with false bravado, her voice tight with grief. "Have Thaddeus fetch me a shovel, if you will, sir, and I'll see to it myself."

"Don't be daft. It's raining, and—"

She spun away, headed toward the back of the house. Clayton moved after her.

He fetched the shovel himself, finding it after a quarter of an hour's search through the garden shed in the dark, buried under rotting grass clippings and discarded weeds—not to mention several apparently greedy mice and as many spiders. With rain pummeling his head and shoulders, forming puddles at his feet, he dug the tiny grave out back of the stables, under a century-old elm tree and a copse of unpruned roses.

Unwilling to watch Miracle place the minute body into the muddy hole, he directed his gaze toward the dark stables. She was hurting unbearably, goddammit. She wasn't just burying her bird, she was burying her mother. Her father, who might as well be dead. Her entire past.

The rain fell harder, so hard he couldn't breathe. At last, he allowed his gaze to fall to the ground, where Miracle, drenched, her white dress splotched with muck, filled in the shallow hole with her bare hands. Only then did she turn her pale face up to his. Only then did he acknowledge the shadows of strain beneath her once luminous eyes. The gauntness of her face. The sadness he saw reflected in her eyes made his chest and throat ache.

"I should have let her go," Miracle confessed through the rain. "Perhaps then she might have survived. Without the freedom to fly, sir, what good is living?"

He closed his eyes, and fell to his knees before her, took her stiff little shoulders in his hands and dragged her up against him. "Cry, damn you," he said through his teeth.

She did, at last. Melting into his chest, the emotions poured from her as thickly as the rain from overhead. Her shoulders shook. Her breasts heaved. She wept until she became too weak to remain upright, so he eased with her to the ground, nestled her wet, shaking body upon his, and wrapped his soaked cloak around her. Lying on his back, he turned his face into the rain, and wept himself for her pain.

Miracle nestled amid the musty bales of fragrant hay and regarded the cozy, much improved confines of the Park House stables as Thaddeus completed his strapping, lacing, and buckling of the racer to the eager horse. The frantic dancing of the lantern flames glowing from the walls only added to the growing anxiousness of the chestnut steed. The horse snorted and stomped its feet.

"You should have seen the looks on their faces," she said to the intense groom, and lifted a handful of hay to Pretender; she laughed as the horse snatched it from her hand and flung it from side to side. "I might just as well have leapt to my feet and proceeded to pull off my clothes. Imagine a woman reading! And riding! God forbid! After all, it's a lady's duty to continually pursue the luxury of idleness."

"Right," he said, and scratched the horse's withers. "But if ya don't mind me sayin' so, milady, ya best get accustomed to it. His Grace ain't known for his patience, ya know."

"It seems that, as the days go by, His Grace and I have less and less to say to one another, unless it's something cross."

Thaddeus stepped back from the horse and shook his head. "Cross ain't gonna come close to describin' His Grace once he's discovered what yer up to. I'll say it again, milady, I wish you'd reconsider drivin' this contraption on Sunday. It ain't safe."

"Of course it is. The trick is to know the course, and having driven it every night for the last week, I know it like the back of my hand."

"It ain't safe," he repeated, his features screwing into a look of concern as he double-checked the buckles.

"Open the doors," she ordered him, then climbed onto the precarious little perch and grabbed hold of the lines. "Now get some sleep," she said to the groom. "I'll see you in an hour."

Miracle drove the horse down the cobblestone drive, out onto the rain-slick street, and through the fog. Closing her eyes, she could easily imagine herself with Napitov again, her hands easily manipulating the reins and checking his collection with a twitch of her fingers to the bit. Oh, how she missed him! Those glorious midnight or dawn rides in the mist—the freedom of the wind in her loose hair. Johnny had always cursed her, begged her not to go, but had always greeted her return with a hug, a shawl warmed by the fire, and a pot of tea or chocolate. Then he would entice from her all the highlights of the experience.

At least *he* understood the freedom of flying.

Of all the coffee and chocolate houses that Miracle had visited while in London, the Cocoa Tree Chocolate House was by far her favorite. Small and intimate, with paneled walls of glowing rosewood and a scattering of Chippendale tables and chairs, the establishment offered its customers an atmosphere of relaxation amid the harried comings and goings of London's busy streets.

Not only that, but tucked into the back of the shop was a cozy library with a corner fireplace, an Oriental rug, and several shelves of books, all newly released. While women waited for their pot of chocolate to be delivered to their table, men could browse through the literary works printed by the three hundred or so publishers throughout England, not to mention the stacks of the most popular newspapers: the *Northampton Mercury*, the *Gloucester Journal*, the *Norwich Mercury*, and the *Newcastle Courant*, not to mention the excessively successful *Times* and the struggling *Morning Post*, both of which shoveled out the city gossip as expansively as a town crier.

Twice since arriving in London, Miracle had come across her name printed there; referring to her as "Lady C——, who aspires to eventually fill the dowager duchess of S——'s shoes by marrying His Grace, H——, the duke of S——." And: "What duke has recently been seen acquiring fashionable threads for himself and his future duchess? Could it be that Lady C—— comes with a large enough dowry to satisfy the duke's beleaguered creditors?"

Casting a look toward Ellie, who appeared mesmerized by the selection of sweetmeats on a silver tray the waiter had placed on their table, Miracle stepped around the corner, into the firelit den, pleased to find it unoccupied. As swiftly as possible, she shuffled through the scattering of papers, her mind preparing for the inevitable. No doubt some publisher would be railing about Lady C—— shocking her guests at a dinner in her honor by announcing she not only studied the philosophies of Homer and Plato, but —God forbid—rode horses with such enthusiasm they would not be surprised to see the future duchess of S—— don field boots and breeches and gallop down Piccadilly Road crying "Tallyho" at the top of her voice.

Miracle grinned. Ah, what a delicious thought!

Her eyes scanned page after page, flew across columns that were intensely and intelligently political, then to the paying advertisements of books, concerts, theaters, dresses, and various kinds of people in want of domestic employment. There were sections occupied by poetry, and serious and comic articles, not to mention letters to the paper signed with the correspondent's name, then the long official reports of foreign affairs. Then the gossip: theatrical, publishing (the editor dissuaded any and all submissions of the feminine intellect), then social snippets.

Her eye caught. She looked away. Then back.

"Have you heard," came the animated voice from the other side of the book wall. "The countess Fanshawe gave a dinner party in honor of Salterdon's fiancée two evenings ago. Seems the future duchess made a spectacle of herself."

"I heard she reads," another feminine voice joined in. "She planted herself smack in the middle of a grouping of men and proceeded to recite a shocking collection of Platoisms—"

"He'll never marry her, you know," still a third voice interrupted. "He's not serious. His Grace has never been truly serious about anyone. Besides, who is Lady Cavendish? Some country lord's daughter? Do you think Her Grace, the duchess dowager, would ever approve of such a match?"

"Of course not."

"No! Certainly not! I shudder to think."

" 'Tis rumored that the only times His Grace has ever presented his grandmother with a possible match, the duchess publicly disapproved, settled money on the unfortuante young woman, and sent her on her way."

"No one could *ever* meet *her* expectations."

"Indeed!"

"Besides . . . I understand that he hasn't even bothered to present this particular upstart to his grandmother—or his brother either, for that matter. Now tell me, ladies, if His Grace were serious about marrying her, if he truly loved her, would it not stand to reason that he would introduce her to his only family?"

"There's only one logical explanation, of course. He simply plans on making her his mistress."

"What on earth would he do with another one? It's all he can do to keep up with the ones he has already."

"Miracle," came the whisper behind her.

Miracle forced her eyes up from the newspaper.

Her hands clutching her reticule, her face slightly gray, Ellie stood rooted to the floor near the end of the book wall. "Don't listen to them," Ellie said softly, urgently, firmly. "They don't know what they're talking about."

"Of course they don't," she replied woodenly, then folded the paper in half, then into fourths, then crumpled it between her hands. "Could we go now?" she asked. "I fear I've lost my thirst for chocolate."

"Certainly. Come along, my dear."

Chin set, paper gripped in her fingers, Miracle walked out from behind the book wall, causing the threesome of young women to look up, startled. Her step slowing, Miracle met each of the women's wide eyes as they clumsily left their chairs and attempted to smile.

"Lady Cavendish," they said in unison. "What a delightful surprise. Imagine meeting you here. We were just discussing what a delightful match you and His Grace make."

Fixing a stony look on her face, Miracle shifted her gaze beyond them, and without acknowledging them, strode past them for the door, Ellie hurrying to follow.

Clayton bought flowers from a humpback woman pulling a cart. There were daffodils and daisies. Then he dropped by Jack Thelwall's Fine Bakery and Culinary Divinities for the Most Particular Inclinations and purchased a dozen sweetmeats.

Then, of course, there was the canary: a plump, sassy little singer balancing on a perch in the gilded cage Trey's strained credit had purchased for Miracle.

Though rainy, the afternoon felt unbearably warm. Coal smoke from the thousands of chimneys and the towering stacks of London's commerce covered the city in a thick fog that smarted the eyes and made breathing labored. Up and down the streets, women dabbed at their watering eyes and coughed in their hankies. Horses stood with their heads down; stray dogs lay sprawled and panting on the pavement.

Clayton had chosen one of Miracle's shirts to wear that morning. Humidity and sweat caused it to cling uncomfortably to his body. Oh, for Basingstoke, where the skies were crystal clear and blue, and a gentle constant breeze cooled the brow and smelled faintly of meadow grass. Throughout the night he had dreamt of nothing but Miracle wandering Basingstoke's vast acres, dancing in flowers, frolicking with her horses, and making passionate love to him amid waving wheat and rustling corn.

At last, the chaise arrived at Park House.

He climbed from the chaise just as Ellie flung open the front door and hurried down the steps, her stride lengthening down the rose-cluttered path toward the street. She carried a newspaper in her hand. Her features were lined in worry.

"Thank God you're here," she said. "Miracle's gone."

"Gone?" His heart skipped. "Where?"

"I can't be certain, of course. She said nothing to me before leaving. She hasn't been herself. But yesterday—I sent word to you—"

"I haven't been home," he said, and watched a flash of irritation cross her face. "I went home. To Basingstoke. There were certain arrangements to be made—"

"It began with a conversation she overheard at the Cocoa Tree. A lot of silly girls talking about how His Grace couldn't possibly love her, that he would never marry her, that the duchess would never countenance the match, that Miracle would simply end up another one of his long string of mistresses—"

Clayton flung the flowers and box of sweetmeats back into the chaise, then he took Ellie by her shoulders and gave her a gentle shake. "Calm down," he said.

Ellie shook her head, then thrust the paper against his chest. "I came across this in her room."

He pried the paper from her hand. He searched the wrinkled columns, frowning. "Speak to me, dammit. What the blazes am I looking for?"

With a trembling finger, she pointed at the lower left-hand corner of the *Post*—at the snippets of less consequential gossip of less than consequential patricians: viscounts and barons and mere sirs.

"The Baron, Lord D. Cavendish, his wife, the Baroness Molly, and their sons, the Honourables Felix and Nigel, have recently occupied their home in Islington for the season . . ."

Take all my loves, my love, yea, take them all,
What has thou then more than thou hadst before?
No love, my love, that thou mayst true love call,
All mine was thine before thou hadst this more.
Then if for my love thou my love receivest,
I cannot blame thee for my love thou usest,
But yet be blam'd if thou thyself deceivest
By willful taste of what thyself refusest,
I do forgive thy robb'ry, gentle thief,
Although thou steal thee all my poverty;
And yet love knows, it is a greater grief
To bear love's wrong than hate's known injury.
Lascivious grace, in whom all ill well shows,
Kill me with spites, yet we must not be foes.

WILLIAM SHAKESPEARE

Chapter Twenty

The hired hackney bounced along the old track from Paddington to Islington. Along each side of the highway the landscape took on a more countrified aspect, lined with gardens and pleasure bowers with wooden arbors and mulberry trees. Miracle had learned enough about London's surroundings to know that this area was the resort of city tradesmen's families on summer Sabbaths. There were fields dotted with dairy farms and merchants' weekend boxes. Beyond Islington's meadows there climbed an enormous circus of aristocratic mansions, grouped round elysian groves and lawns.

With a brief stop at a local pub, the hackney driver learned which residence belonged to Lord Cavendish.

For a long while, Miracle sat in the hackney outside the gates of Cavendish House, staring up at the elaborate filigreed wrought-iron entry with its giant swirling C framed with twining vines. How pretty was the distant brick and stone house, its windows lead-paned and reflecting the sunlight like a kaleidoscope. And the gardens: earthen patches of rich color with an occasional bird path or fountain. Footpaths of crushed shells wove through labyrinths of hedge groves. How her mother would have loved this. Miracle could imagine Lorraina meandering down the pathways, basket in hand, humming to herself as she gathered bouquets for the house. Lorraina, of course, would have known the name of every twittering bird, each blooming flower.

Miracle disembarked and walked to the house. A petite maidservant answered the bell.

"To see Lord Cavendish," Miracle heard herself explain, and thought how disjoined she seemed to be from her own voice. A whisper in her head urgently reminded her that there was still time to leave. She could return to London to her fiancé and forget this incredible scheme.

"Miss?" the servant queried. "Who may I say is here to see his lordship?"

Miracle blinked. She swallowed. "Lady . . ."

"Miss?"

"Aimesbury. Yes. Tell him Lady Aimesbury is here to see him. He'll recognize the name."

The servant scurried away.

A clock ticked somewhere in the distance.

A door opened. Laughter. Then a young man, perhaps a year or two older than she, walked into the foyer, obviously on his way out. Seeing Miracle, he stopped short, a smile on his face.

"What's this?" he declared, regarding her appreciatively. "I certainly hope you're here to see me."

"Lord Cavendish?" she replied. "Of course not. You're—"

"His son. Nigel."

They regarded each other in silence, and for an instant Miracle was swept back in time, to twenty years ago, the moment her mother must have set eyes on a brash, handsome young lord Cavendish, with dark hair and blue eyes and a smile that could melt iron.

Then not so long ago, when she, herself, had looked into gray eyes and felt herself fall under the spell of irrational love.

Had she and her mother both loved too deeply—so deeply that subjectivity had obliterated all common sense, robbed them of dignity, of self-respect? Must love become so all consuming?

"Lord Cavendish will see you now," came the servant's voice from a nearby door.

Nigel shrugged on his cloak and moved toward the door. He spoke to Miracle, but she barely noticed. All senses were tuned to the corridor ahead and how difficult it was to force her feet to move forward.

The servant disappeared through a doorway ahead, and her voice said faintly, "Lady Aimesbury, my lord. Shall I bring tea?"

"No," came the gruff reply. "And close the door when you leave. Should my wife return, tell her I'm occupied with business and not to be disturbed."

"Yes, my lord."

The servant darted from the room just as Miracle moved to the threshold.

Cavendish's presence filled the chamber. He stood by a desk: tall, distinguished, handsome—incredibly handsome. His face looked white, his blue eyes panicked. At last, he cleared his throat and said, "Come in. Please."

She forced her feet to move. The door closed quietly behind her.

His hands in tight fists at his sides, Cavendish opened and closed his mouth several times before finally managing to speak again. "Aimesbury was your mother's maiden name."

"How good of you to remember. I wondered if you would."

"My God, you look just like her. For a moment I thought I was seeing her ghost."

Miracle allowed him a dry smile. "Barely more than a fortnight ago, I would have thought the same about you. All these years, I thought you were dead. How long has it been since I last heard from you, my lord? Eight years?" Her voice mounted with anger. "Of course, I've only recently learned of your *other* family. *This* one. The one you apparently had when you supposedly married my mother."

"I was young, Miracle, and honestly believed—"

"How many other 'wives' did you have scattered throughout the countryside? Were they also doomed to languish away in gloomy, impoverished surroundings? I hope they've fared far better than my dear mother, who continued to love you despite your less than desirable considerations."

"There were no others," he said wearily, his shoulders sagging. "In the beginning, my dear, I honestly believed that I could make things work with your mother. I . . . loved her very much." His eyes became distant. "She was the most incredibly beautiful woman I had ever known. Her lust for life, and living—her laughter filled up my existence. Made me a little insane. Made me willing to sacrifice anything to have her, to spend my days luxuriating in her special sort of madness. I purchased Cavisbrooke with every intention of building her the grandest castle any man could gift the woman he loved."

"Liar," she said through her teeth.

He lowered his eyes. His face went from white to ashen. He seemed to age before her eyes, and he sank against the desk.

"In my infatuated dreams, I imagined demanding a divorce from my wife. But it was my wife's dowry, and her father's wealth that supplied me with this." He motioned around them. "And the respect that my own father's inconsequential position in society could not afford me. Marriage to your mother wouldn't have benefited me whatsoever. By the time that realization had sunk in, I learned Lorraina was with child."

He ran his hands through his gray-streaked hair. "I couldn't just abandon her. An unmarried woman with child, my God. And whether you believe it or not, I still loved her. So I married her, and took her to Cavisbrooke, naively believing that, at some point, things would work out. Then my wife began to suspect that I was keeping a mistress. There were threats, tantrums, her father became involved, and I risked losing everything."

His gaze came back to Miracle's. "Then, of course, you were born, and Lorraina's demands became more frantic and frequent and angry. Eventually, my love turned to resentment. I lived in constant fear that my bigamy would be discovered."

"Did you kill her?" Miracle asked in a dry voice.

"Kill her?" He shook his head adamantly, and clenched his hands together. "No. God no."

"I don't believe you. John told me—"

"John?" He laughed mirthlessly, his lip curling derisively. "John. Groom and trainer extraordinare. The only servant I chose to accompany her to Cavisbrooke. Did John also tell you that he once worked for me, or rather my father? We grew up together, John and I. He was the only person I could trust not to divulge my secret life.

"Well?" he demanded, his voice now rough and angry. "Exactly what did our friend John tell you, my dear? That I pushed your mother off Saint Catherine's Hill? Bastard," he growled. "Lying bastard if he did. He was there. He saw the argument. The wind was fierce. The rain driving. Your mother and I were forced to shout as loudly as we could just to make ourselves heard. She'd demanded an audience of me, informing me that she'd learned of my other family—my legal family and marriage. My sons . . . She threatened to tell them about us, to wreak havoc on my name and my sons. I told her fine. I told her that I would gladly go before any court and demand custody of my daughter . . . of you. I told her there wasn't a court in this or any land who would not grant me the right to take my own flesh and blood, considering the vast differences in our backgrounds. I pointed out that the courts would look upon her as nothing more than a concubine and unfit to raise a gentleman's offspring . . .

"For the love of God, lass, don't look at me like that," he said to Miracle's eyes. "You look just like she did, standing there with rain running down her face, her eyes brimming with pain and outrage." He covered his face with his hands, as if to block out the image of Miracle, to escape the memory of her mother.

At last, he took a ragged breath and lowered his hands; he stared at the floor. In a much weaker voice, almost distant, perhaps lost in the past, he said, "Then she confessed . . . I suppose the reality that she might well lose you, that I might take you—God knows if I would have or not; I knew how much she loved you; you were her life, after all, but I was angry and desperate."

He swallowed. "She confessed . . . that you are not my child."

Silence.

Gradually, he brought his gaze back to hers. "She told me that the child she was carrying when we married, when I took her to Cavisbrooke, was miscarried. I had already returned to London, of course. She was alone. Terrified that it was only because of the child that I had married her. She turned to the only companion and friend she had."

Miracle covered her ears with her hands and shook her head in denial.

"John is your father, Miracle. Not I."

"Liar." She hissed it.

"My God, you don't remember, do you? You were there, Miracle. You followed John to the hill when he came searching for Lorraina. You were watching the entire horrible incident from a distance—a weeping child in the rain. I'll never forget your terrified little face."

"No. You would've known. My birth would have come too late—"

"She went to a woman—Ceridwen—and got from her herbs that brought on her labor. You were born over a month early—at the time when the first child would have birthed. No one expected you to survive—you were so weak and tiny. It was a . . . miracle that you survived."

Miracle.

"My mother," she began quietly.

"No sooner was the confession out of your mother than she turned to discover you in the distance. John ran to fetch you, and Lorraina believed you had overheard everything. One moment she was standing there on the edge of the precipice, her face turned into the wind, a distant, peaceful look on her features, then the next she spread her arms out to her sides and . . . for a moment it actually appeared that she was flying, hanging there suspended. I tried to reach her, Miracle. Then she was gone."

"My lord," came the urgent voice behind Miracle, worming its way through her numb senses. "The man come bursting in the front door with no warning, demanding to see you and the young lady—"

"Meri," Salterdon implored.

Standing, Cavendish demanded, "Just who the devil do you think you are—"

"Says he's duke something or other," the servant squeaked. "That he come for Lady Cavendish? I told him her ladyship is out for the afternoon, but—"

"Meri." Salterdon's big hands closed gently over her shoulders. "Meri, come with me." He turned her around, but when he attempted to pull her close, she shook her head and backed away. It seemed that she shook from the inside out. Her blood felt cold, and her teeth chattered.

"He's not my father," she said, staring up into Salterdon's intense eyes. "I'm not certain if I should shout for joy or . . ."

She moved toward the door, did not look back or hesitate as she left the house and boarded the waiting hackney. Salterdon climbed in beside her, filled up the small chamber with his presence, then rapped with his fist on the ceiling. When he reached for her hand, she slid it away, buried it in the folds of her expensive gown. Only when the hackney rolled under way did she speak.

"It seems that, not only am I illegitimate, I now learn that I'm a product of the most common class—a squire's daughter and a groom for parents. It seems sadly and laughably ironic that I came here in hopes that I would confront my father and possibly convince him to acknowledge me so that I might at least be marginally worthy of marrying you. After all, if your grandmother hasn't approved of the other marriage prospects you've presented her—"

"Had my grandmother been presented to any marriage prospects whatsoever by either of her grandsons, she would have fainted with relief and pleasure, I assure you. Meri Mine, you must learn not to believe every catty comment you hear muttered under an envious woman's breath."

She fixed him with her eyes. "Then tell me, sir. Have you any mistresses?"

He set his jaw. And shifted on the cushioned seat. His countenance turned dark and agitated, and his eyes became hooded.

"Well?" she demanded. "Has the duke hidden away anyone that I should be aware of? Lovers? Children? Wives? Speak to me, damn you." She waited.

"Meri," he finally began.

"Stop the hackney," she demanded in a rising voice. "I said, stop this conveyance this instant before I jump!" She leapt for the door. He grabbed her back, struggled with her as she pounded on his chest and shoulders and struck at his cheek. "I don't want to hear your excuses!" she screamed. "I won't make the same mistakes as my mother. I won't be used, Salterdon. I won't allow you to break my heart—"

"Listen to me, dammit!"

"If you truly cared, you would have presented me to your family long ago, the duchess, your brother. But you never intended to marry me, did you? It all makes sense now. How could I have been so blind. I suppose it must run in the family.

"Let me go, sir. It will be a cold day in hell before I marry you. I would rather spend the rest of my days digging potatoes with an Irishman before I wed the bloody duke of Salterdon."

She yanked her wrists from his hands, breathing hard. "Get out of this hackney—now—or I shall."

He opened his mouth but said nothing. Then, with a guttural growl and a curse and a muttered, "I'm going to murder that son of a bitch when I get my hands on him," he jumped from the hackney and slammed the door hard enough to cause the horses to snort.

"Go," Miracle snapped at the driver.

The hackney lurched forward.

Miracle briefly closed her eyes. She wouldn't cry. Silly girl. There was nothing to cry about, after all. She should be thankful that Cavendish wasn't her father. Oh, poor John. How he must have loved her mother—how he must have loved her—his only daughter. He loved her enough not to ever hurt her with the ugly truth.

Opening her eyes, she stared first at the canary in the cage, then down at the bouquet of yellow and white flowers near her feet. She picked them up and slowly turned to look back down the road.

He stood there, in the growing distance, his hands on his hips, his head down.

Damn her heart for drumming at the sight of him, even now. For loving him despite everything. A cry worked up her throat. Traitorous emotions. Disloyal heart!

Furious, she flung open the birdcage, watched as the canary took flight, soared toward the blue sky and white clouds. Then she went to her knees, and as hard as she could, flung the bouquet of flowers into the air. They scattered, the yellow and white blooms floating over the road as lightly as feathers. She watched, with hot tears running down her cheeks, as Salterdon's image faded behind the rising wall of dust.

Mistress Ellesemere's face turned white as a sheet at first sight of Miracle. "Oh my," Ellie cried, wringing her hands and jumping aside as Miracle stormed through the front entry and headed for the stairs. "Whatever has happened, dear? Where is—"

"I don't wish to talk about it now or ever," Miracle declared so loudly Gertrude and Ethel came running. "And his famously handsome and distinguished—not to mention philandering—duke is somewhere along the highway to Islington, sufficiently boot sore by now, I should think. Bloody serves him right."

Ellie scrambled up the stairs behind her.

Entering her bedroom, Miracle flung open the wardrobe doors and snatched for her clothes: the ones she came to London in, the ones she had sewn herself, the browns and simple calicoes, the unadorned chemises, worsted stockings, worn kid slippers.

"What are you doing?" Ellie demanded.

"Leaving. I'm going home. To Cavisbrooke. To be with the only friend—family—I have in the world."

"Miracle. Please, let's discuss—"

"I'm finished talking. I'm done with understanding. I'm through allowing him to change me into something or someone I'm not just so I don't cause him embarrassment—"

"Oh no! That was never his intention!"

Miracle dragged a valise from under the bed and slammed it onto the mattress. Not bothering to fold the limp garments, she shoved them unceremoniously into the bag. "You must have thought me a naive ninny, thinking I could make a man like him happy. That I could be enough for him. That I could fill up his empty days, replace his hours of frivolous debauchery with something so insubstantial as love and companionship. Seems he's got more companionship than he knows what to do with."

"Meri—"

"Don't call me that. *He* calls me that. And do you know why? Because I make him happy—"

"You do!"

"Because I make him smile and laugh—"

"But you do!"

"A hunting hound can accomplish the same thing, my dear Ellie, and will be far more willing than I to lick the back of his hand."

Hefting the heavy valise from the bed, Miracle turned toward the threshold, just as Ellie stepped from the room, slammed the door, and locked it.

Dropping the bag to the floor, Miracle sprang at the door, grabbed the knob, and attempted to turn it. She banged on the door with her fist. "Unlock this door!" she demanded.

"I won't until you calm down and think rationally."

"This is the first moment I've entertained a rational thought since I met him!" she cried, and kicked the door. "Now open the bloody door before I . . . I throw myself out of the window."

"Quickly, Gertrude," came the urgent plea. "Have Thaddeus fetch a ladder and nail shut her ladyship's window."

Hands on her hips, glaring at the door, Miracle exclaimed, "Surprise! I'm not a lady, either. I'm just the misbegotten daughter of a groom—a mere groom. Imagine that! The man who raised me, who taught me how to read and encouraged my admiration for the man whom I *believed* was my father is actually my father. Are you sufficiently shocked, Mistress Ellesemere?"

Nothing.

"Can you understand now why my remaining here would be sheer folly? The duchess dowager—the cranky old crone—would never approve of my marrying her precious grandson."

A gasp. Frantic whispers.

Finally, "Miracle, I don't intend to unlock this door until you've calmed down. When you wish to discuss these unfortunate circumstances in a mature and adult fashion, without this angry tantrum, then I shall allow your release."

Miracle stubbornly crossed her arms. Tapped her foot on the floor . . . and listened to the ensuing silence. Finally, she pressed her ear against the door, strained hard for any sound. Nothing.

She spun toward the window, just as Thaddeus popped up atop the ladder, his lips pressed around several nails, a hammer in his hand. He waved to her. She glared back, making his Adam's apple quiver and bob in his scrawny throat. Then he proceeded to nail closed her window.

As the light of the moon spilled through her window, Miracle softly blessed three white candles and made the sign of the cross on each one. Then she lit them. According to Ceridwen's bible, silver ones would have been better, but white was all she had and would, therefore, have to do. Her hands clasped, her head bowed over the flickering flames, Miracle chanted:

Angel of the Mirror, Angel of the Moon,
Grant to me your presence as a precious boon.

She dragged a chair to the dressing table mirror, then took the candles and placed them before the looking glass which she had earlier polished to a high shine. She climbed onto the chair, and repeated the chant, and waited, watching the white glow of the flames reflect from the glass as she whispered:

"Does he love me? *Truly?* Do I love him? *Truly?* If so, why have I continued to experience this confusion? Why, in my heart of hearts, do I feel as if the one I love is so different from what or who he appears to be?"

She waited. According to Ceridwen, soon she would perceive a form taking shape within the candlelit mirror. If the figure that appeared was that of a fair angel, exquisite in shades and swirls of purest white, gentle silver, and pearly moonlight, like unto a vision of peace, it is the Angel Gabriel, the angel of the moon, and the answer to her question would be that which she most craved to hear.

But if a dark lady should appear, lovely and terrible and full of shadowy enchantment, hung with a dim veil as if it were made of raindrops falling at the darkest midnight, then that was Morgana, the Dark Angel; she would come to warn Miracle that what she desired most must not be pursued.

Swirl and swirl, the candlelight flickered and dimmed. Her heart racing, Miracle bent toward the mirror, her eyes focusing on the vague shape coming into focus upon the looking glass—the face sharpening to one of—

"Blazes," Miracle whispered, squeezing closed her eyes then opening them again to fix on the wrinkled, fire-eyed wretch glaring back at her. "Morgana. You ugly old—"

"Ugly!" the voice barked behind her, and Miracle leapt in startlement, nearly upsetting the chair. "Come down from that ridiculous perch this minute," came the strident demand. "What the devil are you doing up there, anyway? Conjuring up leprechauns or some such nonsense? Stop staring at me as if I were an archfiend, girl, and present yourself accordingly."

"Present myself?" Miracle said, growing angry now that her momentary fright had subsided. Glaring down into the old woman's steely eyes, she declared, "Just who do you think you are to come barreling into my room unannounced? Furthermore, should I decide to conjure up Old Scratch himself, I'll do just that."

"Not in my house, you won't. Now get down from there before you break your neck."

"Your house? Madam, this domicile belongs to my fiancé, the duke of Salterdon. Should you have some business with him, then leave your card and come again later, preferably after I've gone."

Ellie and Gertrude popped their heads around the doorjamb, their eyes wide. They shook their heads frenziedly. Then Ethel barreled into the room, pointed chin quivering, feet tripping, as she attempted to clumsily curtsy.

"Milady Cavendish. Her—Her Grace, the duchess of Salterdon." Then she endeavored another curtsy, and fled the room, along with Ellie and Gertrude.

Miracle snapped her mouth closed.

Her hair was as white and soft as goose down, and her slender body was draped in a simple, dark frock that accentuated the pallor of her delicate skin. The duchess Salterdon pursed her lips and looked Miracle up and down. "You might try to appear the tiniest bit mortified, young lady. It's the least you can do after inferring that I'm ugly."

"Oh, you're not in the least ugly," Miracle assured her. "Stern, perhaps. And severe."

"I'm the duchess of Salterdon. I'm expected to be stern and severe. And dominating. And cantankerous. You, however, are expected to be—"

"Meek and awed by your rubric."

One gray eyebrow raised a fraction. "Do you intend to remain up there the entirety of the evening?" the duchess demanded.

"Should I choose to do so," Miracle returned.

"Hmph. You're not at all what I expected."

"And what, exactly, did you expect?"

"I heard you were a timid little mouse who apparently doted on my grandson to nauseating extremes. That you trailed along behind him like a pup on a leash."

"Then you heard wrong, Your Grace."

"Apparently." The duchess glanced toward the stuffed valise, but made no comment. Instead, she moved to the window, leaning her weight slightly on the crook of an ivory and walnut cane. "Are you always so volatile?" she asked.

"When I've cause to be."

"And you have cause?"

"Yes." She nodded, and shuffled around on the chair seat to face the duchess's back. How erect the dowager stood, her slender shoulders back, her spine ramrod straight, a portrait of contumacy that was as unflappable as Miracle's own.

"They didn't exaggerate your honesty, I see," the duchess said, staring out at the dark street.

"They?"

"Never mind."

Finally, she faced Miracle again. "Tell me, youngster. Do you love him?"

"Who?"

"My grandson, of course. Don't go daft on me now."

"I . . . don't know."

Both eyebrows went up. "What makes you think you would make a suitable duchess?"

Miracle jumped from the chair and blew out the vaporizing candles. "I don't think any such thing, Your Grace. In truth, I would make a terrible duchess. I'm neither cold nor cruel nor intolerant enough toward others. I enjoy the company of servants more than I care to spend time with narrow-minded peers. I find more pleasure in mucking out stables than penning guest lists for social teas and inconsequential gatherings that accomplish nothing more than wounded feelings. I care nothing for people who care more for a title than they do for the person himself. Nay, I would not make a suitable duchess, Your Grace, so spare yourself any unnecessary disquietude. I shan't marry your grandson. So if that's why you've come here—"

"It's not, so stop putting words in my mouth, impertinent pup." She moved toward Miracle, her cane thumping the floor. "Do you imagine I would allow you to leave now that word has spread that he intends to marry you? Can you imagine what the lot of imbecilic high-stockings would say if you walked out? The embarrassment and humiliation you would cause him? Especially since it's so apparent his feelings for you run so . . . deeply."

"I beg to differ," Miracle stated softly, diverting her gaze.

The duchess roughly caught her chin, forcing Miracle to meet her eyes. "What? Do I see a chink in her thorny armor? Does that tear in her eye glisten of uncertainty where my grandson's affections are concerned? Her chin quivers. She longs to cry, but won't, of course, because she thinks it would give 'the old crone' too much pleasure. Look at me, child. So. You're a romantic. You wish to believe in fairy tales. Of happily ever afters. Is that what you were doing when I found you? Beseeching the moon spirits to reveal your future with my grandson? Dear, naive girl, not even your angel of the mirror can do that."

"But there are others. Women. Mistresses—"

"Ah." Dropping her hand back to her cane, the duchess studied Miracle intently, her thin mouth curled in something short of amusement. "What difference does it make if you have his name, his wealth, and his children, not to mention his title?"

"None of that matters," Miracle argued, beginning to tremble. "It's what's here." She pressed one hand to her heart. "If it's not here . . . I won't be left alone. I won't spend my life loving a man who would rather be with someone else—"

"Like your mother."

She blinked. Shock and abashment stabbed her as sharply and coldly as an icicle, and she shivered.

"I know all about her," the duchess explained in her most efficient voice. "The instant word reached me of this . . . betrothal, I had your past looked in to. It wasn't difficult. While Cavendish is hardly my equivalent, I was certainly familiar with his family. I spoke with him, of course. Privately."

Miracle moved to the bed and seized the valise.

"Don't be stupid," said the duchess.

Eyes flashing, her face going from cold to burning, Miracle turned on the old woman, her voice shaking. "Then you are well aware of who my father is, Your Grace, and therefore have no doubt come to the irrefutable conclusion that I'm hardly duchess material."

"Cease putting words in my mouth."

"Then you simply came here to humiliate me."

"I came here expecting to find the kind of woman who would sacrifice her entire existence in order to keep her children safe and happy. Who would raise her children to be dignified and proud, despite prejudice. Who would be a partner to my grandson, be it hosting a dinner in honor of His Majesty, or turning field dirt with her bare hands. A woman who would fight for what she wants, and once attaining it, fight to keep it. Perhaps I came here expecting too much."

"Perhaps you did," Miracle declared in a dry voice as she stared at the door.

The duchess moved around her, her step slow but steady. She paused at the threshold and looked back. For an instant, she appeared as if she would say more, but she shook her head and quit the room.

Dropping the valise, Miracle hurried after her, stopping at the top of the stairs as the duchess descended. "Did he send you here to reason with me?" Miracle called after her.

"Who?"

"Your grandson, of course."

"Certainly not. Why should he?"

Ethel hurried from the parlor, a hat and pelisse in her arms. Pausing on the bottom step, the duchess took both from the tittering servant before making her way to the front door. "I taught my son and my grandsons to honor their family above all else. I taught them how to fight for what they want, and how to fight to keep it. Occasionally, I must confess that I question the results of my persistent endeavors. They can often be damnably mule-headed. But then, my dear, so can I."

A smile flickered over her stern lips, then she floated from the house, and Ethel gently closed the door behind her.

There are three principal postures of love. It gives with joy, receives with appreciation, and rebukes with humility and hope.

ALBERT M. WELLS, JR.

Chapter Twenty-one

There was trouble brewing. Clayton could sense it. The fact that he had spent the last two days and nights buried up to his chin in hazard tables and markers didn't help. He smelled like a bleeding brewery, and smoke, and forty-eight hours' worth of sweat. He wanted a bath and to sleep. He wanted to forget the last weeks had ever taken place, that Miracle Cavendish had ever existed.

He wished the goddamn sharks had eaten him twenty years ago. *And* his brother. *Especially* his brother.

Standing in his town house doorway, located in the center of the city near Gray's Inn on Holborn Street, Clayton stared out at the chaise and postillions on the street while, somewhere in the bowels of his meager residence, his grandmother was busily settling in. Not that he had seen her, of course, and wouldn't until *she* was ready, which could be in five minutes or five hours. The only word he'd heard from her personally was the cryptic note a nervous and agitated Benjamin had been forced to deliver to him at Brookes': "Come home this instant. Or else. The D."

The D. Enough to strike fear in the heart of any grandson who had not lived up to Her Grace's noble expectations, and she knew it, which was why he had continued playing hazard, not to mention whist, for another two and a half hours after receiving the message. Best not to let her get the upper hand.

A hackney pulled up. His brother, Trey, the duke of Salterdon, exited and stalked up the path toward him, his face burning with color, his jaw working. Upon seeing Clay leaning against the doorjamb, a smirk on his mouth, arms crossed so casually across his chest, Trey's stride hesitated momentarily; then his anger intensified, as Clay knew it would. Nothing rattled and frustrated his brother more than knowing Clayton wasn't at all bothered by the wielding of their grandmother's all-powerful fist . . . and purse.

"You son of a bitch," Trey growled and moved up the steps.

"And a good afternoon to you too, Your Grace. How did you find York these last days?"

Topping the steps, coming face to face with Clay, standing nose to nose, Trey clenched his fists. "Just what the blazes have you done to me now?"

"Meaning?"

"Meaning I've heard from a number of my creditors that I owe them some unimaginable monies for garments I supposedly purchased—"

"For your bride-to-be. You *do* remember her, don't you? The strange one? The lass who is slightly short of intelligence? Can't have the future duchess garbed like a ragamuffin, can we? What would your peers say?"

"And jewels," Trey choked, starting to shake. "Rubies and sapphires? *Big* ones. Costing a sizable fortune."

"They'll look beautiful on her. She'll be the envy of all of London."

"All of London. Oh my God."

"She's made quite an impression, Your Grace. You'll be hard-pressed to tuck her quietly away, now that she's got a taste of the finer things in life."

"She knows, doesn't she?" Trey looked beyond Clay, into the house.

Clayton smiled. "I assume you're referring to grandmother."

"You know to whom the devil I'm referring."

"I suppose that wouldn't be beyond the realm of reason, considering the news of your upcoming nuptials has been brandished across every newspaper in the city. Ah, but speculation does run rampant, Your Grace. There are even wagers put down at Crockford's and Brookes' on whether or not you'll go through with it. My guineas are on the positive, of course, now that grandmother is aware of Miracle's existence—and so is all of London."

"Where is she?" Trey asked.

"Meaning—"

"The girl, dammit. Is she here?"

"No." Clayton watched an old blind Tobit meander down the pavement, his dog walking obediently at his side. "I haven't seen her in two days. Not since she deposited me along the road to Islington. I thought it best to give her a few days to calm down. You know how unreasonable women can be when they think their affections are being toyed with."

"Your Grace. Your lordship," Benjamin said behind them. "Her Grace, the duchess of Salterdon, will see you now."

Clayton stepped back, swung his arm toward the distant closed doors, and grinned. "After you, brother."

Trey glared at him, adjusted his coat more comfortably on his shoulders, then tugged at the cuffs of his sleeves.

"She's waiting," Clayton said.

They moved together toward the door, their steps synchronized. They cleared their throats at the same time and smoothed back their dark hair from their brow at the exact instant. And they thought, *All of this because of a woman. I hope to hell it's worth it.*

Before them, Benjamin shoved open the double doors that led into a small, sparsely decorated chamber which, in most town houses, would have sufficed as a comfortable library. Here, however, the walls of shelves were mostly empty. The fireplace had not been used since Clayton had purchased the residence some years ago.

Four chairs occupied the otherwise empty room. One sat before the distant French doors, which led to a tiny garden surrounded by a tall brick wall. Two others were placed side by side, facing the one now occupied by their grandmother, who applied her infamous withering study of her grandsons with as much expression of distaste as her regal deportment would allow.

"Your Grace," Trey exclaimed in a voice tight with anxiety and forced delectation. "How wonderful to see you again."

One gray eyebrow drew up, but the duchess's sharp eyes watched Clay as he rounded his chair and dropped into it.

You're late, her look said.

I know, his shrug replied.

You look like hell, her sniff proclaimed.

I dressed for you, darling. He smiled.

Bending over her offered hand, Trey pressed a kiss on her bejeweled fingers. "As always, grandmother, you look positively enchanting. And well! By gosh, doesn't grandmother look radiant, Clay?"

"Radiant," he parroted, and winked at the duchess. "Positively."

Drawing her hand away, the duchess cut her gaze up to Trey's. "Sit down and quit fawning," she told him.

A thin smile on his lips, Trey eased down into his chair.

"I don't intend to beat about the bush," she declared, drumming her fingers on the chair arm. "It's never been my way to prattle at you boys. I'm too bloody old to start now."

"You're hardly old—" Trey began, leaning forward and rewarding her with a bright smile.

"Be quiet," she snapped, and waited until Trey sat back in his chair. "I've recently been informed that in the process of reforming a certain young woman, Your Grace has expended a fortune, much to your creditors' dismay. *My* dismay comes from the fact that you assured them that I would satisfy the debts."

Clayton looked away, out the French doors, and hid his satisfied grin behind the tips of his fingers.

Trey said nothing, just crossed, then uncrossed his long legs. He shifted on the chair seat.

Clayton thought, but he couldn't be certain, that his brother groaned.

"Well?" the duchess barked.

"Grandmother," Clayton said, bestowing upon the duchess a patient smile, "there's a perfectly logical solution to the problem."

"And that is?" Trey ground through his teeth.

"Trey will simply satisfy the debts he's incurred with the money you intend to settle on him for marrying the girl."

Sitting straighter, Trey gripped the chair and glowered at Clayton. "Considering the size of the debts, my dear brother, there will be nothing *left* of the settlement once my creditors have done with me."

"What does it matter?" Clay laughed lightly and shrugged. "Think about what your generosity has bought you: a beautiful wife, beautiful children, and a duchess all of London can look up to. You'll be the envy of every man, from His Majesty to the lowest pig farmer. Every door will be open to her. You won't make a move in this city without your society watching anxiously for the briefest glimpse of her."

Falling back in the chair, Trey fixed his gaze on his grandmother, each angle of his face turning to chiseled marble.

"You seem to be well enough acquainted with the young woman," the duchess said to Clayton. "You've been introduced?"

"No."

"I understand she's incredibly beautiful."

"Yes . . . so I understand."

"And intelligent. She even reads."

Clayton crossed his legs and shifted in his chair. "Imagine that," he replied in his most matter-of-fact tone.

"And rides like a jockey."

"Shocking."

"She was seen not long ago bartering with a market fowlman over chickens. She's determined she can save His Grace a guinea a fortnight by raising her own hens and thereby producing her own eggs. Had it not been for Mistress Ellesemere's interference, I fear Park House would now be home to a dozen brooding birds." A smile flickered across her stern lips, then as quickly disappeared. She focused again on Trey.

"There will be wedding plans to make, of course."

"Then you approve of the girl?" Clayton asked.

"Of course. Did you think I wouldn't?"

Silence.

Clayton left his chair.

Her gray eyes followed him. "Is something wrong?"

"I shouldn't think you need me for this," he replied, and moved toward the door.

Just then it opened and Benjamin stepped in. Before he could get the introduction out, Thaddeus stumbled around him, face flushed, brow sweating. He dragged his hat from his head upon seeing the duchess, then his gaze flew frantically to Trey, then to Clay, then back to His Grace. "Yer Grace, I was hopin' to find ya here."

Trey left his chair.

Gulping, Thaddeus did his best to catch his breath. "It's yer lady, sir. Miracle—er, Lady Cavendish. I thought ya should know— Lud, she'll kill me fer sure fer comin'; I promised not to breathe a word, but—"

Clayton grabbed the boy by his shirt. "What the devil has happened?"

His eyes fixed on Trey, Thaddeus blurted, "The Pretender, Your Grace. The lady is drivin' 'im today at the park."

"Driving?" Clayton demanded.

"The racer," Thad said to the duke. "She's been practicin' every night for the last two week. She's goin' up against the men from the club, sir."

"Good God," Trey muttered, then turned on Clayton. 'What the devil am I supposed to do now?"

"Stop her, of course," the duchess said, leaving her chair.

"Well?" Trey demanded.

She's your responsibility now, Clayton expressed with the set of his shoulders and the stubborn thinning of his mouth. *I'm finished.*

With a curse, Trey hurried from the room. Clayton stared after him.

"You don't intend to join him?" the duchess asked.

"Why should I?"

"Curiosity, I would think. Or family loyalty."

"I grow weary and impatient of family loyalty."

The duchess moved to the door. "You always did take loyalty to the extreme," she said under her breath, then added, "I'm finding that loyalty can be a damned nuisance occasionally."

Having given Trey enough time to have departed for the park, Clayton allowed his grandmother a slight bow, then exited the room, stride lengthening, his mind scrambling over alternative routes to Hyde Park. Certainly avoid the way by Westminster, which meant Blackfriars Bridge was out of the question—too many Sunday worshipers, the snare would be murder: perhaps down Fleet Street to The Strand, out by way of Saint James's Square then to Piccadilly—

What the devil was she doing climbing into that feeble little racer? Didn't she *care* that she could be killed? Or was this just another spiteful ploy to needle him—or rather Trey—the duke—

"Clayton! Darling!" Blanche Delarue-Madras, his mistress, who he had virtually forgotten the last weeks, stepped into the foyer, stopping him dead in his tracks. Throwing open her arms and greeting him with a brilliant, delighted smile, she cried, "I'm home from Paris at last!"

At the commencement of the running, bets were five and six to four on Lady Cavendish. Indeed, the oldest sportsmen gathered had wagered on her and declared they never, surely, did see a woman drive in better style.

Word of the future duchess challenging members of the Jockey Club had obviously run rampant throughout the city. It was all Clayton could do to elbow his way through the pressing throng, men and women craning their necks, standing on their toes to watch the spectacle. By the time he arrived at the frenzied scene, the race was over.

Miracle stood up in the racer and waved at the cheering crowd, which only excited the spectators more.

"Another race!" several cried.

"My money's on the gel!" another shouted.

They cheered again.

Miracle threw them a kiss.

Bumped and jostled, Clayton allowed himself to relax. She had obviously survived the race—and won it. Why was he not surprised?

"Clayton! Darling, what is all the commotion over?"

Huffing, yanking her skirt hem from beneath a man's foot, Blanche said, "This is hardly the sort of welcome I had anticipated—being practically dragged from the house—"

"Spare us the theatrics," he told her, watching Miracle's hair tumble as she removed her purple cap and waved it in the air. Her waistcoat was purple, and she wore nankeen skirts, purple shoes, and embroidered stockings.

Blanche went to her toes, hopped up and down, as she attempted to see over the people's heads. "Scandalous."

"Isn't it?" he replied with a grin, and glanced askance at his mistress, who regarded him with a curious eye and a pout on her full red lips.

"And beautiful," she added with a tip of her head.

"Isn't she?"

"Obviously, the rumors I've heard about her are true."

"No doubt."

The crowd parted in that moment. Suddenly, the duke appeared, red-faced and agitated, but in fine form, certainly: It wouldn't do to exhibit flagrant anger in public, especially not at Miracle.

The spectators roared again.

Trey said something to Miracle. She said something to him. Clayton knew that look. Recognized the flash of fire in her blue-green eyes. Knew only too well what the set of those shoulders and the thrust of that chin portrayed. If his brother thought that bullying her in front of a hundred or more people would accomplish anything, he was sadly mistaken. "Careful, big brother," he said aloud to himself. "She bites when bitten."

Wrapping one arm around her waist, Trey dragged her off the racer. With a smile plastered across his face, his brow sweating, he maneuvered himself and Miracle through the pressing crowd toward Park House. Men slapped him on the back. They demanded to know the date of her next race, and hoped they would be invited to the wedding.

Clayton stared after the departing couple.

The realization that she was his now—*his brother's*—hit him like a blow in the stomach.

He turned and discovered Blanche regarding him curiously. "Shall I have my driver take us to my place?" she asked softly.

Sliding his hands into his pockets, Clayton nodded.

Salterdon kicked open the front door and dragged Miracle across the threshold, squirming. Gertrude, Ethel, and the cook scattered. Ellie planted herself on the bottom step of the staircase as if barricading it with her body. Upon seeing her standing there, stiff as a pillar of salt, he declared with a snarl, "You! I might have known."

"Your Grace—"

"Traitor. You always did like him best."

"Let me go!" Miracle snatched and hopped, paying little attention to the odd, angry words Salterdon shot toward her flushed and agitated friend. "How dare you handle me in such a way? You've no right! We're not married and—and if I have any say-so, we won't—"

"You have no say-so, brat." He dragged her into the drawing room, shoved her away, then slammed the door behind him. He looked, Miracle thought with a sluice of despair and a momentary twinge of fear, like a madman: face purple with rage, eyes wild, fists clenched so hard his knuckles shone white. Reason. Obstinacy would only aggravate matters.

She backed away, rolling her velvet cap in her hands. "I was never in any danger," she imparted as he paced like a leopard, hands on hips, head down, dark hair waving over his brow nearly to his eyes, before the only escape route from the room. "The trick is to know the course—"

"Be quiet." He flashed her a telling look. "I'm attempting to decide whether I want to choke you or not."

She raised her chin. "Would I be wrong in supposing that your temper is aflux over how this looks to your beloved peers, and not because I might have been injured or killed?"

A thin smile curved his hard mouth.

"Well." She sniffed. "At least you're at last being honest. Does this also mean I'm free to return to Cavisbrooke?"

"Is that what you want?" he shot back so quickly that Miracle was left momentarily speechless. The realization that whatever she admitted might well mean her future made her face go cold as ice. For the last days, since leaving Salterdon in a cloud of dust, she had thought of nothing but returning to Cavisbrooke—to her father, her horses, and her life as a hermit—and never setting eyes on the duke of Salterdon again.

"Answer me, dammit!"

She jumped, and wrung her hat harder. "I . . ." she began hesitantly, "I . . . yes . . . no. I don't know."

"You don't know? Is that my understanding? You don't know if you wish to be married?"

"Perhaps if I had more time—"

"Time? Why? So you can further humiliate me? What next, Lady Cavendish? Perhaps ride nude down Piccadilly? Dance on a stage and flash your bottom? Or perhaps something a bit more dignified. Have yourself appointed to the House of Lords . . . or should I say, Commons? Tell me what you want, Miracle."

With a little shrug, she lowered her eyes. "I've given that a great deal of thought these last weeks. I suppose what I would like best is to leave London—oh, not necessarily return to Cavisbrooke—it is rather bleak and very lonely, once I allowed myself to admit it. And there are those terrible memories . . ."

A cloud of unhappiness crossed her features. Her throat tightened. "I've imagined myself in the country. Where the air is clean and the sky is blue. Where I can have my chickens and pigs and rabbits . . . and, of course, my horses. Napitov. Hasan. Salifa. I've even given some thought to breeding them to English horses. I understand that it's been done. That the cross breeds excellently. With the English horse's ability for speed, and the Arabian's for endurance, the resulting horse would be untouchable on the track." Realizing her voice had risen with enthusiasm, Miracle glanced at Salterdon, who, having stopped his pacing, stared at her oddly.

"I'm sorry if that upsets you," she said, "and I'm sorry if that doesn't meet with your approval of what your wife should be, but it's what I am, sir. And what I will be until the day I die."

The duke dragged his hands through his hair and shook his head. The anger having drained from him, he declared in a weary, resolute voice to himself, "I must have been crazy for becoming involved in this. No amount of money is worth this worry and humiliation."

* * *

Blanche's deceased husband's money had purchased the house on Drury Lane, as well as one in Paris, and another in Rome. But she wanted Basingstoke. Badly.

Pouring himself a healthy brandy, Clayton tried his best to imagine Blanche occupying his home—all two hundred rooms of it. Perhaps it wasn't such a bad idea. She was certainly beautiful, in the run-of-the-mill sort of way. She understood his appreciation for privacy. While she didn't understand his love of labor, of tilling the soil and watching it burst forth with abundant treasures, she allowed him his "pastime," claiming he would eventually outgrow it.

No doubt they would produce handsome children together. But Blanche didn't care for children. She had gladly handed over the custody of her only son to her deceased husband's family for the settlement of £100,000.

His grandmother didn't like her. Called her a "dollymop with a pedigree."

And the fact that Trey had slept with her had come as no surprise. He'd suspected it from the beginning. He hadn't cared then, and he didn't care now.

Perhaps he *should* marry her. As the duchess had pointed out more than once—always after she had attempted to arrange a relationship with some vapid and vain daughter of one of her peers—"You'll grow fond of her in time."

Besides, marriage to Blanche might get his mind off Miracle.

"My lord," a servant said behind him. "Her ladyship is ready to see you now."

He poured Blanche a drink, refreshed his own. He took the stairs slowly, feeling as if he were scaling a mountain.

Blanche was already in bed, her black hair loose and thick and spread over the white silk sheets. Her skin looked just as white. Her lips were red. And smiling.

"Took you long enough," she teased, and patted the bed beside her.

Clayton glanced around the room. Blanche's clothes were tidily folded and put carefully into place, and it suddenly occurred to him that all their many lovemaking escapades had always been in the bed, with their clothes folded neatly, put aside carefully.

Until Miracle, spontaneity hadn't existed. Passion had been something to harness. And lust—inappropriate for a man of his station to even acknowledge, much less act upon.

Until Miracle.

He had never wanted a woman so badly as he did Miracle.

He quaffed his brandy. Then he quaffed Blanche's. He dropped the glasses to the floor, and her eyebrows went up.

"Get out of the bed," he ordered her.

"I beg your pardon?"

"The bed. Out. Get on the floor. The window. The chair. Anywhere but the bloody bed."

She sat up in bed, hugging the sheet to her breasts. "You're drunk."

"No, I'm not."

Her wide dark eyes regarded him fixedly, then, slowly, she left the bed, reluctantly releasing the sheet.

She had exquisite breasts, full and heavy. And while her waist was slightly thick (she blamed it on childbearing, but he suspected it was too much French cuisine), her hips were nicely rounded, and her thighs long and firm.

"You're beautiful," he told her gently.

"But . . ."

He glanced at the glasses on the floor, wishing he had another drink.

"There's someone else, isn't there, Clayton? Don't give me that look. You could never lie. It's not in you. You carry a wealth of emotions in those eyes, whether you realize it or not." She reached for the sheet and wrapped it around her. "I suspected it the moment I saw you this afternoon. You looked right through me. I was certain of it at the park. You're in love with Miracle Cavendish."

A smile crossed her lips, then she moved to her clothes and began to dress. "I arrived in London over a week ago. I heard the talk: His Grace was to be married. A lass he'd met on the isle some months back. He'd been so smitten he'd returned to the isle to court her. There was only one hitch in the story. Trey's current mistress is one of my dearest friends, and she confided in me that His Grace was with her those weeks."

Blanche tied the ribbons on her chemise. "I've told you all along that if you didn't cease trying to keep your brother out of trouble and under control, you would eventually become as bogged up as he. Now you've finally found the young woman of your dreams, and you've succeeded in winning her for another man—your brother. How like you."

She stepped into her gown, walked to Clayton, and offered him her back.

"You're taking this very well," he said as he fussed with the tiny pearl buttons.

"Have I any choice?"

"You could pitch a fit. Most scorned mistresses do."

"I like you too much for that."

Finished, he dropped his hands.

Blanche faced him, her smile a little sad. "What will you do now?"

"Leave London as soon as possible."

"For Basingstoke?"

"I'm not certain."

"You can't avoid them forever, you know. Eventually, you'll have to see her again."

Saying nothing, Clayton turned away and left the room. Hurrying after him, Blanche stopped at the door, her voice shaky as she called, "Perhaps I'll drop by Basingstoke to see you occasionally, if that's all right."

"You're always welcome," he replied.

Fog had set in just after dusk. It settled over everything like a gray, wet blanket. There were few hackneys on the streets and even fewer pedestrians. The lights shining through house windows were like dim candle flames in the dreary darkness.

Clayton stood on the pavement outside Park House. Benjamin hovered at his side.

'It'll be good to get home to Basingstoke," the servitor said, and unstopped his flask of brandy. "Agreed, my lord?"

'Yes," Clayton replied, staring up at the dark house. His brother's coach waited at the curb, and had been since earlier that day, when Trey had escorted a belligerent Miracle away from Hyde Park.

"What the blazes is he doing in there?" he said. "It's midnight, for God's sake . . ."

Ben turned the flask up to his mouth. "Perhaps they've kissed and made up, my lord."

Clayton glowered, causing Ben to raise his bushy gray eyebrows and drink again, then he corked the flask and slid it into his pocket. "Pardon me for saying, sir, but you had every opportunity—"

"I know that, dammit."

Ben snapped shut his mouth.

"That day she went to see Cavendish, I'd had every intention of telling her. I came to Park House with flowers. But after the meeting with her father, with Cavendish, she was in too much pain. She'd just learned the man wasn't who or what she'd always believed him to be. How was I supposed to reveal the fact that neither was I? She's been lied to all of her life, Ben. I simply couldn't do it to her again—not then."

"Now?"

"No. Not now. Not ever. She'll make one hell of a duchess, Ben. I knew the minute I saw her standing in that racer, the people at her feet cheering. They weren't cheering for the victory, but for her. She's won them, my friend. Maybe now the lot of blue-blooded sheep will at least have an acceptable icon to emulate. Before you know it, women will be reading, racing, and raising the roof off legislature, you can count on that. Places like Saint Luke's and Bethlem hospitals for the insane won't know what hit them. She's exactly what England so desperately needs. A heroine."

"And what about your needs, sir? And hers?"

"Trey will come to love her in time, despite himself. How could he not? Perhaps then he'll be capable of fulfilling her emotionally."

"But yourself, my lord. How will you manage?"

"I . . . don't know." At last, Clayton looked around, into the concerned features of his servant and friend. "I don't know," he repeated, then moved toward the hired hackney he'd left parked in the dark at the end of the street. "Let's get the devil out of here, Ben."

Love comforteth like sunshine after rain.

WILLIAM SHAKESPEARE

Chapter Twenty-two

The duchess's townhouse was located near Saint James's Square, a stone's throw from Saint James's Palace, and a short walk from the House of Parliament. As Miracle was forced to sit quietly in a tiny room off the foyer, waiting to see the duchess, who had commanded her appearance in no uncertain terms, Ellie explained that the decision to build on that particular spot had not been because either the duke or duchess of Salterdon wished to be so close to their royal cousins, but because His Grace, the duchess's husband, had been so fond of strolling to Parliament every morning, rain or shine.

"He was a most distinguished and handsome man," Ellie explained, "and greatly loved by all who knew him. He believed in advanced education, and attended Oxford himself, as did his son and grandsons. He was a dedicated philanthropist."

Grown weary of the wait, Miracle paced.

"Do sit down, darling," Ellie pleaded. "There's nothing to be nervous over. I'm certain Her Grace has gotten over the shock of seeing you fly down Rotten Row in a racer. After all, it's been over a week since the race. Had she intended to dress you down, she would have already done it."

Coming to a painting of a horse on the wall, Miracle stopped. Her heart pounded in her chest.

Ellie moved up behind her. " 'Tis a painting by Virgilius Erichsen. The woman on the gray Arabian is Catherine the Great. Like his father, the duchess's son loved Arabians passionately and traveled to Egypt with his family in hopes of purchasing a number of their stallions, intending to bring them home to England and cross them to his blooded horses."

"But the ship went down," Miracle finished.

"Having lost her husband only a few months before, then her only son, the duchess grieved for years."

Miracle walked to the open door and regarded the strangely decorated interior of the house. Its walls were hung with mandarins and fluted yellow draperies that resembled Chinese tents, with peach-blossom ceilings and canopies of tassels and bells. Imperial, five-clawed dragons darted from every chandelier and overmantel. Along with this were scattered statuaries, carpets, pictures, china, and ormolu of Dutch masters.

"The Orient is Her Grace's passion," Ellie explained. "His Grace took her there soon after they were married. She says it was the happiest time of her life."

"Why are you telling me this?" Miracle asked.

"So you'll understand her reasons for being the way she is. She was young and in love once as well. She only wants what's best for her grandson."

A servant appeared and led them down a corridor to the duchess's receiving room. Her Grace sat in a high-backed throne of a chair; she wore a Chinese garment of wine red silk, emblazoned with tiny dragons of gold thread. Her silver-white hair was loose, and beautiful, and fell over her shoulders to her waist. She no longer looked like a woman of eighty years but much younger. The fires of youth and vitality burned in her eyes.

Her grandson, the duke, Miracle's fiancé, stood attentively at her side, as always, well-dressed, hair in place, that infuriating and obnoxious curl of disdain Miracle had come to loathe on his handsome lips.

Only it wasn't her fiancé. She no longer knew this man. She no longer wanted to.

The man she had fallen in love with would not have dragged her off that racer and proceeded to chastise her so heartlessly for hours. The man she had fallen in love with would not have ridiculed her so mercilessly until she had burst into a fit of tears, despite her attempts to withstand the verbal barrage. The man she had fallen in love with would not have frightened her, shamed her so, or forbade her to come within ten yards of a horse again for the rest of her life—or his.

She would rather die.

The doors closed behind her.

Standing slightly behind her, Ellie curtsied, and flashing Miracle a telling look, mouthed, "Show your respect."

Miracle curtsied.

"So," the duchess said, "you decided to ignore my first two invitations to see me. Why?"

"I had nothing to say, Your Grace."

"And your reasons for refusing to see my grandson?" The duchess flipped her hand at the duke. He pressed his lips and set his broad shoulders. His gray eyes were hard as stones as he regarded her, and Miracle shivered.

"I have nothing to say to him as well."

"Why?"

She lifted her chin and chewed her lip. Finally, "He was rude to me. Nay, not rude, mean. Terribly mean. He called me an imbecile. An idiot. A featherbrain, dim-witted female whose name should be Disaster instead of Miracle."

Her eyebrow drawing up, the duchess drummed her fingers on the chair arm. "Did he?" she asked.

"Among other things."

"Tell me why you attempted such a spectacle."

"Because I wanted to."

"And do you always do everything you want, my dear? Even if it means putting your life or the lives of others in danger?"

"I wasn't in danger. His Grace is perfectly aware that I'm a more than capable rider." Turning on the duke, she declared, "You've seen me ride Napitov—"

He stared at her blankly.

Drawing back her shoulders, Miracle returned to the duchess. "I suppose you'll be sending me home, now that I've brought such discomfiture to Your Grace."

"Ah. I begin to understand, I think. You thought that if you did this silly thing, I would send you packing. No more marriage. My grandson would be saved the humiliation of your breaking off the engagement yourself. Clever girl. But not that clever. No, I shall not send you packing, my dear."

"But surely you cannot still want me to marry him!" she cried.

"You've given me no logical reason why I shouldn't."

"What about what I want?"

"Which is?"

Miracle covered her face with her hands. She tried to breathe. To reason. She felt like she had been dragged before a magistrate to defend her life, and at that moment, her life made no sense whatsoever. The tangle of emotions inside her was excruciating.

Finally, she focused on Salterdon's hard face again. "I *want* to love you still," she told him, her voice quivering. "If I could find a semblance of the man you were on the island, then perhaps . . . *He* was gentle. *He* laughed at my pigs, even spoke to them. Oh, don't deny it, Your Grace, I saw you when you thought you were alone, chatting to Chuck."

His mouth pursed.

"You treated John like your equal. You enjoyed my porridge. You encouraged my dreams. Your eyes were soft, your hands were warm. You liked my hair down, blowing in the wind. You called me Meri Mine. You rallied for my honor—a knight in shining armor. You turned your face into the wind, and I showed you how to fly.

"You were vulnerable. I could touch you then. You cared nothing for convention.

"You looked like a farmer.

"And you cared enough about my happiness to buy a dozen silly shirts because I'd sewn them."

The duchess cleared her throat, and in a kinder voice, said, "There will be wedding plans to be made, of course. In the meantime, I feel you should leave London. Occasionally, time away from one another helps to mend emotional rifts." She left the chair and walked to Miracle, took Miracle's chin with her gentle fingers that were cool and soft and sparkling with rings. "I can see why my grandson came to love you so." She turned away. "Mistress Ellesemere?"

Ellie moved up and curtsied.

"See that Miracle's belongings are prepared. I think a little time in the country will help her spirit, not to mention her heart."

"Yes, Your Grace. May I ask to where Lady Cavendish will be traveling?"

"To Salisbury," she replied. "To Basingstoke."

There had been little time to dwell on her circumstances. The sudden banishment to Basingstoke had taken both Miracle and Ellie by surprise. By the time they had returned to Park House, their belongings had been trunked. Gertrude had prepared a basket of food for their journey, and Ethel had presented Miracle with a bouquet of yellow roses she had plucked from the garden. Miracle had rewarded Thaddeus with a kiss on the cheek, and his face had turned beet red.

Leaving the house that had been her home for such a short time, Miracle wondered if she would ever see it again. She wasn't certain that she cared. She felt numb. And unhappy. She wanted to go home to Cavisbrooke, to see her horses and her father. Would he forgive her for leaving him like she had, with nary a look back and no good-bye? Imagine: After all these years, the many times she had wished to herself that Johnny had been her father, now he was.

The foremost thing that struck Miracle during their journey to Basingstoke was the beauty of the countryside, from the exquisite turf and foliage and soft, moist atmosphere, to the buttercup meadows and vales covered in huge elms that lifted to airy heights against the blue sky.

They passed farmhouses of beautifully fashioned brick and stone with enameled meadows and filigree hedges. Outside each hamlet there were alehouses with placid drinkers gathered beneath the spreading oaks and chestnuts, old men who lifted their tankards in greeting as the chaise lumbered by, and always there were the old gray churches and barns rising up from the ground as if they were a part of the earth themselves.

As it was Sabbath day, the church bells pealed a continuous chain of music that rang like angels over the countryside. Families milled about the grounds, the road, the meadows, children in white gowns, prancing in carpets of flowers while the choir's voice reverberated their lyrical message to the heavens.

"Lovely, isn't it?" Ellie commented as she gazed out at the passing countryside.

"The most beautiful country I've ever seen," Miracle replied honestly, and for the first time in days, she smiled. A butterfly of excitement had taken wing in her stomach, and the confusion and despair she had experienced the last days, nay, weeks, now seemed less monumental. There was something about the land and sky and the freedom to enjoy them that was a panacea to the soul. 'Will we be arriving at Basingstoke soon?" she asked eagerly.

"My dear, you've been on Basingstoke grounds for the last quarter hour."

Surprised, Miracle searched the hills and vales even harder. Yes, she could see it now, the uniformity of the countryside. There were great oaks and hedgerows of elm and ash and a scattering of forest trees in the distant meadows.

Ellie called out to the driver to stop, then she climbed from the chaise and said to Miracle, "Come along, my dear. One can hardly appreciate the beauty and serenity of the countryside when it's flying by so fast. Here, take my hand. We'll walk to the top of the hill."

Miracle took Ellie's hand. It was warm and as small as her own, and gripped her with a firm fondness that brought a tightness to Miracle's throat.

Reaching the top of the knoll, they stopped, and Miracle caught her breath. As far as she could see, the lush landscape spread from horizon to horizon. There were cultivated plots of young corn, a field of barley, another of wheat. Sheep grazed on the east grounds and cattle on the west. Amid it all were the labyrinths of woody lanes, crossroads, and cartways leading up and down hills to straw-roofed stone houses that were buried in leaves and wreathed to their clustered chimneys with vines. Everywhere, along the wagon roads, the footpaths, and even where Miracle and Ellie stood, were hedges of shepherd's rose, honeysuckle, and wildflowers.

"Basingstoke?" is all Miracle could manage to say.

"All of it," Ellie told her, her voice proud. "The houses yonder belong to Basingstoke's tenants. There are the farmers, of course, and their families. But there are also craftsmen whose workmanship is some of the finest in England. There are the drovers for the sheep, the woodcutters, hurdlers, spoke choppers, faggoters, and the rake and ladder makers. Not to mention the blacksmiths, wheelwrights, masons, and carpenters. They build the fences, the barns, the windmills and watermills. The church we passed several miles back, Lord Basingstoke had built for his workers, not to mention the alehouses. The church is used as a school for the tenants' children on every day except the Sabbath. Lord Basingstoke doesn't allow children under twelve to toil in the fields. He feels that education is of foremost importance to the young mind. I might add, his lordship finished Oxford magna cum laude, you know, then went on to study at Gray's Inn."

"Shall I meet him at last?" Miracle asked, and a look of slight consternation crossed Ellie's brow.

"I'm not certain," she replied. "I've heard he's out of the country . . . gone to Paris, I'm told."

"A shame," Miracle sighed. "I should like to meet him. He sounds quite . . . exceptional." She closed her eyes and turned her face up to the sun. The wind kissed her cheeks and toyed with her hair. Ah, the solitude, broken only by the whirring of partridges and pheasants. She had not enjoyed such quiet and peace since leaving Cavisbrooke.

"We've not got much farther to travel," came Ellie's voice, and Miracle reluctantly opened her heavy-lidded eyes to see Ellie pointing toward the very distant hill. "Just beyond there is Basingstoke Hall."

Nothing could have prepared her. Nothing.

Stepping from the chaise, Miracle stared, speechless, at the house. Only it wasn't a house. It was a palace. Even the term *palace* seemed to understate the structure before her.

"Basingstoke won the estate in a card game ten years ago," Ellie explained, nodding to the driver to unload their baggage. "He was only twenty at the time. The house you see before you was little more than a ruin."

Miracle moved down the wide bricked pavement leading to the sprawling marble entrance of immense pillars, while around her the lawns stretched out like green lakes, broken only by meandering footpaths that led to fountains and walled gardens. How cunningly blended was the artificial with the natural, lawns merging with park, which glistened with sun-kissed ponds. Miracle's heart raced as a deer grazing in the distance raised its head and regarded her in so tame a fashion she was certain she could have walked up to it.

The doors opened before her.

Ellie spoke softly to the majordomo, but Miracle didn't listen. Standing in the center of the vast entrance hall, she slowly turned round and round, her senses taking in the porphyry columns and cornices adorned by Etruscan griffins. The ceiling, rising at least fifty feet, depicted cherubs and angels amid clouds, all of which had been painted in a manner to reproduce Italian classics of centuries ago. A fairylike chandelier was suspended there as well, hanging from carved monastic heads. At night it would glisten with hundreds of candles.

Ellie said, "According to Marvin, Lord Basingstoke is in residence after all. However, since no mention of our arrival was made to the staff, we can only assume Her Grace failed to communicate our visit to Basingstoke. In other words, he wasn't expecting us."

"Where is he now?" Miracle asked, still studying her surroundings in amazement. "Shall I meet him? Perhaps we shouldn't stay."

"Oh, we'll stay," Ellie replied stubbornly, "and you'll meet him . . . if it's the last thing I ever do. Come along, my dear, and prepare to be sufficiently astounded."

Marvin shoved open immense double doors, revealing a continuous chamber some three hundred feet long. Its ceilings were spandreled and traceried in the Gothic taste, its walls paneled with golden moldings and shields emblazoned with the quarterings of England. The spread of windows along the left wall were curtained with crimson velvet, and every fifty feet, chandeliers, exactly like the one in the entrance hall, hung from the ceilings.

They passed the circular dining room, whose walls were lined with silver and whose pier glasses reflected forests of Ionic columns with silver capitals: the crimson drawing room with a blue velvet carpet and a breathtaking chandelier whose three circles of lights surrounded a cascade of crystal glass; the vestibule; the anteroom; the rose satin drawing room; the blue velvet room; and then they came to a circular double staircase, which they ascended on royal blue carpets to another set of apartments, the corridor sweeping past a library with shelves of leather-bound books so high one would be forced to mount a ladder to reach them.

Next came the golden drawing room, then the Gothic dining room, and right to the anteroom, dining room, and conservatory. Then, at last, to the private apartments. There were twenty-six in this wing alone, Ellie pointed out.

Finally, they arrived at a room so large it would have easily swallowed the great hall at Cavisbrooke. On both the north and south walls were massive fireplaces, big enough, Miracle thought, to roast an entire ox. In the center of the room, upon a circular dais, was the largest bed Miracle had ever seen, with yards of lilac sheers spilling from the tester canopy.

"I think you'll be comfortable here," Ellie said. "I'll be just down the hallway. After you've rested, we'll discuss your desire to return to Cavisbrooke."

Miracle said nothing as her friend quit the room. What could she say? She had made up her mind. There was no turning back, no matter how nagging was the pang of putting the hopeless love she continued to feel for Salterdon behind her.

Why did it continue to hurt? To disturb her and confuse her? Had she been so ridiculously naive as to believe he could so totally change from the man he had been months ago?

She tried to nap. Sleep refused her. She paced for a while, then discovered a vestibule leading from double French doors off one side of her room. She wandered out onto a quiet garden where a nightingale perched on a tree limb and heralded the encroaching dusk.

What delicious serenity. How she had missed the birds, the trees, and the sky. Wrapping herself up in the peace of it all, she could almost put everything else from her mind. But, as always, his memory wormed its way back in: images of their passion paraded before her mind's eye in shameful and disquieting array, until her blood warmed and her breathing quickened, and the alarming realization came to her that she might never again experience the sort of desire and longing for a man that she felt even now for His Grace.

So she walked out across the lawns in her bare feet. Dusk dew beaded upon her toes. The crisp breeze of encroaching nightfall kissed her cheeks and made them tingle. Her spirits lifted.

Ah, freedom! To run again, to dance again. She spun on her toes. To leap again. Surely, this was heaven.

In the distance were twinkling lights. Pausing upon a hilltop, she gazed down on the sprawling stone barns—the most beautiful she had ever seen—with tiled roofs and arched windows and Dutch doors. There were arenas as well, full of soft sand encircled by white-painted fences.

Raising her skirt slightly, she ran slowly at first, then faster, like a naughty child on some clandestine mission to disobey her parent. She startled a grazing deer and laughed as it bounded away, white tail rising and falling, zigzagging, until it diminished into the dark.

Panting, she fell against the barn wall, closed her eyes, allowed the sounds and smells to enfold her. Fresh hay. Grain with molasses. Dung. Horse . . . And something else. Perfume? Incense? No, not here.

Voices.

She moved toward the open door where golden light spilled over the ground.

"Thief. That you are, sir. I wager you've a card or two slipped up your sleeve," came the familiar voice.

"That's an entire shilling you owe me now, Ben."

The men laughed.

Miracle stepped through the door and focused on the gentlemen with their gray heads bowed over a table strewn with cards.

Benjamin looked up first. His eyes became saucers. He leapt to his feet, capsizing the milk stool on which he was perched. "Good God," he declared, then stuttered and exclaimed again, "*Good God*! What are you doing here?"

"Benjamin? Oh, Benjamin!" she cried, and breaking into a smile, and laughing in pleasure, she flew across the floor and flung herself on the stunned servant, hugging him fiercely, even as he stood stiff as a corpse in her arms. "I've missed you," she confessed. Then, drawing back, she stared up into his ashen face and round eyes. "What are you doing here?"

"I . . . ahem. I . . ."

"Have you come back to work for Lord Basingstoke?"

"Back to work?" He blinked and swallowed and nodded.

"Yes. Yes, that's right. I was working for His Grace . . . temporarily. I believe that was the arrangement," he muttered to himself, then relaxed and smiled. "Right-o. I've come back to work for Basingstoke."

She gave him a fond squeeze, then turned to his companion, who no longer sat at the table. Against his empty milk stool, however, lay a walking stick with a horse-head grip. Her gaze flew to the distant stable door, where John was apparently attempting to escape.

He froze. And slowly turned.

Miracle could say nothing. She forgot to breathe. Tears filled her eyes and spilled down her cheeks. She thought she might faint.

Lowering his red-rimmed eyes, he said faintly, "Well now, imagine this. A man sits down to share a nip and a game with an associate, and who drops by for a cheery hello but an old friend."

"A friend, sir?" she replied softly. "Would you hurt me further by refusing to acknowledge me for who I really am?" She shook her head. "How could I have been so blind all these years? How could I not have known? Of all the times you tucked me into my bed and told me stories and kissed me good night, I would ofttimes go to sleep imagining that you were my father."

Drawing back his shoulders, clearing his throat, John met her eyes at last. "I loved her, ya know. More than life itself."

"I know that."

"But she loved Cavendish. And what's buried that deeply in the heart don't change overnight, if ever. Not if it's real. In love . . . ya take the good with the bad, knowin' that the good will make the bad seem inconsequential. That's the sacrifice I made to stay with her . . . and you. I'll make no more excuses for what I done."

Smiling, she went to him. He opened his strong arms and she fell into them. He hugged her fiercely for long minutes, each gaining control of their emotions.

At last, she sniffed and pulled away, fixed him with her old belligerent stare, her eyes widening. "Just what the blazes are you doing here, anyway?"

He looked beyond her, to Benjamin, who continued to stand stiffly, regarding the emotional scene. "Tell her why I'm here, Ben ol' boy," John said.

"Why you're here? Ah . . . er . . . hmm, well . . ."

"A weddin' gift," John blurted so suddenly Miracle jumped. "That's it. Yer fiancé brung me. His Grace. Felt ya couldn't be married without yer only friend and family bein' in attendance."

"But to Basingstoke? Why not to London?"

"To London?"

Somewhere in the distance, a horse snorted. Then came the thunder, the powerful pounding of hooves clashing upon the cobblestone floor of the long string of stables. Slowly, Miracle stepped around John, and peered down the barn corridor, into the dark. Her heart pounded, and her breathing quickened.

Napitov emerged from the stables, neck arched, ears pointed, nostrils flared and drinking in the wind. He emitted a roaring greeting upon seeing her, and tossed his exquisite head, his black eyes flashing.

Miracle ran to meet him, threw her arms around his sleek neck, and buried her face against it. "John, you darling man, you brought them—" Laughing and crying too, she turned back to John. "That's why you didn't go to London—the horses."

"Aye." John glanced back at Benjamin, who cut his eyes to John, then back to Miracle.

"They were to be a wedding gift," Benjamin announced. "Right. A wedding gift. A surprise. To be given you after the ceremony. From Lord Basingstoke."

John scowled.

Benjamin pressed his lips.

"Basingstoke?" Miracle asked. "Why Basingstoke?"

"His Grace mentioned the horses to his lordship," John hurried to explain.

Miracle's face turned cold. "He promised he would never say a word about the horses to anyone. If word got back—"

"You needn't worry," Ben proclaimed. "Basingstoke understands your love of the horses."

"Why would Basingstoke understand anything about me?" she demanded, her panic rising.

Obviously deciding he had already said too much, Ben closed his mouth and set his shoulders.

Napitov lowered his velvety muzzle into her hand, and Miracle felt her irritation subside. "It doesn't matter," she said more softly. "Because I'll be returning to Cavisbrooke soon. There shan't be a wedding."

Both men stepped forward. "No wedding?" they said in unison.

"Nay. No wedding. I fear His Grace and I have come to a parting of the minds and hearts." To John, she said, "I can't be something or someone I'm not. I would never fit into his world, and he obviously has no desire to fit into mine. So you see, John, you came all this way for nothing. I've made up my mind, and I don't care what Her Grace or Ellie or any of you say. I won't marry the duke of Salterdon. No matter how much it grieves me to admit it, I just don't think that I love him any longer."

Along with the laborers employed to cultivate and manage the hundreds of sections of crops, Clayton had worked until well after sunset. He enjoyed the peaceful ride back to the hall. After a strenuous day of toiling with his body under the sun, he was too tired to think, too exhausted to dwell on the last weeks. Astride the bay horse, he allowed the reins to fall loose and closed his eyes, concentrated on the burning of each muscle, the swirl of hunger in his belly, the stirring of drowsiness in his mind.

Perhaps tonight, at last, he would find sleep . . . without the dreams. Without waking in the middle of the night with Miracle's eyes haunting him and the memory of her unabashed lovemaking driving him from his bed to pace.

The horse stopped suddenly. Its body tensed and quivered. Clayton searched the darkness up ahead. Finally, the sound came to him: A wagon, crashing along the stony path at breakneck speed.

Clayton's eyebrows raised at the sight of Ben bouncing up and down on the driver's perch, hands desperately clutching the reins, his suit coat flapping with each exaggerated bounce.

"Whoa!" the servant shouted upon seeing Clayton. "Whoa! I said whoa, you bleeding sack of larvae infested dung! Whoa, I say!" As the horse, wagon, and driver careened past Clayton, the valet shouted, "Help!"

Clayton whistled. The wagon stopped.

His gray hair standing on end, his face white, and his hound's eyes bulging, Ben stared at Clayton dumbly. "Good gosh," he finally uttered. "I thought I was going to die."

"Chester." Clayton pointed to a bony, mulish horse that, upon hearing his name, looked back at Clayton with his upper lip curled up and his teeth showing. "I bought him from gypsies. He's a trick horse and responds only to certain whistles. Would you like to see what he'll do if I warble like a nightingale?"

"I would not," Ben declared.

He laughed. "Mind telling me what you're doing here?"

"A situation has arisen. An unannounced guest has arrived at Basingstoke. Just thought you should know."

Clayton waited. Unannounced guests were hardly out of the norm. There wasn't a solitary member of society who had not happened by Basingstoke conveniently at nightfall. Inevitably, their overnights would linger for several days.

"Lady Cavendish," Ben announced.

Meri.

"It seems your grandmother sent her here to 'think over, and hopefully reconsider' her decision to scrub her engagement to His Grace." Keeping a wary eye on Chester, Ben smoothed down his hair and straightened his coat. "Seems the lady has misgivings about His Grace. Can't find much to like in him, she says. Not the man she . . . fell in love with at Carisbrooke."

"And John—"

"Blundered upon as we were wagering at cards in the barn."

"The horses—"

"An emotional meeting, to say the least."

"You explained—"

"That the horses and John were to be a wedding gift—"

"From Trey—"

"From you." Ben smiled. "The jig is up, my lord. Mr. Hoyt and I have come to the conclusion that, for the lass's sake and yours, the truth should be revealed."

"The hell you say." Spurring his horse, Clayton reined the startled animal toward home.

Ben cried out behind him, "What about Chester, my lord? My lord? Basingstoke? *Basingstoke!*"

Love looks not with the eyes,
But with the mind:
And therefore is winged Cupid
painted blind.
WILLIAM SHAKESPEARE

Chapter Twenty-three

Hidden in the dark, Clayton watched Miracle curry Napitov. She braided his flowing silver-gray mane. She fed him carrots and apples and corn from her hands while Ismail saw to the others—all twelve of them, their beautiful dished heads extended through the opened Dutch stable doors, eagerly awaiting their evening feeding of grain and hay.

She carefully cleaned Nap's hooves and polished them with a soft cloth until they shone, and she spoke openly of her time in London, while John sat near and whittled on a stick, occasionally raising his head to watch her, his brow creased in consternation.

"He can't help being what he is any more than I can. He has such potential. Such great kindness and generosity. I saw it when he was on the island. I miss that man desperately. But he's happy in London. And he has a responsibility to his grandmother, and his title. He's the duke of Salterdon, and he must live and act accordingly. Oh, but I shall miss him," she added more softly, her eyes becoming distant.

Much later, he sat on a marble bench below her room and gazed up at the glowing windows until the lights went out. Then her French doors opened, and she moved out onto the balcony and stood there, staring off over the moon-drenched countryside, the wind blowing her hair and white nightgown.

Why the blazes didn't he say something? Reveal himself and his secret? Go on his knee and beg her forgiveness and understanding. Explain that he was obligated to his brother—Trey had saved his life, after all—as twins they were closer than brothers, which was why he was flailing now in this mire of guilt. He was in love with Miracle Cavendish, had made love to Miracle Cavendish, had purposely charmed his way into her heart, portrayed his brother as someone and something he wasn't. She had fallen in love with a fraud. Was it any wonder that her only desire now was to return to Cavisbrooke, the only reality she had ever known?

As usual, Miracle joined John and Ellie for breakfast on Basingstoke's east veranda. She nibbled her crumpets and sipped her chocolate, looking back and forth between her father and Ellie, who had eyes only for one another. Miracle had dressed to ride, hoping for an earlier lesson on Napitov, only to learn that John had already made plans to take Ellie on a buggy ride through the countryside. She felt inordinately piqued. Then again, such irritation was only one of the emotions she had recently dealt with. She just couldn't seem to get a handle on her feelings. She felt like crying one moment and laughing hysterically the next.

"Don't you think it odd," Miracle suddenly announced, bringing her companions' attention around to her, "that we've resided at Basingstoke an entire week and have yet to meet Lord Basingstoke himself? I'm beginning to think he's as low as his brother."

"Miracle," Ellie scolded. "That's not a very kind thing to say about our host. Especially after he's so graciously opened his magnificent home to us."

"No doubt because his grandmother ordered him to."

Ellie scowled.

Wringing her napkin in her lap, Miracle raised her chin. "I want to go home."

"Not yet," Ellie replied sternly.

"Why ever not? I don't intend to change my mind, if that's what you think. I shan't marry a man who cannot be bothered to come to Basingstoke and attempt to win me over."

"Is that what this is about?" Ellie smiled and glanced at John. "You're angry because His Grace has not come crawling on his knees in hopes of winning you back?"

"If he loved me, he would. Obviously, he doesn't."

"You said you never wanted to see him again."

Miracle sipped at her steaming chocolate and burned her tongue. "I don't."

"Then what the blazes are ya complainin' about," John said, then shook his finger at her. "You've got that damnable stubborn set to your jaw, lass, and we both know what that means. You'll work yerself up into a tizzy if you're not careful, then we're all in for trouble."

"Really, Miracle. You're acting like a spoiled child," Ellie added.

"Well!" Flinging her napkin onto her plate, Miracle jumped from her chair, and with her hands on her hips, glared first at Ellie, then at John. "I can certainly see that I'm not wanted here this morning. Good day to you both."

She stormed to the stables. As she waited for Ismail to saddle Napitov, she paced. It was then she noticed a servant emerge from a thicket of trees beyond the barns. Miracle had previously paid little attention to the distant, mostly hidden brick building, thinking it was a forgotten outbuilding.

The realization occurred her, however, that that was where her unsociable hermit of a host probably resided.

Miracle hurried to the servant, stopping the surprised girl with a "Wait!"

"Milady?"

"His lordship . . . is that where he resides?"

"Yes, milady."

"Is he there now?"

"No, milady."

"When will he return?"

"I wouldn't know, milady."

Miracle frowned and tapped her skirt with her riding crop. "Is he always so rude as to completely ignore his houseguests?"

"Milady?"

"Nothing . . . Tell me this: Is his lordship in residence, or has he fled the country?"

Smiling, the girl nodded. "Oh, yes, milady. His lordship is definitely in residence."

With a curtsy, the servant continued on her way, and Miracle returned to the stable.

As usual, she allowed Napitov the freedom to work off his excess energy. With the wind roaring in her ears, they galloped cross-country, taking the hedges in high, clean leaps. By the time they reached the tenant's cottages, Nap was lathered and content to trot.

A half dozen children ran out to greet her. Their mothers hurried behind. They curtsied and smiled, first at Miracle, then at the children who clustered about their skirts.

"Our apologies," a woman declared, and mussed her son's hair. "It isn't often that we're visited by gentry—unless it's his lordship, of course."

Miracle slid from Nap's back. A boy hurried to her, hefting a bucket of cool water, which he placed before the horse. Miracle glanced about the cluster of houses. She noted there wasn't one among them that needed repair. All were beautifully kept, their gardens immaculate, as were the tenants themselves. The children were rosy-cheeked with good health. There wasn't even a tatter on their freshly laundered clothes.

"Does his lordship get by often?" she asked.

"Several times a week, milady."

"To make certain the work is being done properly, I assume."

"Yes. And to see to our general welfare."

"Are you happy here? Is Basingstoke a considerate landlord?"

The women all exchanged smiles and soft giggles. Lifting a toddler in her arms, a yellow-haired woman in a calico dress and apron replied, "I've never known another landlord to be so generous and mindful of his workers. Before he sells a bushel of his crops, he makes certain we have all that we need. He sells what he needs to see a slight profit, then the excess he contributes to London charities."

"Such as the Charterhouse—"

"And the Foundling Hospital," another woman added.

"Not to mention the schools—"

"And free dispensaries. The food his lordship supplies them is enough to feed a thousand children."

"He's ever so kind," a tiny lad with a skinned nose declared.

Smiling, Miracle went down on her knee before him. "Is he?" she asked softly. "Why do you think so?"

"When I hurt me leg, he sent all the way to London for a doctor. And 'cause I was so brave, he said someday he wanted a son just like me."

"Does he like children?"

The lad nodded and beamed.

The child's mother laughed. "As we said, his lordship is most generous. Just a week back, he presented each of our husbands with a new shirt—the most exquisitely made garments we've ever seen."

"They came from the Isle of Wight," another said.

Slowly, Miracle stood. She looked from one face to another. "The Isle—?"

"I have one here." A short woman with her arms full of laundry stepped forward and handed the shirt to Miracle. It was her shirt, one that she had sewn with her own hands.

As they had for the past several nights, Ellie and John talked softly in the moonlight, each sitting a respectable distance apart, but their occasional smiles and Ellie's soft, feminine laughter bespoke their growing fondness for one another. With her French door slightly ajar, Miracle sat in the darkness and listened to their murmurings and wished they would find someplace other than Ellie's balcony to do their courting. How damnably inconvenient.

Miracle waited until midnight before slipping from her room. At the far end of the corridor, a manservant snuffed the last burning candle, and complete darkness fell with a silent implosion around her. Quiet voices touched her ear: servants bidding each other a good night. Then silence.

Miracle fixed her path straight down the center of the hallway, moved carefully, cautiously, her hands out before her, every sense straining, ears roaring with her own breathing, her heart thumping loudly. For the last two days she had memorized every hallway, corner, and piece of furniture down the corridor walls, counted strides, knew exactly when she passed the dining room, the anteroom, and reaching the top of the stairs, her hand sought for and found the smooth banister. Thirty-five steps to the floor, then left, down the long corridor with its draped windows, then into the entrance hall and out the front door.

Having escaped the house, she ran quickly down one meandering walkway after another, was forced to stop and catch her breath, then continued on, like a mouse in a maze, winding through hedgerows, rose gardens, fleeing over footbridges, slowing past the awe-inspiring marble carving of rearing horses, then hurrying toward the stables.

By the time she reached the stables, she was gasping for breath and asking herself if, possibly, she had truly lost her senses.

Easing through the shadows, she moved beyond the stables, paused on the footpath, and gazed through the thicket of trees and bramble to the window twinkling pale light into the darkness.

"Very well, Basingstoke," she said aloud. "Tonight we shall meet at last. After all, I should know my husband's brother, should I indeed decide to marry the arrogant, ill-tempered duke of Salterdon, who is apparently appallingly governed by his grandmother's every wish."

She would know this man who garnered such loyalty from his tenants yet was apparently too reclusive to bother with houseguests. She would know how he came about owning the very shirts his brother had purchased on the isle, and why he had given them to the help.

Reaching the cottage, she stared at the door. Setting her shoulders, taking a deep breath, she banged on it.

Silence.

Miracle frowned and knocked again.

Nothing.

She eased open the door, squinting at the intrusion of light on her eyes. The neat, comfortably furnished room was empty.

"Blast it," she muttered, then casting a guarded glance over her shoulder, eased into the apartment, and closed the door behind her.

What had she expected to find? There was nothing unusual here: stacks of books, well-worn furnishings, and a partially finished glass of liquor placed beside an open book.

Miracle moved to the table and picked up the glass. She smelled it. Tasted it. Brandy. She would be certain to inform Earl Fanshawe, if she ever saw him again, that Basingstoke had not turned to port.

She left the small house, stood in the dark among the trees and vines, and laughed to herself. Dear heavens. She must be becoming horribly bored. Whenever had she been driven to sneak about the world at night, clandestinely entering houses, searching out reasons for peoples' eccentricities. God only knew, she had enough of them herself. That made her laugh even more.

She had become one of them. Those curious, small-minded people who looked on anything out of the ordinary as strange and something to be dissected in order to discover what, exactly, it was that made a person odd —as if it might be contagious.

She heard a sound in the trees.

Her heart skipping, Miracle stared into the dark, reason giving her a swift kick on her bottom. How would she explain to her host that she had been meddling around his house?

Swiftly, she took to the path, gripping her skirts, not bothering to weave her way back to the hall by way of the paved or gravel walks. As she rounded the east wing of the house, she stopped short. A couple loitered there—a man and woman—servants, who suddenly flung themselves upon one another and began to kiss passionately.

Her face flaming, Miracle spun on her toes and dashed in another direction, her eyes searching frantically for another way into the manse. At last finding a door, she tried it, gasped in relief to find it unlocked, then leaped through the threshold and slammed it closed behind her.

She stared into the dark like one peering into the mouth of an unexplored cave. Where the blazes was she?

Inching forward, she felt her way through the dark and hit a chair, bruising her knee. She stubbed her toe against the foot of a settee and bumped into a table, causing something glass to clatter. She envisioned the dawn light revealing a path of shattered china and crystal all the way to her bedroom. How would she explain that to Ellie? To John? To her host? And her fiancé? She imagined the duchess of Salterdon looming up over her in an Oriental gown, breathing smoke like a royal dragon.

A door—an exit, which meant a hallway. At last. She took a deep breath.

Where now? Which staircase? Which corridor? One wrong turn and she could very well wind up in the coal room.

There was a sound behind her. She froze, heart thumping, lungs bursting. Someone was near. She could feel it. His presence stole over her like warm air.

"Lady Cavendish," came the soft, gruff voice through the darkness.

"Yes?" she replied, doing her best to sound as normal as possible, considering the abnormal circumstances.

"Are you lost?"

She nodded her head.

"I thought so." Hands closed gently onto her shoulders, turned her partially to one side, eased her forward. She obliged, reluctant at first, feeling vulnerable.

"Did you enjoy your midnight stroll?" came his voice again, still little more than a breathy whisper.

"Yes, thank you," she replied, more curious over the warm tenderness of his hands on her shoulders than the fact that he apparently was aware of her sojourn through the moonlight.

"Are you enjoying your stay at Basingstoke?" he asked, a touch of tempered curiosity sounding in the words.

"Very much."

"Good." The word smiled. "If there's anything we can do to make your visit here more pleasant—"

"There is."

"Oh?"

"I would meet Basingstoke."

The hands turned her again. Instead of carpeting beneath her feet, there was cold marble.

"And what would you say to Basingstoke?"

"That he's incredibly rude, of course, for not presenting himself."

"He's a very busy man."

"There's no excuse for being impolite."

"You're absolutely right. Careful. Turn left here, step down two—watch the pedestal—we haven't far to go now. A few more steps. There. Straight before you is the corridor to the west wing. I'm certain you can find your way from here."

Miracle breathed a sigh of relief and, as the hands left her shoulders, she turned around. The shadow of a man had moved off. "Thank you," she called, her heart racing for some odd reason.

"You're most welcome, my lady," came the distant reply.

The next night, at precisely midnight, Miracle stood beside the towering marble statue of rearing horses, shivering slightly in the cold, which had roused that afternoon with a brief rain. There were no stars, no moon. The night seemed as dark and cloistering as the hall had the midnight before.

"Where the blazes are you?" she said aloud. "I know you're out there. I sense you've been watching me. I should have realized last evening who you were. Basingstoke. I didn't realize until later, lying in bed. Had you been a mere servant you would have lit a candle. You would have seen me to my room. Why won't you reveal yourself?"

Nothing.

She sighed. How preposterous this must seem. No doubt she was simply allowing her imagination to get the better of her. Why would the lord of this immense and awe-inspiring manor choose not to reveal himself?

"Hardly an evening for a rendezvous," came the voice from the dark.

Miracle spun around, searched the shadowed grounds.

"Do you always meet strangers at midnight, Lady Cavendish?"

Heart racing, Miracle called, "I do if it's the only way to acquaint myself with recalcitrant hosts, sir."

"Do you ever sleep, Lady Cavendish?"

"Do you, my lord?"

Laughter?

Frantically, she searched each of the brick pathways leading to the statue. There! A shadow—a form— She took a step toward it.

"No," came the firm command.

"But why?"

"I'm simply not . . . ready."

"Ready for what, sir?"

"To end this."

"To end what, sir?"

"Your being here, in my home. I've enjoyed watching you fill up the emptiness, Lady Cavendish."

"Emptiness?" She laughed brightly and took a tentative step forward, hands clasped at the small of her back, weight balancing lightly on the balls of her feet. "Basingstoke Hall is hardly empty, sir. In truth, I never saw such glorious and abundant furnishings."

"Then you like my home?"

"Like it? Oh, sir, *like* is an understatement. What woman wouldn't care to live in such palatial surroundings?"

"Women who enjoy frolicking in cobwebs and haunted old castles," came the amused response.

"Oh." Miracle pursed her lips and took another step forward. "I suppose His Grace has informed you about Cavisbrooke."

"Yes."

"Then I'm obviously at a disadvantage. You know much more of me than I of you."

"You know me. You've seen how I live."

"I know you're a romantic, sir. You refuse to live in the hall until you've found the woman you wish to marry. I know you're very kind. Your tenants are happy and tell me that you put their welfare above your own. You love horses. I can tell by the stables. They're the finest stables I've ever seen. Clean. Airy. Warm. The animals glow with good health."

Silence.

"Basingstoke!" she called, feeling strangely frantic with the idea that he had left her.

"Yes."

Miracle relaxed. "Since you know so much about me, I suppose you know that I might possibly be returning to Cavisbrooke. I've reconsidered marrying His Grace."

"Why?"

"I fear I no longer love him."

"Why?"

Leaning back against the cold, smooth marble of the horse, Miracle hugged herself. "I can't explain it, really," she replied in a soft, contemplative voice. " 'Tis said that Cupid's eyes are blind. Mayhap I listened to my heart and not my mind. Mayhap I wanted to love him, and saw only that which I craved to see. I fear reality revealed him for what he was."

"Which is?"

"My eyes see him as a pompous aristocrat who cares more for title and peers and his grandmother's fortune than he does for me. I see him as selfish, self-centered, often cruel. My heart, however, sees him as he was on the isle, where I fell in love with him. There he was kind and gentle and giving. Tell me, my lord. Which man is he? Truly?"

"You're asking me?" The query sounded gruff and angry . . . and anguished. "My God. *She asks me.* What will you do if I confess that he *is* selfish and self-centered and often cruel? Run as fast as you can back to Cavisbrooke to live out your life in some falling-down old haunt? My God, what a waste. If I allay your fears and assure you that he's kind and gentle and giving, that you'll never know a moment's unhappiness as his wife, you'll marry him. Either way, I've . . ."

"You've what?" she called when the silence stretched out like an eternity. "Basingstoke? Basingstoke!" Miracle ran down the path, to the place where the shadow had lingered the last minutes. She searched the dark the best she could, disappointment lodging in her breast like a hot stone with the realization that he had vanished again.

Then her gaze dropped to the path. Falling to one knee, Miracle carefully picked up the long-stemmed white rose lying there, and smiled.

Love—what a volume in a
word, an ocean in a tear.
A seventh heaven in a glance,
a whirlwind in a sigh.
The lightning in a touch, a
millennium in a moment.

M. F. TUPPER

Chapter Twenty-four

"Oh, my dear, you look dreadful," Ellie exclaimed and dropped her crumpet to a saucer. Leaving her chair, she hurried to Miracle and gently took her face in her hands. She tipped it from side to side, frowning. "You haven't slept again. You simply cannot continue this way. You look positively gaunt. And your eyes— Jonathan, dear, talk to her. You simply must convince her to rest more."

Sitting back in his chair, his fingers laced over his rounded belly, John regarded Miracle as she pulled away from Ellie and slid into her chair. She gazed despondently down at her plate piled high with scrambled eggs, ham, and scones swimming in melted butter and honey. She wondered if she were going to be ill.

Taking her place at the breakfast table, Ellie said, "I have some powders. They'll make you sleep."

"I don't want any powders," she said flatly, and shoved her plate away. "For that matter, I don't wish to sleep."

"But why?" Ellie and John asked at once.

"Because I . . ." She bit her lip.

"Y've been off ridin' that damn horse all night," John scolded.

"I haven't."

"You've been reading all night," Ellie declared.

"I haven't."

"Then why?" they asked in unison.

"I've been waiting for *him* to return," she admitted.

"*Him*?"

"Basingstoke."

Ellie's eyes opened wide. John sat up in his chair.

"I've met him," Miracle said, looking from John to Ellie, who gaped at her as if she had grown two heads. "In a manner of speaking," she hurried to add. "Several nights ago. First in the house, and then in the garden. It was dark. I couldn't see him . . ."

Ellie sank back in her chair. John cleared his throat.

Miracle fidgeted with her silverware, an intricately carved fork and knife emblazoned with the family crest. "He's ever so kind. And seems very timid. Is he ugly?"

"Ugly?" Ellie laughed before catching herself.

"I envision him as a beast of a man. Why else would he not show himself to me? Perhaps he's disfigured?"

Ellie busily buttered another scone. John poured himself chocolate.

"It wouldn't matter to me if he was," Miracle informed them, and smiled to herself. "The most beautiful things in life cannot be seen or touched. They must be felt with the heart. I feel Basingstoke has a tremendous heart. Look around us, Ellie. Everything is perfection. Beautiful. The home, the grounds, the people—all radiate love."

"Would you care for more sugar?" Ellie asked John.

"Please. Would you like more honey?" John asked Ellie.

"Oh, yes. That would be nice."

Raising her voice slightly, Miracle said, "We spoke at some length three nights ago, near the statue. Every night since, I've gone there and waited for hours, but he hasn't come again."

"Miracle." Ellie smiled understandingly. "Stop chasing fantasies. Besides, you'll need all the rest you can get these next days." She glanced at John, and took a deep breath. "I've received word from Her Grace. She and her retinue will be arriving shortly."

"Retinue?"

"I suppose it's time that you knew. The wedding date has been set. The invitations posted. My dear, you'll be marrying the duke one week from today."

Miracle's jaw dropped. She clasped the table edge with her fingertips. "A week—"

"I know what yer thinkin'," John started.

"No. No, you couldn't possibly. Have I no say in this whatsoever? I haven't even decided if I want to marry the ninny-headed—"

"Miracle!" Folding her hands in her lap, Ellie waited until Miracle relaxed, jaw set, shoulders tense, back into her chair. "People like the duchess don't have the time to dally with wishy-washy young girls who don't know their minds. Therefore, occasionally, their minds must be made up for them." Her countenance softening, Ellie reached over the table and squeezed Miracle's hand. "I understand how you feel. We both do. But what you're experiencing now is nothing more than prewedding jitters. We all get them. 'Tis only natural to question your feelings—your future."

Turning her eyes to John, Miracle said, "And you? Do you wish this marriage for me, sir?"

"Yer askin' me?"

"Yes. You're my . . . father, after all."

John swallowed. His face flushed with soft color. "Aye, that I am." Toying with his napkin, he collected his thoughts. His first decision as her father. It would have to be just and stem from a father's love, devotion, and concern, not as a companion's or friend's. At last meeting her gaze, he said, "I'd rather die than see ya waste away alone on that isle. Like yer dear mother."

"I . . . see. Well, then . . . I suppose, as any devoted daughter would, I shall bow to my father's wishes."

The retinue arrived that afternoon: seventy servants, landscapers, ladies' maids, valets, interior decorators, eight cooks (each of whom declared the kitchens his), coiffure experts (each of whom declared Miracle's hair hers), and three coach loads of seamstresses.

Virtually dragged from Napitov's back, Miracle was ushered into Basingstoke Hall, stripped, measured, pinned, pricked, poked, while all around her the covey of excited women argued, debated, mused, conferred over what her wedding gown would look like. The issue wasn't settled until the door flew open and a thread-thin man dressed in a cream colored silk suit swept into the room, flung open a massive leather-bound book of sketch paper, on which an outrageously extravagant wedding gown had been drawn, and announced, "*Voilà*!"

The seamstresses oohed and ahhed. They clapped their hands and tittered among themselves, while the designer peered down his narrow nose and smirked. When the women had sufficiently fawned, he pinned Miracle with his beady eyes and declared, "Well? Does the mademoiselle approve?"

"Does the mademoiselle have a choice?" she mimicked him, causing his thin eyebrows to shoot up to his hairline. Then, with a huff, he stormed from the room.

"Well?" Miracle demanded of the gaping seamstresses. "Does she?"

Then came the fittings for her trousseau. Enough dresses, Miracle surmised, to clothe her several times a day for the next year. There were morning dresses, tea dresses, luncheon dresses, afternoon dresses, evening dresses. Then there were nightclothes. Shockingly frail little things that made her cheeks grow hot, made the memories of hers and Salterdon's times together rouse to remind her that she wasn't exactly marrying a stranger, and that she had felt very passionately for him . . . once.

He came again to the statue that midnight. Having waited for what felt like an eternity in the dark, Miracle had given up hope and turned to leave.

Moving silently up behind her, he gently took her shoulders in his hands.

"Do you mind," he asked softly in her ear, "if we stand like this for just a moment?"

A smile lifting her lips, Miracle sighed in relief and shook her head.

He moved against her, his big body hard and warm against her back, making her feel oddly safe and secure. He rested his chin on the top of her head and said, "I've missed you."

What could she say? Could she admit, even to herself, that the confession thrilled her? She certainly didn't care to let him know that she thought of him constantly throughout the day, that the hours were filled with the anticipation of meeting him again.

"The wedding date has been set," she told him, drowsily aware of his strong heart beating against her back, of his warm breath brushing the side of her face, of his thumbs gently massaging her shoulders where he held her. "A week from today I'm to become Salterdon's wife. Your . . . sister in marriage. Does that please you? Will you attend the wedding? Shall we finally meet face to face?"

"No," he replied flatly. "I won't attend the wedding."

"But—"

"I've urgent business to attend to . . . out of the country."

She shivered in disappointment.

He held her tighter. "You're cold."

"Nay, I'm not. I was just thinking . . . about my future."

"As the duchess?"

"As your brother's wife."

She leaned more against him, comforted by his strength and gentleness. These were arms that would offer a woman sanctuary and love. They would brace her when she felt weak and give her freedom should she desire to fly.

"Tell me about your day," she prompted—anything to make the moment last—anything so she would not be forced to return to her room and dwell on the upcoming week.

"I rode to the farthest section of my property to judge how barren the soil has become. The crops growing there are sickly, not nearly so lush as last year and the years before."

"Mayhap your soil is depleted, sir." Her face warmed with chagrin. "My apologies. I'm certain you don't care to hear advice from a woman."

"If you've something to impart, then do so."

"Well . . ." Miracle gazed out over the dark landscape, her heart quickening with enthusiasm and the fact that he would invite her opinion. "During the last days, I've ridden Napitov over this vast estate. And all that I've seen has astounded and impressed me. However . . ." She cleared her throat. "I feel there are monies to be saved in ways of cultivation and the raising of your stock."

"Go on."

"Gather your sheep, sir. Tether them in a singular field where they stand on crops of vetch, mown grass, clover, and tares. Feed them turnips, sir. Then, before planting, take those soiled straws and cuttings and till them into the earth, which will enrich it and cause your hay crop to double and be ready to thrash by midsummer. When the corn is cut, instead of allowing the stubble to remain, feed it to your pigs. The combed straw left over by the threshers, use it for the thatched roofs of the tenants' cottages, and the timber that you cut from the forests to construct your buildings . . . erect a temporary shed around it so that every piece can be work for the exact purpose for which it's suited, leaving nary a splinter on the ground and precious little warpage." In a stern voice, she added, "The object of successful farming should not be to seize maximum profit from sales against costs in the minimum time, but to secure over the years the highest possible increase from the soil, plant, and beast. The goal is the productive fertility of the land rather than the immediate salability of a particular crop . . . at least that is the way of thinking on the isle, and everyone knows that the isle produces seven times more crops than its inhabitants can consume."

Soft laughter. A gentle squeeze on her arms. A light kiss on the top of her head, making Miracle glow with pleasure and satisfaction. "Ah, Meri," he said, "you do astound me."

The moment froze. Miracle stopped breathing. Her heartbeat rang like bells in her ears.

He had called her *Meri*.

She blinked, and when the world stopped spinning, she realized that he was gone again. Slowly, she turned and searched the darkness, her body shaking from the inside out.

He had called her Meri. The memory of it would not let her alone.

Like one drugged, she slept late into the day, dreaming of those moments in the garden, with his warm hands on her, filling her with a sense of security and divine pleasure.

He had called her Meri.

And desire. Oh, yes, that stirring in her stomach had been desire: pure, arousing desire. Desire for a stranger?

Upon rising and dressing, she left her room to discover servants dashing like maddened ants to the east wing, the duchess's residence when she visited Basingstoke. The maids and servitors trooped through the hallways with trunks of clothes, furniture, and flower arrangements. Having never ventured into the east wing, Miracle wandered down the carpeted corridors, unsurprised to discover that the rooms reflected the duchess's taste for the Orient. There were black-lacquered screens with embedded mother-of-pearl mountains, flowers, and petite Oriental women with coal-black hair and beautiful slanted eyes. There were chairs with arms resembling dragons. Low lacquered tables surrounded by plush pillows. Red silk rugs and throws filigreed with gold cords, and jade Buddahs occupied every available corner.

Coming to the duchess's bedchamber, Miracle found it decorated much like the dowager's townhouse in London. Only here, there were glass cases displaying her most prized possessions: the sceptre of the King of Candy, a dagger once belonging to Ghengis Khan, and the palanquin of Tippoo Sahib.

She wandered on, into less frequented rooms that were no doubt being opened simply to air out and dust. That is when her eye spied the shawl-draped portrait propped upon an easel. Miracle glanced around. She was alone, for the moment. Just a peek beneath the blue silk shawl . . .

She slowly raised the silken veil and stared down into warm, kind, and twinkling gray eyes. Ah, that sensual mouth, curved up slightly on the ends, hinting of humor; that casual pose, sitting so elegantly relaxed in a chair, long legs, clad in leather breeches, crossed at the knees, the loose, white linen shirt draping softly across his broad shoulders; those bronze hands falling relaxed on the chair arms; dark curling hair looking as if it had been kissed by a breeze.

Her farmer. Her gypsy. The man she had fallen in love with at Cavisbrooke. The man who had won her heart completely, who had filled her with joy and laughter and hope. All those emotions came rushing back to her, filled her mind and heart and body with clashing clarity.

"Lady Cavendish?"

She jumped and turned.

A servant, with her hands full of flowers, smiled at Miracle. Saying nothing, Miracle stood with her hands clenched at her sides, like a child caught pilfering sweetmeats from her mother's pantry.

"Is something wrong?" the girl asked.

"Wrong? No. I was only wondering why His Grace's portrait is here."

"It's a birthday gift for the duchess." Placing the flowers in a vase near the window, the servant arranged, then rearranged them before glancing back to Miracle. "And that's not His Grace," she added.

The words vibrated in the close air.

"Of course it is. I should know my own fiancé," Miracle pointed out sharply. There was a stirring going on inside her, winding like a taut spring in her belly.

The servant only laughed. "No, milady. That's his lordship. Basingstoke. Amazing, isn't it? They're identical, you know. Even their parents had trouble telling them apart. And the duchess . . ." The servant shoved open glass doors, allowing a gust of fresh wind to tumble into the room, stirring the drapes, washing aside the mustiness with the smell of roses. "I understand they gave the duchess a perplexing time, switching identities back and forth. She was never very certain whom she was chastising or rewarding. Though it's my understanding she did more rewarding for Basingstoke than she did for His Grace . . . oh, begging your pardon, milady. Not that His Grace wasn't worthy of reward . . ."

Miracle said nothing, and the servant left the room. Miracle turned back to the portrait, and looked into Basingstoke's eyes.

The next two days were a whirlwind of activities. She was fitted again for her wedding gown and trousseau. There were long discussions between the hairdressers on how to arrange her hair to best accentuate her veil. She was shown list upon list of foods and wine, and the first wagons bearing gifts arrived, as did a portion of the five hundred guests the duchess had invited to the wedding.

Five hundred: at least a hundred of them were Her Grace's closest friends, who were, of course, invited to reside at Basingstoke as her guests. Those evenings were spent with Ellie and John at her side, as graciously as possible entertaining the lot of aristocrats, making idle chitchat about weather, fashion, and menus. It was well into the morning before Miracle was allowed, at last, to fall into her bed, only to spend the next hours tossing and turning and reliving those midnight moments in the garden, and the very instant she tossed back that silken veil to reveal Basingstoke's portrait.

On the next night, she pled a headache. At midnight, she waited by the statue, hoping against hope that he would come, afraid he wouldn't.

He did.

As he had the time of their second meeting, he remained at a distance, a shadow slightly darker than the night surrounding them.

"My lord," she said, forcing her voice steady. "I've missed our talks."

"You've been busy," he replied.

"Your guests are curious of your whereabouts."

"They are not my guests, but yours."

"Your grandmother's," she stressed.

"Yes. I suppose so."

"I understand she and Salterdon will be arriving tomorrow."

"Grandmother enjoys making her entrances."

Miracle moved through the dark toward the voice, heart thumping erratically. "My lord, I have a request of you. Consider it a wedding gift."

"Anything."

"Make love to me."

There came a sudden intake of breath, perhaps a gasp of disbelief and surprise.

"Here," she said forcibly, and began to remove the simple gown she had worn for the purpose. "Now. Upon this very grass. Amid these very flowers. Make love to me, Basingstoke, I beg you."

"You're insane." He growled it.

The garment slid from her shoulders and pooled around her ankles. With a tug of the heavy pearl combs, her hair tumbled over her body like a waterfall. "If I am to become Salterdon's wife and forced to endure a lifetime of his cold hands and eyes, I will have the memory of you, at least, to warm my heart and body."

"Don't do this to me," he pleaded in a voice so desperate Miracle felt shaken and shamed. But she had to know. It was the only way to know if her instincts were right, or whether the thoughts clamoring about her head were simply idiotic fantasies she had constructed in an effort to deny the reality that in four days she would be marrying a man she didn't love—had never loved.

"Please," she said in a trembling voice.

The shadow moved, then vanished with little more than a rustle of hedge branches.

Miracle closed her eyes, disappointment a stone in her breast.

Suddenly, he moved up behind her, his calloused hands on her shoulders, sweeping down her arms, sliding beneath her bare breasts and gently cupping them. He pressed warm kisses on the back of her neck. His tongue traced a moist path to the back of her ear.

Her body melted. It swayed against him. She clenched her teeth to stifle the groan of instantaneous pleasure that streaked through her and centered between her legs. She moaned then, as the pleasure there washed through her, mounting and mounting until it became a hot, throbbing pressure. As his hand slid to that apex, her hips writhed. Her breasts grew heavy and her body quivered with heat.

She spun suddenly to face him, caught only a glimpse of the planes of his face and his white teeth clenched, lips pulled back slightly as if in pain, before he twisted his hands in her hair and pressed her face against his chest. With her fingers, she groped at the straining buttons on his breeches, releasing his stiff organ into her hands. It pulsed and prodded her belly, searching. Then he lifted her up, his hands beneath her smooth little buttocks, and impaled her on the distended shaft.

Hands clutching his shoulders, she wrapped her legs around his hips.

He dropped to the ground, first to his knees, then onto the blanket of her hair and wet grass. Her breasts pressed to his chest, she strained her hips against him, her sex filled with him, throbbing with the frenzied rhythm of his driving, pumping body. His thrusts were brutal, powerful, as if he were overcome by his own long denied passions.

Too swiftly, the surcease came. Rising up, clawing at his back, she cried out her relief, her legs thrashing, then becoming paralyzed by the glorious release. With one final thrust and animal groan, he filled her with his hot fluid, bursting, flooding, bathing, then fell onto her with a moan like death.

Too weak and depleted to even open her eyes, Miracle lay beneath him, his heavy body a welcome weight. She drifted on a tide of pure pleasure. Satisfied. Complete. Secure and happy, at last, in his arms.

"My darling Basingstoke," she murmured, and reached for him, only to discover that as she dozed, he had left her again. She lay alone, on the crushed bed of dew-kissed grass.

Standing before the portrait, hugging herself against the cold that had settled into her bones, Miracle stared down into the eyes of the man who had made love to her so passionately a few hours before.

Why? was all she could think. *Why? How could it be?*

There was a sound at the door. Miracle looked up.

In a halo of candlelight, the duchess of Salterdon, as well as the duke, moved into the room.

"Your Grace," she stated flatly, and attempted a curtsy. "When did you arrive?"

"Hours ago. After you had taken to bed with a headache."

Miracle's gaze shifted to Salterdon's face: those stony eyes, the set of his mouth. His was the stranger's face: aloof, slightly discomfited by their meeting.

The duchess moved up beside her and regarded the portrait with raised eyebrows. "He could have dressed," she muttered.

"But that wouldn't have been Basingstoke, would it, Your Grace?" Miracle said. "Basingstoke is a farmer, after all. A simple farmer, who cares not a fraction for fashion or society's proprieties. He much prefers the sun on his face and wind in his hair."

Raising the candle between them, her white hair falling softly over her shawl-covered shoulders, the duchess said, "We must talk, my dear, and now is as good a time as any."

Her countenance fell, and she was silent a while. He regarded the red berries between them over and over again, to such an extent that holly seemed in his after life to be a cypher signifying a proposal of marriage. Bathsheba decisively turned to him.

"No; 'tis no use," she said. "I don't want to marry you."

from *Far From the Madding Crowd*
by THOMAS HARDY

Chapter Twenty-five

The message arrived just as Clayton was leaving the cottage, intent on getting the hell away from Basingstoke as fast as he could. He'd dallied too long as it was. Last night's escapade should never have happened. It was his damnable weakness where she was concerned. He had knowingly, and without reserve, made love to the woman his brother intended to marry in a matter of days. What was more, she had invited him to.

What the blazes had come over her? That she would turn to another man, a virtual stranger, knowingly, blatantly, cheat on her fiancé with his brother.

According to Benjamin, the duchess and his brother had arrived the previous midnight. Rumor among the servants was they had taken Miracle aside and kept her in a closed, locked room with them until just before dawn. Then Ben had handed him the note: "I will see you and your brother in my chambers at ten this morning. Not a minute before, not a minute after. You will present yourself accordingly, of course. Yours, the D."

At precisely eleven fifteen, Clayton dressed in his usual breeches and linen shirt, marched across the lawn, ignoring the groupings of curious guests meandering about the gardens, taking tea in the gazebos, playing croquet on the close-cropped grass. He entered the duchess's drawing room through the open French doors, paused, scanned the confines with a quick glance, and stopped short as Trey left his chair and moved gracefully toward him.

"Close the door," the duke said firmly.

"Where is grandmother?"

"Detained. Now close the door."

Impatiently, Clayton did as he was told.

Trey, as always dressed splendidly, moved to the liquor cabinet. "I fear I'm going to need a drink for this. And so are you."

"A bit early, isn't it, Your Grace?"

"Never too early for a quaff of fortitude, my good brother."

Having poured two drinks, one of port, the other of brandy, Trey offered a glass to Clayton and ordered, "Sit down."

Reluctantly, Clayton sat. He held the drink lightly between his fingers and watched his brother's face. No doubt about it, something was wrong. The normal cavalier, devil-may-care look on Trey's features was absent, the hard angles grim, if not outright nervous.

"About Miracle," Trey began.

"I don't intend to discuss Miracle. I fulfilled my obligation to you. I succeeded in winning her over for you. Now take your bloody settlement and—"

"I never intended to marry her, Clay."

Clayton frowned.

Trey took a drink, waited until it hit his belly and spread like a fire. In a huskier voice, he said, "It was grandmother's idea. She was determined to see one of us married. When it became obvious it wasn't going to be me, she turned to you. Months ago, after returning home from the isle, I mentioned to the duchess about the girl. Miracle. In passing, I said I thought she would be just the sort of lass for you: earthy, challenging, rather . . . common . . . in an acceptable sort of way."

He took another drink. "Soon after, she came up with this scheme. I was to convince you that the girl was for me. You would go there with the intention of winning the girl, of causing her to fall in love with you, at which time you would also fall in love with her." A thin smile on his mouth, the duke of Salterdon shrugged and laughed dryly as Clayton stared, unblinking, up at him, his fingers gripping the glass more tightly by the mounting seconds.

"Well," Trey ventured, "you most obviously fell in love with her. The trouble was, it seems your loyalty to me ran a little deeper than grandmother and I had anticipated. Instead of storming back to London and announcing that you had no intention of subjecting the lass to the likes of me for the remainder of her life, you practically wrapped her in a ribbon and plunked her at my feet. Not only that, but you made certain the entire country was made aware of her, and me, and our upcoming nuptials. I don't mind admitting, grandmother and I found ourselves in a bit of a crack. So . . . grandmother sent her here, certain the situation would be resolved once you met face to face and the truth was revealed. But, dammit, Clay, you continue to play the martyr—"

"No," Clayton said in a soft, low, and threatening voice as he slowly stood. "I continue to be your brother. Your brother, dammit. Who's been sick to my gut in love with the woman I thought you had chosen as a wife. Who cared enough about you to sacrifice my sanity . . ."

Slamming the drink onto the table, Clayton stalked toward Trey, who backed away. "Let's be reasonable," Trey said.

"Name your seconds, you lying bloodsucker, who would sell his own mother for a few hundred guineas."

"One hundred thousand pounds is hardly a few guineas. And I didn't sell our mother. Never would. I have *some* scruples, you know. Besides, I don't see what you're so upset about. Thanks to me, you met the woman of your dreams. You fell in love with her, and she with you. What does it matter that I receive a small fortune for my efforts? Christ, it's the least I deserve for having my good name and reputation diced to bits the last weeks. Imagine my marrying a lighthouse keeper. Good gosh."

"Where is she?" Clayton demanded through his teeth.

"I wouldn't know."

With a guttural curse, Clayton spun on his heel and stormed out the door, into the sunlight, ignoring the occasional greetings from the curious guests as he strode toward the barns.

She always took her riding lessons just before noon. He knew, because he would take a break from his own chores to return to the stables and watch her from a distance.

He wasn't certain what he would say or how he would say it. But at last, he was free to prostrate himself before her, if he must, and beg her forgiveness. If she hated him, he would understand. If she slapped his face and announced she was returning to the isle, he would regretfully allow her to go.

The hell he would.

Entering the stables, he searched up and down. The aisles were empty. "Meri!" he shouted. "Meri Mine! Miracle? Answer me, damn you!"

He spun around as John walked to the door. Mopping his sweating brow, his eyes bothered, the old man said, "I've looked everywhere for her, Clay. When I come out this mornin' at just after dawn, Napitov was gone from his stall. I figured she had gone off on another one of her mornin' rides. When she didn't return by breakfast, I had Ismail and a few others ride out. No one's seen her."

Ellie showed up then, breathing hard. "I checked her room. Her valise is missing. Clayton, darling, I fear she's gone."

He rode Majarre to the island. The dapple gray mare, though small, carried Clayton's weight with little effort. And while his own blooded horse would long since have given out from the distance, the Arabian carried forth with hardly a break in her stride.

Hot wind from the south collided with cooler winds from the north. The humid air smelled of rain and an impending storm. Dark, boiling clouds rose like a bruise-colored monolith on the horizon, and churned the waves into high, frothy caps beneath the delicate ferry. Clayton had been forced to pay the ferryman five quid to make the journey in the inclement weather. He sat on a box on the deck, bent at the waist, his face buried in his hands, praying the entire five, horrifying, watery miles from Portsmouth to Ryde. Once reaching Ryde, there would be another grueling twelve miles to travel before reaching Rocken End. He hoped to hell Majarre had enough stamina to make the journey.

He drove the horse with whip and spur to Cavisbrooke.

The old castle perched on the precarious Undercliff like a giant gray stone swirling with fog and clouds. Seabirds and rooks circled its crumbling parapets. Wind pummeled its empty windows and sprayed the first spears of rain upon the shell of its burned walls.

Gone. All but the grim, ash-blackened stones. There were no ceilings, no turrets, no battlements, no chimneys. All lay in a great heap within the walls.

With the sharp bite of rain on his face and shoulders, Clayton stared numbly at the holocaust. There, once, was the door on which he and Benjamin had pounded upon that gloomy midnight. Yonder lay the fallen stones of the round tower in which Miracle sewed her garments for pennies.

When? he wondered wearily. *How?*

"They came," said the scratchy voice behind him, and he turned, blinked the rain from his eyes, and focused on the bent and gnarled form of an old woman, her coarse gray hair trailing the muddy ground at her feet as she shuffled toward him, resting her weight on a stick. "Soon after John left. The young imbeciles. Wrought havoc with all they put their greedy hands on. Made no matter to them that it was once a home. It frightened them, you see. It was . . . different."

Stopping feet from him, she raised up her head, revealing the white, sightless orbs of her eyes. "Basingstoke," she said. "You've come for milady."

"Is she here?"

"Nay. She's there." She raised up the crooked stick and pointed down the Undercliff. "At the lighthouse."

He grabbed for Majarre's reins.

The crone slammed her stick across his arm. "She'll know how much you care once this is over. Let not fear be your enemy, my lord. Her life depends on it. Now quickly! Make haste. The storm builds even as we speak."

The storm was the least of his worries.

Napitov loyally remained near the ledge where Miracle had left him, rear turned into the wind, his head down as rain pummeled his withers and back. Upon hearing Clayton and Majarre ride up, the stallion lifted his head, ears forward, nose tipped toward the sky, and blew a greeting, but he didn't move, and wouldn't until his mistress returned to him.

The tide was in, surrounding the chapel and lighthouse, writhing waves climbing up the tower and swirling around the mostly submerged crucifix. As if the ocean floor had heaved, great green curls rose up and careened forward, propelled by the wind, and slammed so fiercely against the Undercliff walls that the ground trembled under Clayton's feet.

Helplessly, shielding the rain from his face, bracing his body against the howling winds, he watched the erratic firelight in the house, saw it gyrate and dance, grow brighter, then dimmer, then waver from side to side.

No. It was the tower that moved—swayed. The tower was crumbling beneath the onslaught of the gale.

A movement? There! Upon the widow's perch, that horrid little landing hanging so perilously to the side of the tower. Miracle!

He shouted her name. Useless. He couldn't hear his own voice. What the blazes was she doing out there?

Clinging to the balustrade, her dress torn by the wind, her hair swept straight back, she stumbled to one end of the perch, then the other, as if, out of desperation to escape the tower, she was actually considering jumping into the turbulent sea.

"No!" he shouted, and began the descent down the slippery stone grooves of steps, his hands frantically grasping the jagged wall to steady himself, skinning his knuckles, abrading his fingers.

A spear of lightning erupted from the sky, streaked once toward the ocean, danced over the waves, exploded upon a shelf of rock not far from him. A fireball flashed; Clayton covered his head and huddled against the stones as the heat electrified the air so brightly he felt momentarily blinded. Another—a blue-white jagged sword that smashed against the roof of the lighthouse with a crack so sharp the sound trembled the stone ledge on which he crouched.

Timbers flew. Windows shattered. The fire within, fed by the sudden influx of wind, leapt like some hungry, untethered beast to engulf the lighthouse. To Clayton's horror, the widow's perch disintegrated and plummeted to the sea.

Where was Miracle?

Had she tumbled into the water?

Had she fled into the lighthouse before the lightning struck? If so, she was caught in that internal inferno.

He skidded down several slick steps. Below him, the ocean churned and swirled and crashed.

Impossible to swim out there.

Oh God, he hadn't submerged his body completely underwater since . . .

"Clayton, darling, give me your hand! Jump, darling, jump!"

Gasping air through the rain, Clayton focused on the shadowy form resting on the lower ledge. The boat. Miracle had once mentioned a boat. Could it be?

"Yes!" He yelled it and fell upon the overturned wooden craft barely large enough to seat two people. How light it was, constructed of little more than splinters. An oar lay underneath. Waves this fierce could so easily bash the less than substantial dingy against the walls and smash it to pieces, and him as well.

He dragged the boat behind him, to the edge of the hissing water. Waves rose up and crashed against his legs, wrapped around his ankles and gripped, pulled hard; they seemed to scream, "This time you won't escape me. This time we'll drag you down into the watery grave with your mother and father. You escaped us once, but not again."

With a heave, he flung the dinghy into the water, and threw himself into it. It rolled threateningly from side to side; water crashed over him, spun the craft around and hurled it toward the wall, but just as it seemed he would be catapulted onto the rocks, the boat was snapped up by the back wall of a wave and driven out toward the open sea, and the lighthouse.

Using the oar as best he could, he battled the tidal currents and storm-driven waves, the muscles of his arms screaming with exertion, his mouth and nose gasping for air amid the salty spray and rain. Again and again he came close to the jutting crucifix; again and again he was dragged away, as if the ocean were teasing and taunting him.

At last! He flung the loop of the boat rope over the stone cross. The line snapped taut as a wave swelled up beneath the boat and sent the craft hurling against the wall of the lighthouse, causing Clayton to spill hard into the bottom of the dinghy.

Above him, the sky boiled with clouds and smoke. Fire leapt up through the rain, hissing, cracking. Stones crumbled and fell to the sea, missiles that, should a solitary one hit his insubstantial vessel, would smash it to pieces. So little time . . . he had to reach Miracle . . . if she was still alive . . .

The realization struck him then. There was no way in. The only entrance to the lighthouse was by way of the chapel and it was a dozen feet underwater.

He couldn't do it. An impossibility. It would mean diving. Fighting the currents. Submerging, holding his breath. The water would surge up his nose and down his throat and fill up his lungs . . .

He gasped for breath.

"Do you believe in miracles?" his Miracle had once asked him, there, at the entrance of this very chapel.

He removed his boots and flung them away. He tore off his shirt and watched as it floated like a ghost in the air momentarily, then fell to the water, swirled round and round, then sank from sight.

"Clayton, darling, jump. Jump!"

He dove into the frigid water. It swallowed him. Sucked him down. And down. His lungs were going to burst. Down. He kicked his way down until there was no sound, only movement, power around him drawing, thrusting.

His lungs were going to burst. Don't panic.

Salt burned his eyes as he searched the dense, murky depths, following the wall of the chapel, down, deeper.

At last! The entry! He kicked hard, dragged himself through the opening, into darkness, into stillness—a watery tomb of four stone walls and a ceiling. He followed the wall with his hands—bursting, his lungs were bursting—his head would explode any moment—the burning in his brain was excruciating.

His hands passed over the Virgin's face. Her eyes stared out at him. Her lips were smiling.

Not far now. Here! Through the passageway, now up—where the hell was the surface? Up— He clawed his way up the slimy stones of the spiraling stairwell—up—he had to breathe or—

Bursting out of the water, he gasped for air, thrashed, scrambled up the steps before collapsing. He retched seawater. It ran from his nose and mouth and seemed to weep from his eyes.

Then the heat from above hit him like a furnace. Rousing his strength, he dragged himself upward, through the ceiling of condensing smoke, until he emerged at the top of the stairwell where fire roared, engulfing most of the ancient wood. Frantically, he searched the burning interior, and there, huddled against the farthest wall—

"Meri!" he shouted, and stumbled to her.

Her head came up, and she stared at him blankly, but as he fell to his knees and reached for her, anger replaced her stupor.

"No!" she screamed at him, and batted at his hands. "I would rather die—"

"Listen to me," he pleaded.

"I've listened for weeks and heard only lies. All lies!"

"I love you, Meri."

"You love your family's precious name—"

"I love you, Meri."

"It was all for your brother—all of it—all the promises, the endearments—you must have thought me a fool—I believed you. I worshipped you. I would have done anything to make you happy. But you meant none of it."

Gripping her shoulders in his hands, he shook her. "A mistake. My mistake. I fell in love with you immediately, and I was too goddamn weak to deny a worthless obligation I owed Trey. Listen to me. What could I do? If I confessed, even from the beginning, would this very thing not have happened? If you'll forgive me, Meri Mine, I'll spend the rest of our lives making it up to you."

She shook her head, turning her scratched, sooted face away.

He released her. In a resolute voice, he said, "Very well, then we'll both die."

Slowly, her wide, tear-filled eyes came back to his. Her chin quivered. "What are you saying?"

"That I'm not leaving here without you. That my life wouldn't be worth living without you. If you've chosen to die here, then so shall I."

She regarded his wet hair, his damp, shirtless body and saturated breeches. "How did you get here?" she asked him softly.

"I swam."

"But the tide, and storm—"

"It wasn't easy."

A timber groaned above them. Burning embers rained over their shoulders. With a muttered curse, Clayton grabbed Miracle and dragged her to her feet. This time, there was little hesitance. Sweeping her up in his arms, he fled across the burning floor and down the smoke-filled stairwell to the water.

He slid Miracle to her feet, stared down into the murky green water while the heat grew more intense and the air impossible to breathe. The panic and fear were there still, knocking at his subconscious.

Then Miracle's fingers entwined with his. She said very softly, "Do you believe in miracles, my lord?"

"I believe in you," he replied.

They waded into the water, and with one last breath, dove under.

The current wrapped around them and gently ushered them out of the chapel. With his arm around Miracle's waist, Clayton kicked his way to the surface. He helped Miracle into the boat, then he clamored aboard, released the rope that moored the dinghy to the crucifix, and battled the next eternal minutes to drive them toward the elusive steps.

Miracle leapt first, then held out her hand for Clayton. He grabbed, and missed. The boat whirled. It slammed against the face of the Undercliff, and for a heart-stopping moment, it seemed the fragile craft would disintegrate around him.

"Jump!" came Miracle's voice through the crash of waves and thunder. "Clayton, darling, jump!" She held out her white hand to him. He grasped it. Clung to it. If he went into the sea now, he was a dead man. He would be crushed in a matter of seconds upon the rocks.

He jumped, and hit the steps hard.

Suddenly, Miracle was there, her slender arms around him, holding him close, her soft lips pressing kisses across his salty face and mouth. Feeling as if every muscle had been bruised, every bone broken, Clayton wearily caught her little face in his hands and laughed.

"Does this mean I'm forgiven, Meri Mine?"

"How could I doubt a man who conquered his greatest fear to save me, my lord?"

Pulling her close, Clayton shut his eyes, and with a smile, whispered, "My greatest fear was losing you, my love."

Enter Juliet

Here comes the lady; —O, so light a foot
Will ne'er wear out the everlasting flint:
A lover may bestride the gossamers
That idle in the wanton summer air,
And yet not fall; so light is vanity.
JULIET: Good even to my ghostly confessór.
FRIAR: Romeo shall thank thee, daughter, for us both.
JULIET: As much to him, else are his thanks too much.
ROMEO: Ah, Juliet, if the measure of thy joy
Be heap'd like mine, and that thy skill be more
To blazon it, then sweeten with thy breath
This neighbour air, and let rich musick's tongue
Unfold the imagin'd happiness that both
Receive in either by this dear encounter.
JULIET: Conceit, more rich in matter than in words,
Brags of his substance, not of ornament:
They are but beggars that can count their worth:
But my true love is grown to such excess,
I cannot sum up half my sum of wealth.
FRIAR: Come, come with me, and we will make short work:
For, by your leaves, you shall not stay alone,
Till holy church incorporate two in one.

WILLIAM SHAKESPEARE

Epilogue

Certainly, the wedding would be talked about for the next several seasons. Imagine! Five hundred guests had converged on Basingstoke Hall, believing they were to witness the duke of Salterdon's marriage to . . . what was her name?

Instead, the bride had wed Salterdon's brother. His brother! What could the girl be thinking? To marry a mere lord, instead of a duke. Obviously, her mama had never instilled in her a sense of priority.

Miracle felt like a princess. Her gown was white satin and lace, the bodice fit snugly across her tiny waist and slightly flared over her hips to spill in multiple layers to the ground. The pearl-studded lace sleeves formed points on the backs of her hands. A band of lace and pearls encircled her pale, graceful throat and flowed in a heart shape down over her chest. A bustle of white satin spilled from the small of her back, and tiny pearl buttons ran the length of her spine, where her back was exposed by a heart-shaped film of sheer lace.

Her veil, two partial garlands of embroidered olive branches met in a vee in the center of her forehead, and upon that tiny point dropped a tear-shaped pearl. Small bouquets of embroidered flowers, with pearl pistils and pearl-encrusted leaves spilled just behind her ears, and from there, a diaphanous webbing of lace flowed to the small of her back.

She carried a bouquet of white roses.

The sun shone bright on her wedding day. Barely a breeze stirred. The guests had spread out over Basingstoke's grounds, the ladies fanning their warm faces with peacock feathers, occasionally whispering to themselves.

Sitting comfortably on Napitov's back, lightly gripping the silver reins, which connected to his headstall of silver formed into a pearl-studded vee across his browband, Miracle smiled down at her father, as John led the silvery white Arabian stallion down the red-carpeted aisle to her husband to be.

Basingstoke, with His Grace at his side, smiled at her with as much pride and love as she felt that moment in her heart. How could she doubt his devotion? He would have gladly sacrificed his life to save hers.

Oh, to be so loved at long last! To be so cherished! To look forward to her future, not with whimsy or a fear of loneliness, but to dream of long, spectacular nights in his arms, of the children they would conceive together, of the dreams they would strive for and attain.

Clayton's hands lifted to her. She slid from Napitov's back and into his arms.

They exchanged their vows.

He slid a diamond and pearl encrusted ring on her finger.

With champagne flowing like water from a fountain, Lady Basingstoke and her husband, who obviously worshiped the rose petals on which she walked, greeted each guest with a smile. The last to approach them was the duke and the dowager duchess of Salterdon.

Her cheeks turning warm, Miracle raised both eyebrows as His Grace caught her hand in his. His eyes were no longer cold, but surprisingly warm. His smile was genuine, and not so unlike his brother's.

"Welcome to the family, my lady," he said in a fond voice. When she thought to withdraw her hand in one last show of feigned disapproval, he gripped it more tightly. "You would have made one hell of a duchess, isn't that right, grandmother?" he said to the duchess, who regarded Clayton and his bride with a sense of smug satisfaction.

"Obviously," she replied, her eyes surprisingly glassy, her smile a trifle unsteady. "Would I have chosen less for Clayton's bride?" Then raising her dignified chin, she turned her gaze to Salterdon and announced, "You're next, of course, if it's the last thing I ever do."

"Never," he declared and, hooking his grandmother's arm through his, they moved away. "As God is my witness, grandmother, you will never manipulate me into matrimony."

"No?" Glancing back over her shoulder, she winked at Miracle and smiled. "We'll see, my darling boy. We'll see."

Clayton slid his arm around Miracle's waist. He bent and kissed her and pressed a paper into her hand. "A gift from my brother; a peace offering, so to speak, just in case you were skeptical about his sincerity."

Miracle gazed at the writing, her heart climbing into her throat.

"Trey had a word with cousin George about the horses. Pointed out they would make one hell of a wedding present—"

"They're mine?" She smiled. "All mine? Legally, I mean. I needn't worry—"

"You never need to worry over anything ever again, Meri Mine. Not as long as you love me."

She swayed against him, allowing the warmth and strength of his body to fill her up and his love to enfold her.

"You asked me once if I believed in miracles." He smiled into her sparkling eyes. "I didn't, until I found my own Miracle . . . and she made me believe in forever."

Laughing, Miracle danced away. Seeing Ellie and John walking together, she called, "Ellie! Quickly!" then tossed the bouquet of roses into the startled woman's hands.

Lifting her satin skirts, she ran down the path toward the vine-covered cottage. Tomorrow they would begin their life together in the manse, but tonight, ah, tonight they would spend their hours in the simple privacy of the carriage house . . . and mayhap she would whisper to him of the miracle that stirred even now inside her. *Their* miracle—conceived in true love.

Their promise of forever.

Acknowledgement

My thanks to Tracy Caruth, of Caruth Arabians for allowing me to use the name of her beautiful silver-white stallion, Napitov, in this book. Thanks also for allowing me the opportunity to share in Nap's greatness by purchasing his awesome young son, NapPoleone.